HIS JET-SET NIGHTS WITH THE INNOCENT

PIPPA ROSCOE

AN HEIR FOR THE VENGEFUL BILLIONAIRE

ROSIE MAXWELL

MILLS & BOON

First published in Great Britain 2023
by Mills & Boon, an imprint of HarperCollins*Publishers* Ltd,
1 London Bridge Street, London, SE1 9GF

www.harpercollins.co.uk

HarperCollins*Publishers*, Macken House, 39/40 Mayor Street Upper,
Dublin 1, D01 C9W8, Ireland

ISBN: 978-0-263-30695-8

09/23

This book is produced from independently certified FSC™ paper to ensure responsible forest management.
For more information visit: www.harpercollins.co.uk/green.

Printed and Bound in the UK using 100% Renewable Electricity at CPI Group (UK) Ltd, Croydon, CR0 4YY

Pippa Roscoe lives in Norfolk, near her family, and makes daily promises to herself that this is the day she'll leave the computer to take a long walk in the countryside. She can't remember a time when she wasn't dreaming about handsome heroes and innocent heroines. Totally her mother's fault, of course—she gave Pippa her first romance to read at the age of seven! She is inconceivably happy that she gets to share those daydreams with you. Follow her on Twitter @PippaRoscoe.

Rosie Maxwell has dreamed of being a writer since she was a little girl. Never happier than when she's lost in her own imagination, she is delighted that she finally has a legitimate reason to spend hours daydreaming about handsome heroes and glamorous locations. In her spare time she loves reading—everything from fiction to history to fashion—and doing yoga. She currently lives in the North-West of England.

Also by Pippa Roscoe

The Wife the Spaniard Never Forgot

A Billion-Dollar Revenge miniseries

Expecting Her Enemy's Heir

The Royals of Svardia miniseries

Snowbound with His Forbidden Princess
Stolen from Her Royal Wedding
Claimed to Save His Crown

This is **Rosie Maxwell**'s debut book
for Mills & Boon Modern

We hope that you enjoy it!

Discover more at millsandboon.co.uk.

HIS JET-SET NIGHTS WITH THE INNOCENT

PIPPA ROSCOE

MILLS & BOON

For anyone who grew up loving adventures, treasure hunts, pirate stories and romances as much as I did.

This one is for us.

(Any mistakes are very much my own!)

xx

CHAPTER ONE

IT WAS A surprise to many that Evie Edwards didn't *hate* the room she'd been assigned for her lectures. At the far end of the London campus, down the back stairs of the smallest building, along a corridor with less than fully functioning lights was a door to what looked like a store room, bearing the bold declaration of Lecture Room Four.

While the room was considered a lecture hall, there was nothing remotely academic about it. Not the rows of black plastic chairs placed awkwardly in a semi-circle around her chair, or the large A3 clipboard that looked more boardroom than school room. Part of the issue was that, much like her lecture hall, she just didn't *look* the part of the University of South-East London's Lecturer in Archaeology.

At the age of twenty-five, she was mistaken for being either a PhD student or a teaching assistant, which Evie could begrudgingly understand. She had never truly fitted in, having finished her A levels by the time she was sixteen and her degree by eighteen. Her Masters rolled into her PhD at nineteen and she had passed her viva for her doctorate by twenty-one.

And with an IQ higher than one hundred and sixty Evie either failed to live up to anticipation or confounded those with lower expectations. Her adoptive parents, Carol and

Alan, leaned towards the former, where mostly everyone else leaned into the latter.

'It doesn't matter what they think at the beginning, it's what they think at the end that counts.'

Professor Marin's words echoed through her mind and she felt the sting of his loss throb a little as a group of fresh-faced students filed into the room. But she buried it deep, knowing that, as the first lecture of the year for the new crop of undergraduates, *this* was Evie's only chance to grab and hold her students' attention. Positioning herself in the centre of the room, she took in the familiar sense of expectation, excitement and a little trepidation universal to all students on their first day. She counted heads and waited a few more minutes, aware of just how many students would come in late, having struggled to find Lecture Room Four in the back of beyond.

'Good morning,' she said in a bright, confident voice after the door closed behind the last few stragglers. 'Welcome to the BA Programme in Archaeology.' Evie's glance skimmed the faces of students who sat up a little taller, eyes a little wider, recognising her finally as their new professor. 'Archaeology is the study of the past, but from investigation of the material remains left throughout history we can see what it means to be human. In your first year, your modules will cover…'

Evie slipped into the rehearsed welcome, soothed by the familiar outline of the lecture programme she would give over the next year. This was her domain and she was happy here. It was comfortable, even if there was a sense of disappointment that muddied the waters.

As she was wrapping up, she ignored the door to the lecture hall that opened and closed, refusing to be knocked from her stride. Perhaps it was the Dean, come to deny her conference proposal request. Again. She'd spent the entire summer on it and knew its merits; it was excellent, but the Dean was wary of being tainted by the reputation that she had already earned herself in her four-year career. A reputation that would have been made precarious enough by her age and gender, but that had been damaged irrevocably by her work with Professor Marin and their research area. Stubbornness and loyalty steeled her spine, even now. She wouldn't take back her work and time with Prof for anyone or anything.

So, as the students filed past her on their way out of the room, she gathered her lecture materials and prepared herself for the overbearing obsequiousness of her boss. But when she turned round, she was so shocked she nearly dropped everything she was holding. Rather than the red-faced, sweaty visage of the Dean of USEL, a shockingly beautiful blonde-haired woman stood before her.

'Your Majesty,' Evie stated, somewhat obviously, to the Queen of Iondorra, immediately dropping into an awkward curtsy.

By the time Evie had straightened, she could just make out a few figures placed around the small lecture hall in shadows.

'Professor Edwards,' the Queen said with a perfect smile. 'It is nice to finally make your acquaintance.'

Evie nodded as if they'd had an arrangement to meet when she knew that they'd had nothing of the sort. She was as shocked by the sudden appearance of the ruler of the small European kingdom as she would have been had Cleopatra stepped right out of the pages of a history book.

Queen Sofia of Iondorra gestured towards the front

row of seats and waited for Evie to sit down before taking a seat right beside her.

'So this is where they put a prominent professor whose thesis was focused on eighteenth-century Iondorran history?' she asked, looking around her and appearing somewhat dissatisfied.

Alarmed at the thought the Queen would take it as a slight against Iondorra, rather than what it was—a slight against her—Evie rushed to reassure the Queen that she liked teaching in this room, a reassurance which was gently waved away with the sweep of a gloved hand.

'I was sorry to hear of Professor Marin's passing,' Queen Sofia said. 'I know that we weren't able to acknowledge his theories publicly, but they were of interest to…my family.'

Evie looked down, unsure—as always—that it was for her to accept sympathies as if she were a family member. He had been family to her. Not on paper. But the professor had understood her, accepted her, in a way that not even Carol and Alan had. But every time she received condolences she couldn't help but remember the looming figure of the son who had barely made it to stand at the back of the graveyard where Professor Marin had been laid to rest. The son who had not spoken a word to his father in the three years before his passing. But before the well of a familiar resentment stirred, she brought her focus back to the Queen.

'Professor Edwards, I would like to talk to you about a very sensitive matter. A matter that, I'm afraid, would need the utmost secrecy and discretion, which is why, before I explain anything further, I would like you to sign a non-disclosure agreement.'

Queen Sofia held out her hand and a man appeared from the shadows with a sheaf of papers and a pen.

'Personally, I detest the things and I understand if you feel that you—'

'There is no need to explain, I'll happily sign the NDA.'

Evie missed the slight reddening of the assistant's cheeks from the way she had accidentally interrupted the Queen of Iondorra as she bent over the legally binding document and signed her name. Evie might not know what was going on, but there was a heaviness about the woman who had once been known as the Widow Princess, before finding true love with a Greek billionaire. Theo Tersi had become the Queen's consort when her father, King Frederick, had stepped down and Princess Sofia had claimed the throne.

The Queen's assistant retrieved the document, placed his signature in what must have been the witness box, tore along the perforated edge of the paper and returned what looked like a bound thesis to her. Frowning, Evie scanned the blank cover, unable to resist running her hand over the royal insignia embossed into the thick red cartridge paper.

'I'm afraid we don't have much time,' Queen Sofia explained, 'so I have to be quite blunt. There is an item up for auction in Shanghai in three days. An item the vendor is claiming to have once belonged to the pirate Loriella Desaparecer.'

Evie stared at the Queen. 'Loriella?'

Along with Gráinne Mhaol, Mary Read and Ann Bonny, Loriella Desaparecer was one of the most renowned female pirates of the eighteenth century.

'Yes,' Queen Sofia confirmed. 'My father…he has…'

Evie waited while the royal gathered herself, sensing an emotional turmoil that was probably rarely seen by anyone. 'It is not openly known yet, but my father has been suffering from early onset dementia for some time now and for the most part we have been managing quite well. He rallied at the birth of our daughter five years ago, but…there is something about this auction item that he has become fixated on. He has become quite adamant that we obtain it.'

'Why is he so interested in this particular item?' Evie couldn't help but ask.

'My father is convinced that it is the octant that was gifted to Princess Isabella before her travels by the English crown.'

Evie's attention snapped like a band pulled tight. A thousand thoughts and conclusions were weighed, considered and discarded. While one part of her mind delved into what she knew about the eighteenth-century navigational equipment invented only years before Isabella had set sail for Indonesia, another part delved into her own personal history. For years Professor Marin had been working on the theory that Iondorra's eighteenth-century princess had not, as believed, died during the sea journey that would have taken her to her Dutch fiancé in Indonesia, but had in fact become one of the most notorious female pirates of that tumultuous period. And Evie had assisted him. They had scoured research and resources across the world, chasing the tale of the Pirate Princess.

But in doing so they had become the laughing stock of the academic world, made worse when their work was renounced by Iondorra. Evie couldn't blame them for laughing, because it *was* fanciful and *was* the stuff of movies rather than reality. But she had believed in Professor Marin and she had believed where the research had taken them. They just hadn't been able to find concrete proof. But if the Queen was here, taking the sale of the octant so seriously, then perhaps…

'For obvious reasons, we cannot purchase this ourselves. So we would like you to attend the auction in Shanghai, assess the item, and if you feel that it is authentic and identifiable then we want you to obtain it at auction. The Dean of USEL has been apprised that I am in need of your services and has granted you a leave of absence, and we will, of course, pay for any and all expenses incurred.'

Evie's mind was spinning, not with confusion but with what would need to happen if she agreed. The Queen had delivered a summation that was an order she could hardly refuse, but it was one that could cost her greatly. Returning to the research that had made her and Professor Marin a professional laughing stock could be the end of her career.

'I must warn you, even if you are able to find a link between Isabella and Loriella, Iondorra will not be able to acknowledge it. We will soon have to release the news of my father's condition. Talk of Pirate Princesses would be…'

'Devastating,' Evie concluded. 'I understand.' More than most, she supposed, knowing how damaging it had already been to her reputation and her fledgling career. Evie looked around the small lecture hall. For the two years since Professor Marin's death it had been all she had known. No field work, no research. No one wanted to risk their precious funding on a 'girl with no life experience with her head in the clouds rather than the past'. Just stepping outside of the comfort and privacy of her teaching position here at USEL was an enticement. But the Queen was also representative of the palace, who had refused to validate any of Professor Marin's theories, or provide him with access to items and artifacts that would help.

But when Evie looked up at Queen Sofia, beneath the poise and grace she saw a grieving daughter, struggling with losing her father before her very eyes. A daughter who wanted to help her father find peace…find the *truth.*

'Your father, he needs this?'

'I've not seen him so fixated on anything before,' the Queen admitted, the tears of a child for their parent glistening in her eyes.

'"It is not always important that the world knows our history. Sometimes it is enough for just one to know,"' Evie quoted.

'Professor Marin?' Queen Sofia asked with a gentle smile.

Evie nodded, wondering who would be most deeply impacted by this particular truth, if the auction item turned out to in fact have belonged to Isabella.

'I would be happy to go to Shanghai,' Evie decided.

The relief that softened the Queen's tense features was fleeting but enough for Evie to know she had made the right decision. And if the auction item proved to be both from the Pirate Loriella *and* the Princess Isabella, then perhaps she might even be able to prove that Professor Marin had been right all along. Not immediately—as Queen Sofia had said—but eventually, perhaps. It would have to be enough for her. 'But before I go to Shanghai I will need to go to Spain,' Evie added.

'Spain?'

'It's something I need to help with the octant's authentication,' Evie explained, thinking of Professor Marin's old notebook. And in her mind's eye, she saw a broad, dark figure walking away from her at the graveside.

'Happy birthday!'

Mateo Marin pulled his mobile away from his ear as his mother's squeals of delight pitched into static. He punched the speaker button on the phone and found a space for it on his desk.

Grabbing the presentation for the first meeting of his afternoon, he took a sip of coffee and nearly spat the tepid liquid out. Grimacing as he swallowed, he glared at the phone as he heard his mother ask what he was doing to celebrate.

'Henri is coming over for drinks and a meal.'

'Mateo! Is that all you are doing? How are you ever going to meet anyone if you just sit around drinking whisky with that boy?'

Mateo had no intention of letting his mother know that he met plenty of women—just none that he would spend more than a couple of mutually beneficial and pleasurable evenings with. He had learned that any more and they got ideas that he had no intention of fulfilling.

'Henri isn't a boy any more,' Mateo chided instead.

'You will both always be boys to me, Mateo,' his mother replied. 'But enough. It is time for you to settle down. When are you going to make me happy?'

Mateo stopped, his hand stuck halfway towards the bin with the now crumpled paper coffee cup clenched in a fist.

'Am I not enough to make you happy as I am?' he demanded, the mockery in his tone hiding the bitterness at the heart of his question.

'Of course you are, *mi hijo*.' His mother's soft words

barely reached him as his gaze blurred in the middle distance.

She was still talking but all he could hear, all he could see, was her crying in the corner of the kitchen after they had first returned to Spain from England when he was ten years old and utterly helpless to do anything. Over the years he had never stopped trying to make his mother happy, but settling down? No. He slashed a mental hand through the thought. That would never happen.

'Mateo? You *are* still coming over for dinner on Friday?'

'Of course, Mamá,' he replied, finally throwing the cup into the basket, noticing the spray of cold coffee across the paper. 'But I have a meeting I must get to.'

'Mateo, are you at work? On your birthday?'

'Mamá, it's a weekday. Where else would I be?'

'Meeting the woman who is going to give me grandbabies—'

'Bye, Mamá,' he said, hanging up the phone and cutting her off before she could do more damage.

Mateo checked the calendar on his computer, eyeing the back-to-back meetings he had all afternoon with relish rather than distaste. He purposefully made sure that his birthdays were like this. After all, it was just another day in the year, he told himself.

His mobile rang again and he punched the button on the screen without looking at the caller ID.

'Mamá, if you're that serious, I'll go out onto the street, grab the first woman I meet and make as many grandbabies as you need—'

'Well, that's a rather alarming thought,' came the accented male voice that was most definitely *not* Mateo's mother.

'*Cristo*, Henri!'

'What? You answered the phone like that.'

'I didn't see who was calling.'

'That's not on me, *mon ami*. I'm just checking that you're on for this evening. What time do you think you'll be home?'

'Now you really *are* sounding like my mother,' Mateo growled.

'And you're sounding like a child. You're always so moody on your birthday,' Henri practically whined.

As would you be, if for most of your life the day meant either upsetting your mother or being forgotten by your father.

Mateo bit back the retort and checked his watch. 'You know why, so stop complaining. I'll be back by seven. You, me, a bottle of whisky and a pack of cards. *Perfecto*,' he said before hanging up.

He had five minutes before—

The knock on his door interrupted even the thought of five minutes to himself and before he could even answer, the temporary secretary covering for his utterly faultless, but in this instance flu-ridden assistant, walked in looking half terrified. Mateo bit back a groan. He liked to fill his birthday with as much work as he could to keep himself distracted, but this was getting out of hand, even for a workaholic like him.

'Yes?' Mateo asked of the terrified assistant.

'There is a woman out here, waiting. She's been here some time,' the young man answered, twisting his hands in knots.

'Who is she? And exactly how long has she been waiting?' he asked.

'She said her name is Edwards and she's already been waiting an hour.'

'An hour?' Mateo groaned. He'd wanted to give the young assistant a chance, but clearly he was out of his depth. 'I'm about to go into back-to-back meetings for the rest of the afternoon. She won't rearrange?' he asked, half hopeful.

'She says she can't, as she has to leave for Shanghai tomorrow.'

Mateo cast a look over his afternoon schedule. 'Tell her that I'll try and fit her in, but I can't guarantee it.'

Any other day of the year he had wiggle room in his schedule for things just like this, but not today.

'Did she say what it was about?' he asked just as the young assistant was leaving.

The temp shook his head. 'Only that it was personal.'

Mateo frowned. He made very sure not to have 'personal' turn up at his office, so he couldn't begin to think what it might relate to. Edwards. The name sounded as if it should be familiar, but he couldn't put his finger on it.

He dismissed the assistant, picked up the file for the Lexicon deal and left his office by the opposite door to the one his assistant used to take him more quickly to the meeting rooms on the floor below.

Evie crossed her legs again and pulled at the form-fitting white shirt she'd thought suitable to make her look professional enough to approach Mateo Marin in his office. But four and a half hours of waiting and she was feeling distinctly *unsuitable.* The seating area she was in was out of direct line of sight of the assistant's desk, but she could hear him typing away, answering phone calls and sighing. A lot.

She'd arrived at the office as early as possible after her flight from London and had come straight to the imposing building that bore Professor Marin's son's name. It should have been familiar, but the sleek, industrial feat of architecture was so far removed from the world she'd shared with Mateo's father, it felt unnerving. And she wished for the hundredth time that he'd answered one of her many calls, or replied to the several emails she'd sent in the last twenty-four hours so that she hadn't had to come in person.

She glared at the picture of Mateo looking out of the magazine cover with one eyebrow cocked arrogantly, his arms folded across a broad chest that must have had some kind of Photoshop trickery done to it to make it look so imposing. She'd turned to the first page of the article and there he was again, staring directly at the reader—half-arrogant, half-dismissive and all ego—and the first time she'd seen it, the sudden intense heat that had flashed across her cheeks had stung. By the second look the flutter in her stomach had morphed into an angry buzz as she remembered how hurt the professor had been by Mateo's absence from his life. His son's refusal to resume even the most basic communication had devastated Professor Marin, who had not once blamed or resented his son's choice.

But it was the third time she scanned the article that made her gasp—because there in a picture captioned as 'The Library', she caught sight of several objects sitting on the wooden bookshelves. A magnifying glass, a watch, a wooden box, a compass. They looked as if they had been placed there absentmindedly. Things that had been chosen to be preserved, but easily accessible. Things that had made her wonder about their significance, in the same way as she wondered at a copper bracelet at an ancient burial site, or the earthenware jugs recovered from a lost village. Evidence left behind, for years to come. Like the item in the corner of one shelf that pulled on her heart.

The professor's notebook.

The sight of it so familiar that she'd nearly reached out to touch it on the glossy page of the magazine. She heard the assistant sigh and checked her watch. Frowning, she saw it was nearly six pm. Rising uncertainly, she approached the young man's desk, when he looked up at her half in horror.

'You're still here?' squeaked the assistant.

'Of course. I said I'd wait,' Evie replied, unaware why he would think anything different.

'But Mr Marin has left.'

'Left?' Evie asked. 'He left?' she repeated, her voice rising an octave in outrage. 'But I need to see him. It's matter of the utmost urgency.'

'I... I...' the assistant stammered, and Evie couldn't help but feel sorry for a man who was so clearly terrified of his boss. Her anger at being so easily dismissed by the professor's son receded behind the practicality of what she needed to do now that he had left.

There was no way the assistant would share his employer's home address with her, a complete stranger. She had one night to get the notebook before flying to Shanghai and she couldn't waste it.

'Would you...? I'm sorry,' she said, feigning sudden weakness, not even feeling a little bit bad about brushing her palm across her forehead. 'I'll leave, I don't want to be a burden,' she forced sincerity into her words, 'but I feel a little... Could you make me a cup of tea? And then I'll leave?' she offered.

'Of course, of course, I'm so sorry, Ms Edwards,' the assistant rushed out and practically fled from his desk.

Checking the corridor, Evie bit her lip at the act of deception that came worryingly naturally and, heart pounding in her ears, she flicked through the stacks of paper on the desk. She was about to reach for a drawer when she saw a green Post-it note on what looked like a contract with a company called Lexicon.

Courier to M. M, Villa Rubia, Sant Vicenç de Montalt.

Without a second thought she grabbed the note, fisted it in her hand and, grabbing her bag from the sofa where she'd wasted an entire afternoon, she ran to the lift and pressed the button, desperately praying it would arrive before the assistant returned.

When the doors closed and the lift began its descent, she exhaled her relief at not getting caught in a little laugh, and warned herself from getting too addicted to the adrenaline coursing through her veins. She still had to face down Mateo Marin and get him to hand over his father's notebook. But she would do it, because she *had* to.

CHAPTER TWO

MATEO FLICKED AN angry gaze from the road to the display of his ridiculously expensive car. He wasn't ostentatious by nature, but when it came to travel, he liked luxury. He cursed as he palmed the wheel to take the turn that led to his home. He was twenty minutes late. Henri would probably have let himself in already and made himself comfortable, but one thing Mateo detested was making people wait.

It was because of that that he was late himself. He'd got to the underground car park of his office building when he'd remembered the woman waiting for him in the office. By the time he'd got back up to the sixteenth floor, both his assistant and the unknown woman were gone.

Edwards. There was something about that name that rang a dull bell somewhere—

His thoughts screeched to a halt when he saw at least twenty cars on his driveway waiting to drop their passengers off outside *his* front door. Passengers dressed ready for a party. A party that he was apparently hosting but had not yet been invited to.

Henri.

Mateo was going to kill him. Violently. And publicly.

Having parked his car in the garage which, thankfully,

was free of guests, he made his way through his house, calling Henri on his mobile. Keeping his head down, Mateo passed uniformed waiters with silver platters of food or champagne, marvelling at his friend's organisational skills, whilst simultaneously worrying at how easy it was to arrange a party at someone else's house without their permission.

'Explain yourself,' he demanded when Henri answered the phone as he nodded a greeting to a couple who recognised him.

Someone stopped him to shake his hand, the face a blur through Mateo's frustration. All he'd wanted was some peace and quiet.

'It was my New Year's resolution to ignore your wishes,' the Frenchman replied with absolutely no shame.

'Excuse me? That was months ago.'

'I know. It's been a great source of pain that you've not noticed me ignoring your wishes all this time, but I'm glad it's now out in the open.'

Mateo came down the hallway and peered into the living area to see Henri, in a tuxedo, surrounded by several people dressed as if this were The Ritz, phone pressed to his ear, grinning back at him.

'I didn't want this,' Mateo said through gritted teeth.

'I appreciate that you hate your birthday, but I'm bored and wanted a party,' Henri pouted. 'Besides, you work too hard. It's time you let off a little steam.'

Mateo groaned down the phone.

'Go get changed. You look like you've had to work for a living today.'

'Yes, *darling*,' Mateo replied sarcastically to Henri's mock snobbery, spinning on his heel and turning towards the staircase that would take him to his private suite, narrowly avoiding a waitress carrying a silver tray with empty glasses.

'And wear something nice!' Henri called out before Mateo could hang up.

Today had clearly been sent to test him. But at least now the surprises would be done with.

Evie watched the red lights of the taxi disappear into the night before looking back to the sprawling estate before her. Men in full tuxedos and women in sequins and diamonds passed her, barely sparing her a glance as they all eagerly made their way towards the open doors of the brightly lit home.

Evie wasn't exactly unfamiliar with wealth. Carol and Alan had certainly had enough money to have her schooled from home the moment they'd realised her potential. And no one could argue that anyone who owned a townhouse in Mayfair could be anything short of incredibly wealthy. But this? It just…it just didn't fit with Professor Marin. But it *did* seem to fit with the arrogance she had seen of Mateo Marin.

The article had speculated about the life of the wealthy billionaire bachelor. It had covered the charities and foundations that Mateo had sponsored or founded, and barely skimmed the surface of the investment company he'd started with the help of his mother's family connections. The journalist seemed impressed rather than disparaging of Mateo's easy acknowledgement of the help he'd received as a young entrepreneur, and had lauded the fact the billionaire gave back more than he'd been given, not only to his mother's family, but also to other young business-minded people. It seemed that while Mateo traded heavily in the practical, he also dedicated much of his time and focus to clean energy and newly emerging technologies. In short, the journalist—in Evie's opinion—had clearly been swayed by charm and a good PR team, because nothing she'd seen, or heard, had proved a word of that article to be true.

She came to a stop. She'd hoped to speak to him about his father's notebook in private and throw herself on his mercy. But as she took in the party guests she knew that even at her most socially inept she would have realised now was most definitely not the time to approach him.

She was about to leave when someone shouted at her in Spanish.

'What are you doing? Don't just stand there. You're late, so we'll dock your pay, but we still need the help.'

Her knee-jerk reaction was to apologise, to try to explain in Spanish that he was mistaken. He was dressed in a white shirt and black trousers. Almost identically, Evie realised, to how she was dressed. But…wasn't this an opportunity to at least see if the notebook was still there? And Mateo Marin *had* left her waiting all day. And that *was* after ignoring all her attempts to reach him otherwise. Did a man who had ignored his father for the last three years of his life even *deserve* to have his father's notebook? A familiar heat crept up her spine as she remembered how hurt the professor had been, even as he'd never once spoken badly of his son.

The man was staring at her now as if she was stupid.

Perhaps fate had intervened and given her an opportunity.

'Pues?'

'Sí, señor,' she replied, quickly rushing to follow him as he stalked towards the back of the house.

I'm sorry, Professor, but it's the only way I can see to get what we need.

She quickly gathered that this man was a manager as he directed various waiting staff through the kitchen and around the house, and before he could give Evie a direct order she picked up a tray and decided that the safest option was to collect empty glasses. She exited the kitchen into the hallway just as Mateo came towards her with a phone pressed to his ear.

Her heart thudded once, hard, and then seemed to stop for a second. He was much taller in person, the width of his shoulders—which clearly had *not* been a trickery of Photoshop—taking up nearly the entire breadth of the hallway. He wasn't bulky, but lean. His features, even creased into a scowl, were alluring, the richness of brown in his eyes so deep, she nearly tripped. Her gaze went to the sharp cheekbones and strong jaw he'd inherited from his father. But, unlike the unruly mess the professor had barely bothered with, Mateo kept his beard trim, cut close to the skin—as if he'd made absolutely sure to be as different from the man he'd shared those features with. Everything in him was contained. Neat.

Apart from his hair, which was thick, dark and unruly, as if a lazy hand had flicked a slow curl and it had stuck that way. It matched the way the top two buttons of his shirt were undone, as if he'd just pulled off his tie after coming home from the office.

Once again, her cheeks heated to an almost painful sting, and she pressed a palm to her skin there, for once thankful that her hands were always cold.

'I don't want this,' she heard him say into the phone.

She slowed her steps, worried they might actually collide, as it didn't seem that he'd seen her.

The groan he sent down the phone raised the hair on

the back of her neck, and it turned into a shiver that fell down her spine.

'Yes, *darling*,' he growled as he disconnected the call and slipped his phone into his pocket. Evie had to press herself against the wall and nearly lost the tray of glasses as he passed her, barely sparing her a cursory glance.

Oof.

She struggled to right the tray—and her equilibrium—and just about managed it as Mateo Marin disappeared up the large staircase in the middle of the house. Fury pounded in her chest. That was the second time she'd been ignored by Mateo Marin. And the poor woman he'd been speaking to, Evie thought, shaking her head. To have to put up with a man like that! Evie clenched her teeth together. So much for being a bachelor. *Charming*, the magazine had called him. The man was a menace!

Mateo removed his cufflinks and flicked open the buttons of his shirt, tossing it aside onto his bed. There were strangers in his house. There were *waiters* in his house. He rolled his shoulders, trying to ward off the tension headache beginning to form at the back of his neck and temples.

He stared at the half-empty bottle of whisky on the mantelpiece above the fireplace. This was the one safe haven he had. His suite. He had bought the estate for his mother, but she had never lived there, instead claiming to prefer the smaller apartment in the heart of Almería. Rather than sell it on, Mateo had moved in himself, mainly just for this room. His sanctuary.

If the photographer hadn't promised that it would only be the two of them taking the pictures, and not the army the journalist had brought with him to do the interview his CFO had badgered him into last month, Mateo would never have agreed to doing the shoot in here. Thankfully the suite was large enough so that his bed had been out of the picture.

Reaching for the bottle of whisky and the glass beside it, he poured himself a couple of fingers' worth. Maybe he could just hide out here for the rest of the night, he thought, before huffing out a reluctant laugh. Henri would track him down and pull him out by the ear, no matter what he was wearing.

He took a sip of the amber liquid, relishing the explosion of taste and heat of the alcohol on his tongue, and turned to look at the shelves that lined the entire side wall of the room. *His library.* There were several serious work tomes—hardbacks, academic books from his degree—and there were many history books, which would have surprised most of his acquaintances, and were also academic rather than recreational. There were even the adventure stories he'd loved as a child and had somehow not been able to part with all these years.

On those shelves also sat the compass his uncle had given him on his fourth birthday, the magnifying glass his grandfather had given him when he had first returned to Spain with his mother, the wooden box that had held the cufflinks his mother had given him on his sixteenth birthday, and the watch—the first thing he'd bought himself with his first pay cheque. All of those he knew had been captured by the photographer's keen eye. But in the far corner, was an old beaten-up leather-bound notebook that he was barely able to look at, let alone think about.

With a sigh, he threw back the remainder of the whisky and put the glass down on the side. Perhaps it wasn't such a bad idea that Henri had decided to host a party. Mateo flicked the top button of his trousers and stalked into the en suite. Worried about what on earth Henri would get up to next, he decided he didn't have time for a shower before getting back downstairs to check what havoc his best friend had wreaked upon his life.

He ran the taps in the sink and splashed water over his face and neck, and in his haste got water in his eyes.

Cristo!

This just wasn't his day.

He slammed his eyes shut, hoping that the water wouldn't do enough damage for him to need to change his contact lenses, when his phone beeped. Prising open his clear eye, he peered at the screen to see a text message from Henri.

I left your birthday gift in your room. Indulge away, but don't stay up there all night! It's YOUR party after all.

Mateo bit back a groan. Henri was in one of his Shakespearean-level nefarious moods and frankly Mateo could expect anything from a peacock to a Picasso when he opened his bedroom door.

Although it couldn't have been that big, or surely he would have seen it before he came into the bathroom. Frowning, he pocketed the phone and gingerly opened the door to his bedroom. With one eye still clenched tight to ward off any damage to the contact lens, he peered into the gloom, his gaze finally resting on the outline of a woman's figure.

Bare hands. He would use his bare hands to kill Henri.

Evie had checked all the rooms on the ground floor and there wasn't even sight of a bookcase in any of them. Biting back an internal groan, she'd realised that she would have to follow Mateo upstairs to the second floor. An area that she'd been told was 'strictly off-limits'. Forcing a confidence she didn't feel, she took the stairs one at a time, the gentle sounds of music and easy conversation dying away as she reached the upper floor. Her heart was thumping so loudly and painfully in her chest that the moment she stepped out of sight, she put down the silver tray and rubbed her sternum, taking slow, deep breaths, just as the therapist had taught her.

She'd never once not been thankful to Carol and Alan for making that resource available to her. While they had never been demonstrably affectionate or even comfortable with emotional intimacy, they had done the best they could to meet her practical needs, with nannies who engaged her interest, or tutors to engage her intellect, and a therapist after recognising that being adopted from birth might result in a certain amount of trauma that would need processing.

As she waited for the breathing technique to work, she wondered once again why they had adopted her. They seemed only to want some kind of legacy that befitted them and Evie was never sure that she'd been able to live up to that kind of expectation, no matter how high her IQ.

She brushed the old hurt aside and focused on what she had decided to do. She doubted Mateo would give her the time to explain why she needed the notebook, and with her flight booked for Shanghai tomorrow morning, rather than risk his refusal, Evie had no other option but to simply take it. The idea of something as illegal as theft rankled, but, given that he had ignored his father for the last three years of his life, Evie had a hard time believing he would even notice the notebook's disappearance.

The corridor stretched out to the left and right of her,

four doors on each side. She started with the right-hand side of the corridor and pressed her ear against the first door she came to, her hand resting on the doorknob. Mateo Marin had disappeared into *one* of these rooms. But what were the chances he wanted to seek out the library in the middle of a house party? They weren't, after all, in a Victorian romance novel. Her hand paused on the door handle, heart racing, when…

A drunken giggle and a squeal startled her, leaving her with no option other than to pull open the door, throw herself into the room as quickly as possible, and pray that the room was empty.

Eyes clamped shut, half afraid of what she might see, she heard the couple's steps immediately outside the room. Heart in her throat, she spun round and grasped the handle just before someone tried to open it from the other side.

She couldn't be found in here!

'I think it's locked.'

'We're not supposed to be up here, remember?'

'Oh, come on, Marin has so many rooms and we have such little time.'

The door thudded and Evie got the impression of a body backed against the door, followed swiftly by a moan so explicit her cheeks pinked.

'Let's try the next one.'

Thankfully the couple moved off and soon their hushed giggles drifted into a different part of the house, leaving Evie to give a sigh of relief. She turned around, peering through the darkness at the room she found herself in, and gasped. In front of her were rows and rows of bookshelves, all carefully and meticulously ordered, with a compass on one and a wooden box on another. She'd found it!

Pressing her cool hands against cheeks hot from adrenaline, she took in the rest of the room, frowning at the bed she had not expected to see. The magazine had called this a library. Why would anyone…? Her thoughts trailed off the moment she saw the worn leather-bound notebook that had never left Professor Marin's pocket. Along with his glasses, it was what she most remembered about the man who had been more than a mentor to her.

Half convinced she was seeing things, she crossed the room and plucked it from the shelf. She half imagined that the leather was still warm, as if the Professor had only just put it down. Suddenly she was hit with a tidal wave of emotion she simply wasn't prepared for; a sweeping sense of grief, loss and longing for the steady support and belief that only the Professor had ever really given her. Yes, her adoptive parents had met her every material need, but the Professor was the first and last person who had believed in *her,* not in what she could do or what she could provide.

Holding the notebook to her chest, she had half turned to leave when a door behind her opened, and she turned to find, shrouded in light from the en-suite behind him, Mateo Marin staring right at her.

Wearing nothing but a pair of dark trousers, her gaze consumed the sight of him. Her hand reflexively fisted at her side as she took in the breadth of his chest, the dip and curve of the muscles tensing into a v at his waistband, and her breath sighed out of her in a shockingly feminine way.

With one contact lens still a little fuzzy from the water, Mateo ran his gaze up and down the woman in his room standing, somewhat precariously, on a very high, very tantalising pair of heels. He could tell that she was doing the same to him, the heat of her mutual interest reaching out like a tentative touch across his skin and making his breath shake in his chest.

Even for Henri, this was extreme. The almost constant refrain of his closest friend to leave work at the office and indulge in some play time had become boring in the last few years. Mateo had goals he wanted to achieve professionally in order to secure the personal; to make sure that his mother was happy and that those under his care, his friends, his staff, were safe. He had little time for the distraction of women.

'Listen, I'm not sure what you're here for, but I think it's probably best if you just leave,' he said.

The woman simply stared at him blankly and he wished his eye would clear so he could see her properly.

He sighed. 'If you're after money…' God only knew how much money Henri had promised her and once again he cursed his friend. He'd always skated very close to inappropriate, but hadn't once reached it, until now.

'Money?'

He frowned, her accented Spanish a little clunky, and he switched to her obviously native English.

'Yes, money. If that's what you want—'

'I don't want your money,' she said, the stress on the word 'money' almost distasteful in tone.

Cristo, Henri had actually sent him someone who just wanted to bed the bachelor billionaire. He'd been inundated ever since the article had come out. Some wanted the notoriety, some just the challenge, and this one? He wasn't sure.

'*Querida*, what is it that you *do* want?'

He blinked and his contact lens finally settled to focus

on features he'd already become intrigued by. Long dark hair had been gathered into a ponytail, making her appear fresh-faced and innocent in a way that was a refreshing change to the dates he was used to meeting.

Beautiful. She was *beautiful.* In a very classic way. The curve of her cheek drew his gaze and the temptation to reach out and cup it in his palm burned in his chest. Long, thick lashes framed eyes he couldn't quite see and unconsciously he closed the distance between them, wanting to know their colour. She took a half-step back as if surprised by his movement, halting him instantly.

Something about her clothing, the simple white shirt, rang a bell of warning in his mind, but it was barely audible over the blood rushing in his ears. It was enough to distract him from the fact she hadn't answered his question. Her hands were behind her back, pressing her chest forward, and he tried gamely not to stare at the sliver of skin he could see between the buttons of her shirt.

'What's your name?' he asked, surprised by the gravel in his own voice.

'Evelyn.' Whether it was fake or real, the breathless intonation of her name raised hairs on the back of his neck.

He nodded, disconcerted that his body's instinctive reaction to her was threatening to supersede the moral ambiguity of accepting such a 'gift'.

He took a tentative step towards her, and when she didn't back away he took another until he could finally see what he was looking for. Gold, green and mahogany clashed in eyes that to describe as simply as hazel would have been an insult. Swept back from her face, long, dark tendrils of hair cascaded down her back but it seemed that she was as incapable of looking away from him as he was from her.

Something strong and utterly unyielding wove between them and all sense of propriety left his mind. He reached for her then, his hand cupping her cheek, as he had wanted to do, the strangeness of unfamiliarity mixed with a rightness that almost made him dizzy.

What on earth was this woman doing to him?

He saw his own confusion mirrored in her gaze, as if she was as utterly confounded by this as he.

What is this? he wanted to ask, but was also half afraid to. In the back of his mind, something wasn't quite right, but the day, the significance of it, the past few years suddenly pressed so heavily against him that he wanted to throw it all away and lose himself just for one moment.

Evie didn't know what was happening. Only she did. And she *wanted* it. A small part of her mind was banging against an invisible door, trying to remind her of exactly who this was, but she couldn't hear it over the blood rushing in her ears. The scent of his cologne filled her head, a subtle spice and something deeper beneath that, darker and more masculine. Him. She could smell *him*.

Her heart fluttered in her chest and she felt an internal tremble whip through her body. Her body felt heavy and thick as if she was moving through honey. She should tell Mateo to stop. He clearly didn't know who she was or why she was here. But he was looking at her in a way that made her feel *alive*. As if she were taking the first true breath of her entire life. And before she could say anything, he had closed the distance between them and his mouth was on hers and, *oh…*

His lips, soft but determined, were already in motion when they pressed against hers, enticing her mouth to open to him. When his tongue pressed against hers, she was flooded with an intoxicating, brain-fuddling need that started at her toes and raced up to cover her entire body. He tasted like honeyed whisky, heat and hunger. It flashed over her like a fire and only then did she heed the alarm sounding in her mind.

Shaking out of her stupor, she yanked herself back away from him. Her chest heaving as she gulped in desperate breaths. Desire and shock thundered across her over-sensitised skin and a heat she misunderstood morphed into outrage.

Yes, darling.

The words he'd uttered into the phone hit her a little too late, and before she could stop herself she delivered a quick, sharp slap against his cheek.

CHAPTER THREE

THE SLAP SENT a shock through Mateo that he was, frankly, half thankful for. *What was he thinking?* Immediately he stepped back and raised his hands, more to show he wasn't a threat than in surrender.

It had been short and sharp, rather than powerful, and although he felt a gentle burn across his jawline, the woman in front of him appeared to be more surprised by her own actions than he was. Her knee-jerk response seemed shockingly innocent rather than incited by fury.

'Are you okay?' he asked, concerned by the wide eyes staring up at him.

'No, I'm not okay!' she cried. 'Why would you do that when you have a girlfriend?' she demanded, much to his confusion.

'I don't have a girlfriend,' he replied, bemused by the naïve description of his mythical lover. 'Why would you kiss me if you thought I had a lover?' he retaliated.

She frowned, presumably both at his question and his choice of words. 'I didn't kiss you, you kissed me! Do you always go around kissing women you don't know?' she asked as if outraged by the mere thought.

It was on his lips to protest that he didn't, but he just had. He watched as she raised a hand to her mouth and began to suspect that the surprise he'd seen on her features wasn't from the fact that she'd slapped him, but because of the kiss. But surely that much innocence was feigned. He ran a hand through his hair, frustrated with himself as much as the situation. 'Listen, I don't know what you agreed with Henri—'

'Who is Henry?' she asked, nothing but genuine confusion in her gaze.

'Henri,' Mateo said, stressing the correct pronunciation, even as he quickly realised that no one would ever make the mistake of saying his friend's name in such a heavy English accent if they had actually ever met the man.

'You don't know Henri?' he asked, his throat thick with deep discomfort. Had he been so utterly mistaken?

She shook her head.

'I thought you were a gift from my—'

'You thought a *woman* was a gift?' she asked in outrage, as if the arrogance of it alone was a crime.

'Birthday,' he finished lamely, anger at the way she made it sound painted in guilty red slashes on his cheeks. Because he *had* thought she was a gift and he could see now how that *was* bordering on criminal.

Would the ground please swallow him up now?

'What kind of man—?'

'It was a misunderstanding,' he said, taking a step back further away from her as if it could somehow make up for things. 'Please accept my sincere apologies.' He bowed his head, hoping to convey his sincerity, but when he looked up she was frowning at him as if she thought he was worse than the dirt under those rather spectacular high heels, which he could concede, in that moment, he was.

'But if you don't know Henri…' he said, his mind apparently dulled from the illicit kiss that still had its hooks into his brain and body in a rather alarming way, 'then who are you and what are you doing in my bedroom?' he demanded, anger at himself fraying the thin thread of his patience.

'My name is Evelyn and…' She had started out with confidence but faltered on her explanation, by which time he'd finally realised that she was one of the waitresses for the event.

He supposed at least that he should be thankful she *wasn't* here to seduce him. He caught her gaze, it was swimming with so much—anger, heat, but also anxiety—and he stepped back again. He bracketed his temples with one hand and sighed. *Cristo,* what a mess. 'I'm sure that you were told this area is off-limits,' he said with more exasperation than anger.

She stared at him for a moment, looked down at her own clothes, and something flashed in her gaze just before she answered that made him pause.

'Absolutely, sir, I'm sorry. I…needed just a moment and this was the first room I found. I'll leave. Very sorry,' she said, backing away from him.

'About the—'

'Not to worry, sir. Happens all the time.'

It happens all the time.

Why had she said that? She could see that it had confused him too. That kiss…that kiss had fuddled her mind and dissolved her rational faculties. She shouldn't have slapped him. He hadn't deserved that, but she'd been so shocked by…*everything.* How could she have kissed Mateo Marin? The man that had ignored her and devastated his father? She needed to get out of the room, urgently. And without him seeing that she had the Professor's notebook.

'I'll just be going—' she said, trying to avoid his gaze and turning in time with the hand she'd concealed so far, holding the notebook. She was halfway across the room—the *bedroom*...how had she failed to see that?—when he called out to her.

'Evelyn.' Her name stopped her and she half turned, reluctant to meet his gaze.

'If you are...having trouble with any of the clients you cater to, you should let your manager know.'

Evie stared back at him in genuine surprise. 'You just kissed me. In your...*bedroom*,' she whispered as if that would make it any less outrageous. 'And you are advising me to speak to my manager?' She posed the question slowly in the hope that he would realise just how ridiculous his suggestion had been. And finally, he had the decency to look ashamed.

'It was a mistake.'

'Of course it was,' she said, turning back towards the door, confused by the feeling of hurt and disappointment twisting through her chest. She bit her lip to silence herself. Because that kiss had awoken a desire in her that had emerged gasping for air as if it had been suffocated for years, as if each press of his mouth and plunge of his tongue had breathed life into a need she didn't recognise. And now she wanted more and she didn't know what to do with that.

She could accept that he was telling her the truth—that it *had* been a misunderstanding. But couldn't help but feel disappointment that Mateo Marin was a man who had been so willing to simply indulge in such an intimate moment with a woman who had been presented to him as a *gift*.

And then, beneath that, a deeper part she wasn't quite

ready to listen to whispered that of course it was a misunderstanding. A man like that would never be interested in a woman like her. That she would only have been kissed if she'd been paid for.

You couldn't even pay me...

She slammed the door shut on those thoughts, too painful to delve into here, where she was still vulnerable after that kiss. Closing her eyes and summoning the strength she had used to get through much more difficult moments than this, she steeled herself and took a step towards the door, when—

'Stop.'

As if he had control over her body, it did as he commanded. Frozen, she hesitated. Should she run for it? She was so close…

But his hand closed around her wrist and drew her back round.

When had he got so close?

Her breath stalled in her lungs as he peered down at her with an intensity that raised the hairs on her neck. Would he try and kiss her again? she wondered, half hoping he would but half terrified of the thought.

But when she looked up at his face, she saw a mask. A mask that should have concealed the anger thrumming in his body, but didn't. He shook his head and tutted, slowly. 'Now, Evelyn. There I was, thinking that I was in the wrong, and all this time it was you,' he taunted, his voice a honey-covered growl.

'Me?' she asked, heart in her throat as he reached behind her and plucked the notebook from her hidden hand.

'You little thief.'

Mateo clenched his jaws together before he could say whatever else was on his mind. He'd been feeling utterly disgusted with himself when he'd seen what she was trying to conceal in her hand. And this woman—this *thief*—still had the gall to stand there looking at him as if he were *still* in the wrong.

Evelyn. He frowned. The name finally ringing the bell to the end of its peal. Edwards. The woman who had been waiting for him outside his office that afternoon, the same woman who had been his father's assistant.

He huffed out a cynical laugh.

'Nice to finally meet you, Evelyn Edwards.'

She pulled away from his grasp, rubbing at her wrist as if he'd burned her.

'Well, if you hadn't left me waiting for *four* hours I might not have had to resort to *this*,' she said, her hand gesturing around the room as if it explained everything.

'*This* being breaking and entering, theft, and aggravated assault?' he demanded, astounded at the woman's audacity to sound indignant, given the circumstances.

'I did not break a single thing, and as for assault, that was self-defence.'

He rubbed his jaw, her gaze snapping to the place where her palm had connected with it. Yes, he'd definitely deserved that, but he didn't deserve this, he thought, his grip tightening on the notebook she'd tried to steal.

'Was this what you wanted to see me about?' he asked, holding it up. The silly woman could barely contain her desperation. As if connected to the object, her whole body shifted towards it, and he was unaccountably irritated by the motion, his male pride smarting that her only interest in this room was his father's scribbles. It had been all about the notebook from the very beginning. He was such a fool.

'There are many ways you could have gone about this, Evelyn. *This* was not the right one.'

He turned on his heel and walked past her to put the notebook back on the shelf where it had been.

'Wait.' The word punctured the thick, heavy air in the room.

'I…am sorry,' she said, the words ground out between clenched teeth, betraying the fact that she clearly wasn't sorry at all.

He cast a glance back at her, his raised brows showing the truth of his thoughts.

She sighed and tried again. 'I *am* sorry. But it really is a matter of some urgency. You hadn't replied to any of my emails or phone calls—'

'How do you have my number?' he asked, surprised that a woman he barely knew five minutes ago had become a lot more tangled with his life than he could have imagined.

'Your father gave it to me, in case of emergency.'

He felt as if he'd been slapped a second time that evening by her easy, familiar reference to his father. With a follow-up sucker punch that he had been his father's emergency contact, despite the fact that they hadn't spoken in the three years before his passing.

He wasn't sure how to process that information. His relationship with his father had been more than strained at the best of times. It was as if they'd spoken different languages—something about their interaction always rubbed the wrong way, painfully, abrasively and inevitably. Something that seemed to be repeating itself with Evelyn Edwards.

'I didn't come here to stir up old wounds,' she offered apologetically, as if he could even believe that.

'No? Then why is my father's assistant here?' he demanded, just stopping short of adding, *In my bedroom* and *messing with my head.*

'Your father's *assistant,*' she replied with not an inconsiderable amount of bite to her tone, 'is now Professor Edwards.'

Mateo was impressed, piecing together what little he remembered hearing of her. Child genius, high IQ. And yet, she'd clearly been naïve enough to follow his father down the rabbit hole of what amassed to little more than pirate stories and treasure hunts.

'Good for you,' he replied as he looked away in disappointment.

'Do you think you might be able to...?'

He looked up to find a pretty blush on her cheeks again.

'What?'

'Do something about that,' she said, her hand sweeping a circle in the air around his chest, and belatedly he realised he'd held the entire conversation with her whilst shirtless.

Cristo, this woman short-circuited his brain.

'Don't move,' he said, glaring at her for good measure, before he turned and pulled open the door to his walk-in wardrobe, leaving it ajar so that he could hear her if she tried to leave. He grabbed a pale grey shirt from the hanger and thrust his arms into the sleeves with angry, awkward movements. The kiss, his father, the notebook—they all bled together as he pulled at the shirt cuffs and started doing up the buttons slowly enough to buy himself some time to get his head on straight.

Citrus was what she'd tasted like. Sweet citrus and sunrise.

And since when had he become a poet?

Since the first second of that kiss. It had been as if a switch had been flipped and he'd been utterly overwhelmed. It was probably a good thing she'd stopped it when she had because he wasn't completely sure he'd have been able to end it. And she'd been in just as deep as he had, he'd *felt* it, known it as sure as his own name. She was right, it had been utterly wrong of him to kiss her. But the heat and want from her…it had been there beneath the simmering confusion in her gaze, it had been in the little gasp he wasn't sure she even knew she'd made, the opening of her lips beneath his and the tentative tongue—at first—and then…

Whoosh.

They had gone up in flames.

A flicker moved in the mirror in the corner of the room and he clenched his jaw. It didn't matter if they'd burned down Rome, she wasn't here for him. All she'd wanted was his father's notebook. Mateo turned back, finishing doing up the last button on his shirt, came out of the walk-in wardrobe and stalked towards her.

'Better?' he asked, somewhat peevishly.

'Much, thank you,' Evie replied primly and could finally stop averting her gaze so much. Though she wished he wouldn't glare so much. Something about the way he peered at her beneath those strong, dark brows made her feel too similar to how she'd felt when he'd… She cleared her throat. 'As I was trying to explain, I've been hoping to speak to you about your father's notebook.'

'And when you couldn't, you thought you'd just take it instead?'

While she searched for a way to answer that question, her eyes tracked him as he crossed to the mantel above the fireplace and poured a finger of whisky into a crystal-cut glass.

'Want one?' he asked far too casually for her liking.

She shook her head. All she wanted was to take what she'd come here for and get back to her hotel. Being near him after that kiss, it was all too confusing. Her pulse was still racing, and every time he looked at her she felt it almost like a physical touch. She cursed her pale skin as she felt the blush rise again on her cheeks, because without taking his eyes from her once, he lifted the glass, drained it, and poured himself another.

She opened her mouth to advise him to perhaps take it easy, and once again his raised eyebrow dared her to intervene. Pressing her lips together and biting her tongue, she looked around the room, hoping for a reprieve from the intensity of his focus.

She took it all in, even as she felt the hot, heavy press of his gaze. The bed had surprised her at first, but that was because she had imagined the bookshelves as part of a bigger library. A desk sat between two impossibly large bookcases, in front of a bay window. But the desk itself was oddly familiar; that deep forest-green leather topping the dark mahogany table-top, with drawers either side of the seating area. Perhaps if she got close enough, she'd see a ring mark in the top right-hand—

'It's a different one.'

She glanced back at him, unnerved that he had read her thoughts so easily.

'The desk. It's not his,' Mateo clarified unnecessarily, his tone so balanced she couldn't read the emotion that lay hidden beneath it.

'Mr Marin. This really has been an unfortunate misunderstanding.'

'Of course it has,' he replied, throwing her words back at her.

She ground her back teeth together to prevent herself from saying something stupid. Inhaled, counted to five and exhaled slowly. 'I waited. Outside your office, this afternoon, and when I came here—'

'How did you get my address, by the way?' he interrupted easily, infuriating her—in part because she still felt guilty about it.

'I saw your address on the desk while your assistant was making me a tea,' she said, hoping Mateo wouldn't blame the young, out-of-his-depth staff member.

'Huh,' was all the reply he gave as he watched her over his whisky glass. 'He's a temp,' he said, half apologetically. 'Of course, had my usual secretary been present, you would have been seen, and sent away again within minutes, I assure you.'

Without the notebook. That was the unspoken conclusion to the sentence she heard. And once again his absolute refusal to listen or try to understand her—just as he had done with his father—grated on nerves already raw.

'I came here to speak to you and explain,' she tried again, 'but there was a party and I was mistaken as a waitress,' she said, gesturing to her clothes and then regretting it as Mateo's slow gaze tracked her body, 'and before I knew it, I had a tray in my hand.'

'Clearly it would have been too much for you to simply explain that you weren't the hired help for this evening?'

She bristled at the superiority in his choice of words.

'Well. Here I am now, listening. Why do you want the notebook so badly?'

'I need it to…to…' Evie bit her lip, remembering the NDA in time to stop herself from breaking it, but clearly managing only to look even more idiotic to Mateo than she had before.

Something flashed in his eyes—as if he'd come to a realisation. 'I can't believe this,' he scoffed. 'You're going after the treasure?' He shook his head at her as if he was disappointed in her. 'It's a fool's errand,' he stated, looking at her as if she had utterly lost her mind. He was shaking his head, even before he said his next words. 'No. You can't have the notebook. I'm doing this for your own good. You'll thank me one day,' he said, pointing a finger at her that she wanted to grab and pull—*hard.*

Anger shot through her, twinning with frustration. How many times had—and would—people tell her what was best for her?

You're not ready for it.

You don't have the life experience for it yet.

It's for your own good.

That heat boiled over into her words. 'Your ego is utterly inconceivable,' she growled at him. 'What on earth would you know about what is good for me? You know *nothing* about me. And yet you think you have the right to decide what is "good" for me?'

He stared at her, all mulish stubbornness, but she thought she had struck a chink in his determination. Until he replied.

'Did he ever tell you of the other historical academics whose careers were wrecked on the shores of this particular pirate story?' Mateo asked. 'Do you know the name Professor Wheller or Kritsen?' It was clear that the names meant nothing to her. 'They were the first two who believed they could prove that Princess Isabella of Iondorra was Loriella Desaparecer. And the reason you've never heard of them? Because they were blacklisted from academia. Men have been driven mad trying to find the Desaparecer treasure.'

'I am not a man,' she replied hotly. 'And I am *not* looking for the treasure.'

'I don't believe you,' Mateo replied. And he didn't. How many times had he heard from his father that it wasn't about the treasure? That it was about history and uncovering the truth, about giving people 'their place' in the story of the past, not the one assigned to them by the victors? And yet still his father had chased the pot of gold at the end of the rainbow as if finding it would somehow make up for the fact he'd lost his wife and son to his madness.

Mateo ground his teeth together. So, no. He knew it was overbearing, and an inconceivable arrogance that Henri would be proud of, but he could not help Evelyn Edwards throw her career and whatever else she had away on a search that she had only pursued because of his father.

'I don't care if you have the backing of the King of England—'

She reared back, shock exploding in her gaze before she tried to blink it away from her eyes. He had strayed too close to the truth. He must have.

'You've *got* to be kidding me?' he groaned, realising that *someone* had to be backing this wild goose chase.

'I don't know what you think is going on but—'

'Enough. I don't want to know and I don't care. Whatever damage you want to do to your reputation from here on in, you do without my help.'

She glared at him. A thousand furies all spitting hell

and something in him roared in delight. He felt it, the passion and the heat, boiling the surface of her outrage, until it came to a screeching halt that he felt shockingly jarred by.

She nodded. 'Okay,' Evelyn said, her shoulders slumped, and he had to stop himself from reaching out to her in concern. 'I'm sorry for ruining your birthday. This clearly wasn't what you had in mind,' she said.

Reeling from the sudden about turn, he was so busy trying to find his feet that she spun on her heel and left him alone in his room with the taste of citrus still on his tongue. He reached for the glass of whisky and knocked back the last mouthful, hoping that the burn would erase the last trace of Evelyn Edwards.

Refusing to acknowledge the spool of disappointment that unwound in his chest, he rested his gaze on the bookshelf where he'd placed his father's notebook.

The *empty* space where he'd placed his father's notebook.

That little thief.

CHAPTER FOUR

'YOU ARRIVED SAFELY?'

'Yes, Your Majesty.'

'And the hotel is to your liking?'

'More than, Your Majesty. It's the nicest room I've ever stayed in. I can't thank you enough,' Evie replied sincerely.

Already Queen Sofia had shown more concern over her preferences than her adoptive parents. It wasn't, Are you at the hotel? but, Do you like it? Not, Did you arrive? but, Did you arrive there safely?

'I believe of the two of us,' the Queen said through the phone speaker, 'it is you that needs to be thanked. Did you get what you needed from Spain?'

Did she?

Evie had come to believe that she got a lot more than she'd bargained for.

'Yes, Your Majesty. I got the Professor's notebook.'

'And it will help you ascertain the provenance of the octant?'

'Yes, ma'am. The auction is this evening and I will let you know the moment it's done.'

Ending the call as politely as possible, Evie turned and pushed back the curtain on the incredible suite the Iondorran palace had arranged for her at one of Shanghai's most famous hotels.

The view of the river took her breath away. As the sun crept upwards to meet the day, mist hazing the edges of the serene vista, she knew she was seeing a different image from the typical neon-bright, futuristic marvel that most people associated with the Huangpu. A golden glow pushed at the night's blue slowly, edging it back to make way for the sun. It felt as if she was witnessing a glimmer of the *real* Shanghai.

Evie had wanted to come here for years. She and the Professor had been due to attend the Shanghai Archaeology Conference two years ago but Professor Marin had passed just before. And to be here now, alone, made her feel a little sad.

Seeking comfort, she looked to the notebook she'd left on the bedside table. In the twelve hours of the flight from Spain she'd pored over every page, some of the Professor's notes making her smile, some of them making her cry, and some making her wonder if Mateo had read the words written down by his father.

From his reaction when they had met, she doubted it, sadly.

And just like that, the thought of Mateo did it again—made her heart thud a little heavier in her chest, made her skin a little too sensitive. She pressed her fingers to her lips again, and tried to catch a breath. She bit down gently against her lower lip, hoping to relieve the ache that had taken up place the moment she'd pulled away from his kiss.

And then, just like when she'd tried to get some sleep on the plane, the memories of that kiss morphed into an earlier memory—one that was half-nightmare.

You couldn't even pay me to kiss you.

The one time she'd ever had the temerity to ask someone out and, in her naïvety, had forgotten that she was a sixteen-year-old girl, surrounded by university students in their twenties. Of course, it had ended badly. Shame and embarrassment crawled up her neck in hot, ugly inches. And no matter how she tried to tell herself that what had happened with Mateo was different, the exact opposite even, something had connected them in her mind and she couldn't seem to separate them.

She swallowed the lump in her throat and turned back to the bed. It was six am now and she had five hours before she could see the octant, and then, if it proved to be authentic, she would need to find something suitable to wear for the glamour of the evening's auction. But as she crept between the covers of the bed, yawning, her last thought before falling asleep was of deep brown eyes and hot caresses.

Mateo descended the short flight of steps from the private jet that had brought him from Spain to Shanghai in a fraction of the time it would have taken Evelyn on a commercial airline, with Henri shouting down the phone in his ear.

'A bottle of whisky! I left a bottle of *whisky* in your room, not a woman! How could you think I'd do such a thing?' Henri demanded.

Mateo pinched the bridge of his nose.

'I mean, I'm a lot of things, Marin, but a procurer of women is *not* one of them.'

'And *that* is the most important part of everything I've told you, is it?' groused Mateo.

'Right. Your Father's pretty assistant—'

Mateo pulled up short. 'I didn't say she was pretty.'

'You kissed her. Is she *not* pretty?'

Mateo clenched his jaw together, cursing that, no matter how much coffee he'd drunk that morning, or whisky he'd drunk last night, he could still taste a sweet citrus on his tongue. 'That is not the point,' he reluctantly replied. 'She stole from me—'

'So you kissed your father's pretty assistant—'

'She's a professor,' he reminded Henri, much in the same way that she'd reminded *him* last night.

'Evelyn Edwards stole your father's notebook and you're in Shanghai to get it back,' Henri replied in loud, sharp words down the phone.

'Yes,' Mateo said, pulling the phone away from his ear and wincing slightly as one of the cabin crew took his suitcase to the black town car waiting for him on the private landing strip. He smiled perfunctorily at the woman who had ideas in her gaze and suggestions on the tip of her tongue, and, ignoring both, he got into the back of the car…alone. 'And while I'm here, I'll be able to meet with Léi Chen.'

'Only you would try to do a business deal while following a woman halfway around the world.'

Mateo pressed against the dull throb at his temples. Contrary to what women—and Evelyn Edwards—seemed to think, he wasn't a notorious playboy willing to bed anyone that entered his bedroom. He still couldn't work out what had come over him last night. He counted his drinks before she had appeared in his room. He'd only had one and that was most definitely not enough to fuddle his mind to the extent that he grabbed and kissed, *thoroughly* kissed, a strange woman in his room, no matter why he'd thought she was there.

'Your message said that you'd left a present in my room.'

'It. Was. Whisky.'

'*Where?* Where did you leave this mythical bottle of whisky?' Mateo demanded for the hundredth time.

'I left it beside your bed.'

'You left it in the darkest corner of my room, not known as the best place for leaving presents!'

'That is beside the point. When you find her, you tell her it's your mistake. I cannot have people out there thinking that I *buy women.*'

'I hardly think that's the most important—'

'You promise me *right now.*'

'Okay, okay,' Mateo said, pulling the phone away from his ear for long enough to give the driver the name of his hotel, and returned to the call, 'I promise I'll let her know.'

'Listen, don't worry about Lexicon. I know the deal as well as you do,' Henri assured him. Mateo bit back the thread of discomfort at the idea of handing it over to anyone, but he trusted Henri with his life. He'd already caught enough grief when he'd called to cancel dinner with his mother, and leaving work rankled, even if it was just long enough to get back the notebook.

'But are you sure that meeting Léi Chen is the right thing right now? You've not taken a holiday for *years*.'

'This isn't a holiday,' Mateo growled.

'But you're in Shanghai, and with a pretty professor too—'

'I'm hanging up now,' Mateo announced, despite the smile pulling at the curve of his lip. When his entire life had changed in an instant, Henri—the first student he'd met at the exclusive boarding school his mother's family had sent him to—had been the one to make him laugh until his stomach hurt, and smile when he'd thought he'd not find anything to smile about again. Family—Mateo knew—was made of more than just DNA.

It was made from being there when needed. Present and in person. Time and time again throughout his whole life his father had made him wait. Second to a treasure hunt that was scribbled about in the pages of a notebook Mateo couldn't bring himself to read. There had been so many times over the years when his mother had needed her husband. When *they'd* needed him. But instead, it was Mateo who had stepped up to comfort his mother when she cried. He'd been the one who had made sure that his mother had what she'd needed, the security she'd needed. And his father? He'd buried himself in his research, or some dig site that might finally prove his utterly baseless theories about princesses and pirates true.

So yes, he'd come to Shanghai because he wanted that notebook back. If only to burn the thing and be done with it for ever.

In the viewing room of one of Shanghai's most famous auction houses, Evie felt the hushed silence, as reverent as that in any museum. The large warehouse-sized space stored all of the items up for auction over the next forty-eight-hour period, and what she saw was a veritable feast of exquisite historical artefacts, some impressive, some simply beautiful.

Feeling much better than when she had landed, and dressed in clothes that were much more comfortable and familiar to her than the black and white suit she'd chosen to wear to meet Mateo Marin, she made her way slowly towards the area that displayed the items of the auction she was interested in.

Her heels clipped on the concrete floor, polished to a gleam. Her high-waisted, wide-legged trousers concealed the ferocious height of her favourite pair of shoes. It was her only indulgence, she thought, smiling a little at the rather shocking amount of money she'd paid for this particular brand. It wasn't that she was short. In fact, if anything, at five feet six, she was almost tall in some circles. But shoes had become the thing she'd relied on to see her through whatever she faced. She'd been walking through Cambridge, shortly after her first—and last—May ball, her confidence in tatters and her heart low. She'd passed a shop and stopped to stare at the beautiful high heels in the display window.

A girl wearing those wouldn't be laughed at, she'd thought. *A girl wearing those would be confident, alluring. A girl wearing those would be a* woman.

At sixteen years old, not even able to legally drink, having just been humiliated and rejected by her first crush, she'd wanted all those things so desperately. Even now, Evie's breath shuddered in her lungs from the memory of that need. It felt like a lifetime ago, but she remembered the hurt, the pain and the hope. That was the day she'd bought her first pair of heels and she'd worn them for hours and hours, practising to walk in them until she'd mastered it completely.

Yes, she would be embarrassed again, and yes, laughed at too, and she might even have to fake that confidence a little. She might never quite be alluring enough, but she was a woman from that point on in her mind, heart and soul.

And in *this* moment? Utterly sure in her ability and

her knowledge of the item she was about to assess, she relished the clip of her shoes echoing in the large space as she drew closer and closer to the very item that could, one day perhaps, give credence to the Professor's final research paper. And maybe, just maybe, help prove her own theories about Princess Isabella too.

There were a few other people in the brightly lit area but she let their hushed whispers disappear into a haze of background noise as she came to the raised glass case containing the gold legs and semi-circles of the eighteenth-century octant up for auction.

A beautiful example of an early edition octant from John Handly (1682-1744), made of gold and ivory. Unique for its unusual design and materials for the period, and the thicker, graduated arc along the bottom. The navigational equipment has exquisite and unusual detailing, with the following engraving:

'Presented by J Berry Aberdeen on behalf of His Majesty King George II. May your travels be swift and take you where you need to go.'

Item reported, without proof, as having belonged to Loriella Desaparecer.

It was a thing of beauty, and not just because of how well it had been preserved. Despite the fact that every inch had been intended to aid navigation, there was elaborate artistry in every curve. And as she came around to the back of the glass box, allowing her to see the back of the octant, she searched for the mark that the Professor had written about in his notebook. It had been a habit of Isabella's father, the King, to place his own mark upon any expensive gifts, in case ownership ever came into question. And there it was! A small but perfectly identifiable etching of the five petals, single stem and leaf of a clematis; the national flower of Iondorra. Just like the one from the old charcoal rubbing Professor Marin had folded into the pages of his notebook.

She peered closer just as she felt someone behind her. When she moved a step to the side to see more clearly, a shadow again fell across her line of sight. Sighing irritably, she turned to confront the person and stumbled the moment she saw who it was.

A strong arm swept out around her waist, holding her, when she would have fallen from heels that had never once let her down before, ever. As she looked up into the eyes of the man who held her, rich dark whispers of heat were interrupted by a cynical glare.

'Fancy meeting you here,' Mateo Marin said with absolutely no surprise whatsoever.

Her hands clutched at his waistcoat and the *heat*… He felt burned, deeper than his skin, so much so that he nearly dropped her.

Mateo cursed. He could read volumes in the gaze staring up at him, marvelling at the clarity of each emotion he saw. And while his mind chose to ignore the flash of desire he sensed she struggled with, his body didn't. Fighting back his own arousal, he righted her and looked away from the pink flush across her cheekbones. He pulled once sharply at the points of his waistcoat, needing something to do with his hands other than reach for her again.

'What are you doing here?' she demanded with a bite no more dangerous than a papercut. She glared at him angrily from beneath long lashes he remembered being fascinated by. 'Wait, how did you…how did you find me?' she demanded, passing a leather briefcase from one hand to another.

He shrugged as if he hadn't paid an inconceivable amount of money to hire someone to find precisely that information out. 'It wasn't that hard.'

'You had me investigated?' she cried in realisation. 'That is a violation of my privacy!' Her outrage would have been laughable, had it not been for the increasingly concerned glances being cast their way from the other people in the warehouse.

'You can't have expectations of privacy while committing a crime.'

'Oh, for the love of—'

'Give me back what you stole and I'll be out of your life for good,' he said pleasantly, even though he felt anything but pleasant.

Her hand flexed around the strap of her bag as if she thought he might try and take it from her with force. *Joder*, what kind of man did she think he was? And then he remembered that she had been grabbed and kissed by a stranger in a dark bedroom and told that she had been mistaken for a gift.

'And to…erm…' Mateo rolled his eyes to the ceiling. 'Henri wishes for it to be known that he doesn't buy women.'

'What?' Evelyn's hazel eyes peered up at him in confusion.

Mateo cleared his throat. 'I promised that I would explain to you that Henri did not buy a woman for me as a gift.'

'Oh.' She bit her bottom lip and snared his attention away from the conversation. 'Okay,' she said on a little laugh. This was *not* going how he'd intended. People didn't laugh at him; they usually did what he said. But Evelyn Edwards seemed to oppose him at every turn.

'Now, the notebook?' he asked, holding his hand out in expectation.

'I can't give it back to you,' she said.

'I believe you can. It's really quite simple. You reach into your bag and you place it in my hand.'

'I don't have it with me,' she replied, the pretty blush becoming slightly angry on her cheeks now.

He raised an eyebrow, disbelieving her entirely.

'And even if I did,' she started, 'why do you want it?' she asked, for once genuinely. 'What is it to you? You didn't speak to him for the last three years of his life, Mateo.'

And there it was again. The knife that cut too close to the heart of an old hurt it left him almost breathless with anger.

'You think you have more right to it than I do?' he demanded.

'Maybe, yes,' she replied, and the sheer honesty of her response was more cutting than a thousand knives.

'Well, you're wrong,' Mateo stated sharply. 'I deserve every page of that notebook because while he was scribbling notes about his research on his trip to the research dig in Indonesia, he'd promised to be there for the results of my *bachillerato.* And when he was delivering his lecture on Iondorra's Economic Impact on Europe in the Eighteenth Century, it was my twenty-first birthday. And you know what? I don't even know where he was to celebrate my company's IPO launch because all I *need* to know is that he simply couldn't be bothered to show up.'

Evelyn looked at him with a sympathy that grated rather than soothed.

'Have you read it?' she asked.

'I don't need to read it. And neither do you. You were there with him on every dig and every research paper,' he bit out, unable to prevent the mean words from spilling between them.

'I don't—I'm sorry, Mateo.'

'But you won't give the notebook back to me?'

Evelyn bit her lip as if to stop herself from saying more.

'Fine. You don't want to give me the notebook? Then I'll have to take something you want even more.'

Concern filled her gaze, blotting out the thousands of questions he saw there. Honestly, her eyes were like a constellation, mapping the course of her thoughts. The woman should never play poker. Because he'd already beaten her at her own game.

'A word of warning. If you're planning to go to the auction dressed like that, think again.'

With that parting shot, he turned on his heel and stalked out of the auction house, leaving her standing alone in the middle of a near empty room.

Evie flexed her hand, before running the black liner across her eyelid, working carefully so as not to stab herself. Much like the heels, she'd practised make-up but it had never made her feel the way that the shoes did, so she tended not to wear it. She always thought that when teaching, it made her look as if she were trying too hard. To fit in, to look older, to try to make them take her seriously. She pulled her hand back as she got a little upset.

Why was she thinking like this all of a sudden?

Because she was still upset about Mateo. Only upset didn't seem to cover the seething mass of emotions that twisted and turned whenever she thought about that afternoon. She felt guilty, because at the beginning of their encounter she truly hadn't wanted to give the notebook back to him. She *hadn't* believed that he'd deserved it more than her and facing that thought was difficult and painful.

Mateo's words had conjured a side of the Professor unknown to her and it seemed he was not entirely blameless in the one-sided relationship she'd seen and that was also difficult. But Mateo had also been wrong about his father not being bothered to be there for him, and once she had returned the octant to the Iondorran palace, she would make sure that Mateo not only had the notebook, but also understood that the Professor had bitterly regretted some of his choices.

And between anger and guilt, she was annoyed with herself for the utter extravagance of the dress she had eventually bought. She'd let Mateo's taunt get to her and, even though she hadn't quite understood what he'd meant by it, it had sunk teeth into her vanity and hurt.

She turned side-on in the mirror, casting a critical eye over what she saw. Red sequins covered every inch of the material that clung to her skin like water, flashing and sparkling in the bright bathroom lights. The deep v on her chest was replicated on her back, and the ruby-rich red colour of the material made her skin glow. The skirt flared out from the knee and pooled in a half-train behind her.

A secret feminine part of her was both giddy and thrilled, she really did look good, but the other more practical part chided the waste of it. Would Mateo even see her in it? The warning he'd left her with…did that mean he intended to come to the auction? Evie was confused by her feelings. That she wanted him to see her like this, that she wanted him to...*want* her.

Not that it mattered. It wasn't as if she would ever act on it. Mateo had already proved how utterly unsuitable he was. Someone like him would never understand someone like her. She rolled her shoulders and pulled herself together. Tonight, she would bid on the octant, tomorrow she would travel to Iondorra, and the following day return to her flat in London, where her normal life would resume.

Barely an hour later and Evie found a seat near the large, heavy-curtained window as the seats at the auction quickly filled up. Tuxedos, velvet, silks, and jewels were as on display as the items up for sale. While the evening auctions often held fewer lots than those in the daytime, the money changing hands that night would likely exceed sixty million, and people dressed for the occasion. People that, she was sure, would bid on the octant.

She sat through the early lots trying not to think of where Mateo was. Casting her eyes almost constantly around her, she'd not yet seen him. Maybe he wouldn't show up after all?

'Lot Thirty-Two, ladies and gentlemen, an unusual octant thought to have belonged to the great pirate Loriella Desaparecer.'

A gentle ripple of laughter broke out, cresting against her like a wave, and Evie fought back the irritation and frustration it caused in her.

'While octants of the period usually sell for much less, this unique piece made with gold accents not only increases interest, but so does the inscription, connecting the item to the British royal family. Owing to significant interest, we'll start the bidding at five hundred thousand.'

There was a gasp across the audience. Even Evie hadn't expected the guide price to be so high. It differed from what was in the catalogue. A gentleman near the front started with the first bid, she countered, and so it began. The three or four other interested parties soon dropped away as the bidding got closer and closer to one million. Her heart was pounding and a cold sweat was breaking out across her skin as they got closer and closer to the Queen's financial ceiling. Evie had a certain amount to play with, but any more would bring too much attention to the item and Iondorra still couldn't risk anyone discovering their interest.

Back and forth she went against the man in the front, who didn't seem bothered in the slightest. Unease filled her as they were now at the nine hundred thousand mark. So much for avoiding attention. The other bidders were now watching a tennis match as she and the man bid back and forth. She wanted to scream. Gripping the white card with her bidding number on it, she raised it to bid nine hundred and ninety thousand.

Her heart beat painfully in her chest as she saw the man waver. It was going to be hers. She would win the bid on the auction and be able to return to Iondorra with it. The Queen would be able to give her father the peace he deserved and she might be able to use it to find proof that would finally validate the Professor's research. Wet heat pressed against the back of her eyes and she willed herself not to cry with hope.

'The bid is with the lady in the middle. Back to you, sir?'

She bit down on her lip. She couldn't afford to bid any more if he chose to counter.

The man shook his head.

'Going once…'

She stifled the sob of hope and excitement that filled her chest. She was going to do this. She was going to get the octant.

'Going twice…'

'Two million dollars.'

In unison with every other person in the bidding gallery, Evie turned to look at the man who had just doubled her bid and the gasps of shock were drowned out by the sound of blood rushing in her ears.

There, at the top of the aisle at the back of the room, dressed in a black tux, sexy as sin with his hair in effortless disarray, was Mateo Marin, who had just bought the octant for two million dollars.

CHAPTER FIVE

MATEO MARIN FIXED his stare on the auctioneer, because if he caught even the merest glimpse of Evelyn Edwards he might just implode. He should have spent the last six hours since he'd seen her working on the prep for his meeting tomorrow with Léi Chen. The merger would be a real coup if they could pull it off, bringing untold solidity to his financial base. That security…it was important to him. But instead, he'd been distracted by thoughts of Professor Edwards, so much so that he'd sent at least five emails to the wrong recipient and had nearly caused an internal incident. Henri had finally got on the line and told him to switch off his laptop, making him feel even more frustrated. And now? The victory he thought he'd feel at snatching away the precious item she'd clearly come to buy from her at the last second…it hadn't helped one bit.

Evelyn turned to glare at him, ignoring the gossips in the seats beside her flicking their gazes between the two of them. Eyes rimmed with kohl made the deep chestnut of her irises glow golden. Her lips were a shade more intense, not powerfully rouged, but accented in a way that made her look freshly kissed. The subtle make-up stirred far too much of a reaction in him and he made to turn away, and then she stood up.

Cristo.

Tension hummed through his body as if he'd been shocked by mains electricity and he was forced to almost violent levels of self-control to stop himself from doing something monumentally stupid like reaching for her the way he had in Spain.

A red shimmering film clung to a body he'd not even had the faintest idea about. Hidden beneath the trousers and shirts he'd seen her wear was a body that rooted him to the spot. He failed terribly to stop himself from consuming her with his gaze, lingering over the span of a waist he wanted to encase with his hands, the shoulder he wanted to slide the silken strap of her dress from, the breasts he wanted to take into his mouth and hear her cry her pleasure. And then, when she started to walk towards him, the sheer sensuality of the glide of her hips on those incredible heels, and he had to turn away or embarrass them both. It had been too long since he'd allowed himself to be distracted by a woman and he had no intention of starting now.

At the back of the room an assistant was waiting to direct him to the clerk to process the paperwork for the sale, but he too was as lost to Evelyn as Mateo had been. The young kid's blush put Mateo firmly back in his place and by the time Evie had reached him, Mateo had regained control over his wayward body.

'What was that?' she demanded in a furious hiss.

'That was me showing an interest in eighteenth-century pirate treasure.'

'Don't be absurd,' Evelyn dismissed. 'You have never once shown an interest in—'

'Cara,' he said, interrupting her, 'please know that when I show an interest in something my focus is absolutely, utterly and irrevocably fixed.'

She glared at him, and golden fury rained down on him like the bright embers of a children's sparkler. Everywhere her gaze touched him burned bright but left no damage other than to his libido.

'You are holding it hostage,' she growled, and he was half surprised that she hadn't stamped her foot.

'The octant? Yes. I am,' he replied and had to work to stop himself from smiling at her indignant outrage.

He took her arm, ignoring the sparks the physical contact sent up his skin to his chest and, turning them away from the curious glances, led her out of the auction room into the reception area.

'I would have given you the notebook back,' she said from between clenched teeth.

'Would have?'

'Well, I'm not going to now, am I?'

'It's sweet that you think you can stand toe to toe with me on this. You *will* give it back to me,' he warned, before turning to find the office where the clerk waited to process the paperwork.

Evie paced the reception room, waiting for Mateo to return. She told herself off for letting him get to her. It was the octant she needed, not the notebook. Of course, she should give it back to him, as she'd intended from the beginning. But Mateo's high-handedness had riled her usual peaceful and happy equilibrium. And to think… she'd been actually hoping that he'd show up to the auction and see her in the dress!

And now everything that the Queen had wanted was at risk. Yes, Evie had hoped that she might be able to prove her and the Professor's theories true, but more than that she had really wanted to give a daughter the chance to do something kind for her father.

Just then the devil walked back into the room and she hated that even through the angry red mist she could see how gorgeous he was. His hair was tousled as if he'd been running his hands through it, his eyes looked darker against the midnight colour of his tuxedo. At some point Mateo must have pulled his tie loose, as the ends hung down, stark against the white cotton shirt, making him look every inch the billionaire Lothario.

She bit her lip and dragged her gaze upwards, to discover that he had caught her staring. He raised his eyebrow as if to dare her to keep looking, but she couldn't and turned away.

'Are you coming?' he asked her.

'Where to?' she asked hesitantly.

'Somewhere we can talk privately.'

Gone was the surface civility from before, the good-natured, easy-going façade he had hidden behind. The tone of his voice and the taut lines holding his body stiff all spoke of the fact that the games were over. Even the slight undercurrent of flirtation that had simmered between them ever since the kiss was gone.

She nodded and followed him from the auction house. They didn't speak a word to each other in the taxi that took them back to the hotel they were both staying in. She didn't object as he led them through the exquisite foyer of the hotel, towards a bank of lifts that looked very different from the ones she used to get to her room.

She didn't say a word as he gestured for her to enter the lift and swiped a card that permitted access to the penthouse. She barely registered that the doors opened directly into the suite that looked out over the river and the stunning nightscape of Shanghai as she tried to find a way through thoughts that circled between the octant, the Professor, Princess Isabella and Mateo and his father. And lost amongst all of them, buried deep in there, were thoughts about herself.

She placed her wrap over the arm of the sofa and turned to where Mateo watched her from the entrance of his suite. The wooden box containing the octant was tucked under his arm, possessively.

'Can I see it?' she asked tentatively.

He seemed to consider her request and for a moment she thought he might refuse it, but he slid the box onto the coffee table in front of the sofa.

'Knock yourself out,' he said before going to the wet bar and pouring himself a drink.

Evie rounded the sofa and, sitting, took a breath as she opened the box.

'How much do you know about your father's research?' she asked as she took in the exquisite craftmanship of the octant up close. It really was a thing of beauty.

'Assume I know ninety per cent and understand eighty per cent.'

She smiled sadly at his response. 'Your father used to say the same thing.'

'I remember.' The sharp edge of his tone lashed and stung.

Forcing down the feeling, she delved into the legend that had captured her attention at a very young age and been the driving force behind her desire to delve into archaeology in the first place.

'Princess Isabella had been sent by her father, the King, to her fiancé in the Dutch East Indies—a Dutch colony in what is now known as Indonesia—when her ship was attacked by pirates.'

'There was a great battle,' Mateo said, picking up the train of the story in an overly dramatic fashion. 'The Princess's people put up a valiant fight, enough so that the pirate captain was killed in the skirmish,' he concluded, and then he frowned as if, for the first time, realising the story had a plot hole. 'Everyone thinks Isabella also died during the attack, but my father believed she survived. So why didn't she make it to her fiancé?'

'Rumour was that he was a particularly vile man with a reputation for cruelty who only wanted the dowry, not the wife. And he'd already received the dowry.'

'He intentionally let his fiancée get set upon by pirates? If she survived, why didn't she just go home?'

Evie let out a half-laugh. 'She was betrothed to a Dutch duke in a trade exchange. She was nothing more than a chattel and her father would simply have sent her back to Indonesia to her fiancé. There's reason to believe that she was ignorant to that.' Unwanted by parent and fiancé. Even as a child she had unconsciously identified with a princess disowned by her family and her future.

'And she just walked into the position of captain? A princess?' Mateo asked sceptically.

'I doubt it was that easy. But within eighteen months, Loriella Desaparecer was sailing the high seas and causing more damage to the Dutch East India company than any other pirate or privateer operating during that time. The records are sparse and much of what we know is hearsay. But that's not surprising, as the records are from the VOC—the Dutch East India company. And it's unlikely that her ex-fiancé would want any specific details getting out about the beating they were taking from his betrothed.'

'You believe it,' Mateo observed, 'that they were the same person.'

'Yes, I do,' she answered honestly, squaring up to him as if she expected him to meet her with a barrage of doubt and derision.

'And you think this octant is proof of that?' he asked.

'No,' she replied, immediately confusing him a little. 'It is clearly possible that Loriella stole it from whoever ransacked Isabella's boat, or was given it, or it fell into the sea and was discovered later. There are many, many ways in which the octant that once belonged to Isabella ended up with Loriella.'

'Then why do you want the octant?'

'I don't, but someone else does, very much. And I will do anything I can to make that happen,' she said.

'Even give me back my father's notebook?' he asked.

She was torn. He could see that. Her connection to his father was almost visceral and tied to that damn note-book.

'You paid two million dollars for the octant,' she stated quietly.

'A price I am willing to pay to put an end to this once and for all,' he replied before finishing his glass of whisky in one mouthful.

'But don't you want to know?' she asked, her large eyes glowing with an earnestness he felt too old for.

'Know what?' he asked, suspecting he didn't want to hear the answer.

'Know if he was right? Know if this could help even with the smallest possibility, prove that your father's the-ories about Isabella were true?' The plea in her voice, the eagerness, the desperation to redeem his father…it was as painful as it was obvious.

'No. The veracity of his claims about Isabella in no way makes up for all the time he spent ignoring his duties as a husband and as a father. He just wasn't there, Evelyn. He was *never* there. Again and again he was absent from my life and you don't know what that's like, how it makes you feel.'

He could have bitten off his own tongue. Even if he hadn't just remembered that she had been adopted and taken in by an rich, older English couple, the look on her face—the way that the blood had drained instantly from her features, the sheer excavated wound that her eyes exposed—was enough. He remembered his father's complaints from back when they were still talking; frustration and incredulity at the behaviour, the *absence*, of his assistant's parents. He'd called them cold, aloof, and utterly unfeeling. Mateo had remembered because he'd not been able to understand how his father couldn't see the irony of what he was saying. That his father was raging against the injustice of bad parenting had been a knife in his gut. And even now he remembered the twisting feeling of it but still that gave him no right to trample all over her pain.

'Evelyn—'

She held up her hand, bringing his silence while she gathered herself.

Guilt scratched against his skin like sandpaper and he couldn't stay still. He put his glass on the side and came to the chair angled ninety degrees from where she sat on the sofa. He sat and braced his arms against his thighs.

But before he could speak, she stood, rubbing her hands on the silk of her dress.

'You want the notebook in exchange for the octant? You're willing to do that?'

'Evelyn—'

'Are you?' She looked up at him as if she wanted this over and quickly.

'Yes,' he replied, the word ground out between clenched teeth, ignoring the swipes his conscience was taking at him.

'Here,' she said, reaching into the briefcase she had brought with her to retrieve the notebook she'd taken from his estate in Spain. 'I never should have taken it. And if I had any other option, I would not be bartering the octant for it now. But before I go, I want you to see something,' she said, unwinding the leather string keeping the cover bound and preventing several loose pages tucked neatly into the spine from coming free. She turned to a page bookmarked by an old Polaroid.

Just the sight of the black square backing the old photograph brought a deluge of memories of the way his father had eschewed the modern technology of digital cameras over the old-fashioned physicality of his Polaroid camera. His mother still had several pictures his father had taken from when he was younger and when they were still together.

'I know that things had become strained between you. And I know—more than most—how lost your father could get in his work. His focus and drive was something that very few people could match, but it came at a cost. One he regretted bitterly.'

Her words should have soothed—wasn't it what he'd always wanted? For his father to have known how much he'd missed out on? For his father to have recognised the damage he'd caused? But they were too little, too late, and he wanted her to stop. Stop explaining and justifying his father's absence.

She plucked the Polaroid from the notebook.

'We were coming back from a conference in Toronto and he'd made sure that our flights stopped in New York. He'd been so excited. So proud.'

Mateo's jaw was clenched so tight, a headache had begun to form. He didn't want to know what she was alluding to, didn't want to hear it. He'd become a child again, pressing his hands over his ears so as not to hear his mother's heart-wrenching sobs.

'We arrived just as you were being interviewed,' she offered as she held out a photograph he couldn't bring himself to look at yet. 'You'd just taken your company public in a record-breaking launch. And they were asking who you had there with you to celebrate.'

'And I said I had everyone I needed,' Mateo replied, remembering how angry he'd been that his father hadn't been there. 'My mother, my grandfather and my friends,' he said, repeating the words he'd said to the journalists that night. It had been the final straw. That his father hadn't been there for his greatest achievement had drawn an uncrossable line between them. But now Evelyn was saying that he *had* been there?

'We left shortly after. He didn't want to spoil your day.'

Finally, Mateo looked at the Polaroid she held out to him.

In the picture his father was standing in the foyer of the New York hotel Mateo had hired for the launch party celebration. His father was staring straight at the camera, beaming with a pride Mateo barely recognised. Mateo's heart pounded as he searched the image for the incontrovertible proof of what his heart wasn't ready to accept.

And there in the background, over his father's shoulder, looking up and staring towards the camera he saw *himself.* Goosebumps broke out on his skin as he stared at the little Polaroid. A moment in time he'd never known about.

His breath left his lungs in a gush as if he'd been punched in the chest. 'I…' He didn't even know what to say.

'I know that this doesn't make up for things, Mateo, but you should know that he did love you,' Evie said, hoping that he believed her. 'He did regret the distance between you.'

'Why didn't he just stop? Stop this ridiculous search,' he asked of the only person who might be able to answer.

'I think…' She hesitated and his heart held its beat. 'I think it's because he wanted to prove to you that it was worth it, That his sacrifice had been for something real.'

'Then why didn't he say anything?' he demanded, his voice like gravel.

'He didn't think he deserved your forgiveness,' she said quietly.

Mateo cleared the thickness from his throat with a cough and reached for the whisky to swallow all the other emotions clamouring to escape. He couldn't stop himself from wondering if things had been different, if he'd seen his father there before giving that interview, would there have been peace before his father had died? Would they have reconnected?

He felt the weight of Evelyn's gaze on him, almost as palpable as the dawning realisation that he had got things so very wrong.

'Who was he to you?' Mateo asked, looking to Evelyn, now standing by the window, having given him some space to process his emotions.

The question might have appeared strange but Evie didn't mistake it for anything other than a child trying to understand their parent.

'He was a lot,' she admitted truthfully.

'How did you meet?'

Evie huffed out a gentle laugh. 'Carol and Alan, my adoptive parents, took me to meet him when they realised my interest in Iondorran history wasn't just a phase. We'd taken a summer holiday to Iondorra when I was about five. They'd already started to notice that my intellect was high. I was apparently dissatisfied with explanations that would pacify other children; my reading skills were beyond above average. At first it was thought that I was an only child used to adult company—Carol and Alan were hardly ones for baby talk or play. But they'd been advised to take me away on holiday and it happened to be to Iondorra.'

Evie turned away to the stunning nightscape reflected in the river just beyond the hotel. 'They had picked up a travel book, hoping to perhaps keep me from asking them questions every two minutes, and I'd read it front to back in less than an hour. There was a small history of the monarchy in it and something about Isabella caught my imagination. I wanted to know more. I needed to know what happened to the woman who had been sent away from her home and never reached her destination.

'We visited the museum and there was a section with Isabella's room recreated with some horribly frightening waxwork figures and pieces of her clothing and jewellery that had remained behind to be sent on once she'd arrived in the Dutch East Indies. And that was it. I was fascinated by the idea that there were belongings, proof, evidence of a life even after it had been left behind.' Evie ran out of steam and realised that she'd just let that all blurt out and her cheeks flamed, and she was suddenly embarrassed. Pressing her cool hands to her skin, she smiled ruefully.

'So it was Isabella that led me to your father. And it was your father that seemed to be the first person I'd met that understood me,' she finished with an apologetic shrug, hoping her words didn't reignite Mateo's hurt.

When she looked up, she was surprised to find that Mateo had left the chair and crossed the room. He was further away than he had been in Spain, but her heart still fluttered in her chest like a bird. The scent that had almost hypnotised her before was still there, taunting her. Hope for something she did not want to name still filled her lungs, making it hard for her to catch a breath.

He looked at her, his gaze unfathomable, but long and steady, as if telling her that he saw her too. Not that he understood her, but that he *saw* her, and that was almost too much for her to bear.

She went to turn away, but his hand caught her chin and gently guided her back. 'Don't. I… I'm glad you had that with him. I'm glad he was there for you in a way that you needed.'

She wished he wouldn't use words like *need* when he was that close to her, when she was this vulnerable. He was talking about his father, and all she could think of was how he'd kissed her. How he'd prised open her lips with his own, how his tongue had filled her in a way that made her both full and hungry at the same time.

Her breath caught and he dropped his gaze to her lips. Desire flashed like fireworks in the espresso-rich depths of his irises. For an exquisite moment he leaned towards her, the move barely perceptible, but enough for her to feel the puff of his breath against her lips. She angled her head towards him just when he released her from his touch and stepped back as if to emphasise the distance he wanted between them.

Desire turned to shame in a single twist of a heartbeat. Once again she was that naïve girl with her first crush, humiliated by how badly she had misread the situation.

A sob replaced hope, hurt replaced desire and she quickly spun away from him, half running to get her wrap and the box containing the octant. She had to get out of there before she made an even bigger fool of herself.

'Evelyn, wait,' he called after her, but it was too late. Tears were already blurring her vision, but as she blindly reached out for the wooden box it slipped in her cold hands and crashed to the floor, hitting the side of the table, cracking open and landing on the octant.

The gasp that cut through the room echoed with Mateo's own shock as he pulled her back just in time from reaching for a jagged metal piece and cutting herself. Cursing, he led her over to the couch, leaving her only long enough to pour a measure of whisky into a glass and making her drink it. His own shock was almost as acute as hers.

'It's okay, Evie,' he said, using the shorter version of her name for the first time and not even noticing.

'Oh, my God.' She looked up at him, eyes wide and tears gathering. 'I'm sorry, I don't… I'm sorry.'

He shushed her gently and took the octant carefully from her to inspect the damage. Casting his eye over it, he could tell that the bottom arc of the device was a little bent, but it was the crack in the bone inlay along the back of the arc that was the most obvious. His heart dropped, even as he tried to comfort her.

'This can be repaired,' he lied.

But she shook her head back and forth. 'It doesn't matter. It's not about whether it can be fixed…' She held her hand out for it and he gave it back to her, watching as she gently ran her finger over the crack. She shook her head again, but then stopped. Frowning, she brought it closer to her face as if she'd seen something.

'What is it?'

'I don't know… I think… Is that paper?' she asked, seemingly of herself. 'Can you pass me my bag?'

He retrieved the leather briefcase she'd dropped by the door of the suite and gave it to her, taking a seat in the chair beside the sofa.

After rummaging around in the bag, she took out a pair of tweezers and gently went at the crack in the octant, poking the tweezers into the crack and retrieving what looked like the smallest roll of paper he'd ever seen.

He stared in disbelief as she put the octant to one side, and gently prised open the ancient piece of paper.

'What are they?' he asked, even though he had a sneaking suspicion that he knew very well what the figures were.

Evie looked up at him, shock turning to surprise, excitement replacing horror. 'I think… I think they might be coordinates.'

CHAPTER SIX

MATEO WISHED SHE wouldn't pace like that in the suite. With every movement she made, sequins shimmered and shivered across her lithe form and he couldn't look away. He ran a frustrated hand through his hair and bit back a curse, turning to glare at the tiny piece of paper with numbers scratched onto it from four centuries ago as if it were to blame.

'I understand,' Evelyn said into the phone she'd been on for the last half-hour. 'Yes, I agree.'

Angry. He was angry. A worryingly large amount of pent-up energy was coursing through his veins and he realised that he'd subconsciously been echoing Evelyn's movements and pacing the suite himself.

Basta ya.

He caught her eye and gestured to the door to the bedroom and en suite. She nodded absently and went back to her phone call. He stalked through the door, past the large bed that taunted him, and into the bathroom.

Running the cold tap, he splashed water on his face in an attempt to shock him out of whatever funk he was in. But in his heart of hearts, he knew it wouldn't work. Because what he felt in that moment was guilt. Guilt, anger, frustration. Had his father been right? All these years, all the anger and hatred he'd directed towards him for choosing to chase a fantasy over his responsibilities, and in actual fact his father had been the only one to see the truth?

He punched the marble countertop in a fit of fury. He wanted to roar, to yell, to swear and break, but Evelyn was only a room away and he didn't want her to see that. Evelyn, the woman who had been the only one to support his father.

It didn't make up for the fact that his father had never been there for him—even if he had been there at the IPO launch. It didn't make up for the fact that his mother had been devastated by his absence, it didn't make up for the years of feeling second best to a myth, a legend only his father believed in. But…if it was real, if those co-ordinates, or whatever lay at the end of them, proved that his father had been right, that *Evelyn* had been right, then maybe he could at least see his father's search through to the end. It was all that was left of their relationship and he owed it to them both to see it through. He could work with Evie, they could take some time to make a plan. He could still see Léi Chen tomorrow and then—he nearly laughed at himself—they could go on a treasure hunt?

Mateo had looked up the coordinates on his phone while Evelyn had called the person she had been acting on behalf of. Mateo was half-sure it was the Iondorran palace, but he doubted she'd tell him even if she was allowed to. The coordinates had pinpointed an island in Indonesia and he knew that she would want to go there.

Cristo, *he* wanted to go there. It became an urgent refrain in his mind, needing to know if his father really had been right. Maybe knowing one way or another would finally bring him and his mother some peace.

He stared at himself in the mirror.

And instead, he saw Evelyn looking up at him, her entire body throbbing with want so clear he felt it beat against his skin in tidal waves that pulled him closer and closer. And he'd wanted her with a kind of feral insanity—the strength of which he had never experienced before. But he couldn't. She was innocent. If he hadn't known it before, when he had first met her in Spain, he knew it now for sure. It was written in every single part of her body and, although he'd hated himself for crushing the desire he so easily read, it was far better than for him to have toyed with her knowing it would and could not go any further.

But she was as dangerous to him as he was to her. She wreaked havoc with his focus and was far too tangled up in things with his father. No. He needed to keep her at a safe distance.

He splashed water over his face again, hoping it would take a bite out of the desire he felt simmering just beneath the surface of his skin and his civility.

Reaching for a towel, he swiped angrily at his face and threw it aside. He might want to keep a safe distance from her, but he also knew that she would get herself into trouble if she ran off to Indonesia on her own. They just needed to make a plan, he decided as he left the bathroom and made his way back to the suite. He would speak to Evelyn about this and perhaps—

He came to a halt, knowing immediately that she was gone.

Evelyn exited the cab and thanked the driver, turning to gaze up at a train station that looked far more like an airport. Yes, she could have waited until tomorrow for the quicker train. She could even have taken a flight. But she'd needed to go *now*. And not just because she'd stolen from Mateo *again*. Her hands shook as she reached for the strap of her briefcase. She had left with both the octant *and* the notebook, knowing that she would need the notebook when she reached the coordinates and unable to trust Mateo that he would let her have it until then.

She felt faintly sick, but it wasn't because of yet another instance of morally ambiguous behaviour she seemed to engage in since meeting the Spaniard. No. In her mind, she watched as Mateo released his grasp on her chin and stepped back, the apology clear in his gaze. He didn't want her. It was that simple and Evie decided then and there that she'd take disdain over pity any day and she hoped beyond all hope that he'd have the decency to at least let her go.

She made her way into the sprawling international train hub and was thankful that there were signs in English to point her way. She ignored the looks she drew as she rushed through the station, having only had time to grab a handful of clothes and her wash bag before leaving the hotel. She'd not even had time to change.

She found her way to the platform, urgency nipping at her heels. Her heartbeat raced as she boarded the train and found her cabin, an instinct telling her she needed to hurry, while a voice whispered that she was running away.

Of course she was running away, she wanted to cry.

Shame and embarrassment were one thing, but to be rejected like that again… It was too much. It *hurt* too much. She'd tried to pass her encounter off with Jeremy, the boy from Cambridge, as a universal childhood experience. And she'd hoped that the derision and near-exile from her colleagues because of her association with Professor Marin's research would peter out. But it hadn't. Instead, all that rejection and all that hurt had snowballed, accumulating the weight of an avalanche, and she just... she just wanted to breathe.

She put her bags down and sank onto the bottom bunk of the small cabin. It was just big enough for her, with a little table between a small seat on one side and the bunk on the other. A minuscule bathroom was wedged next to the seat and she vowed to change out of her sequinned dress the moment the train left the station. But until then she let the wave of hurt washing over her bring tears to her eyes. Here, alone in the small cabin, she let a few of them go, sweeping them aside with shaking hands before they could fall. She was about to give in completely when a knock pounded against the door. She reached for her ticket and opened the door, only to step back in shock.

'What the hell do you think you're doing?'

Mateo Marin loomed impossibly large in the small doorway, still wearing the tuxedo from the auction earlier that evening. An announcement sounded over the speaker, buzzing in the background, but she couldn't understand it. Her sadness morphed into anger and frustration in a heartbeat. He'd come to stop her because just like everyone else he underestimated her. And she couldn't take it any more.

'I'm following the coordinates. Are you here to stop me? To tell me that you won't "let" me? Please. Tell me that I'm going to "thank you one day",' she challenged him, *dared* him. Something hot and fiery twisted in his gaze.

'You rush off in the middle of the night—'

'It's not even ten pm,' she cut in.

'Without even letting me know—'

'I don't *have* to let you know!' she yelled, her anger rising to unprecedented levels.

'Without a single care for your own safety—'

She huffed out an incredulous laugh. 'Trains are far safer than planes.'

'I wasn't talking about your preferred mode of transport,' he growled and walked her backwards into the small cabin. 'You can't just rush out without a plan, having stolen from me *again*. The octant is mine. The *notebook* is mine. I'm now in this as much as, if not more than, you. Now, we're getting off this train and returning to the hotel to figure out how best to get to these damn coordinates.'

'You want to follow the coordinates?' Evie asked in surprise.

'Of course I—'

This time it wasn't Evie that interrupted him but the jerk of the train leaving the station, shoving her forward and throwing her against his chest. He reached out a hand to brace it against the overhead bunk, his other arm wrapping around her, holding her to him before she could hurt herself.

Instinctively she clung to his waist, her fingers fisting the black tuxedo jacket, and she could hear the strong pounding of his heart where her cheek had landed on his chest. For just a second the wind lodged in her lungs before coming out on a whoosh.

For a blissful moment he just held her, his hands firm, his scent intoxicating, but it was the *holding*. She couldn't remember the last time…*a* time…when she'd just been *held*.

She heard him curse under his breath and tried to disentangle herself, embarrassed for weaving a fantasy from an accident.

'We'll just get off at the next stop,' Mateo said dismissively.

Evie bit her lip and winced a little.

'What is it?' he demanded.

'Well, it's just that the next stop...' she said, looking into a stormy gaze.

'Yes?'

'It's Hong Kong. In nineteen and a half hours.'

Mateo furiously jabbed out a message to Henri on his phone. He didn't know what he would have to do to make it up to Léi Chen, but he would find a way to do it. Mateo absolutely hated letting people down. In fact, this might just be the first meeting he'd ever missed. Tension and frustration roiled in his gut, and with Evelyn in the bathroom he had nowhere else to direct his ire than into his phone.

He fired off a message to his assistant asking him to arrange for his things to be collected from the hotel and for a car to meet them when they arrived in Hong Kong. Along with his passport. After a rather tense negotiation with the train inspector, he'd been given a fine and forced to buy a ticket for the cabin, although only once the inspector was convinced that Evelyn had no objections.

For a moment, he thought she would object. He'd seen the temptation in her eyes as she glared at him, before finally nodding to the inspector that he could stay in the only free space left on the fully booked train.

He leant back into the small seating square beside the cupboard posing as a bathroom, wincing as his shoulders hit the sides, and mulishly glared at the two bunks on the opposite wall. The top bunk had yellow tape across it, with what he presumed was Chinese for 'out of order'. Hence why the inspector had needed Evie's permission. He rubbed his eyes. His contacts had become dry and were already hurting. By the morning he would be in agony.

Only one bed.

Of course there was only one bed.

The thud of the water shutting off in the cubicle beside him was the only notice he got before Evelyn emerged from a cloud of steam, having *finally* changed out of the dress that had been designed with the sole purpose of driving him out of his goddamned mind. He blinked, hoping to lubricate the lenses.

She took one look at him and sighed. 'I really am sorry about your meeting. But it's not my fault,' she repeated for the hundredth time.

'Really? If you'd just told me where you were going—'

'Mateo,' she snapped, using what he thought of as her teacher voice, 'I am not prepared to fight over this for the next nineteen and a half hours.'

Which was a shame. Because he wanted to fight about *something*. Anything, rather than the unwanted desire coursing through his veins that had grown exponentially when he'd imagined Evie under jets of hot water.

He blinked again.

She slid onto the bunk to sit opposite him, the small plastic table wedged in between them, and peered at him in an unnervingly analytical way. She sighed again and reached into her briefcase, rummaging around until she found what she was looking for.

'Here. These should work.'

She thrust a pair of glasses across the table at him.

Mateo stared at them as if they might bite. They were his father's. He shook his head, less in denial and more in confusion.

'You have the same prescription. He told me that once.' She smiled sadly. *'"Blind as bats we are. Both of us,"'* she quoted, getting his father's intonation just right. 'He was always losing them, so I got used to carrying a pair around with me. And when I came out to Shanghai I wanted…' She shook the sentence away with a wave of her hand.

She'd wanted a part of his father there with her, he realised.

He nodded, taking the glasses into his hand. Refusing them would reveal more stubbornness than he was willing to concede. If he'd expected some kind of 'there, I told you so', he'd been wrong. Evelyn was still avoiding his gaze and he was pretty sure he knew why.

'Thank you,' he offered reluctantly.

Evelyn finally brought her eyes to his and accepted his thanks with an equally reluctant nod. She pulled a notebook from her briefcase—her own, not his father's—and she started to make notes in it. Something about it was achingly familiar and utterly strange. He had never met her as his father's assistant, but he could see it so easily. The two of them working together. What she had shared with him in the hotel had given him a much stronger understanding of what his father had been looking for in the search for Isabella. But he wasn't quite sure what was driving Evelyn. She'd clearly identified with Isabella but he didn't quite feel that was the whole truth.

'You said that…' He paused to choose his words carefully. He knew that he was treading on painful and dangerous ground for her, but maybe once he understood her, this insane fascination with her would end. 'You said that my father was the first person who understood you. Your adoptive parents… Carol and Alan…they didn't?'

Her pen paused mid-sentence, and everything about her tensed before she seemed to make herself relax with some effort. The table was barely a foot wide and this close he could see every flicker in her eyes, reminding him of embers in a fire. He saw her debate whether to answer him or not and then saw the end of the fight.

'No, I don't think they ever have understood me really. Alan is a retired inventor with several successful patents under his name and Carol is a retired housewife.'

It wasn't that her voice had gone cold, Mateo realised. It was that it had become…clipped. As if compartmentalising as she went. Careful. But there was no warmth, no mess or anecdotes. He felt as if he had been formally introduced to her parents at a cocktail party, without the cocktails or the parents. If he'd been asked about his own mother? He'd probably have complained about a million different things, but all with a smile and all with the knowledge of love, no matter what. That was blisteringly absent from Evie in that moment. And as if by that very absence he heard what they hadn't given her.

'You weren't happy with them?' he asked before he could stop himself.

Evie bit her tongue against the surprising desire to reply honestly. She would always have been truthful, but to be *that*? Honest? About something so personal? The urge was strange and unfamiliar.

'They gave me so much more than I could have ever asked for,' she replied genuinely. 'But they are unaccustomed to…' Torn between loyalty to the people who had taken her in when her birth parents hadn't, and to herself, she simply struggled to find the words for how painful it had been to grow up without the comfort of easy affection. 'They are not the kind of people who eat meals in their kitchen and laugh at daily anecdotes. They are not the kind of people who call weekly and invite you round for dinner at the weekend,' she said, suddenly aware that she was describing things that she'd always wanted from them. 'They care for me, I know that, but showing their feelings isn't something that comes naturally to them,' she said, choosing her words carefully. 'It's not personal to me, because they are the same with everyone.'

'Evelyn, you are not everyone. You are their child,' Mateo insisted gently.

She didn't want to look at him, didn't want to read the sympathy in his eyes that would remind him of his father. The Professor had tried to keep his feelings to himself about her parents, but had often failed spectacularly. The thought softened the hurt radiating out from the bruise she had felt born with, deep in her heart. His defence of her had warmed and soothed in a way she'd never experienced before. But when she did finally meet Mateo's eyes, the fierceness of his gaze, the burning heat of his anger on her behalf made her feel something else entirely. It made her feel *seen*.

'They give me what they are capable of giving and I know and understand that—I know and understand their limits. There simply wasn't any "more" to ask for from them.'

'Did you ever want to look for your birth parents?' he asked hesitantly, as if he was aware he was bashing around the fragile contents of her life and smashing them accidentally.

Evie looked out into the dark beyond the train's window, remembering the sessions she'd had when she was younger with her therapist. Remembering how she'd first been so bewildered by the idea that wanting to be wanted, wanting *love*, wasn't something to be ashamed of. That there wasn't something needy or grabby or desperate within her as she reached again and again for things that weren't there for her. It would have been logical then, perhaps, to search for her birth parents—as Mateo himself had seemed to wonder. But she'd spent years putting words to her feelings and understanding to her emotions, and she'd known then, just as she did now, that she just hadn't been able to face the idea that the people who had given her up for adoption might not want to know her. Might never have regretted their decision. What if, every day, they were thankful that she hadn't reached out to find them? The thought bloomed fresh blood on an old wound and she knew she couldn't risk it. She had stored up her hurt and the room it was locked in was full. There was no more space for her to ache.

Evie exhaled hurt and looked up to find him watching her closely. Instead of answering his question, she asked one of her own. 'Why did you stop speaking to your father?'

His body's reaction was almost imperceptible. Almost. But she'd seen the emotional flinch that had braced his features, the hitch in his breath, the tightening of his shoulders. 'Because I couldn't wait for him any more. I couldn't…' He nodded slowly, understanding and equally unable to put into words the hurt of a child who couldn't trust that they would get what they needed. And it was a need. A need that if not met, it would have been devastating.

'But Evie,' he said, reaching for her hand, laying his

over hers in a gesture of comfort that, rather than startling her, she wanted. Welcomed. *Needed.* 'I regret that so much. I regretted it even before you told me about him being at the IPO launch. I regret that I will never get the chance to make peace with him.'

But you still have time, his words whispered.

'You shouldn't let fear hold you back from the things you want to know, Evie.'

She shook her head at his words, as if she could avoid them from finding a painful landing spot on her heart. Avoid the possibility that he might be right. Because…

'If I discovered that my birth parents still didn't want to know me, that they never regretted giving me up for adoption, if their lives are better off without me in it… I don't think… I don't think that I could survive that much rejection,' Evie confessed in the smallest of voices.

When I've already survived so much.

Evie had been so good at pushing aside this hurt, but she suddenly felt it hit her now like a tsunami. It had made her feel vulnerable and ashamed to admit her feelings. And she pushed back at the wave of the other smaller rejections that snowballed in her heart. The boy from Cambridge, the academics that should have supported her. *Him.*

She silently whispered the promise she'd made years ago.

I won't beg to be loved by anyone ever again.

It was a promise that taunted her now as she looked at Mateo, the glasses he wore framing eyes that saw too much and too deeply. But it was precisely the depth of those feelings that made that promise so important even now.

Unable to hold the intensity of his gaze, she looked

out of the window. It was late, but they hadn't eaten yet, and even though she wasn't remotely hungry they would need to eat at some point. 'I was going to get some food from the service counter.'

'I'll go,' Mateo offered, getting up quickly, clearly forgetting the tight space he was in, and must have hit the table across his thighs, *hard*, from the wince in his features.

She nodded, not even able to find humour or sympathy in his need to escape. She should be using this time to look at the research on Isabella and Loriella, not in a getting-to-know-you session with Mateo Marin. She barely spared him a glance as he squeezed out into the hallway, her gaze blurred by tears, staring at words she couldn't see, hoping that she could at least hold them back until the door closed behind them.

Mateo cursed himself all the way to the food service counter and back again, ignoring the funny looks he got from his fellow passengers. He should never have asked her that question. And for what? To satisfy his own curiosity? To help shore up his own defences at the expense of hers? That was a low point, even for him. And as much as he hated to admit it, hadn't he already rejected her too? He couldn't lie to himself. He'd seen it in her eyes in the hotel. He'd known what she'd wanted and he'd backed away, and in trying to protect her he'd quite possibly done more harm than good. He prised the door to their cabin open with one hand, while he juggled a mound of unhealthy packaged food in the other, only to discover that Evie had fallen asleep. Head resting upon her arm, which was stretched out across a notebook with a pretty sloping scrawl, she looked serene in comparison to the high emotions that had driven him from the cabin.

He sighed, and sat down beside her. He couldn't leave her like that, she'd feel awful in the morning. He had intended to lift her up and place her properly down on the bunk, but the moment he had her up, she drifted against him and settled there. His only option was to remain like a statue and crick his own neck in the morning, or lean back against the cabin wall and let her sleep against him. His body knew what it wanted, and for the first time since he'd met her, Mateo gave in to the path of least resistance.

He toed his shoes off and, holding her with one arm, managed to slip out of his tuxedo jacket and pull his shirt from his trousers to make himself as comfortable as possible. Giving up, he leaned back against the wall and arranged her as comfortably as possible. Her hand slipped around his waist, while her cheek rested against his chest, and as much as he wished to curse himself to hell and back, he decided that it was the least he deserved. He could undergo a few hours of the sensual torture of having a beautiful woman pressed against him. From here, he could pick out the red and gold strands that took her hair from dull brown towards auburn. Assured that she was asleep, he picked up a lock of the soft threads and ran them between his thumb and forefinger. Smooth and silky.

In his mind, he plunged his fingers through her hair to scrape gently against her scalp and she leaned her head back into his touch, exposing her neck to his lips, and on his tongue he remembered the taste of citrus and heat and…

Cristo, what was he thinking? Not only was she so clearly innocent, but she was also vulnerable on a deep emotional level thanks to the very people who should have protected her. It angered and infuriated him in a way that made a mockery of his desire and need for her.

She stirred beneath him and he quietly cleared his throat, the sound cutting through the small cabin. He forced his frustration to the back of his mind, and without moving her too much reached for the notebook Evelyn had been reading. He supposed if he was to go on a treasure hunt, he should at least try to be prepared.

He peered at the notebook held in one hand through the glasses she'd given him. She'd been right. They were a match for his prescription and he hadn't even known that. As he read through her notes, he saw the questions scribbled in the margins about what his father would think, whether he would have seen it the same way as she did. And in his mind, he saw a student missing her mentor, finding her own path and making her own discoveries, but alone in those discoveries with absolutely no support from the academic world. And even as his conscience stirred, she nestled deeper against him.

Evie fisted her hand in the cotton sheet as she began to wake. Her felt heart bruised and raw but that was background to something much more persistent in her mind and body. Heat surrounded her, and the scent that filled her senses was woodsy and salty, sharp with a bite of bay. She remembered that scent, but couldn't quite place it in her half-asleep state. Desire crawled across her skin, heat slipped between her heartbeats and need throbbed between her thighs. She shifted her legs in an attempt to soothe the ache and stopped when she felt the superfine wool of a man's trousers. Not just *a* man. *Mateo.*

Her eyes sprang open to find her hand fisted in the

cotton of his shirt, her other hand wedged between her cheek and his chest. Frozen still, she felt a gentle press against the back of her head, and in the reflection of the cabin's window she realised she was lying practically on top of Mateo, his hand pressed against her head in an almost possessive way. She bit her lip to stop herself from moving, terrified he might wake to find her draped all over him.

His head faced the other way to her, his chin angled down towards the top of her head. His glasses were on the tip of his finger, dangling from his free hand, hanging off the side of the bed and hovering above her notebook that was now on the floor. She must have fallen asleep at the table, she realised. Not that it explained how she was currently sprawled across him.

The sound of his heart thudded in her ear again, slow, powerful and unstoppable. That was what he made her think of, that was what he was like; powerful and unstoppable. She was fascinated by that kind of force, that kind of self-assurance. She had tasted a hint of it in the moments before he kissed her in his bedroom, before he'd discovered who she was. A hint that had remained in the back of her mind like a drug, one she wanted again. Even now her breath caught in her lungs, pressing her chest against his side, arousal and want hardening her nipples to painful points that only he could appease…and never would. Because instead of erotic fantasies, she remembered the way he had pulled back from her in the hotel, apologies in his eyes and barriers between them. And if she continued to lie there indulging in silly schoolgirl fantasies she would only hurt herself more. He stirred beneath her, his free arm coming up from where it had dangled off the bed, to wrap around her and hold her in place.

In her shock she squeaked, but he mumbled at her to go back to sleep. And she wanted to. She wanted to go to sleep with someone holding her tight, wrapped in a warm heat and the unspoken promise of what could happen when she woke. But she couldn't. Because at that precise moment, the train began to slow.

'What's going on?' a sleep-fogged voice asked from beneath her.

'We're here,' she answered.

CHAPTER SEVEN

THE CAR MATEO'S assistant had arranged to meet them from the station in Hong Kong took them to a small private airport where Evie's benefactor had arranged for a small flight to take them out to Amahai Airport on Maluku. From there, further 'transport' would take them to the coordinates. Transport turned out to be a one-hundred-and-five-foot yacht with a twin engine, a Jacuzzi, three impressive suites, with a galley and staff accommodation, worth more than he'd just paid for the octant.

'You need a plan, Evelyn,' he argued, standing on the jetty beside the exquisite boat that gleamed in the morning sun.

'I have one,' she said, passing her briefcase to a young woman in a white uniform.

'Really?'

'Yes, this boat will take me to the island the coordinates pinpoint.'

'An *uninhabited* island, buried deep in the Kei Islands. What if the weather is bad?'

'The yacht has state-of-the-art stabilisers, sir,' the woman in the white uniform informed him. He glared at her in thanks—she was *not* helping.

'Why are you making this so difficult?' Evie asked.

'Because for a genius, you are not thinking this

through. You need a base of operations. You need to do your research, gather your information and then go to the site.'

'You sound a lot like your father at the moment.'

'Said no one ever,' he growled.

Evelyn sighed. 'This will be my base of operations. We will dock…moor, berth—?'

'Drop anchor, ma'am,' clarified the woman in the white uniform.

'Thank you,' Evelyn said. 'Drop anchor as near to the coordinates as possible and I'll assess from there.'

Mateo glared out at the sea.

'Tell me,' she asked, 'when you muscled your way onto a journey that, for me, has been almost twenty years in the making, and for you twenty-four hours, did you think that you would suddenly be in charge?'

'What? Absolutely not,' he replied, disliking the transparency of his thoughts.

'Okay, then. I'm sorry you got stuck on a train here with me, and I'm sorry you missed your very important meeting—'

Her words stopped short as he closed the distance between them with a single step. He leaned into her space, not to intimidate but to make his point completely clear. And if his whole body felt on fire being this close to the woman who had slept with him, *on him*, for the last eight hours, then he ruthlessly ignored it. Only it wasn't so easy to cast aside the flare of desire he saw burst to life in her eyes.

'I'm coming with you,' he said, determined to see this through.

'Well—'

'And you are forgetting the most important thing, of

course. That it is *mine*,' he said, plucking the leather notebook carefully from her grasp, and stalking past Evelyn, and up the ramp onto the yacht, ignoring all the alarms going off in his head.

He strode down the steps that led him to the lower salon, through polished wood, luxurious leather, and opulence towards the captain, who stood outside a fairly impressive cabin with ten windows.

'Ms Edwards suggested you sleep here while on board,' the uniformed man said before disappearing.

Mateo threw his suitcase angrily onto the bed. Why was he so annoyed that she was trying to get rid of him? His ego was healthy enough to survive it even if he'd taken it to heart, but that wasn't it. And no, he was not concerned about following her lead in this—it *was* her world, she had the knowledge and the experience here. But he was invested too. And not just because he wanted to validate his father's legacy, he wanted to validate *hers*. He wanted all the academics who had turned their back on her to know that they had been wrong to do so. The urge was so strong and so urgent, he had completely forgotten to check in with Henri about Léi Chen.

Having taken the hour since they'd left the dock to freshen up and change into new clothes, Evie arrived for lunch at the upper salon to find a beautifully set table covered in a crisp white table-cloth. She'd felt a little awkward unpacking the clothes that Mateo's assistant had, surprisingly, procured for her, worried about the size and style. But whether he was redeeming himself or had a very good eye, she was eternally thankful. There were enough clothes for a week packed into the brand-new case, along with the kind of clothes she would happily wear for her field work. But it was the ankle-length green dress with twisted straps that she loved the most. It clung to her chest and waist and fell from her hips, making her feel feminine and pretty. She had paired them with the other thing in the suitcase that had made her smile—a pair of wedged sandals. Just one of the pairs of heeled shoes and sandals that she would have bought for herself. As she turned to check her reflection in the mirror, the press of the material against her waist reminded her of Mateo's hand wrapping around her to hold her against him. Her heart leapt, skin warmed, and once again she felt breathless with want. She would have changed out of it, if it hadn't been for the fact that lunch was waiting on her. And now, as she walked towards the table, the dress leaving her bare skin cool in the warm breeze, she told herself not to hope for some kind of reaction from him.

The man in question leant against the railings at the bow, looking out at the horizon. She hadn't thought he could look any more impressive than when he'd been in a tux, but dressed in tan linen trousers and white shirt he was lethal. Wind came off the South China Sea and ruffled the heavy, lazy curls of his hair.

Her gaze was drawn to the breadth of his shoulders, wide and strong, and she let the desire to be surrounded by those shoulders drift away on the breeze. And once she had let go of that want, she noticed how stiffly he held himself, as if he were weighed down. She remembered the Professor getting this way when he couldn't get what he wanted. Evie nearly smiled. It had always reminded her, somewhat, of a slightly stroppy child. And while there was nothing childlike about Mateo, it was fascinating to see that, despite their estrangement, there were similarities that could only have been hereditary. Before the thought could take her on a tangent as to what characteristics she might have inherited, she thought back to her earlier accusation. She had meant what she said earlier about him muscling his way onto this journey with her, but secretly…she was pleased. Not just because he was the Professor's son, but because of him. The last two years had been quiet and…lonely, she was beginning to realise.

Evie reached the table where Annie, the steward who had met them on the jetty, filled two glasses with a chilled white wine before retreating to leave them alone.

Evie felt, rather than saw, Mateo's attention turn to her, as if he had run a palm down the outside of her arm. Goosebumps followed the imaginary caress perusing her body like a forbidden touch. Did he know the effect he had on her? Surely he wouldn't be so cruel as to taunt her in such a way, especially having rejected her at the hotel? Frustration dampened her desire. Despite the promise she'd made, she found herself vehemently wanting someone who didn't want her back.

Willing back the wave of emotion that swelled as strongly as the sea beneath the boat, she took a seat at the table and faced a selection of incredible fish—cured, seared, roasted from the look of it—even though any hunger fled the moment that Mateo sat opposite her. If Mateo had looked good against the bow, he looked almost devastating up close. Her pulse flared at his proximity, as if it was responding to some silent call from him, and heat inched across her skin like a trail of fire. Ordering herself to snap out of it, she focused on the job she was here to do. The Queen had decided not to tell her father about the coordinates found in the octant until Evie had been able to assess the situation. Once they knew what they were dealing with, further decisions could be made. And now, here, finally she allowed herself to feel that thread of professional excitement. The hope that they might finally find proof of what the Professor had searched so long and so hard for.

But what are you *looking for?*

Evie looked up to find that Mateo was holding out her glass of wine to her and she took it, careful to avoid even the most accidental of touches.

'What do you think we'll find?' he asked, sitting back in his chair, apparently content to sip at his wine for the moment. She could feel the sense of determination about him now that he'd decided to join her in following the clues left in the octant. It seemed to have refined his features, given everything focus and clarity. And she wished it hadn't, because it made him seem even *more.*

'At the island? I have no idea,' she confessed, following his lead and taking a sip of the delicious wine. Perhs she would find her hunger again in a moment. 'I'm hoping for a ducatoon, stiver or guilder—coins used by the Dutch East India Company. If we're really lucky, maybe some jewellery that could be linked to someone specific.'

'You're hoping for so little?'

'Little,' she repeated incredulously. 'That would be *huge.* It's not like it is in the movies, Mateo. You don't just stumble across a chest of buried treasure.'

'Or a pirate ship,' he added.

Evie smiled reluctantly. 'Or a pirate ship. I honestly can't imagine that there will be much to find after more than four hundred years. Surely anything to find would have been found by now, so to find even *something* would be incredible.'

'You're excited,' he observed.

'Yes, aren't you?' she asked him, as if incredulous that he might not be.

Mateo wished he could tell her truthfully that he wasn't. But in that moment, he did feel it. Rushing through his veins a strange lightness, coursing through him, making him *hopeful*. He could see it though, that bright, open excitement in her eyes that reminded him of his father.

'You're just like him,' he said, the words falling from his lips before he could call them back. But he meant them. He remembered the almost childish joy his father would express, infectious and thrilling, so that when Mateo would listen to his father's stories of pirate princesses and the legendary Dutch East India Company, Mateo wanted to go with him. As a child, he'd dreamed of hunting treasure and sword fights and laughing as he played with a father who indulged his imagination with history tempered with a little bit of fairy-tale.

'If you *could* find anything, what would it be?' he asked, wanting to see just a little more of her when she was like this. Wanting to see a little more of his father.

'I would like to find just some sense of them,' she replied instantly, utterly unguarded.

'Them?' he questioned, not sure what Evie was talking about.

She blinked as if she'd only just realised what she'd said and sat back a little as if to distance herself from what she'd revealed.

'Evie?' Her name called her back to his question.

'I think Loriella and her first mate were married,' she explained.

'I don't remember my father ever talking about that.'

'He didn't…it wasn't his theory,' she confessed.

'It's *yours*,' Mateo stated.

'Yes.'

He stared at her patiently, daring her to tell him her theory about Isabella.

'You don't know what you're asking,' she said to him, a plea in her voice he chose to ignore. She shook her head as if she could shake him off. 'I've been ridiculed enough just aiding Professor Marin's research. A female archaeologist, following such a romantic, unproveable legend? I would never work again.'

She reached for her glass and took a sip of wine.

'It's just me, here,' he said, suddenly convinced that this was the most important thing he could know about her.

She sighed, and he wondered if she realised that she was looking out over the same sea that she believed Princess Isabella to have sailed, to have waged a war against her ex-fiancé, against the injustices the Dutch East India Company were committing.

'I believe that after Princess Isabella survived the attack on her ship, she became close to the first mate, who taught her everything she needed to know. I believe that she proved herself to him and to the crew and that the change of her name was intended to show that she was more loyal to them than her own family. I believe that rumours were spread to denigrate her and destroy her spirit and she didn't let them.'

He wondered if she could see it, the parallels that had consciously or otherwise drawn Evie to Isabella. Because how could she not see that the strength she admired in the Pirate Princess was the same strength she showed every single day against the colleagues who had turned their backs on her, or the family that had abandoned her? 'You admire her,' he stated.

'Absolutely. When she had been left for dead by everyone she knew, instead of giving up, she pushed on—overcoming an incredible amount to lead some of the most dangerous mercenaries in the world at that time. And it led her to a man who respected her, rather than resenting her gender or inexperience. A man who followed her rather than taking a lead that would have pretty much been his right to take as First Mate. But instead he brought her into his life, he shared that with her, supporting her and letting her shine. It was a true partnership.'

He heard the yearning in her voice, added it to the bits and pieces she'd shared with him about her life. Mateo's heart thudded once, heavily. A cloud passed in front of the sun, the cool descending over the table as if she'd reached out with her cold hands and touched him.

He could see it in her eyes. The wistfulness, the hope. And it dawned on him that Evelyn wanted something that was as far removed from what he could even begin to imagine from himself. A chasm opened up between them and, somehow, she felt it happen too.

'Mateo?'

'It's nothing,' he dismissed.

'It's clearly not nothing,' she said, frowning at him as if trying to see what he was thinking.

He looked up at her and realised that she might have misunderstood. 'No, Evelyn, I… There is nothing to be embarrassed or concerned about with your theory of Loriella and her husband, if that was what he was.' He'd hate to think that he had offered her a safe space to share her thoughts and then taken that space away. But… He shook his head. 'I just… I just don't think those kinds of partnerships are real or lasting. I think that what you're looking for in Isabella and her first mate are as much fantasy as—'

'As the treasure?' she demanded, the warning signs of an angry flush painting her delicate cheeks.

'No, I just think it's naïve to—'

'Naïve?'

Cristo. He was getting this wrong, but he was frustrated, annoyed by her outrage. Because he had seen what happened when those once-in-a-lifetime loves went wrong. Wasn't that precisely what had happened to his parents? An age-old anger rose, unfurling and twisting, adding heat and hurt to words he could barely stop himself from saying.

'Yes, naïve,' he said, shaking his head. 'My mother believed in that kind of marriage, that kind of partnership, and what did it get her? Nothing. Nothing but crying herself to sleep every single night for a year after we returned to Spain. Nothing but having to start over again under the pitying, watchful gaze of a family who had never thought she should marry an English academic anyway. Of having to pretend that everything was okay, when inside she was being torn apart. But do you know what the real kicker is? Why she actually left him? It wasn't because she didn't love him,' he said, sounding as surprised as he'd always felt. 'It wasn't because she didn't want to be with him. It was because of *me*. It was because she couldn't bear to see me disappointed every single time my father would forget a birthday, or a celebratory meal, or that he'd promised to read me a book that evening, or that he'd promised to attend my graduation. So, if that's what partnership and true love get you? I'll take a hard pass, thank you.'

'Mateo…' Evelyn reached across the table, but he pulled his hand away, unable to put the roiling mass of emotions back into the box he usually kept them safely locked away in.

'Do you know what? I honestly don't know one single marriage that has lasted. Henri's mother raised him by herself, even my board of governors has two failed marriages behind it and one impending divorce between them.'

'Carol and Alan are still married,' she pointed out.

'And what a fine bastion of the institution of love and affection they are,' he snapped, watching as she flushed pink and then pale, so pale as the blood ran from her cheeks. Guilt fisted his chest. 'Evie, I'm—'

She stumbled up from the chair and he cursed, seeing the tears that gathered in her eyes. 'If you'll excuse me, I…' Without finding the words to finish that sentence she disappeared and he damned himself to hell and back. He hadn't meant to upset her. Why was he getting everything wrong when it came to her?

Three hours later, Evie stared out of the window of her cabin, her eyes a little less puffy than they had been before. The conversation with Mateo had been painful, but more so for him than for her, she'd decided. Yes, what he'd said about Carol and Alan had cut, but she could hardly say that it wasn't true.

It was the glimpse of the little boy who had been so badly hurt by the breakdown of his parents' relationship that had clutched at her heart. A little boy who had taken responsibility for something not of his own making. She could see it so easily. A mother who had tried, but failed, to hide her pain from her son. A father who had been so distraught by the breakdown of his marriage, he'd buried himself in his work. And Mateo… Mateo, who had closed himself off from the one thing that might have healed his wounds.

She let a sad laugh escape as she imagined Mateo's sardonic response to that observation.

And what have you closed yourself off to?

Everything.

The response was immediate and sounded so very much like her childhood voice that it shocked Evie. The instinctive reply screamed in her mind as she recognised how again and again she had pulled herself back from things and people that might reject her. Might cause her hurt. What if Mateo was right and she *had* let fear hold her back from what she wanted? What if she had stopped looking for the truth about Isabella because she was worried about doing even more harm to her reputation? What if she had held herself back from the possibility of a relationship with her birth parents because she was fearful of their rejection? What if she was doing it even now, with Mateo? Holding herself back because…because…?

A knock sounded on the door, interrupting her thoughts and, thinking it was Annie coming to take away the tea tray she'd ordered to her room earlier, she called out, 'Come in.'

The door opened and Mateo stood there, filling the frame with the breadth of his shoulders, looking for all the world like a rakish seducer. His shirt was undone at the neck, sleeves rolled back, his hands fisted in his pockets, hair mussed and tousled and something unreadable in his gaze.

Oh, *why* did he have to make her heart pound like that? Why did he have to make her *want* so much?

'I came to apologise.'

His eyes were clear from the storm that she had seen

earlier at the table on the deck. The bronze depths sparking with truth.

'You don't need to,' she said a little more sharply than she had intended.

'I belittled your feelings,' he admitted.

'And I underestimated yours,' she replied.

He nodded, acknowledging the truth of her words. 'Still, I shouldn't have said what I said about Carol and Alan.'

'Thank you. I appreciate that.'

'I also wanted to let you know that we'll be dropping anchor shortly.'

'Why? Are we there already?' she asked, eagerness and excitement a flashover through her body.

'No,' Mateo said, shaking his head. 'But we've arrived at Kei Island and I've booked us suites there for tonight.'

'Why? We need to push on to the coordinates, Mateo.'

He held his hand up. 'Evie.' Her name was almost a plea, making her waver in her determination to keep the distance she needed between them. 'Let's take this evening and get our feet back beneath us. Tomorrow could throw anything at us.'

It was so tempting. To take a pause in the storm of emotions swirling in her heart. But she wasn't sure that being even closer to Mateo was what she needed right now.

'What about the yacht's staff?'

'They'll remain on board.'

'I still think I should stay…' she hedged.

He held up his hands as if in surrender. 'If that's what you want…'

He had turned regretfully away, but something about the words he'd used…

If that's what you want.

'Wait,' she called after him, and this time when he turned she couldn't help but return his infectious smile.

Evie didn't know what she had expected from the island that Annie had taken Mateo and her to on the yacht's small speedboat. After a day at sea, with nothing but the blue sky and daydreams of pirate ships, she'd been surprised by the hustle and bustle of an island so clearly dedicated to upmarket tourism.

They'd bypassed the marina, where yachts matched or even surpassed the upscale boats she'd seen in Hong Kong, and disembarked at a much smaller wooden jetty, empty of people or boats. Mateo had held out his hand to help her off the boat, and she'd ignored the zap of electricity that had arced from his touch.

He had waved Annie off as she turned the boat back to the ship and led Evie confidently up the jetty to a thicket of palm trees and green vegetation. The sun was beginning to set and the entire island was painted in a soft yellow glow that was beginning to burn red at the edges. And when Mateo looked back over his shoulder to check she was still with him, she half fancied she had been touched by its rays.

She had packed some overnight things in her briefcase, along with her notebook and the Professor's, and as she looked around she felt at peace for the first time in a long time. It was something that settled into her skin and sank into her bones. The call to relax, the urge to let go a little, and she thought she'd seen the same thing in Mateo's eyes. The wooden jetty turned into a path that cut into the grove of palm trees and she was about to ask Mateo where they were going when the trees opened up and she stepped almost directly onto a beach of pure white sand, the likes of which she'd only ever experienced in her wildest fantasies.

She couldn't help the gasp that fell from her lips as she took in the curve of the sandy bay and the azure-blue sea gently lapping rhythmically at the blond grains of the beach. Halfway across the bay, widely interspersed between palm trees, were four huts, open to the elements, with thatched roofs and string lights hanging from the eves.

There wasn't another soul on the beach and something unfurled in her chest as excitement and hope lifted the lid on her desires. She dared to cast her gaze to Mateo, praying not to find disinterest or boredom in something that was so magical to her, but she should have known better.

Because there, looking back at her with the same sense of barely repressed excitement, was Mateo, and the words next on his lips stole her heart.

'Welcome to paradise.'

CHAPTER EIGHT

ONCE AGAIN MATEO found himself marvelling at how expressive Evie's face was. He could have described every single feeling she experienced as she looked out across the beach at dusk. But wonder was the one he recognised the most. That was what he'd wanted when he'd asked Annie to let them off here at one of the Kei Islands. To take away the hurt he'd carelessly inflicted and cover it with something beautiful.

There was a much larger hotel on the other side of the island, but this? This was perfect. He had no intention of telling her that he'd hired out the entire hotel for just the two of them. He bit back a laugh at the thought of how she would berate him for the waste of money. But he didn't consider it a waste at all.

He'd bitterly regretted the things he'd said over lunch. It didn't mean that he'd changed his feelings about it, but he should never have said what he'd said, nor spoken of her adoptive parents. If he was honest with himself, he knew where his anger came from, a deep realisation of what they could never be to each other; of what they could never have. But he also knew that he'd have to make it up to her. And from the look on her face, he was right. Something hot and heavy eased in his chest and he breathed his first full breath since that afternoon.

'Dinner will be served on the beach in an hour, but until then you can get settled in your suite, or you can take a swim, or...' The way she was looking at him stopped his words. 'What?'

'I'm not quite sure that this is how I'd describe getting my feet back under me. It's more like sweeping me off them,' she half laughed, but stopped suddenly as if she'd realised what she'd said. She bit her lip as his gut clenched, but then... 'Thank you,' she said, simply. For a moment he thought she was going to rise on her toes and press a kiss to his cheek. For a moment he *wanted* that. But then she was gone, walking past him towards the huts in the apex of the bay.

Walk away. Walk away now.

A familiar internal warning ran through his brain, and for the first time since he could remember he wanted to ignore it. He followed behind her, trying to ignore the allure of the sway of her hips and the way that her wedged sandals sank her a little lower into the sand. He kept pace with her until she came to a stop a few feet away from the huts, sensing her reluctance to tear herself away from the view of the sea.

That he was just as reluctant to tear himself away from the view of her was all he needed to know that he should find his suite before he did something he couldn't take back. Maybe he was the one who should have stayed back on the yacht, not Annie.

Evie remembered telling Queen Sofia that she had never stayed anywhere more beautiful, but this? Mateo wasn't wrong. It really was paradise. She looked around her at the achingly stunning surroundings. It felt like serenity and she hadn't realised how much she'd needed it. The hut

Mateo had pointed her to was on one side of the beach, his was at the far end of the small settlements. She'd known that because she'd all but hidden behind a curtain and watched as he'd walked to the far side of the encampment and up the steps of a hut that mirrored hers, half thankful and half bereft for the distance between them.

The front of the exotic suite faced the sea and was open to the elements. Even now a gentle salt-scented breeze pushed at the tendrils of hair that escaped the loose plait she'd wound her hair into. Behind her, a series of reed walls allowed both for a sense of liberating openness and discreet privacy. The bathroom was enclosed, and there was a shower out on the decking that wrapped around the hut completely hidden from view.

A canopy bed was placed in the centre of the hut with views of a beach now dusted with dusk and from which she could already see a few twinkling stars in the sky. She had seen a few people dressed in white and black uniforms discreetly passing before the huts, presumably getting their dinner together.

It served only to remind her of the night she had met Mateo. Had it really only been three days ago? Before, when she'd thought of the Professor's son, there had been resentment towards an undefinable figure who, in her mind, had taken his father for granted. But now? Now that she had seen so much more in the *man,* could she really continue to lie to herself and deny that she wanted him? That, even knowing he didn't want the love and marriage she secretly was so hopeful she would have in her own life, she *still* wanted him?

She was almost sure that he desired her—she felt it press against her when he looked at her, burn in her skin when he touched her, fill her lungs whenever he was near—but it was clear that he didn't *want* to want her. Something in her fought against that, wanted to push and prod and poke at the barrier between them.

They had clashed from the very first moment they'd met, and in that fire, in that friction, was something alive and twisting, needing to get out. It simmered beneath her skin, making her restless, making her…*reckless*. Never before had she understood more the phrase 'throwing caution to the wind'. The thoughts and hope for her future, they belonged to someone else, to some other time. He had brought her to paradise and it was whispering desires and wants from her most secret fantasies.

Could she really just ask him for what she wanted?

Could she take just this night, perhaps?

There was something seductive in the thought of just one night. Not because he might agree, but because surely, if she knew that there was no possibility of the kind of future she wanted, then she would be safe from hurt? Her *heart* would be safe?

She started at the gentle tinkle of a bell. Frowning, she made her way out onto the decking and the sight made her heart leap. A wooden dais had appeared as if by magic. Large fire torches marked each corner, illuminating a white cloth-covered table set for a feast and decorated with local flowers and shells. Mateo was standing in front of it, waiting expectantly for her.

She was thankful she'd taken the time to freshen up and change into the sarong that had been waiting for her on the bed. The material was soothing against her heated skin and the colour, a deep turquoise, was beautiful. She'd never worn anything like it, but when Mateo's eyes finished his slow, intense perusal from top to toe, returning to meet her gaze, she felt absolutely incredible—invincible almost. It was only when she took the first step onto the sandy beach that she realised she had left her heels behind, and, barefoot, she made her way towards him with a self-confidence that was empowering. Her heart shifted in her chest as she drew level with Mateo, who hadn't taken his eyes off her once.

'You are beautiful,' he said, the words not intended to flatter, or to manipulate. It was simply a fact for him, but she wanted more. They fired something in her breast, as if they had been a call to arms that only she heard. He poured her a glass of wine and passed it to her.

'Where are the other guests?' Evie asked.

'It's just us tonight,' he replied, trying to swallow the heat in his throat.

The table was full of lots of little dishes, all of which he was sure were utterly delicious, but Mateo couldn't have described a single one. He was simply unable to draw his attention away from Evie. As if by tacit agreement, they avoided speaking of the Professor or the coordinates, but instead shared happy stories of their childhoods. Over the starter, Mateo dutifully described the trouble he would get into at boarding school with Henri. He couldn't have said when the plates were cleared, because of the way her eyes shimmered at hearing about his achievements and his own sense of accomplishment at providing his mother and friends with the security he felt they deserved. He barely noticed the main course as Evie regaled him with amusingly awkward stories of Carol and Alan, and through dessert, she entertained him with the more humorous disasters she'd experienced as a young girl as she'd tried to navigate her intelligence in an environment meant for much older children.

'Do you feel you missed out on things?'

'Absolutely,' she said, nodding. 'I was tutored at home until I was sixteen and then went straight to university. All of the normal experiences you had with Henri—'

'I'm not sure I'd call them normal,' Mateo laughingly interrupted.

'Maybe not,' she conceded with a smile, 'but things like school dances, or walking home with friends, or sharing gossip and crushes on the cool boys…' Her breath shuddered in her chest, just a little, just enough for him to hear the longing for things she hadn't had or known. When she looked up at him from across the table, he suddenly realised that they had wandered into dangerous territory. Because the way she looked at him pulled his pulse into a faster beat, it filled the air between them with a heavy sensuality and everything in him wanted to respond to it—a siren's call that would dash them both on the rocks if they were not careful.

'There are things that I—'

'Evie.' Her name was a plea on his tongue, needing her to stop. He'd seen so much of her in the last few days. Not just his father's assistant, or a woman determined to follow an ancient treasure hunt. But also the woman she was…incredible, powerful, proud, intelligent. He admired her. And he didn't want to hurt her. He didn't want to give her false promises of a future he had no intention or ability to offer her.

She bit her lip, and once again he regretted dimming that light, thinking wrongly that it had been extinguished. But when she looked back up at him, anger shimmering with desire, he realised the spark had been lit and now threatened to *burn*.

'There are things that I want,' she repeated, her voice trembling a little, but no less clear for it. Her determination pushed him to the brink. Everything in him warred between walking away and pulling her to him.

He started, when she pushed her chair back and stood, slowly coming around the table, her bare feet sandy and soft on the wooden platform.

'There are things that I want and if I don't say it now, I…' She paused and he thought he understood. He expected that she might not find the courage again, but he was wrong. He had underestimated her again, and that would be the last time he would ever do it. 'If I don't say it now, I will be smaller. I will be less. And I don't want to be less. I want to be as strong as Isabella was when she faced down the pirate that attacked her ship. I want to be as fierce as she was when she defended her crew against her fiancé. So I know that you might turn me away, but,' she let out a small laugh, 'this actually isn't about you. It's about me,' she said. And as if realising the truth of her words as she spoke them, she *shone*. Her eyes sparkled and her skin glowed beneath a milky moon.

He stood to take her hand, gazing into all that was her glory.

'I'm listening.'

'I want you to kiss me,' she said, and heat burned his lungs on an inhale. 'I want you to crush my lips to yours and fill my mouth with your tongue.' Her words were an erotic fantasy, the imagery of it, slashing red marks across his cheeks. 'I want to taste you,' she said, 'and I want you to taste me,' the soft wishes morphing into something hot and carnal. 'I want you to touch me, to cover my body with your hands.'

Evelyn's breath was coming in pants he could feel against his lips. *Cristo*, it was taking every single ounce of strength to hold himself back.

'I want you to touch me in places that will make me moan with pleasure,' she said, as heat and need built in his chest until he thought he might explode. 'I want you to relieve the ache burning across my body and delight in doing it,' she all but begged.

'And I know,' she said as he opened his mouth to speak, 'I know it wouldn't be more than tonight. But just for tonight, I want that,' Evie said, her hands bunching the beautiful turquoise material at her thighs, as he bit back a moan of need so strong he wanted to tear the world apart.

'And I wanted you to know that,' she said before turning away.

Before she could take a step, he reached for her wrist and drew her back, pulling her against the length of his body, relishing in finally, *finally*, having her against his skin. With one hand he cupped her jaw as the other pressed her against him.

'You wanted to be as strong as Isabella?' he asked.

She nodded, trying to avoid his gaze.

'How did you not know that you already are?' he asked, searching her eyes for an answer he wasn't sure he didn't already know. And, unable to deny them both what they so desperately wanted, he claimed her lips with his.

Her mouth parted on a cry, as he hoped it would, opening for him, welcoming his passion. Her hands threaded through his hair, holding him to her as if she was worried he might disappear. He cradled her neck in the palm of his hand, half terrified of exactly the same thing. An urgency overwhelmed him even as he gentled his desire, remembering her innocence and inexperience. He wouldn't turn away from her, not unless she asked it, but he knew that he should ease back a little. He slowed the kiss, closing it with a careful bite of her bottom lip.

'I know you want those things, and I know that you've thought it through, in here,' he said, tapping gently at her temple. 'But what you feel in here,' he said, pausing to lay his palm against her chest, 'might be different to what you expect.'

'If you're asking me—'

He cut her words off with a kiss, lips pulled into a slight curve by his smile from the indignance in her tone. 'Evie,' he said, resting his forehead against hers, 'I'm not asking if you've changed your mind. But I have to make sure you understand that I cannot offer you more than this,' he said, searching her level gaze, thankful she clearly had no idea of the storm raging within him. She had offered him everything he had wanted from her and for her and only the thinnest thread of selflessness was holding him back. But it was strong enough. Because he needed her to know that he could not be what he knew was in her dreams. 'I cannot give you forever and happy-ever-after, Evie. It's just not in me.'

Solemn eyes stared back at him, green and gold flickers in the hazel-brown depths.

'I understand,' she said sincerely, and half of him urged, now! Now! But that thread still held him back, so very careful of her inexperience.

'I want you to know that if you want to stop at any point, I'll stop. If you think it's too far, or even if you just need a moment, I'll stop and it won't change a thing between us. I need you to know that.'

It was as if a hand had swept aside all the obstacles muddying the waters between them. In that moment, Evie understood him perfectly and she felt understood completely. Trust. That was what it was. She trusted herself with him utterly and irrevocably and he trusted that she would be true to herself with him. It spoke to her soul in a way that made Mateo's words true. She didn't know what to expect to feel from this…but everything in her wanted to find out.

She rose onto her toes and pressed a chaste kiss against his lips, once, then twice. By the third, her tongue swept out to taste his lip, then his mouth, and then…oh, then it was heaven. As he opened for her, he pulled her into him, his arms sweeping around her as his tongue filled her mouth and she felt possessed. Not owned, but joined. Her skin ached and the juncture of her thighs throbbed with want. Her legs became restless, and just when they began to tremble he swept her up into his arms, and without breaking the kiss he walked them to his cabin, up the wooden steps, and into a suite that mirrored hers.

He placed her on the end of the canopied bed and she barely spared a glance for the hundreds of tea lights glittering around the cabin. With the night sky in the distance and the shimmering candles around them, she felt as if she were on a bed amongst the stars.

He stood before her, slowly undoing the buttons of his linen shirt, his eyes not once moving from her. She bit her lip, aching at the sight of him. Intellectually she didn't quite understand her reaction to him, but instinctively she knew that it was unique. That she had never, would never feel the same way again. Because it wasn't just the breadth of his shoulders, the defined musculature, the dusting of dark hair that whispered the word *man* in her heart and soul, it was him.

She lost herself in the heady sense of power arcing between them, being passed back and forth and shared in a way she could hardly put into words. She raised her hands to release the tie of the sarong at her neck, wanting to be as naked as he, and just as he shrugged out of the shirt, the silky material fell from around her neck to her waist, leaving her top half completely bare to his perusal.

Something powerful and feminine soared at the heat slashing his cheeks and the sparks of ferocious need in his gaze. And she, who had spent years feeling shame and fearing embarrassment, felt almost invincible. He prowled towards her, forcing her back, even as she felt in control. He leaned over her as she lay against the large bed until he covered her body with his own.

'Evie, if I'd known that you were naked beneath the ties of your sarong,' he whispered against her neck as he placed upon it little kisses that showered her skin in goosebumps, 'we wouldn't have eaten a thing. You are so utterly beautiful,' he said, and she wondered if he'd realised that he'd slipped into Spanish.

His hand smoothed across the skin of her side, skating perilously close to where she wanted him to cup her breast, the gentleness of his touch beginning to grate, offering only a taste of what she truly wanted. Him, unfettered, and as lost to passion as she. But when his hand curved her hip and slipped beneath the material that had rucked up beneath her, her heart leapt with want. Her pulse pounded so hard in her chest, she half imagined he could hear it.

His fingers dug in, not so gentle now, and she almost came off the bed, desperately pressing her chest against his, wanting relief, needing release. His hands swept around her thigh and gently parted her legs beneath him. He had barely touched her and she was sobbing with need.

Back and forth he soothed the sensitive skin of her thigh, before he slipped his fingers beneath the band of her panties and she gasped and shivered at the first of his touches. She turned away from him, seeking the safety of his shoulder as she bore the exquisite sensations that he gave her, heat turning her skin pink and pleasure shortening her breaths. Oh, God, it was the most exquisite thing.

His mouth found her breast and she arched from the bed, the sound of her own pleas almost as erotic as his fingers. She was panting in need and he pulled back to watch her, his own arousal clear for her to see. Her pleasure was *his*. She understood that now. She felt that as he held her with his gaze and, completely safe in his hands, she reached higher and higher until she could barely breathe past her pleasure and then she felt him inside her, his thumb against her, but a finger deep within her, filling her nearly to how she wanted to be filled, but it was close enough to push her into nothing but sheer bliss.

Mateo had never seen anything more perfect. His pulse thundered as if it had been his own climax he'd just experienced. Sweat had beaded his brow and tipped down his back as Evie began to slowly blink her eyes open, constellations of wonder and pleasure and satisfaction and just that little bit of giddy excitement he could always sense in the background for her.

He wanted to kiss her, he wanted to touch her, he wanted to find every single one of her expressions and gaze at them in his own wonder. He had always put his partner's pleasure first, enjoying theirs as much as his own, but this was an addiction and he wanted more, he wanted to hunt her pleasure to whatever extremes it went to.

She looked for a moment as if she might try to make light of what had just happened, but as she read his intent, her gaze cleared and instead he fell deep into a connection that scared him more than he'd ever admit.

The blush on her cheeks deepened, her eyes flaring wide, and the swift inhale expanding her chest had him biting his lip to stop himself from taking her mouth with a passion that would have shocked them both. Her hands went to the clasp on his trousers, but he caught her hand.

'We can stop here, Evie.'

'Thank you,' she said, lifting her hand to press against his chest. 'But I don't want to stop,' she replied. 'Do you?' she asked in return. The dull alarm sounding in the back of his mind made him waver for barely the space of a heartbeat, but it was drowned out by a wave of desire that flooded his mind. The need to see her fall apart beneath another orgasm was like a living thing in his veins.

'No,' he replied as he nudged her hand out of the way and made quick work of removing the rest of his clothes, her eyes burning caresses into his skin he thought might scar him for life, and instinctively he knew he would walk away with the marks of their combined need imprinted on his soul.

He looked to her before returning to the bed, his chest locked in a vice as she lay back regally against the plush pillows, surrounded by a silken canopy, hundreds of little tiny lights flickering in the breeze like a meteor shower. She looked wanton and wanting and he nearly pinched himself to see if he was dreaming.

As he came back to the bed, she rose from the pillows and they met in a tangle of limbs and lips and tongues and teeth. Passion was an unstoppable force, but even then his first care was for Evie. He whispered his worship of her in kisses and touches as she made room for him between her legs. He honoured her with every moment he could, knowing that the seconds were slipping through his fingers. He hated the morning in that moment, resented the sun, and pleaded with the moon to stay in the night sky, just so he could have one more taste, one more touch.

He filled her slowly, but fully, and it hurt his heart to see home in her eyes and know that he could not be that for her. But he could give her everything in this night, so he slowly withdrew, before once again filling her, luxuriating in the feel of her wrapped tightly around him, thrilled by the cries of her pleasure-filled moans as they drew closer and closer to oblivion. Pleasure built hot step by hot step and sweat slicked their bodies. Time lost meaning as desire drenched touches, and kisses became as sensual as the glide of their hips. Their bodies danced together to a rhythm unique to that night and known only to them, until the final crescendo pushed them into a starlit moment that stretched beyond the capture of words. It was the most intensely erotic experience of Mateo's life and he knew—in that moment—no one else would ever match it.

CHAPTER NINE

STANDING AT THE bow of the yacht, Mateo watched Evie talking to Annie and the captain, explaining how long they might be gone. The captain didn't seem happy about letting the two of them go to the island alone, and his genuine concern over their safety had Mateo double-and triple-checking they had what they needed. The small speedboat was a similar make to one he'd used before, and he'd promised that safety was his absolute priority. He had stowed the small rucksack containing a satellite phone, a flare gun and emergency first-aid kits. They had both listened to the warnings about seismic and volcanic activity in the area, along with the risk of tsunamis. He had recognised, very quickly, that the captain was not exaggerating his warnings and had asked Evie, again, if they shouldn't wait.

'For what?' she'd asked.

Mateo hated that he didn't actually have an answer for that, as Evie must have predicted, because of the knowing gleam in her eye. A gleam that had turned molten when held just a little too long.

If he'd thought spending the night with Evie would have got anything out of his system, if he'd thought that he'd have been able to indulge his addiction to her just once and walk away, then he had been utterly and irrevocably wrong. He didn't know which of them had been worse, which of them had craved the other's touch more, needed the other's kiss more than their next breath, but he did know that it couldn't continue.

If Annie had noticed the red mark on Evie's neck from where his open-mouthed kiss had lingered too long and sucked too hard, she hadn't mentioned it when she came to pick them up from the island that morning. When he'd reached out for Evie, still half-asleep, her side of the bed had been cool. Without opening his eyes, he'd fisted the empty sheet in his hands and remembered the words she'd given him the night before.

Just for tonight.

They were a curse and a promise in his head.

'Are you ready?' Evie asked.

'At your service,' he replied without missing a beat, despite the bent of his thoughts. He held out his hand to her, helping her into the small speedboat.

'If you have any problems,' said the captain, 'just call in.'

Mateo nodded and pushed them away from the side of the yacht, before turning the key in the ignition and firing up the speedboat's engine. He manoeuvred the boat to face towards the island up ahead, surrounded by a series of dangerous rocky outcrops creating currents that needed some careful handling. The captain had explained that the island's layout, with its jagged and steep incline making it inhospitable for development, and the approach so tricky as to permit only one boat at a time in and out, made it unattractive for tourism. Nestled further away from the easier to access and much more pleasant islands closer to the main thoroughfares, it was rarely given a second look. The billionaires had spent their money on much easier islands, but as they approached, Mateo could still appreciate the attraction.

He flicked his gaze between their destination and where Evie sat on the bench seating, holding on to her hat, her face upturned towards the sun, looking for the world like a tourist on her way to a deserted beach. If she hadn't been wearing walking boots, canvas trousers and a loose linen shirt.

He'd been slightly disconcerted when he'd dressed in what she called her field-work clothing. Disconcerted by the shocking jolt of lust that had speared him by her efficient, utterly practical work uniform. Then again, he was beginning to fear that it might not actually matter what she was wearing, because it was her—*her*, unique, utterly spectacular, fascinatingly focused, intently determined *her*—that he was attracted to beyond reason.

'You should stop looking at me like that,' she said, her eyes still closed.

'I don't know what you're talking about,' he replied, a half-smile reluctantly pulling at his lips as he steered the speedboat in an arc to land as close to the small strip of beach the captain had suggested would make the most logical place to land the boat.

The movement of the speedboat mirrored the twists and turns of her stomach. As she hid behind dark glasses and basked in the sun, strangely it was Mateo's attention that grounded her. Grounded her in something tangible rather than the hypothetical that lay at the end of their journey.

The night before had connected them on a deeply physical level; an awareness of him she could never have imagined lay like a second skin over her body. It was as if she were a sunflower turning to face him, seeking him out, and the instinctive independence in her chafed a little. But despite that, she was impossibly thankful that she wasn't doing this alone because she was suddenly nervous.

Nervous that they would find nothing. That she wouldn't be able to validate the Professor's theories, that she wouldn't be able to give the Queen and her father what they wanted. What if she failed them? What if she failed because she wasn't good enough? She pressed a palm to her chest and took a breath, trying to ground herself on a moving vessel.

You want to be as strong as Isabella?

How did you not know that you already are?

The words Mateo had given her the night before whispered the strength and confidence into her soul. Because for the first time, ever, she had seen herself through Mateo's eyes, she had seen herself as he had—as strong and powerful as Isabella, a Pirate Princess.

And as she looked up at the uninhabited island, through the series of jagged rocks waiting to damage and break those who would trespass on its shores, she felt something unfurl in her chest. A knowing, deep and instinctive, as if she was on the brink of discovering something significant.

The island the coordinates had brought them to wasn't quite the small desert island with a palm tree and nothing but sand one imagined for a treasure hunt. Large, dark, craggy rocks loomed unwelcomingly above the sliver of white sandy beach she caught glimpses of as the speedboat surfed the tricky tides, making it appear taller than it was wide. But despite that, she was sure that they would find *something* here. Something to validate the Professor's research, to give the Queen and her father what they needed, and maybe, just maybe, even something for her.

Mateo jerked the wheel as they drew too close to one of the perilous formations dotted between them and their landing point, and Evie cringed at the thunderous sound as the side of the boat scraped against rock.

Mateo grimaced, but said nothing, clearly needing all his concentration to manoeuvre them away. His forearms corded as he yanked the wheel one way and another into the swell of the tide, pushing them back while he gently urged them forward. Not too much throttle but enough to slowly tease the boat away from the rocks.

By the time they made it through the dangerous maze of rocks and tides and to the beach, they were both damp from sea spray, a little breathless, and nearly an hour later than they had imagined arriving. With his shoes tied together by their laces and hung around his neck, Mateo rolled up his trousers, jumped over the side of the boat and pulled the speedboat to shore. He secured the boat and turned to her, holding out his hand, and for the breadth of a heartbeat Evie saw him as he'd been the night before, welcoming her to a candlelit dinner on a bleached blond beach dusted by dusk and heat in his eyes. Her body throbbed in the memory of last night—the one night she'd asked him for. Just one. She would never regret asking for what she wanted. And even though there would be no more nights like it, she would never regret what they had shared.

He called her name as if sensing she was elsewhere and, steeling herself, she took his hand and jumped down onto the sand, adjusting the straps of her rucksack and studying the GPS tracker to locate themselves in relation to the coordinates. She waited for Mateo to put his shoes back on and nod to her that he was ready.

'This is your show, Evelyn. You lead, I'll follow.'

If only he would, she thought.

An hour later of really quite difficult climbing, up a near invisible and definitely deteriorated track, they arrived at the summit of the island. The cover provided by the thick and tangled vegetation that had protected them from the sun gave way to a clear blue sky that balanced on an azure horizon line from the sea. The sun beat down on them, drying her sweat to a salty residue around her neck.

Shading her eyes with her hand, she looked out at the Philippine Sea, and in her heart Evie saw eighteenth-century ships sailing in the hazy distance. The pulse pounding against her eardrums was like explosions from a canon firing at a pirate ship, and beneath it all was a whisper from Isabella asking her to find her. A bead of sweat turned icy cold and fell down her spine as Mateo pressed a flask of water into her hands and gently tugged her into the shade.

'Drink,' he ordered.

She shook her head at the command, reluctant to leave her thoughts.

'Evie, you need some water. You haven't had any since we got off the boat.'

Reluctantly she caved in and went to sit next to where Mateo was perched against a smooth jut of rock beneath a palm casting dappled shade, taking a mouthful of water and only then realising how thirsty she really was.

She half expected him to press to question, or suggest they turn back, or try and take the lead, but he didn't. Not once. She may have been teaching in a classroom for the last two years, but even fellow students had overstepped her when they'd been in the field. Whether it was her age, or her gender, she had been pushed to the back. And yes, it was only the two of them here, but it wasn't that either. Mateo trusted her to know her limits and herself here, and that…that was something incredible to her.

And she wished it hadn't happened just when she was about to fail.

'What is it?' he asked as if sensing her feelings.

'We're here.'

'Where?'

'At the coordinates.'

And there was nothing. No building, or sign of life in the present or the past. She scanned the area again, knowing that she could happily spend days here combing every single inch of the craggy outcrop…but the sight of absolutely *nothing* shook her.

Mateo remembered his father being like this sometimes. The extent of focused frustration almost a physical thing. He checked his watch, aware of the time ticking away, knowing that Evie would be feeling it too, so he chose his words carefully.

'What was Isabella like?'

Evie frowned up at him.

'You've studied her, you *know* her. Would she have been obvious about whatever it was she may have hidden here? Would she have placed it behind another clue?' he asked, unaware of when he had slipped from disbelief to belief that Isabella and Loriella were the same person. 'What would *you* have done?' he asked.

'Well, I wouldn't leave anything exactly where the coordinates pointed.'

Mateo smiled at the indignance in her tone. 'Okay. But there *are* coordinates and they *did* lead us here,' he observed. He considered Evie, who had begun to merge with Isabella in his mind. 'But you'd want to make it harder than that, wouldn't you?'

'Not harder. I'd want to make sure that whoever found it was the right person.'

'The right person being…?'

'Friend, not foe. And friends, they know you. They'd… know *her*.'

'And what would they know about her?' Mateo gently nudged.

'That she was Iondorran.'

'So, we're looking for something Iondorran.'

'Or something that would mean something to someone from Iondorra,' Evie concluded, her eyes once again flashing with the spark of excitement that was swiftly becoming dangerously addictive to Mateo.

She stood up from the rock and made her way back out into the sun towards the summit the coordinates had led to. Standing at the edge of the island, the sea stretched out before her, eyes closed, she looked like the captain of a ship, the wind pulling at her hair and a determination on her features he'd only seen on the deserted beach the night before.

He felt the breath she took calm him as much as her and didn't even question when she had become so known to him. And even if that thought yanked on his pulse, pulled at his heartbeat, he gave them both this moment.

Evie began slowly, as if working inch by inch, methodically scanning the land around them from one side of the island to the other. She didn't use binoculars, or her GPS tracker, she just looked with her own eyes, as

Isabella once would have done. She worried her lip with her teeth, a habit Mateo wasn't sure she was even aware of, but he wanted to reassure her that she was on the right track. That she would find what she needed because he knew that she would, even if he couldn't explain it.

And when she found it, he saw it in her eyes. In the curve of her lip, in the crackle on the air between them—it was almost like magic.

'Do you know,' she asked, taking a step towards a point a little to his right, 'that clematis flowers—the national symbol of Iondorra—symbolise two things?'

'No,' he replied, standing up to follow her.

'They represent both the beauty of ingenuity and the trait of artifice. Both of which are needed for the plant's clever ability to climb around impossible-to-reach places.'

She led them back into the shade provided by the thick chaos of rich green foliage, broken up by bursts of bright white and brilliant purple flowers, clustered around thick, heavy vines.

'The other thing about the clematis is that it is most definitely not native to Indonesia.'

She reached out to thread her fingers through the fragrant vines clinging to the rock behind it and he realised that she was looking for something. No, not for something. *At* something.

'Can you get your father's notebook?' she asked him, without sparing him a glance, as she began more forcefully moving the ancient strands of Iondorra's national plant.

'Of course.' Mateo reached into the bag she had left by the rock and withdrew the notebook.

She pulled out a loose leaf of parchment, the paper older, thinner and darker than the lined notepaper. He frowned, unfamiliar with it, coming to stand to look over her shoulder as she spread out the old folds creased into the paper. It looked like a rubbing, charcoal shades marking out an outline in light and dark.

'What is it?'

'I always thought it was an old doodle, but…'

Evie held the rubbing over the detail she'd uncovered in the stone beneath the clematis vines. It matched perfectly. All along, this had been tucked away in the Professor's notebook. She'd never asked him about it and he'd never mentioned where it had come from, but Evie traced the marks carved into the stone, surprisingly smooth given the type of rocks they'd encountered so far on the island.

The marks were a crude imitation of the same stylised clematis as had been on the octant. The five petals and the single stem and leaf. Five petals… She placed her fingers and thumb on each of the petals and, holding her breath, she pushed.

She felt Mateo start behind her as the stone sank back with a puff of dust. Spanish curses mixed with her awe as the stone shifted and slid to one side. Her legs began to tremble as an entrance appeared in the side of the rock. Retrieving her flashlight, she peered into the gloom and caught sight of the top of a set of wooden steps.

She turned to find Mateo shaking his head. She could read the concern in his eyes, and she felt it too. She was eager, desperate even, but not naïve. He looked off out to the horizon and she hungrily ate up his profile. The proud brow, the stubble crossing a jaw her palm ached to feel, the perfect outline of lips that had brought her the most intense pleasure. All that she collated in a second. But what took a few more moments to process was that they didn't need words for this. She knew his thoughts as much as he knew hers. She knew he was finding arguments for them to turn back, warring with his desire to let her do this. Three days ago, he would have thrown her over his shoulder and left the island. But now? It wasn't just that he was also invested in proving his father's theories. She felt, believed, hoped, that it was also because of her. Because he trusted her. What they had shared last night, that connection, it was more than just physical, even if she tried to keep telling herself it wasn't.

'We do it safe and we do it right,' he said, when he finally levelled her with a gaze.

'Yes, we do,' she agreed.

They checked and rechecked their bags. Mateo pulled ropes, harnesses, torches, flare guns, first-aid kits and water from their bags and put them all back, while Evie stood a little way into the cave that the rock door had revealed.

She passed the torch's beam over the top of the wooden steps that led down into the maw of darkness below. Behind her she heard the snap of an emergency glowstick, and a flash of bright neon swept over her shoulder and down into the pit.

The staircase that wrapped around the inside of the narrow circular well had been protected from the elements, but that didn't mean that it hadn't deteriorated in the last two hundred and fifty years. If they were doing this properly…

'At least one of us should stay up here,' she said.

'There are only two of us,' he replied.

'I know, but—'

'Evie, I know that you're tough and I know that you're

strong—maybe to your own detriment sometimes—but I'm coming with you and that doesn't diminish those things about you,' Mateo stated, and Evie tried not to let the overwhelming relief go to her head.

She was about to take the first step, when Mateo caught her arm. 'And if at any point, any, you want to turn back or you get a bad feeling…'

She bit back the innate knee-jerk reply of 'I won't', and instead replied as she should and as she felt: truthfully. 'We'll turn back. I promise.'

Evie had no idea how much time had passed. She'd been so utterly focused on her footing, on searching for signs of who had made the wooden staircase, scanning the walls for any kind of graffiti, or impressions of who had walked these steps before them.

Had Isabella walked these steps? Who had made them and where did they lead? She had never lied to Mateo… it wasn't about the treasure at all. But she really did want to find something. It was a need in her blood like…like the way she had needed Mateo the night before.

She'd been so lost in her thoughts that she didn't immediately notice when the wood of the next step creaked beneath her foot. It happened in a heartbeat that stretched over an eternity. She just dropped, every nerve ending screaming out in shock, her breath catching in her lungs as she reached out to grasp nothing, and then—

Her arm pulled tight and her body hung in mid-air. Mateo's grip on her hand and wrist a steel lifeline tying her to him.

'Don't look down,' he commanded and nothing in her would have refused his order. His arm bulged beneath the line of the T-shirt sleeve as he worked to pull her up. She had to reach up with her free hand, which he caught and then reached for her elbow, inch by inch dragging her out of the darkness against him until she could get her feet on the same step.

Panting and out of breath, he asked if she could get around the step below. Heart still pounding, legs shaking terribly, she quickly assessed it and nodded.

'We have to go on, I'm not sure how long the rest of the steps will hold out,' he said. Clinging to him for support she gingerly stepped around the broken wood. It was a larger step to make, and on shaking legs wasn't as easy as it should have been, but she made it and slowly, in silence and fierce concentration, they made it to the ground.

She felt Mateo's hand on her arm.

'I'm fine,' she dismissed quickly before he could ask, but her pulse hadn't yet slowed. She shone the torch around the walls, her heart thundering in her chest, but forced herself to breathe. There was something down here, she just knew it, but…

What would you do?

She took a breath, Mateo's hand on her shoulder, not holding her back but grounding her, encouraging her to think. She passed the beam more slowly over the jagged stone and saw a glint of gold. A guilder maybe? She made her way towards where she'd seen it. And gasped.

There, set back about half a foot behind a sliver of rock, was a series of bronzed cogs. It must have been used to open a door or entrance to another part of the island, because there was nothing else down here. The workmanship was exquisite, but…there was no lever. No way of making it work. She searched the cave again but there was nothing.

'May I have a look?' Mateo asked, sensing her frustration and desperation.

She nodded absently and he peered around the shard of granite that had hidden the panel of cogs. They were incredible. Even rusted and old, they were a thing of beauty. His father would have been in his element here. Not because this might prove that he was right, but because of the human ingenuity that he'd always loved the most about history. He could see, though, that something was missing from the cogs—something to connect one half to the other. He turned his head to the side.

'Evie, do you have the octant?'

'Yes, it's in the bag,' she replied. And then, as if sensing his meaning, she hauled the bag from her backpack, retrieving the octant and passing it to him.

He turned the octant in his hands, reasoning that it was almost the perfect shape missing from the cogs. On the back of the octant, where the measuring arm met the mirror, was a tiny cog that had nothing to do with the mechanics of the navigation. It looked as if it would fit right into the…

He pressed the octant into the space and felt it slot into place with a click. He felt Evie's gasp against his cheek as she came to stand, tucked beneath his arm so that she could see. 'I think the measuring arm becomes—'

'A lever,' she finished easily and looked up at him with her excitement sparkling in her eyes like fireworks.

'Go on, then,' he encouraged with a laugh.

It was a little rusty and she strained between being gentle and firm, when just like before, there was a clunk, and a puff of air on the other side of the wall. Grinding gears sounded and they both took a step back, alarm and excitement warring in his chest.

'This is it,' she said to him, gripping his arm with strong hands. 'This is where we're going to find the answers,' she declared, and he'd never wanted to kiss anyone more.

The stone wall slid away to reveal an opening. Evie looked back to make sure he was with her and, after his nod, made her way towards it. Mateo inhaled a breath of air fresher than the stale, gritty air of the cave. Curious, he ducked into the opening behind Evie and followed the curve of the wall until it opened out and…

'*Cristo*,' was all he was capable of saying when he found himself in a giant underground cave system, so large it must have run under the entire island. But it wasn't the cavernous space that awed him, or the beam of sunlight shining down into the space and illuminating it from the cracks in what appeared to be a ceiling. It wasn't even the pool of water that lapped at a stretch of the same white sand they'd landed on.

'Is that a—?'

'Pirate ship,' Evie replied, the words coming out of her mouth on a whisper.

CHAPTER TEN

'HOW DID IT get in here?'

Evie shook her head, not sure. It could have been a volcano, an earthquake or even a cave-in that had surrounded a previously accessible section of the island, but it had effectively trapped an entire sailing ship here.

They walked out into the cave—a space that was easily larger than four football pitches. The light from the crack in the stalactite-covered ceiling illuminated the entire space with a gentle glow. Almost half of the space was water, lapping gently at a sliver of silver sand where the ship had beached. Beyond that, the terrain quickly became rocky, much like what they had found when they'd landed the speedboat earlier. The movement of the water suggested that it must have been coming in from under the walls of the cave somehow.

'What kind of ship is that?'

'It's a *fluyt*. A Dutch sailing ship,' she explained as she made her way towards the ship that had collapsed on its side, signs of damage from age and war clear in the ancient wood. But the name was still bold and proud and Evie couldn't help but press her fingers to her lips in shock. 'And it's not just any sailing ship, it's Loriella's.' She drew level with the ship, a shiver working its way over her skin as she reached out to touch the wood.

Even in its derelict state, it still loomed upwards of nearly twenty feet above her.

'I wonder if this was once part of the island,' she said, thinking out loud, 'and an earthquake caused a landslide, or landfill or something. That could explain the sudden disappearance of Loriella and her crew.'

'But they got out? Or at least *someone* got out if the wooden steps are anything to go by,' Mateo observed.

'Someone who was able to write the coordinates down and hide them in the octant,' she stated.

Mateo nodded. 'But if they could get out, then why did Loriella and her crew simply disappear?'

'In the last skirmish, the Dutch Duke was finally forced into battle. It raged for hours, so many were killed, including the Duke himself. The bounties on their heads would have been enough to tempt anyone to turn against them, so it's assumed that they simply slipped away into anonymity after getting their revenge.'

'For going after Isabella, or killing their captain?'

'Both, I'd imagine,' Evie said, turned to look out across the cavern. Mateo beside her did the same, until she felt him stiffen. Following his line of sght, she turned towards the rocky side of the cave, surprised to find a wooden structure erected between the beach and the cavern wall. Instinctively she began to make her way towards it.

'What is that? I've never seen anything like it,' Mateo said, wonder in his voice.

Evie had a suspicion but she didn't want to voice it until she was sure. She looked at the markings that covered the doorway. Religious symbols carved into the wood with exquisite detail that would have taken much time and dedication. A sense of hallowed stillness fell over them.

She felt Mateo's gaze on her as she gently pushed against the door to the small wooden hut. Shelves lined the walls, covered in jewels, coins, old-fashioned pistols, muskets, cutlasses, chests overflowing with jewels tarnished by age and dust and sea air. But it was the two figures on a bed in the centre of the room that caught her attention the moment the door was opened. Wrapped in each other's arms, there lay the skeletal remains of Loriella Desaparecer and her lover, husband, and first mate.

'It's them,' she whispered, unaware that tears had risen to press at the corners of her eyes. She felt Mateo's hand on her shoulder, and reached up to hold it there, needing his touch in that moment.

She felt him look around the small wooden burial chamber, taking in all the treasure that lined the shelves as she had done in a heartbeat before her focus was drawn to the final resting place of Princess Isabella of Iondorra.

Mateo pointed to several lines of rough writing carved into the wood. 'What is that?'

'It looks like Iondorran,' Evie replied, leaning closer to the words above the wooden bed.

'Why would it be in Iondorran if…?'

'If this wasn't Isabella?' She looked up at him, smiling, knowing—*knowing* that everything the Professor and she had believed was true.

'Can you read it?' he asked.

'I think so,' she replied, moving just a little closer. *'"Our heart, unable to live without he who held hers, chose to stay by his side until his last breath. And then chose to join him in eternity. Long live the Pirate Queen."'* Goosebumps had broken out across her skin, as she realised what must have happened.

'You were right,' Mateo whispered and his words

turned over in her heart, making her feel both elated and deeply sad for what Isabella had lost that day.

'They called her a Pirate Queen here, not a princess.'

'As a sign of their respect for her?'

Evie nodded. 'The first mate must have been injured in the last battle—the one that killed the Dutch Duke. Loriella and her crew must have come here and...' She looked at the ship, and then took a step back out into the cave, her hand pressing against her lips in shock. 'They blew the...they must have used explosives to seal in the ship and...' She looked back to Mateo staring at her. 'And she couldn't live without him, her first mate. Her husband. She...' Evie couldn't bring herself to say that the Princess had taken her own life, but Mateo must have realised, because he came to her and took her into his arms. 'Her crew,' Evie said, needing to finish the story. 'That's how much loyalty they felt for her,' Evie realised. 'They touched hardly any of the treasure and they buried her with her husband. The carving, the wooden mausoleum, that would have taken years. They would have used the wooden staircase until it was done. And no one ever betrayed them, no one ever revealed the location of the treasure for their own needs.'

A week ago, Mateo would have been surprised that anyone had managed to inspire that much loyalty, but that was before he'd met Evelyn Edwards. Somehow in his mind, Princess Isabella had merged with how he saw Evie and he could hardly separate the two. His father had looked for the missing princess for almost his entire life, and now that Mateo stood at her final resting place, he hoped that his father felt at peace.

He retrieved his phone from his pocket and swiped

across the screen to get to his camera. He held it up to take some pictures, to secure the proof his father had always needed, but Evie pushed his hand down gently, shaking her head.

'Don't you want this?'

'Need and want are two different things.'

Sometimes it is enough for just one to know.

He remembered his father's words, back from when he was still a child, when he believed in pirate adventures and treasure hunts. It seemed that even though he had lost his faith in such things, he had been destined to find his way back to them.

'But this could be all you need to restore your reputation. To prove everyone who doubted you wrong,' he said, staring down into the beautiful depths of her hazel eyes that smiled sadly back at him.

'I'm not here for that. I'm here so that a king can know peace, can know what happened to his ancestor, that a queen—a daughter—can help her father, and so that a son can find his father again. That's what I'm here for, Mateo.'

Her words broke something in him, shattering something that hurt, that cost him greatly, but that he couldn't, wouldn't look at right now. He held her to him and he couldn't shake the feeling that, of all the riches and jewels in the room, what he held in that moment was more precious.

'May I have a moment?' she asked, after her breathing had settled—clearly as moved as he had been, if not more.

'Of course.'

He started to leave, when something on the shelf by the door caught his eye. The flash of a memory, his father and a painting, traipsed through his mind, and before he could question it he'd retrieved the object to take a closer look at it in the sunlit cave. But the moment he got outside, he was once again mesmerised by the impressive ship beached on the shore.

He looked around at the cave, realising that Evie must have been right, and marvelled at how Isabella's crew had managed to bring down the rocks in such a way that the ship hadn't been damaged irrevocably. Or perhaps that hadn't even been a consideration, and just…fate.

He sat down in the white sand, staring at the clear blue water, wondering if this was perhaps one of the most beautiful places he had ever been. And for the first time in three years, maybe even more, he wished his father could be there. Without anger, or frustration or resentment, he simply wished his father could see this; the culmination of his life's work.

His father wasn't infallible, Mateo had always known that. But he hadn't understood that, as an adult and not the child he once was, it meant forgiving his father for not being infallible. Acknowledging that his father had made mistakes he bitterly regretted meant letting go of that blame and anger. But when he tried, he still felt the gnaw of heavy responsibility tightening its hold. But the unease he felt swirled around Evie. The absolute and utter shock when she'd nearly fallen through the stairs… His palm fisted instinctively. He heard Evie's footsteps in the sand behind him and buried his feelings when she sat so close to him that she could lean her head against his shoulder.

'Are you okay?' he asked her.

'A bit overwhelmed, but yes. I…' She started, staring

at the way the water lapped against the beach. 'It's the culmination of so much. I wish he could have been here.'

Mateo didn't have to ask who and instead replied, honestly, 'I do too.'

'Will you tell your mother?'

He nodded. Of course he would tell her. But he feared it would cause more hurt and he'd tried so hard over the years to avoid that. And instead of seeing the sand beneath his feet he saw his mother, unable to get out of bed for days at a time, her stare into the middle distance more frightening than any of her tears. And the words she would whisper when she thought no one was looking.

'I did the right thing. I did it for the right reasons.'

His mother had done it for *him*.

Utterly unaware of the emotional maelstrom slowly picking up speed in his heart, Evie sighed contentedly.

'I'm so happy I saw this,' she sighed, and he gritted his teeth together to hold back the hurt so that she could be happy in her achievement.

But when she lifted her head from his shoulder, he sensed the shift in her mood.

'What is it?' he asked.

'The water,' she said, rising up to stand. He looked and it appeared that the tide was much stronger than it had been only moments before. 'I'm not sure that there should be a tide here, if—'

Whatever she was about to say was cut off as the ground beneath them seemed to groan. Alarm shot through him, and in her gaze he saw a stark fear that nearly stopped his heart. He was about to say something when the rocks cracked and screamed as the ground shook.

'Earthquake,' they said simultaneously.

They lurched to their feet, awkward as the sand shifted even where they stood. Evie went to run to the chamber, but he caught her round the waist, practically lifting her off her feet, just as a jagged crack formed in the rocks above the wooden hut.

'Evie, you can't. It's too late,' he shouted over the terrible grinding noise of rock grating against rock. She screamed as if it were her being cut open rather than the rocks, raining down and smashing the final resting place of Isabella and her husband. Mateo looked back to the opening they had come through and knew that they couldn't risk even trying to climb back out the way they had come. He looked out into the pool, the crystalline blue darkening at the back of the cave speaking to a depth he could only hope was achievable.

'Evie, can you swim?' he demanded, but she was still lost, staring between the sailing ship and the wooden hut. He shook her firmly, needing to get her to focus immediately. 'Evie!'

'Yes! Yes, I can swim,' she replied, her quick mind catching up and reaching for her pack. 'We need to find where the water is getting into the cave,' she said, speaking his exact thoughts. 'And we need to do it now. Right now.'

He nodded, glad he didn't need to prompt her further. He kicked off his shoes, thankful to see her doing the same. They stripped out of clothes they didn't need and would weigh them down, even as the stalactites hanging from the ceiling began to tremble and fall.

He cursed as they waded into the pool, fear making their movements jerky and their breaths impossibly fast. He grabbed Evie, hauling her round to face him. There was so much he wanted to say, so much that he saw in her eyes. She kissed him then. Swift, harsh, but enough. It had to be enough.

He followed after her as she ploughed through the water with strong strokes, aiming for the back of the cave. He tried to peer through the surface of the water, searching for any kind of sight of where it was coming in, of where they could possibly escape, but the water was so torn up by the earthquake there was no way of knowing.

They reached the far end of the cave and stopped to tread water.

'We have no other option,' Evie said to him.

'It will be there,' he told her with a confidence he didn't feel but knew they both needed to hear.

Together they deepened their breathing, readying their lungs to take in as much oxygen as possible, and with one last look, one last inhalation, they dived beneath the surface of the water.

What had once been a shallow, smooth pool was now awash with an unnatural tide. Peering through the murky depths, he felt salt water sting his eyes but it was the only way to find out where water was entering the cave. Just beyond his reach, Evie seemed to be heading for an area with purpose. With absolute faith, he followed her to where the rock wall arched and a blessed blue filled the darkness. With a glance back at him and his nod to her, they powered through the gap and out into the open sea, emerging from the depths with desperate gasps of air.

From outside of the cave and further back from the island, they could see the damage the quake was wreaking on the small, uninhabited island. In shock, they stared as rocks broke away from the craggy shoreline they'd stood atop only hours before, crashing down into the sea below.

They needed to swim further out. Evie drew the rucksack from her back and, treading water, searched for something inside.

'We need to get further away,' Mateo called out to her.

'Yes, but we also need this,' she said, pulling out the orange emergency flare gun, and fired into the sky. He watched it shoot upwards into an arc and, glowing a bright red, flare and spark before slowly falling back into the sea.

'Are you okay?' he demanded, resisting the urge to grab her, to hold on to her, knowing that they needed their strength.

'No. Not even remotely,' she replied truthfully. 'Are you?'

He shook his head, unable to confess that he feared he might never be the same again. He was exhausted, every limb impossibly heavy. Consciously, he knew much of that would have been adrenaline and shock. It was a miracle that neither had been hurt by more than scratches and scrapes as they'd passed under the jagged rock, but he wouldn't be okay until the captain of the yacht came to find them. He wouldn't be okay until Evie was as far from harm as she could physically be. And even then, he wasn't sure he'd be okay.

Evie had stripped the wet, salty clothes from her body and thrust herself in a shower the moment they returned to the yacht, desperate to wash off the fear and the sadness. Consciously she knew she was probably in shock, not just from the earthquake but from everything that had passed before that too; finding the cave, finding Isabella. But also, there was a creeping sense of wrongness between her and Mateo since they had been rescued and she scrubbed her skin harder and harder to try and remove that more than the rest of it.

The captain had brought the yacht to where he had seen the flare and found them what felt like hours after they had emerged from the cave, but which had probably only been minutes. He'd explained that it wasn't a particularly bad earthquake and might not have even been felt on the main islands, but the cave would have suffered so many tremors and quakes, it was a miracle that it was still standing.

He'd asked them if they wanted to go back, if there was anything left to find. Mateo's steady gaze had held hers as she'd said 'no', letting Isabella, her husband and their treasure finally find peace. And that was the last time she'd felt his eyes on her. Mateo wasn't ignoring her. He would answer questions, he would even smile, but he had retreated, emotionally and physically.

Even now as she looked across the cabin of the small plane that had met them from the private landing strip of the island where she and Mateo had spent the night, he felt almost a world away. She tried to tell herself that she was wrong, that she was imagining it. That after everything they'd shared, the connection between them was stronger than ever. And perhaps if she said it enough times, she'd actually start to believe it.

'We'll be landing shortly,' the flight attendant announced, and Evie felt a sense of panic.

She hadn't been able to bring her thoughts together enough for herself, let alone for the Queen of Iondorra. Everything was happening so quickly and she couldn't help but feel she was a step behind. She wanted to tell Isabella's incredible story, wanted to do the woman she'd researched for almost her entire academic career justice, because she wasn't just a figurehead to the Queen of Iondorra. She was family. And Evie knew how important knowing about family was, more than anyone.

But at the same time, Evie couldn't stop herself from thinking of Mateo.

She looked across the cabin to where he was speaking to the flight attendant. His words were lost beneath the hum of the plane's engine, but she heard the air staff offer to ask the pilot. She told herself off and instead once again tried to gather her thoughts, but they felt as scattered as sand. She reached into her bag for the Professor's notebook and remembered that she had given it back to Mateo. It was the right thing to have done, but just for a moment there it had felt as if…she had lost something so very precious to her.

The flight attendant returned and nodded to Mateo's waiting gaze. The confirmation of whatever his request had been didn't seem to make him happy though. His firm, powerful lips flattened into a line that spoke only of grim determination. And then he cast his gaze on her and inexplicably her heart dropped.

'Evelyn, when the plane lands—'

'The Queen will probably want to see us quite quickly. It will be about six in the evening when we arrive and I'm sure that she's busy—'

'Evelyn…'

'We might even have to meet her father, after all he is the one—'

'Evie.'

She didn't want to hear it. She didn't know exactly what he was going to say, but it would break her. It would break her in places she was already broken. She marvelled at that. At how, in this moment, she didn't need words or explanations, that what was being communicated to her she felt in her soul. It defied speech or language and her body was reacting more quickly than her mind. Tears pressed against the backs of her eyes. One even escaped and she hastily wiped it away, hoping that he wouldn't have seen it, but he had.

And she wished she hadn't seen the way his eyes turned from hard to soft, to hurt, to determined, all in a heartbeat.

'I'll not be at the meeting with the Queen.'

'Mateo, you have to be there. They will want to thank you for all you've done.'

'I did nothing but follow you,' he said and for a moment she believed him. Believed his words.

'Your father would want you there.'

'Don't,' he said, holding his hand up, a hint of the anger and frustration she had felt simmering in the air between them since they'd been found in the sea. 'Don't use my father against me like that.'

Shame crawled up her neck, heated her cheeks at the truth of his accusation. 'I'm sorry,' she said, regretting the words that desperation had made her use.

'After we land, I'm taking the plane back to Spain. I've already pushed back the meeting with Léi Chen too many times.'

'Is that really what's important right now?' she asked, surprised.

'Yes. It's a meeting that has been years in the making. It's very important to my company,' he tried to explain. 'It's important to me.'

Evie couldn't believe it. It wasn't that she'd expected him to suddenly drop everything, but…

It's important to me.

And she wasn't, she realised with a heart that suddenly felt as heavy as a rock.

Had she been that stupid? Again? To think that someone wanted her when they didn't? Her hand shook as she pressed her fingers against her lips.

No. She had seen the way he had looked at her. Felt the way he had made her feel. Knew that kind of feeling, that kind of *love*, had to be two-sided. It had to be.

He crossed the cabin and came to sit opposite her, leaning forward to snatch her hands into his, and even she wanted to hide from him, hide from what it was he was trying to tell her.

'Please don't make me,' she pleaded, her voice quiet and her throat thick.

'Make you what?'

'Beg,' she whispered as a hot tear rolled down her cheek, her soul aching and her heart breaking.

CHAPTER ELEVEN

THE BOTTOM DROPPED out of his world. He cursed himself to hell and back a hundred times over and even that wouldn't be enough. That he had cowed this strong, powerful, incredible woman made him feel sick.

Nausea, anger, fear, resentment, they rose up in a noxious, heady substance that choked his throat and shattered his words.

'You should never *have* to beg, Evelyn. Can't you see that?'

Another tear rolled down her cheek and he wasn't even man enough to watch it. Coward that he was, he turned away from the pain he knew he was inflicting. But it was nothing compared to the damage she could feel in the future. Damage that he didn't think he could fix this time. No amount of security or promises could heal this hurt. And that was why he couldn't stay. He couldn't.

Panic began to build in his chest. He didn't want to be here. He wanted to get out, to be away from this plane, away from her. He was angry, furious at himself for being so weak that he'd let this happen. He'd let this happen to another woman. But if he stopped this now, then perhaps it wouldn't be so bad for her. Perhaps it wouldn't be so bad for himself.

'It was just one night, Evelyn. That was what you asked for and that was all I could give you.'

Anger flashed in her eyes, an anger that covered an age-old hurt, one that he should have paid heed to, but couldn't.

'Don't dismiss what we shared,' Evie whispered.

'And don't make more of it than what it was like you do with everything else.'

'What do you mean?' she asked, paling even more though he'd thought it impossible.

'You do this over and over again, Evie. You did it with my father and with the Queen of Iondorra.'

'What are you talking about?' she reared back, but he saw it—the fear of what he was about to say.

'I'm talking about the fact that these people ruined you, Evie. They ruined your reputation. My father let you help him in his research, knowing that he could handle the backlash, but that you wouldn't. The damage done to your reputation has been almost irrevocable and he left you with absolutely no support. And the Iondorran palace?' he scoffed. 'They not only stood back and let it happen, all the while knowing how probable your theories were, they then sent you on a treasure hunt, demanding your silence and refusing to change the negative press against you. And you are so desperate for love and acceptance that you would do anything for them!'

He hadn't realised when he'd raised his voice, but the look on Evie's features horrified him as much as the damage caused by his words. If he could have cut off his own tongue, he would have. That there was truth in his accusation made it all the more painful.

'Desperate,' she whispered to herself, nodding as if considering his words, but there was a jerkiness to her movements, as if she were back in the cave, wading through water. As if the ceiling had just come down around her ears. Then the nod became a shake, slow but more and more determined. 'Not desperate, I don't think.' And this time when she looked up at him and the tear fell from the corner of her eye, she swept it away quickly and efficiently.

'But thank you for your advice. On reflection, you're right. I appreciate the reminder. Just one night.' She nodded again. 'It clearly is better that we leave this here. It wouldn't have worked. Because the one thing I know I need—as you have taken great pains to point out,' she said, the breath shuddering in her chest, 'is someone who is emotionally available. And you are not,' she said, shaking her head and twisting a knife lodged in his heart. 'You're just too much like him and the saddest thing is that you don't even see it. Which makes you doomed to repeat his mistakes. And I won't be one of those mistakes.'

'Like who?' he demanded, guilt and anger balancing on that knife's edge.

'Your father.'

'I am nothing like that man,' he spat. 'He shirked his responsibilities…he did nothing while my mother moved us away and set up an entirely new life. I was the one who stepped up,' he said, pointing a finger at his chest, 'I was the one who made sure she was happy, that she was safe and cared for.'

'You shouldn't have had to do that, Mateo. You were a child. But you grew up burying your head in work—just like he did—so that you didn't have to confront how you felt about it. Because it's so much easier, Mateo, to lose yourself in work than to confront the painful and difficult feelings of loss and love.

'But it's worth it,' she said on a half-plea. 'It's worth it to live a full life, not a half-life of hidden feelings and buried anger. It's worth it, and *I'm* worth it, and until you see that...' she took a breath, the constellation of emotions in her eyes for once unreadable '... I don't want to see you ever again.'

Her words wounded him so deeply he was struck silent, utterly incapable of speech. It was only when Evelyn unbuckled her belt that he realised they had come in to land. She barely met the gaze that was unwillingly glued to her every movement as she stood and retrieved the briefcase she always had with her.

'Wait,' he said, the word bursting from his mouth like a bullet.

She paused as she passed by the seat he occupied, her eyes straight ahead. He reached into his pocket for the object he'd been carrying ever since they left the cave. He had always intended to give it to her but suddenly he didn't want to, knowing that it may very well be the last time he saw her. It sat in the centre of his closed fist, warmed by his body and sharp to his skin.

'When they ask for proof—'

'I don't have any proof,' she said, her words clipped and somehow more devastating than before.

'Give them this,' he said, holding out his hand to reveal a red gemstone surrounded by pearls, set in a gold band.

She stared at his hand so long, he thought she might ignore it, ignore him, but while she was staring at the ring he was staring at her, so he saw the moment that the sob worked its way up her body. He knew she'd recognised it, the same way he'd recognised it, from the photograph of his father standing beside the life-sized portrait of

Isabella of Iondorra, with the ring gifted to her on her first appearance at court proudly worn on her left hand.

It was more than proof, and more than a reminder of his father, and more than he could put words to. Inexplicably he wanted her to say something, he wanted to say something. He wanted to take the last ten minutes back, he wanted to be different. He wanted to be the man she needed, but she was right. He was frightened of being responsible for his own feelings, and he had hidden his weaknesses behind hurt-filled accusations of her failings as if his weren't so much worse. And just as he opened his mouth to say something she plucked the ring from his palm and took one step forward, then another, and he realised she was walking out of his life and that he needed to let her go.

'Do you need a minute?' the Queen's assistant asked, peering at Evie in concern.

Evie almost didn't want to know what she looked like. Eyes red and blotchy, she was sure, skin an unhealthy shade of pale. Standing in the corridor just outside the private suites of the Queen and her family, she really couldn't care less. Because Mateo had just torn out her heart. But she took the chance she was offered to freshen up in the bathroom. She splashed cold water on her face and dried off with a hand towel. She just had to get through this, then she could let go. Then she could take in the way her life had just been irrevocably ripped from its roots.

Are you so desperate for love and acceptance?

Her mouth wobbled until she bit down on her bottom lip hard. She willed the tears back, knowing there would be a time to let them fall, but that now was not it. Standing up tall, shoulders back, she stared at herself in the mirror. She didn't look as bad as she felt, and that was a small mercy.

'You will do this,' she told herself. 'And then you will go home,' she said, trying not to break down on the last word. Suddenly realising that home and her life in London felt inexplicably alien to her after all that had happened.

The assistant knocked gently on the door and Evie cleared her throat. She rolled her shoulders and smiled through her hurt, all the while holding the ring Mateo had given her in her hand as if it were her only lifeline, and she emerged from the bathroom and went to meet the Queen of Iondorra.

It wasn't until Evie found herself before the Queen that she realised she was in a bit of a daze. As if half of her was here, present and answering questions, and half of her was back in the cabin of a small plane with Mateo, saying goodbye for ever.

'So, you're telling me that you actually found it? I mean, found *her*.'

'Yes, Your Majesty,' Evie replied, forcing herself to hold on to the present.

'Really?'

The Queen seemed utterly surprised, and Evie supposed she could understand why. She'd initially only gone to Shanghai to retrieve a family heirloom and instead had come back with a tale so adventurous and outlandish she hardly believed it herself.

In the corner of the surprisingly comfortable sitting room, the Queen's consort, Theo Tersi, was making them all a cup of tea. Belatedly, Evie realised, that this was in her honour, and perhaps because he and the Queen had been casting some slightly worried glances in her direction.

'Would you like to sit down?' the Queen asked.

'Yes, that would be… Thank you,' Evie replied eventually.

She sat at the end of a beautifully regal sofa, with pen marks scribbled on one of the cushions and a pile of children's books in three different languages that almost reached the sofa arm. A little blonde-haired girl was sprawled on the floor in the corner of the room, colouring in a design with such fierce concentration, her tongue was sticking into the side of her mouth. Her father peered over her shoulder, pride and love shining from him with an almost ferocious intensity. *This* was what she had wanted as a child, before she had realised that she would never have it with Carol and Alan. This loving, soft, easy, comfortable domesticity…this *family.* Evie paled when the Queen caught her taking in the scene as if she could read much deeper than just the basic envy that had spread across her heart.

'It has cost you greatly, this search for Isabella,' the Queen said, rather than asked.

'Yes,' Evie admitted.

'More than just your reputation.'

Evie nodded. It had cost her her heart.

Suddenly the little girl leapt up from the floor. 'Grand-père! Grand-père!' she cried, rushing to greet an old man with shockingly thick white hair and startling blue eyes. The little girl wrapped her arms around his thighs in a tight band and stared up at him with such adoration, it nearly brought a tear to Evie's eyes. Had she looked at her mother like that? Had she ever thought to look at her adoptive parents like that?

The older man, the Queen's father, placed a gentle hand on his granddaughter's head, but his eyes zeroed in on Evie.

'You found her?'

Evie nodded. 'Yes, Your Highness,' she replied. 'But I'm so sorry, the octant was lost in the cave during the earthquake.'

'Tell me everything,' he commanded.

So there, sat on the sofa, with the Queen of Iondorra on a chair with her husband standing beside her, her daughter at her feet and her father opposite on another chair, Evie told the story of how Princess Isabella became the Pirate Queen. And if she embellished just a little, to please the fancy of a wide-eyed little girl who gave gasps of shock and delight, no one in the room minded one bit. There were looks of thanks as she carefully navigated the subject of finding the remains, and frowns of concern from the adults as she told of the daring escape from the cave, but everyone cheered when she described the captain of the yacht coming to their rescue.

'I'm sorry that I wasn't able to preserve their legacy,' she concluded to the Queen's father.

Again, to her surprise, he waved her off. 'It was never about treasure, was it, my dear?' he said, looking down at the little princess, who shook her head so determinedly her pony-tail nearly came loose.

Absentmindedly her father reached down to tighten it as she replied with a big, gap-toothed smile, 'No, Grand-père.'

He fixed those piercing blue eyes on her, even though Evie knew he was talking more to the women of his family. 'I wanted my granddaughter to know that no matter what happens in life, the women of Iondorra are strong and powerful. They are survivors and warriors, who will fight for their people and their families, no matter if they are princesses, pirates, or queens. The women of *this* family? They have the power to do whatever they set their mind to, don't they, Alize?'

'Yes, Grandpère,' Alize replied with an even bigger smile, until she descended into hysterics as the once King of Iondorra tickled his granddaughter and chased her around the room until they both ran out of breath.

Queen Sofia was looking at her hands but Evie could tell that tears had gathered in her eyes, because they had gathered in her own. Sofia placed her hand over her husband's, where he had rested it on her shoulder. And when the Queen met her eyes, she understood. For just a moment, she'd had her father returned to her. A proud, powerful, eloquent man, who had fought to give something to his granddaughter, more precious than any treasure: hope and possibility.

But it was what Evie saw passing between Queen Sofia and her husband that made her realise what she wanted. It was support, it was companionship. It was *love*. And no matter how much she wanted to have that with Mateo, if he didn't, couldn't, be that for her, then it wasn't love at all.

The clench of her fingers reminded her of the last thing he had given her.

'I might not have proof that would stand up to any real investigation, but I do have this.'

She held out the ring and realised the moment they lost the King. He stared at it blankly and then a broad smile split his features. 'A sweet. No, a…uhm…a treat…no.'

Alize laughed, 'Silly Grandpère. But I know where we can find some sweets,' she confided and started to lead him from the room. Theo pressed a kiss to his wife's head and followed his daughter out along with the neatly dressed man in the corner who appeared to be some kind of medical professional.

Queen Sofia sighed and set her shoulders to look down at the ring in Evie's hand. 'I know what that is. It's Isabella's coming-out ring. We all have one, the women of this family.' A small laugh escaped as if she didn't believe her own eyes. 'Thank you,' she said, finally. 'Thank you for bringing her back to us.'

And beneath that Evie heard the unspoken words the Queen of Iondorra intimated.

Thank you for bringing him back to us.

'You're welcome,' Evie replied, and wondered if she would ever feel the same. Whether, perhaps, there was a future in which she might finally try to find her birth parents.

'Ms Edwards, I know that you are currently employed, but we have a few openings in Iondorra that might interest you.'

Evie couldn't help but smile. Ever since she'd first come to Iondorra she'd been taken by the beauty of it. In her mind, somehow, it had become a country from her very own fairy tale. But the last few days had rocked her sense of self a little and she knew that she needed to regroup.

Mateo really had been wrong. It wasn't that she had been so desperate for the scraps that Iondorra had thrown her way. What had been driving her was her desire to know the past. Only, Evie was beginning to suspect it wasn't Isabella's past she wanted to know, but her own.

'I'm sure they would interest me, very much. But I

think I need some time to think through my next steps,' she replied.

'Of course. Please know that if you would like to take that time here in Callier, we will provide a suite for you and open a line of credit for you too.'

'That is too kind, Your Majesty.'

'No. It really isn't. I am deeply sorry for how you were treated by your peers and regret very much that the palace wasn't—and isn't—able to change that. Yet.'

Evie held the gaze of a queen and accepted an apology that was her due. 'Thank you.'

Mateo had intended to return home. He had. He'd arranged for his car to be waiting for him when he landed and there it was on the runway, waiting for him to drive it the short distance to his villa.

He'd blocked out two days for the rescheduled meeting with Léi Chen, but this time it was Chen who'd had to cancel due to a family emergency. So, he'd got in his car and started to drive.

He was nearly three hours in when he realised his unconscious destination. He both wanted it and feared it. Feared it because of the emotions coursing through his veins. His heart hadn't beat normally since Evie had disembarked from the plane. Who was he kidding? It'd practically been arrhythmic since he'd first met her. An hour later and the muscle memory that had brought him here a thousand times had him turning off at the junction for Almería and he stopped fighting the fact that he was going to see his mother.

She was standing in the doorway, wiping her hands on a cloth when he pulled into the parking bay in front of her villa. He wondered for a moment if she'd somehow known he was coming, an instinct he previously would have dismissed, but after everything he'd seen, everything he'd discovered, he really wasn't that sure any more.

He exited the car and she opened her arms, and for the first time in what felt like forever he let his mother embrace him like a child. He was shamed by the anger and frustration that escaped from the box he'd tried to stuff them in, through the tears that pressed desperately against his eyelids, and he tried to pull away to hide them, but his mother held on tight, refusing to let go. And finally, he gave up the fight and sank into his mother's arms.

An hour later he was in the kitchen with a coffee and a plate full of crumbs, his mother refusing to hear a word until he'd eaten the sandwich he'd denied needing but had consumed in less than thirty seconds.

She looked at him knowingly and he smiled. For a moment it had reminded him of Evie. And then the knife twisted again.

'Speak and don't leave anything out.'

He didn't know where to start…there were things he'd have liked to leave out—the hurtful words he'd delivered, embarrassment and shame hot, crawling things with spikes that sank into his skin—but his mother also deserved to know that her husband's theories had not been pure fantasy, but reality.

He started at the beginning and took the slaps to the back of his head with grace, knowing they were delivered by a mother who had raised her son better than that.

There was a wistful smile on his mother's face when he finished.

'That would have meant so much to your father. That you and she were the ones to find the treasure and the proof.'

'But the world will never know.'

'The world wasn't what was important to him, Mateo. You were. I know…he…wasn't always able to show it. He didn't have a good relationship with his own parents and,' his mother paused and looked away, 'there was a lot of hurt there that was very deep. Too deep. But he loved you. And for *you* to know that he wasn't chasing fantasies, that would have been enough.'

His mother's long-ago whispered words came back to him then and he knew he couldn't hide from this any longer.

'Mama, why did we leave him?'

She looked away, trying to conceal her hurt.

'I… I heard you say that it was for me.'

Still looking away from him, she pressed her fingers against her lips. 'I'm ashamed you heard that. Ashamed and truly sorry. It was not because of you,' she said, finally turning to look at him so that he could see the truth of her words.

His breath shuddered slowly from his lungs.

'We left because, as much as I loved your father, I simply couldn't continue to live in the absence of him. It made me less; it took things away from me and I could see that it was doing the same to you. So no, we did not leave because of you. But telling myself I was leaving my husband for the sake of my child helped ease the guilt of breaking up my family. I…had no idea that you'd heard that, and I'm so deeply sorry for it.'

Something eased in Mateo's chest, but the pressure was still there. Something tapping against the walls of the emotional cage he'd put everything in for the last twenty years.

He looked at his hands, unable to look his mother in the eye. 'Am I like him?'

His stomach clenched, waiting for the gut punch he feared was coming.

Mateo's mother placed her hands over his, drawing his gaze back to hers, and the love shining in her eyes humbled him.

'You are the best bits of him and the best bits of me, *mi corazón*,' she said, the sincerity and truth of her words raising the hairs on his forearms.

'But he let us leave,' he whispered.

'Yes, he did. I think that was because he did not know better. He did not know how to fix the problems between us.'

'I tried so hard,' Mateo said, 'to make it okay, to stop it hurting you so much.'

'I know, *mi hijo*, and it was my weakness that let you do it. Because that wasn't your responsibility, Mateo. It wasn't for you to protect me, but for us to protect you and… I don't think we did such a good job of that,' she said, the tears in her eyes hurting him as much as his own.

Mateo went to interrupt but she cut him off.

'Your father and I were always so incredibly proud of you and what you'd achieved. He loved you so much.'

'But I hadn't spoken to him for years before his death,' Mateo said, the shame almost drowning him now.

'Mateo, that didn't matter one bit. He loved you. It is that simple and that difficult,' she said on a sad smile. 'But he never blamed you.'

'How do you know?'

'Because we spoke. We would always speak on your birthday,' she said, smiling. 'You were the one thing that always brought us back together.'

This time Mateo did feel sucker-punched. All that time he'd missed and he'd never get back. The wasted opportunities because of his stubbornness, his pride…his fear.

'I don't…' he started, struggling to find the words he needed. 'I don't want to make the same mistakes as he did.'

'Good,' his mother replied, with a strength that surprised him. 'Both your father and I made mistakes—I won't let him shoulder the blame entirely. But learn from our mistakes. We turned and ran from our hurts, not realising that we could never fix things alone…but together?'

His mother let the question hang in the air as blood pumped through Mateo's veins with hope and energy and strength.

From where she was brewing another coffee by the kitchen window, his mother turned to look back at him. 'This may sound strange, *mi amor*, but I'd like to thank whoever gave me my son back.'

'Me too, Mamá. Me too.'

CHAPTER TWELVE

'THANKS, MISS EDWARDS.'

'You're welcome. And it's Professor,' she called with a smile after the last of her students left Lecture Room Four. She looked around the dimly lit room and wondered which poor professor they would house in here next. She'd heard that Humanities were in the doghouse at the moment, so maybe it was their turn. In the meantime, her students were to be transferred to Professor Baldick, who was, if somewhat eccentric, an incredible teacher.

Carol and Alan had handled the news surprisingly well. It had never sat happily with them that their adopted daughter was teaching at a south-east London university, and apparently any possible future plans were better than that. She had left them in their townhouse being looked after by their staff and felt that actually very little would change between them, no matter where her future lay. She would most likely continue to see them once every couple of months and, as they had little to no attachment to festive periods, Evie would be able to come and go as she pleased.

A lot had changed in the last four weeks. She'd made decisions that she'd never have imagined making the day the Queen had come to visit her here in this lecture theatre, and she'd done things she'd never dreamed of, she thought, smiling at the adventure she had taken with Mateo.

Yes, his words that last day had devastated her. She'd reeled from his rejection, questioned herself and her belief that he'd wanted more in spite of what he'd said to her, and come out of it alone. But she had survived. And that was the thing she clung to. Because even though his words had been cruel, they had forced her to confront some painful truths.

She *had* let her reputation become damaged by working with the Professor and she *had* willingly followed the Queen's request without thought to the impact it would have on her. And in some ways that showed a reckless disregard for herself which was untenable and would not continue. So now she was putting her wants and needs first. Fear had held her back for so long from too many things and she was done hiding.

She had shied away from the search for her birth parents because she feared another rejection from them. But Mateo had shown her that she was as strong and fierce as a pirate queen and nothing, not even his rejection of what they had shared that night and what they could have had in the future, could take that from her. So, she had begun to look at her adoption paperwork and was considering using her DNA to see if she had any more family out there. But that was a slow process that she wanted to think through and she felt no need to rush it. She might have lost her heart that day with Mateo on the plane, but it certainly helped her find her strength.

A strength that had been pivotal in the decision to leave USEL. Evie looked around the quiet, empty hall, a small smile curving her lips at the affection she felt towards what had been a safe place for her in the last two years. But as she had learned, safe wasn't everything. It was time to push herself, to make waves and be a little more…pirate.

It hadn't taken long after returning to London from Iondorra for her to realise that everything about her life that had once given her peace and contentment felt *lacking*. So she had handed in her notice and was using some of her savings to take some time and consider her options. While she did that, she was taking Queen Sofia up on a rather interesting proposition from a friend of hers.

And in her down time, she would work on the book that she would publish only when the Queen gave her permission to do so. Evie wasn't looking for fame or money and was in no rush, she just wanted people to know of Isabella's incredible story.

She had moved her things out of her flat and into storage, using a hotel for these last few days before she left for Iondorra. It had been a naïve attempt to avoid the Mateo-shaped figure she imagined haunting her. She'd thought, wrongly as it turned out, that if she left her flat she would no longer imagine him lingering in a doorway, or taking up space in her living room. She hoped to never again turn at a shadow in her kitchen, small and ephemeral in ways that Mateo Marin probably had never been in his life. No, leaving her flat hadn't solved anything. She would see him in hallways, corridors and on the streets, but although her mind played tricks on her, she knew in her heart that it wasn't him.

She closed the clasp on her leather briefcase and turned to find, once again, her imagination playing tricks on her. Illuminated by an open door was a figure standing at the back of the room.

She closed her eyes, holding her breath, but when she

opened them again he was still there. And then, slowly, step by step, casually almost, Mateo Marin made his way towards her. It gave her the time she desperately needed, not to compose herself, but to consume the sight of him as if she were starving; hungrily and greedily. His suit jacket was open to reveal a waistcoat that hugged his torso snugly, the open-necked white shirt that indicated laziness or frustration, either of which Mateo had always worn well.

His hair, thick and carelessly tousled, made her want to feel those silken strands between her fingers and she could barely think of anything other than pressing her hand against his chest, to feel the beat of his heart, hoping to feel his own hand pressed against hers as if he'd wanted to keep her there.

She bit her lip, a sharp nip that pulled her out of the daydream.

By the time he reached her, she had pulled hurt around her like a cloak, refusing to be the same weak-willed woman she'd been the last time she had seen him. Just the memory of how she'd nearly begged him to love her cut her off at the knees. He stopped as if reading the change in her expression, his own gaze softening and offering a reflection of her hurt.

Mateo drank in the sight of her as if he were dying of thirst; great big gulps he wanted to gorge himself on. In that moment the constant sense of urgency, the anxiety driving him forward in the last four weeks, began to disappear, just from the sight of her.

He'd worried that it had been a waste of time, that he should have gone to her immediately, but he'd needed that time to get his head on straight. He'd chosen to take a sabbatical from his company. It had taken a while to convince the CFO and the board that he really did only mean six months and that it would not be for ever, but he'd had Henri's support. Henri, who was thrilled that Mateo had finally got his priorities in the right order.

Mateo had worked his fingers to the bone from the moment he'd started his company, and when most people would have stepped back after the IPO, he'd only pushed on further. He'd hidden himself, he now realised, in flings that could go no further and that wouldn't threaten the iron hold he'd had on his emotions—the iron hold he'd felt he *had* to have. All to protect himself from bearing more emotional responsibility than he could take because of the misguided belief that he had to make up for his father's mistakes and absence.

Evelyn had been, without question, absolutely right. Mateo *had* behaved exactly like his father, hiding from his fears and hurts by burying himself in his work. Too scared to confront what it was that he was hiding from. And in those last few weeks, he'd realised that he'd been hiding from himself. From the hurt that he'd never confronted at his parents' divorce. He'd found coping mechanisms that threated only to make him repeat the mistakes of the past and they no longer worked. And now he wanted more. And while those realisations had lifted so much darkness from his life, Mateo had known that there was still something missing. *Someone.*

'I missed you,' he confessed before he could engage his brain.

Her eyes flared with a hope that dimmed far too soon and it was something that he never wanted to see again, the extinguishing of that light.

Unable to help himself, he cupped her cheek and held

his breath until she relented and leant into his palm. This was where he was supposed to be. He just had to hope that she felt that too. She turned so that her lips pressed against his skin, but less in a kiss and more as if to hide her thoughts or her words. He hated that, that she thought she could not be anything but honest with him. It hurt, but it was a pain he'd earned.

He slid his other hand to the side of her face so that he held her in his hands and gently drew her chin up so that her gaze met his.

'How did I get it all so wrong?' he asked her as if she had the answer.

Tears glistened in her eyes, long lashes slowly trying to blink them back, and it hurt to bear witness to the pain he'd caused, but it was also right, earned and deserved.

'I'm so sorry,' he whispered, wanting to kiss the path of the tear that fell. Content to sweep it aside with the pad of his thumb, he needed to tell her, needed for her to know how much he cherished her. How much she had shown him and given him.

'There is so much I want to say to you, but nothing is as important as my sincere and heartfelt apology. I should never have said such an awful thing to you. It came from a place of cowardice so deep and so unnatural that I lashed out in self-defence, and still that isn't an excuse.

'I belittled what we shared—not only that night, but also what we had come to mean to each other. I dismissed it and I will never stop regretting that and the hurt I caused. And more than that, I undermined your relationship with my father and your relationship with Iondorra, and I hope to God that you didn't listen to me, because I had no right and no reason to do it.

'You were a godsend to my father. I know that without speaking to him because you gave him the support and respect that I was not able to. You were as much his family as I ever was and, no matter what my relationship with him was like, I would hate to think that I had spoiled it. Please tell me you understand that—please tell me you know what you meant to him?' Mateo half begged.

She nodded into his palm, the dampness of her tears hot on his skin but not burning nearly as much as he deserved.

'You were right, on so many levels, but the most important being that I *was* just like him. I was hiding from my feelings by burying myself in work.' He tried for a small smile.

Evie placed her hands over his, her eyes widening and her mouth beginning to open. How like her to want to deny the truth of what had happened in that moment. He shook his head slightly and pressed the pad of his thumb to her lips.

'The moment I realised what I'd done, I wanted to come back, I wanted to find you and tell you. But… I needed some time. I talked with my mother. We were finally able to speak about *papá*. For so long I had blamed myself and I would have continued to do so, if you hadn't made me realise how much it was holding me back. I… regret the last years in which I didn't speak to my father, but Evie… You gave him back to me. You healed something for me that I never thought would be healed. Our relationship wasn't perfect, and there are things I wish had been different, but you gave me a peace I never thought I'd have.'

Understanding softened her gaze, and her head dipped ever so slightly to brush her lips against his thumb, as if she was praising him with the smallest of kisses, without realising that she fanned the flames of his hope.

And finally he found the courage to say what he wanted to say, what he needed to say. 'I want you to know that I love you. That nothing you would do or say would change that. There is, and never will be, anyone I will love the way that I love you. I want all the forevers and all the happy-ever-afters with you and only you.'

Her eyes softened and she opened her mouth to speak, and when he silenced her for one last time, she glared at him but allowed him to continue. 'I'm sorry that I made you ask to be loved, so eternally sorry. But I promise you that if you give me this chance to make things right, I will show you every single day how much I love you, how you are the centre of my world and always will be. I love you. I love everything about you. I love the way that when you focus on something, it is your *entirety* in that moment, whether it is a problem to be fixed, or a new piece of information to consume, or a new experience to be had. I love that when you think things through and say it, you mean it. I love the way that you see the world differently and show me just how much there is that I'm missing out on.

'I know that you'll need time to think this out. To poke and prod from every angle intellectually and emotionally, and I'll wait, no matter how long you need, so you take whatever time you—'

Evie crushed her lips to his, urgency and need and happiness and love all mixing together to make one heady, powerful combination. He had seen her. She knew it and felt it in her heart. For a moment she allowed herself to get irrevocably lost in his kiss, their tongues dancing together as if on their own accord, her hands at first clutching at his waistcoat, and then slipping around his torso to bring him even closer.

She ended the kiss only because she had something she wanted to say, and then—hopefully—they'd be able to return to that kiss and many more.

'I'm sorry too,' she said, searching his eyes for understanding she desperately wanted. 'I was hurt and I lashed out at you. I should never have forced that on you. I was hurting but that is no excuse.'

'But you were right and I was wrong,' he argued with a sweet stubbornness.

Evie bit her lip. 'I don't think you were wrong about everything.' She smiled up at him cautiously. 'I *have* let things happen to me that I should have fought harder against. I still disagree that I let myself be taken advantage of,' she said, shooting him a gentle glare to know that she wasn't quite happy with his choice of words, 'but I perhaps didn't push back as much as I could have. There were so many times and so many people who turned away from me, or rejected me…and that fear made me timid in ways that I am sorry for. But…you saw the strength in me in spite of that.'

'It hurts to think that you questioned it,' he said, his eyes sparking in defiance and defence. 'It hurts to think that I caused you to question it.'

She shook her head, eyes damp and cheeks aching from the smile she felt bursting from her heart.

'But you didn't. You showed me that I was strong enough to handle the things that hurt me and survive. You've given me the courage to reach for things I would never have done before. I'm beginning to look for my birth parents,' she confessed, loving the pride and delight she saw in the way he looked at her.

'I don't know what will happen, or whether I'll even manage to find them—'

'You will,' Mateo said adamantly. 'And when you do, if you want, I'll be right there with you.'

She bit her lip again, hope soaring free in her heart. 'Would you?'

'If you'd let me, absolutely. Evie…' Mateo searched her eyes for something, a sign of whatever it was he needed and finally, when she thought he'd not speak again, he dropped to one knee. 'Evelyn Edwards, you are my north star. You are my home. You are my Pirate Queen,' he whispered, sending shivers across her skin and tremors into her heart. 'Would you do me the honour of becoming the other half of my heart and life?'

Goosebumps plucked at her skin as Evie took in his words and the love shining in his eyes, but it wasn't until she looked at the ring in the box that she gasped. There, nestled in the folds of old black velvet, was a gold band, supporting a red ruby surrounded by pearls.

Isabella's ring.

'How did you—?'

'I am under strict instructions to give you this ring whether you accede to being my wife or not.'

'Accede?' Evie repeated, her smile holding back laughter.

'It felt fitting,' he replied, a sparkle in his eyes that ignited fireworks in her heart.

Evie held out a shaking hand, and Mateo removed the ring and slid it onto her finger.

'A perfect fit,' he observed in a whisper and Evie knew they were both thinking of the twists and turns that had brought them here.

He rose from the floor and took her into his arms, and

between kisses he told her of how much he loved her. It wasn't until a janitor walked in on them that they finally realised that they should probably head home.

'So, it looks as if I'm house-hunting in London, then,' Mateo mused as Evie gathered her things.

'Not necessarily,' she said, turning back to him with her lip pinned by her teeth. 'I'm leaving USEL.'

'You've quit your job?' he asked, genuine shock flashing into pride. 'I'm so damn pleased,' he said, as if he was relieved.

'Really?' she asked, surprised by his reaction.

'You shouldn't be back here teaching in the worst classroom ever invented.'

'I don't think they invented—'

'Not the point, Evie,' he said affectionately. 'Do you have another job? Because wherever you're going, I'm coming too,' he informed her in that slightly, but utterly enthralling, autocratic way he had about him sometimes.

'What about your work?'

'I've taken a six-month sabbatical. I've spent too long intensely focusing on my business. Now I want to spend some time looking up.'

'At the stars?' Evie half teased.

'At you. I will never lose sight of what you mean to me, Evie. Never.' It was a promise and an oath. One that would be repeated two years later over their wedding vows. But for now, Evie welcomed the words into her heart with joy and love.

'So where are we going?' he asked as he tucked her arm under his, picked up her briefcase in his other arm and started leading her, for the last time, from Lecture Room Four.

Evie looked up at him, practically feeling the mischief

and excitement rolling off her in waves. 'Well, if you're coming along, you'll have to sign an NDA.'

Mateo turned to her, surprise and something like anticipation in his gaze. 'Has another royal demanded your expertise?'

'Actually, yes,' she replied, unable to stop the smile from pulling her lips.

'How on earth did that happen?' he asked, eyes wide with shock and pleasure.

'Apparently someone reached out to Queen Sofia and she passed on my details.'

'You're a real treasure hunter!' he exclaimed, pulling his arm away as she slapped him.

'I am a Professor of Archaeology,' Evie asserted primly.

He smiled the biggest smile she'd ever seen and then whispered in her ear. 'I want to have adventures with you,' he confided, filling her heart with love.

'Good, because we're about to go on one of the best there is,' she replied, knowing he understood that she meant their lives together.

He leaned towards her and whispered, 'Okay, but can you keep the bag? Because I'm getting sexy teacher vibes and I was never a good student.'

Evie's loving laughter was the only thing she left behind her that day.

EPILOGUE

AS EVIE LOOKED out at the sea of people clapping and cheering, she honestly thought she might need to pinch herself. She stood behind a small wooden podium in the back room of Olland, Iondorra's world-famous bookstore. History practically vibrated from the mahogany shelves, that familiar sense of the past providing a warmth and comfort that was the icing on the cake for Evie as she took it all in.

She had just delivered a reading from *The Pirate Queen*. The book she had written had been five years in the making and, although it had at times felt like an unending task, one that challenged and maddened, frustrated and annoyed, it had also brought her the greatest joy. She had worked closely with the Iondorran palace to ensure that the information and the history was representative but not destabilising to Sofia and her family, who had given their permission for the publication two years following on from the sad passing of the Queen's father.

She recognised the Queen's assistant in the back row, discreetly filming the event, and sent him a small smile, knowing that Sofia—a woman who had become so much a friend in the last few years—wouldn't have been able to attend without drawing attention away from what Sofia had said Evie absolutely deserved; recognition for all the work that she and Professor Marin had done.

Scanning the crowd for the faces she was looking for, she finally found them at the back, cheering the loudest and the hardest. Mateo—her husband, lover, partner and friend—had one hand tightly holding their three-year-old daughter's, and the other punching the air in victory. Isabelle's childish, happy cries reached Evie above all the other cries and applause because a mother would always hear her child, wherever and whenever she was needed. The blonde curls bounced as Mateo jiggled her and her cheers turned to laughter as they both celebrated her achievement. Their joy and support were enough to bring tears to Evie's eyes. Tears of love, of thanks, and of peace, knowing that all that she needed was right here in this room.

Carol and Alan had sent their wishes with a very large, impressive bouquet of flowers and a note, and while a part of her would always wish for just a little more than they were capable of giving, Evie also understood that it was simply that: capability. There was no intent or malice behind their emotional separation, and understanding that had changed and eased a part of her that had always hurt just a little.

Evie smoothed a hand over the twinge in her belly, their second child clearly not wanting to miss out on the celebrations. Mateo must have caught the gesture, as his eyes heated with love and pride, so attuned to her and her feelings. She could never have imagined how close they had become. Living with that kind of love and support, unconditional and unending, had been a balm she'd never expected. Before she had met Mateo, she had intellectually understood her feelings and hurts, but healing them had been done with him. And the love that they shared with their child and the child to come was a magic that she would once have called impossible.

She looked off to the side where another bouquet of flowers was waiting for her. She had read the note before the reading had started and before anyone had taken their seats. In the peaceful moment before her nerves had started—even two years of teaching hadn't managed to get rid of the stomach-churning, knee-trembling jitters—she had opened the handwritten note sent with the flowers.

To my darling, we are so very proud for you and wish we could be there with you as you prove to the world just how incredible you are. With all our love, Edward and Ellis.

She had pressed the small card to her lips and felt her heart soothed in a way that she couldn't explain. Meeting her birth parents had been one of the most terrifying and emotionally draining things she had ever done, but Mateo had been with her every single step of the way.

Evelyn had taken a DNA test a few months before she and Mateo had married in a beautiful ceremony in Spain. But even with that and the adoption papers they hadn't been able to find any information. Eventually she had conceded defeat and they had hired a private investigator who specialised in ancestry and family searches. After eighteen months of hard work and ups and downs, the investigator had led her and Mateo to Edward and Ellis. Her birth parents had been so young—barely sixteen when they had fallen pregnant with Evie. They had made the devastating decision that it would be better for everyone if they were to ensure their child went to parents who were financially able to provide the things their child needed.

Evie had expected to feel resentment; anger perhaps and loss for the things she had missed with them. But she didn't. They had stayed together and had always cherished the memory of their child. Ellis had become a surgeon and Edward had gone into technology. They had dedicated their lives to ensuring that the sacrifice they had all made was worth it. And in fact, Ellis had become pregnant with Evie's brother around the time that Evie had fallen pregnant herself with Izzy. It had created a place where they could bond, rather than harbour hurt or resentment, and together they had navigated both the past and the present in a way that Evie was grateful for.

Mateo waited for her as she slowly made her way through the crowd, people stopping her to congratulate her, others to ask if she had plans for any more books. She caught Mateo's eye, her husband having clearly heard the question, and smiled. There had been a few more adventures since their trip to Indonesia and there were certainly enough stories to tell with more books, but that was for another time.

This was the last event Evie would be doing for a while as they hunkered down as a family and awaited the arrival of Izzy's little sister. Mateo's mother had been thrilled with the news of another girl. Mateo had groaned dramatically, complaining about being outnumbered, despite the fact Evie knew he loved every single minute of it. He delighted in 'his girls', as he liked to call them, even though Henri would often claim that they were more his than Mateo's. Evie had loved Henri from the moment they'd met, realising just how much light and laughter he brought to Mateo, chasing away some of the darkness that had lessened greatly over time. Even though there were still glimpses of that determination he would get, and sometimes she would have to remind him to take a bit of time away, they had found the perfect balance. And it was all because of Professor Marin and the Pirate Queen.

* * * * *

AN HEIR FOR THE VENGEFUL BILLIONAIRE

ROSIE MAXWELL

MILLS & BOON

For my mum, whose love, belief and support
helped turn this dream into a reality.

CHAPTER ONE

A car will pick you up at your hotel at seven-thirty p.m. and bring you to the unveiling of Chateau Margaux. I'll be waiting there for you. Damon x

CARRIE MILLER STARED at the words written in elegant male script and then lifted her gaze to the clock display.

Twenty-five minutes past seven.

She swallowed the emotions swelling at the back of her throat. Only five minutes to go.

Beneath the exquisite silk dress, which had been delivered to her hotel room along with the handwritten note that morning, Carrie's heart raged. Damon was *all* she had been able to think about since their parting the previous night. She had lain in bed, giddily awake, recalling every intimate detail about him. His mesmerising gold-ringed coffee-brown gaze. The low, elegant timbre of his voice that had brushed across her senses like velvet. His crisp evergreen scent that had shot straight through her when he'd moved in close to place that lingering goodnight kiss on her cheek, just a whisper from her lips.

Picturing him at that very moment, awaiting her arrival at a grand, ancient chateau in Paris, one of the most magical cities in the world, was making her blood rush and her heart skip several of its frantic, fevered beats. Yet as she turned to make a final check of her appearance in the full-length mirror and met her reflection, it was a set of dark green eyes glittering with trepidation that stared back at her.

Because there was one other thing about Damon that had kept her wide awake.

His name.

Meyer. Damon Meyer.

A name she was heartbreakingly familiar with.

Because as a young boy Damon had been forced to endure the loss of his father due to the actions of *her* father.

The Meyer-Randolph Scandal, as the shocking events had been dubbed by the media, had seen their fathers' prolific professional partnership end in tragedy when her father's seismic betrayal had unleashed a fury that had cost Jacob Meyer his life. And before the attraction between them went any further Carrie knew she needed to tell Damon exactly who she was.

The fact that she was estranged from her father didn't matter. Although she'd been raised by her mother, far away from her father's influence, and had never been part of the family empire, *and* had long ago divested herself of the name she'd been born with, Sterling Randolph was still her father. And Carrie was always honest. After the way Nate had deceived her, with every word and every look, honesty was of unparalleled importance to her—to always be truthful and to always receive the truth in return.

But the thought of how Damon would react to the truth unleashed a swarm of butterflies as large as bats in her chest. There was every chance that he would walk away without a single second's hesitation, because whilst the person responsible for Jacob's death had been arrested and convicted, in Damon's eyes her father was the real culprit.

Carrie knew he wasn't innocent. Her father's actions had caused a lot of pain, and Carrie would live for ever with the debilitating panic attacks that had been triggered by the media hounding they'd endured in the wake of the scandal, but she'd never considered him entirely responsible, and she hadn't expected Damon would either.

But when her curiosity about him had prompted an online search, amongst the thousands upon thousands of hits that Damon's name had generated—detailing everything from his gorgeous female companions to his celebrity friends and the homes he owned across five continents—she had seen how wrong she was. Every bit of the animosity Damon felt for her father was there in black and white.

His distaste for his business practices. His frustration that Sterling had escaped from the scandal unscathed, as well as his certainty that he was solely to blame for it all.

As Carrie had read, her stomach had twisted into tighter and tighter knots—because had he known who she was the previous night, she knew Damon would not have looked her way.

But he had…and it had been wonderful and exhilarating.

It had been such a long time since Carrie had felt even the tiniest shimmer of attraction for a member of the opposite sex. No man she'd met had come close to penetrating the fear and mistrust that Nate's deception had burdened her with. But that had changed last night with Damon.

A single searing look and slow half-smile from him had jolted her as if she'd been shocked with electricity, setting her heart alight and infusing her blood with streaks of fire. He'd introduced himself and held out his hand, and though the name had sent a shocked charge zipping along her veins, the warmth that had spread to the rest of her body when his long fingers had closed around hers had pushed the significance of his identity entirely from her mind.

Because suddenly every inch of her had been tingling with a sensitivity she instinctively knew could only be soothed by him.

As easily and as quickly as that she had been lost. Except it had felt as if she was found.

A warm shiver danced down Carrie's spine as the feelings she'd been flooded with the previous night rushed back to her. And even as sparks of anxiety continued to flash in her eyes like warning lights she crossed to the door, hoping with all her heart that now he'd found her Damon would want to keep her, even after she told him who she was.

Damon Meyer resisted the urge to glance again at his watch. Carrie was late, and a voice in his head was starting to question if she was going to show up at all—a voice he quickly silenced with the assurance that such a rejection was unlikely.

Every signal she'd transmitted the previous night had

said that she wanted to see him again and continue what had been started. He'd read it in the reluctance of her gaze to part with his, and in the tremor of desire that had rippled through her when he'd kissed her goodnight, their lips tantalisingly close to touching. He'd had to draw on all his control not to pull her tight against him and claim her as his own then and there!

But tonight he was giving himself permission to act on those heady impulses—provided that was Carrie's wish too.

It wouldn't be anything more than a fleeting affair. Damon had neither the time nor the energy to devote to a real relationship. He'd long ago committed himself, heart and soul, to his revenge against Sterling Randolph, and he would not stray from that path until Randolph had paid for putting his father in an early grave.

That score, however, was getting closer to being settled. And once the Caldwell deal was his he'd have done it. But that was business, and for the evening ahead he wanted to focus solely on pleasure…

The hum of conversation surrounding him fell away and all thought vanished from his mind as Damon's gaze zeroed in on the striking figure just arriving. His heart started to pound with an unfamiliar tempo, and as Carrie's searching eyes found his, the same bolt of attraction that had drawn them together the previous evening flashed through Damon, white-hot and stronger than anything he had ever experienced.

'Excuse me,' Damon said to his guests, unbothered by their startled surprise as he abruptly exited mid-conversation.

Never taking his eyes off Carrie, he cut a path through the growing number of guests to where she was on the upper terrace. Coming to a stop before her, he could only stare, a hot feeling stirring low in his stomach, as his eyes were drawn to all the mesmerising ways the magenta silk kissed the gentle curves of her body.

The moment Damon had seen that dress he'd known that he wanted to see Carrie in it. The outfit she'd worn the night before had been stylish, but muted. The dark colour and the modest design had flattered her body—there had been no doubt about that, given the way *his* body had reacted to her in it—but it had been designed to allow the wearer to blend in, and some innate inner sense told him that was exactly why she had selected it.

His choice of gown, however, allowed for no such hiding. Whilst the dress hinted at more skin than it actually revealed, with its deep neckline and invisible leg slit, it was a daring cut, and with her silken fall of raven hair hanging straight and sleek over her narrow shoulders and down her back, she looked sensational. The lightest dusting of smoky shadow enhanced her already beautifully wide eyes, making them look even bigger and brighter. And her lips…*those lips*.

Damon wanted to kiss her. In that second it was the sole thought in his mind. He wanted to banish the space between their bodies, draw her into his arms, hold her against the heat of his body and slant his mouth over hers, finally know the feel and taste of her.

Dazed by the force of his wanting, Damon took a second longer than necessary to locate his voice. 'You look even more incredible than I thought you would,' he said, his voice roughened with a craving that only deepened as his words caused a rosy blush to unfurl across her cheekbones.

'So do you,' Carrie replied, although her exquisite olive-green eyes had yet to break the searing connection of their gazes to take in the flawlessly fitted black suit and pristine white shirt he wore. 'And the chateau is spectacular. I've never seen anything like it.'

'Thank you,' he replied, though he did not care one iota about the chateau in that moment. Only her.

It had been only twenty-four hours since he'd met Carrie, and he had spent no more than a handful of those hours with her, yet to Damon it seemed as though he'd been waiting to touch her for ever. The ache to feel her melt beneath him was deep and visceral, sending heat rushing through his blood and tightening his groin.

His attention was so fixed on her that it only took a second for him to spot the pulse hammering in the sweet hollow of her neck. A rapid sweep of his eyes revealed even more signs of nervousness—the firm way her lips were pressed together, the white-knuckled curl of her fingers around her clutch bag. He didn't want her to feel anything in the slightest bit negative, but he could understand how the extravagance of this evening might be overwhelming to a girl from a small, close-knit community in Santa Barbara.

Everything about the evening was overwhelming: the sprawling chateau designed to resemble a fairy-tale castle, the grandeur of the party upon which no expense had been spared, the few hundred personally selected guests, each of them demonstrating their precocious wealth in the diamonds, rubies and emeralds that glittered around their throats and on their ears and fingers.

And most overwhelming of all was the attraction that held them both in its thrall. Even Damon was finding the ferocity of their chemistry intense.

He took a step forward, banishing the distance between them. He saw the tremble that ran over her shoulders as he breached her personal space and her long dark lashes lowered, shielding the uncertain flicker of her eyes.

'I'm glad you're here,' he said, his voice low and soft. Reassuring.

Carrie emitted a shaky breath. 'I…'

He couldn't stand her lowered gaze. Gently he placed a finger under her chin and tilted her head up, so the full force of her eyes once again rested on him, and as she read whatever emotion it was he could feel burning through him, the conflict and anxiety she was battling seemed to ebb away. 'So am I,' she responded softly. 'I'm happy I got the chance to see you again.'

'Did you really think I wouldn't do everything in my power to make sure we had that chance?' he questioned smilingly, feeling much more at ease as he stood close enough to feel the heat from her body. 'In the interest of full and forthright disclosure, I have spent all day unable to think of little else other than seeing you tonight.'

'I've been thinking a lot about you too.'

'Good,' he responded, and felt a violent kind of euphoria barrelling though him that she was just as enthralled as he was.

But then emotions that didn't stay long enough for him to discern flittered across her expression, and she pulled in a quivering breath. 'But there is something I should mention before we…before this…'

From the corner of his eye Damon detected the multitude of glances being directed their way. Attention was nothing new to him. From the moment of his first architectural success he'd been the focus of countless profiles and interviews, attracting attention for being his father's son and for the unexpected sensation caused by his work. From then his profile had exploded.

Fame had never been something he craved, but he'd quickly realised it could be to his advantage. The bigger his profile, the more publicity his takedown of Randolph would attract—and he wanted the whole world to witness his downfall! So he smiled and waved, consented to interviews and accepted invitations to the biggest dates in the social calendar. And as all that attention turned him into a figure with even more renown than his father, it became impossible for him to attend an event without at least a dozen strangers making a beeline for him, eager to see him and be seen with him.

And, judging by the hungry looks from some of those who'd been lucky enough to make it onto the exclusive guest list, tonight would be no different.

But Carrie was also drawing a fair amount of speculation, which was no surprise given how sensational she looked, and he estimated it would be only another ninety seconds before they were interrupted. That was the last thing he wanted. He was in no mood to share.

'Let's take a walk,' he interrupted, sliding a hand to her lower back to guide her away from the curiosity of the crowds. 'I'll show you the chateau.'

'Can it wait a second? I really do need to say something,' she said, as he extracted a key from the inner pocket of his jacket and fitted it into a lock, pushing open a tall, panelled door and gesturing her inside.

'We can talk inside.'

Carrie looked between him and the open door uneasily. 'Are you sure this is allowed?'

He lifted his shoulders in an unconcerned shrug. 'I have the keys. I'm the architect. I think we can get away with it.'

'I don't want to get you in any trouble.'

Damon couldn't help but smile. He was already in deep trouble where she was concerned.

'It'll be fine,' he assured her. 'Besides, what is the point of knowing the architect if you don't get a private tour?' He gestured for her to step inside. 'Now, what was it you needed to tell me?'

But Carrie wasn't listening to him. She had fallen still, admiring the large room they were in, her eyes wide and her lips parted in awestruck wonderment.

'Damon, this is beautiful,' she breathed, her eyes hungrily taking in the room from floor to ceiling, slowing over all the intricate detail. 'It's like stepping back to a different time.'

'The brief the owner gave me was to restore it to its former glory with just a few contemporary touches.

'The detail is incredible. *All* of it is incredible,' she said.

Her unfiltered awe made his achievement seem even greater. Bigger than when he had declared the project complete. And as she continued to admire the room

Damon was interested only in admiring her: the shape of her body, her graceful movements, the glow the low lighting cast across her smooth skin.

'Is the owner going to live here?'

'I'm not sure. Perhaps. He's also considering utilising it as an investment, renting it out for events. He's hosting his daughter's wedding here in a few months. I imagine he'll decide after that.'

'It's a spectacular place for a wedding.' Carrie turned to him, her eyes lively and curious. 'Was it projects like this that made you want to be an architect?'

Unhappy with how far away she had strayed from him, Damon took the opportunity to close the space between them as he answered her question. 'Not especially, no. Buildings like this are special, and I enjoy getting to work on them, but no. I...erm... I wanted to be an architect because my dad was one.'

He had admitted that a hundred times before, but saying it to Carrie felt different somehow, as if he was placing an old key in a different lock, opening up something new. He hesitated, feeling that sense generating a faint pulse of unease, but then he caught the way she was regarding him from her rounded beautiful eyes and it was a look that was utterly compelling. A look that made him feel that there was no place to hide. Or, even more poignantly, no *need* to hide.

'He specialised in urban planning, development and regeneration, working a lot with local governments, but he was an architect first and foremost. He loved buildings—especially old grand ones like this, with a rich and proud history. He liked delving into the story of a building and using that to guide his designs. He just loved building things in a way that was infectious. So I did too. He took me to every site he worked on…walked me through the structure, showed me the plans and asked what I thought. It was our father-son thing. I once told him I thought a wall was in the wrong place. He went back to the plans and changed the design, then told me I was a natural, maybe even better than him. And he was the best. It was never really a decision to choose the same career. I always knew I wanted to be just like him. And after he died, I was even more set on following in his footsteps,' he admitted, realising as he said the words how much truth they carried.

Damon had allowed himself to believe that it was his thirst for revenge that had been the strongest hand in guiding his future and setting him on the path he'd hurtled along—and, yes, it was revenge that dictated which projects he sought and which contacts he prioritised. But he had been born to be an architect. It was in his blood. His heart.

Somewhere along the way he had forgotten that—a fact that disconcerted him nearly as much as the amount of personal information he'd just divulged.

'How old were you? When he died?' Carrie asked.

Her whole expression had changed, and she was watching him with a tentativeness he usually found offensive. He was not fragile. He was not in pain. His father's death had broken his heart and broken up his family, but it had not broken *him*. It had made him strong, purposeful.

'I was twelve.' Damon kept his face blank, his body straight and tall, even as the excruciating memory forced its way to the surface. The crowds. The anger. The cameras there to capture it all. And then the gunshot.

He heard it as if he was there again in that very moment. He could taste the bitter adrenaline in his mouth, feel the terrified thuds of his heart as he lay on the ground, not knowing what was happening. And then the scream, ripping from his throat when he realised exactly what had happened.

Carrie's eyes glistened with the sudden gathering of moisture and she shook her head. 'I'm so sorry, Damon.'

And he knew she really was. It was unnerving, how her heartfelt sympathy made his insides twist. He was used to the platitude, and the faux sympathy with which it was usually delivered, but from Carrie it was genuine. He could hear it in her words. See it in her eyes. She knew his pain even as he concealed it, even as he fought it. She felt it as though she was holding his heart in her hands and could see how it had been ravaged by that single moment in time.

And yet that was not possible, because he did not give his heart away.

'Thank you.'

And suddenly the despised grief was upon him again, burning the backs of his eyes and obstructing his throat. Making spasms ripple across his chest like tremors of an earthquake. Threatening to bring him collapsing in on himself. The breath-stealing pain advanced as if the loss had happened only yesterday.

Damon turned away, outraged by the upwelling of unwanted sorrow. It was a wasteful, weak emotion. And pain was futile, a burden to his soul. It was for that reason he had skipped right past pain and settled happily into a state of anger. Anger was good. It instigated purpose and action. Anger was his daily fuel.

He concentrated on pulling the face of Sterling Randolph into his mind, the memory of his arrogance and the smugness of his family, wanting to feel the rage those images evoked, wanting it to rise up and smother the anguish racking his heart. But before he could summon any picture of his enemy he felt the warmth of a body, a hand curling around his bicep. Within seconds her gentle touch was bringing him back, pulling him from the edge of that black despair. Her deep green eyes were the first thing he saw, and it was their brightness he clung to until the lash of pain began to subside, to the point where he no longer needed to hold his breath.

Carrie's lips parted, as though she was about to offer words of solace, but instead she gave a small shake of her head. There were no words. Damon knew that already. No words capable of adequately sympathising over how the squeeze of that trigger had changed his life—obliterating his present, casting his future into the wind, altering his landscape of family and love and trust for ever. But the fact that she understood that, too, created a connection that anchored him deeper than what he already felt for her. It hitched in his chest, hooked around his heart.

And just her standing beside him was enough. Her hand against his arm. Her sorrowful gaze reaching into his. He didn't feel the pain. He didn't need the anger. All he needed was her.

Turning his face, he grazed her wrist with his mouth and saw the shudder that shimmied through her. It drew a smile across his lips, as did the beam of hunger that flared in her eyes.

Her lips called to him again. Everything about her called to him. But there was something extra-special about her mouth that was driving him past the point of desperation. The simple act of looking at her, seeing her clear olive-green gaze blinking with a growing dazedness, was stirring his erection, and he knew he could not hold out much longer against this connection zinging between them. Nor did he wish to.

The sudden sound of music floating into the room had Carrie angling her head with curiosity.

'It's coming from the ballroom,' he told her.

Her eyebrows arched, her smile full of wonder. 'There's a ballroom?'

He led her across the gleaming white marbled floor of the hall, opulent with its double staircase coming down in curved arms of intricately designed wrought-iron and its spectacular antique chandelier high above them, and into the ballroom.

The room was as high as it was wide, with intricate gold leaf patterning the walls, another sparkling chandelier hanging from the high ceiling and numerous sets of French doors leading to fairy-lit gardens beyond.

Carrie slipped her hand from his and walked into the middle of the room, spinning on the spot as she absorbed the fairy-tale grandeur. 'This is magical. I didn't think anything like this existed outside of films or...you know, royal palaces.'

She was a romantic. He would have assumed so anyway, but now he could see it in the dreaminess of her expression, in her imagining of a love story unfolding in the very setting they were stood in.

With a gesture of his hand Damon gestured to the practising orchestra to start playing again and walked towards Carrie, his arms catching her as she turned to face him. Before she could react, he pulled her in snug against his body, his right arm curling around her waist, and with her smile of delight still floating on her lips he started to move her across the floor.

'What are you doing?' She laughed, self-conscious colour staining her cheeks.

'Dancing with you.'

He hadn't planned it. It had been a complete spur-of-the-moment decision based on her obvious pleasure and his burning desire to have her in his arms and against his body. And this was something he could give her—a night that very few other men on the planet could offer. He would not stay in her life beyond these few hours and days, but he could ensure she would never forget the time they had together.

'Is that a problem?'

The laughter in her expression faded, turning it serious. 'No.'

There was an intimacy to their movements that he had not expected to come from something as simple as dancing, but Damon found he liked it. At least he liked dancing with her.

Pulling her in closer, he splayed his fingers over the lowest point of her back until she was pressed gloriously against the hot muscled wall of his chest. He heard her sudden intake of breath and kept moving to the gentle music. He was aware of every line of her body, every shaky breath she was taking, and every staccato beat of her heart.

Not for one second did their gazes stray from each other, and as the music built towards its crescendo Damon dipped her, his arm supporting her back as he tilted her downwards, his head following to press a kiss to the hollow beneath her chin, his lips brushing against a flickering pulse-point.

When he brought her back upright Carrie's eyes were glazed with the same need that was pounding through his blood. He didn't remove his arms from around her, and nor did she make any attempt to retreat from him. Her palms were resting lightly against his chest and her lips parted with anticipation.

Damon didn't really know why he was waiting...only that looking into her mesmerising eyes held an eroticism of its own, seeing her hunger as well as his own reflected back at him. Her breathing hitched even higher, and as her eyes dropped tellingly to his mouth he lowered his face and grazed his lips against hers for the barest second. It was just a taste, but it was long enough for him to know that she was paradise.

'Damon. Excellent. I've been looking for you.'

The voice rang through the large, empty room, causing Carrie to jump guiltily free of his arms. Damon turned his head to see the owner of the chateau coming to a hasty stop as he looked between him and Carrie, belatedly realising that he had interrupted.

Damon cleared his throat, smoothing over the moment

of unease. 'Jean-Pierre, this is Carrie Miller. Carrie, this is the chateau's owner—Jean-Pierre Valdon.'

'It's a pleasure to meet you, Mademoiselle Miller,' Jean-Pierre murmured, a smile playing about his lips as he bowed his head in Carrie's direction.

'Likewise. And congratulations. The chateau and everything about tonight is incredible. I'll let you two talk.'

Damon began to protest, turning to Carrie with a frown and tightening his hold on her fingers, but she shook her head lightly.

'It's fine. I could use some air anyway.' She squeezed his fingers and sent him an uneven smile. 'I'll catch up with you outside.'

Before he could react she was hurrying from the ballroom, and only his eyes were able to follow her.

Oh, God, what had she done? What had she *done*?

Sneaking off with him. Letting him confide in her his pain over his father. And then dancing with him. *Kissing* him.

Carrie's head felt on the cusp of explosion, with her heart launching itself against her ribs over and over again as she pressed down on the handle of every door she could find until one opened and she tumbled out into the garden and clean night air washed over her, blessedly cool against her burning skin.

She was supposed to have told him the truth the second she arrived—told him exactly who she was. That had been her intention. She'd rehearsed the words in her head, she'd had them ready, but then…

Then their eyes had met in a way she'd thought could

only happen in fairy-stories. And he had looked at her with a glowing appreciation that had made her dizzy, and she had known that he had been seeing *her*, Carrie Miller, the woman she was. Not her name, not her father's wealth and influence, but *her*. And he had touched her. It had been a tiny, insignificant press of his finger to her chin, but that small, single moment of connection had been so potent that she had almost gone up into flames.

Still, she'd tried. Or at least she thought she had—it was all a bit fuzzy. But then he'd taken her hand and led her into the house and…

It had all just been so overwhelming.

He was overwhelming. And so was the connection between them. Too overwhelming for Carrie, in all her inexperience, to know how to handle.

She'd felt attraction before, or so she had believed. Even after discovering that Nate had not been what he'd seemed, that their relationship had not been at all what she had thought, Carrie had recognised that she'd played right into his hands by being swept off her feet by his traditional handsomeness.

But none of the time she'd spent with Nate had contained the spectacular sizzling electricity of the past hour. Her heart had never beaten so keenly in his company, and her body had never been so attuned to his hands and his eyes, so in thrall to him the way she was to Damon.

Whatever it was that she'd felt for Nate had been a pale and weak prologue.

This, with Damon, was attraction. Passion. Heat.

This, with Damon, was overwhelmingly, thrillingly, terrifyingly real.

So real it obliterated all else—like the truth she needed to tell him. And she could hardly go back and tell him now, could she?

Not after willingly pressing her body up against his and thrumming with a need that his very masculine touch promised to assuage.

Not after letting him reveal to her the depth of his pain over the loss of his father.

A sob of anguish rose in her throat.

When the conversation had turned towards Damon's father her heart had vaulted out of her chest. It had been such an unguarded moment on his part, a raw glimpse of his hurt, and what made Carrie feel absolutely wretched was the sense that Damon didn't lift that curtain very often. But he had let her peek behind it and see his vulnerability, all the while unaware that she was the daughter of the man whose betrayal had kick-started the tragedy.

If he learned who she was now, he would surely consider it a deception of the cruellest kind. And she wouldn't blame him.

She had deceived him. She hadn't told the truth.

With agonising tears pressing against the backs of her eyes, Carrie knew there was only one thing she could do now—leave.

Allowing herself no time to change her mind, and hoping that if she moved quickly enough she could slip away undetected whilst Damon was still engaged in his conversation, she began to move through the shadows of the garden, hurriedly slipping along the pathways bordered by manicured shrubs and trees.

'Carrie!'

She heard the shout of her name over the cacophony of the party, but she kept moving her feet, kept her eyes forward though her heart jolted. She would be able to go faster if she wasn't navigating the ground in five-inch heels, but to stop and take her shoes off would take too much time, and right now she just needed to get away without facing Damon.

Relief raced through her as she realised she was drawing near to a set of steps that would take her to an exit point, but then a figure leapt down in front of her, landing with an agile crouch before straightening to his impeccable full height.

'Damon!' Carrie gasped, looking from him up to the level he had jumped from and feeling her heart catch. 'Are you crazy? You could have broken something,' she admonished, whilst her eyes tracked quickly over his athletic body, checking for any sign of injury.

He dismissed her concern with a careless slice of his hand through the air, surveying her with dark-eyed bewilderment. 'Where are you going?'

'I have a…' But a suitable fib would not rise to her lips and she ended up shaking her head. 'I need to leave.'

'Are you unwell?' His eyes scanned her face, seeking a clue as to what had changed in the space of a few minutes. 'Has something happened?'

'No. I just… I can't stay.'

He said nothing, but his penetrating stare seemed to reach inside her and grasp at her heart, and with that single look the emotion filling up her body grew bigger somehow, and much less easy to contain.

Before she could stop them, words were tumbling from

her lips. 'I shouldn't have come here tonight, Damon, okay? I shouldn't have… I… I'm sorry, but this was a mistake. And now I need to leave.'

Ignoring the shadow that scudded across his expression like a cloud, Carrie moved to sidestep him. But Damon anticipated her evasion and moved quickly, blocking her path with an outstretched arm.

She froze, her heart flailing as she realised she was effectively trapped.

'There is someone else?' he asked roughly, his warm and soft breath hitting the sensitive skin of her ear and making her think of that briefest of kisses.

It had been no more than a graze, but it had sent feeling trickling all the way down to the tops of her toes and the tips of her fingers. And she wanted to experience it all over again.

'No.' She wished it was that simple. 'But that doesn't change anything.'

She summoned just enough courage to raise her face and meet his gaze, and did her best to inject into her voice a conviction that she didn't feel.

'Whatever this is between us, it can't happen. It can't go beyond now, tonight. It should never have started in the first place. So, please, just let me go.'

'No,' he answered, with so much determined power surging into his eyes it was like a fireworks display. 'Not until you give me the real reason you're running away from this.'

CHAPTER TWO

THIS WAS IT THEN, Carrie thought, feeling unsteady as Damon's demand for an answer hung in the taut air between them. The perfect moment to tell him.

She gathered a breath, already knowing what she needed to say.

My father is Sterling Randolph.

That was it. Five small words.

Yet as hard as she tried she couldn't make the words form. Couldn't make her lips move. Because she knew that once she spoke those words aloud to him there could be no going back, and she was terrified of seeing that beautiful gaze, now fixed on her with such heat and passion, turn arctic with the loathing that she knew ran through his veins.

Because without a shadow of doubt she knew that once he learned who her father was her name would, yet again, be the only thing about her that mattered.

It had been all that had mattered to her high school friends, who had stopped talking to her because her father had killed a man. It had been all that had mattered to Nate, who hadn't wanted her as much as he had wanted to ingratiate himself with her father and snag himself a little corner of the Randolph empire. And it had been all that had mattered when she had been headhunted for the dream job of pastry chef at a new Parisian restaurant.

She had been so stupidly excited, so proud of the offer and the hard work and skill that she thought had got her noticed so quickly, but they had only wanted her in order to forge a connection with her father, to invite his patronage, perhaps even his investment.

Discovering that had crushed her.

Eventually she had abandoned her father's name for good. She had returned to Santa Barbara to pull the broken pieces of herself back together and had rebuilt herself as Carrie Miller, creating a life and a business without the weight that accompanied her globally recognisable surname.

It was the best thing she had ever done. Not only did her anonymity feel like a shield against any repeat of the frenzied media hounding that had followed her family and traumatised her as a little girl, it also gave her the luxury of knowing that all her success these past few years was her own, earned by hard work, dedication and skill.

That was all she wanted—to be recognised and treated as her own person, to be judged on her own merits and mistakes, to be accepted and loved for the person she was and not the name she bore.

But, with the past being what it was, would Damon really be able to do that when he was still in so much agony over his father's death?

Would he be able to see her as Carrie Miller and nothing more?

'It's complicated, Damon,' she said finally, trying to contend with the disappointment crashing through her that she ultimately wasn't brave enough to take that chance. 'You just need to trust me. It is better for both of us if this begins and ends right now.'

Displeasure had Damon's jaw tightening, and Carrie braced herself for a further demonstration of truculence, but instead his arm curled around her waist, and before she knew what was happening he had drawn her flush against his hard body and his mouth had come sweeping down against hers.

The sensation of his firm lips moving with slow sensuality against hers had her eyes fluttering closed, and as the sharp sweetness of the kiss pierced all Carrie's levels of resistance her body softened with a surrender she had thought it was impossible for her to feel.

For the last five years the thought of being touched by another man had consumed Carrie with fear and anxiety. The memory of how each and every one of Nate's caresses had been a lie, a mere tool to draw her in and use her for his own ends, had caused her to retreat from whatever small moments of attraction she'd felt and from any physical contact with the opposite sex. But with Damon she was aware of only the heat between them, so hot it burnt away all else, leaving no oxygen for doubts to feed on. She could only feel the rightness of his caresses, could only think of having more—more of his mouth, more of his hands on her body. More and more and more.

'Say that again,' Damon murmured against her lips. 'Now you know how I taste, tell me again that it's better to end this now.'

Carrie couldn't. All she could do was stare at him, dazed and amazed and silent. She hadn't known it was possible for a kiss to be so compelling, to leave her feeling so replete and yet hungry for more at the same time.

With her legs threatening to turn into liquid as the impassioned heat of their kiss continued to burn through her, Carrie curled the hands resting against his strong chest around the lapels of his jacket as her quivering body half collapsed against his. It was a mistake, but one she didn't recognise until it was too late…until she was achingly aware of every solid line and ridge of his body and the awesome power contained beneath the suavely dressed surface and the gentlemanly veneer it projected.

The thrumming she could feel beneath her hands and the steely press of his erection left her in no doubt that beneath the gentleman was a *man*. A hot-blooded man who hungered and craved, who sought and took. Who knew how to use his body to drive a woman wild.

As though to prove that very point, Damon lifted a hand to her face and trailed his fingers lightly across her cheekbone. 'You said this can't go beyond tonight…but what about tonight? Can we have that?'

The question was unexpected, and Carrie blinked with surprise. Damon's eyes held a gleam…a look that sent a thousand shivers skittering across her bare shoulders and had feeling pulsing all over her body. She understood what he was asking, what he was proposing. One night together. No questions asked, no answers needed. A continuation of what they had already started.

She should say no. She knew that. That was the smart thing to do. The *right* thing to do. But the voice urging that course of action had become very quiet, almost muted by the force of that kiss and by her need for this one man that was building with every passing second, blooming into something larger and stronger every time he touched her.

And Carrie knew in that second that there was only one answer she could give to his question. It was not a choice. It was not a decision. It was a need—an imperative. And it had been from the first moment their eyes had locked.

One night with him. That was all. And then she would walk away, as she already should have done.

'Yes, we can have tonight,' she answered, barely able to hear her voice over the riotous beats of the heart.

'Then if that's all we have, let's not waste it. Let's go somewhere. Just you and me.'

'But the party….' Carrie began, looking up to where music and chatter and laughter drifted down to them.

'Forget about the party. I don't need to be here. It's just a chance for Jean-Pierre to show off his chateau. I would rather be with you.'

He wound his fingers through hers, then brought their intertwined hands to brush against his lips. And it was only the lightest press of his mouth, but it completely undid the last bonds holding her together.

'Then let's go,' she said, and smiled before she could think twice.

Damon took her to his penthouse. It was just off the Champs-Elysées, nestled within the architectural beauty and all-round luxury of the city's Golden Triangle. From the large terrace it offered spectacular midnight views across the whole city. With one sweep of her eyes Carrie could look from the Eiffel Tower to the Sacré-Coeur Basilica to the American Cathedral and the Pantheon.

She did her best to concentrate on the breathtaking sight, but she was too aware of the nerves that had her stomach swooping and the whirring of too many thoughts in her head. Doubts and questions over what she was doing...what she was thinking. *If* she was thinking.

She knew she had not yet passed the point of no return. She could change her mind and leave, let the memory of Damon fade until it was as if meeting him again had never happened. But then she heard footsteps behind her, and as she looked over her shoulder her eyes crashed into Damon's, that sinfully slow smile worked its way across his lips, and her head fell silent. The flutters in her chest disappeared. Even her stomach settled. And there was only a peaceful kind of certainty that, even though it was a tangled mess, and even though Damon with his string of previous girlfriends and very public lifestyle was entirely the wrong man to be taking this chance with, she was exactly where she needed to be. Where she should be.

As he arrived at her side, Damon held out a glass of champagne. 'For you.'

'Thank you.'

'I ordered us some food. It shouldn't take long to be delivered.'

Silken heat kissed her skin as he settled himself beside her and he, too, fixed his attention on the illuminated cityscape spread out before them.

'I always forget how incredible it is looking out over this city at night. Living here, I take it for granted, I suppose.'

'How long have you lived here?'

'Not long.'

He set down his champagne glass and shrugged out of his jacket, pulling apart the top few buttons of his shirt with an easy flick of his fingers before doing the same to the cuffs, and then pushing them up his forearms in a mesmerising motion that captivated her attention.

'I bought it when I was hired to work on the chateau. I didn't want to be living in hotels. But I wouldn't say I've *lived* here. More like crashed when I wasn't working.'

An image of him tumbling into bed exploded in her mind, sending waves of heat crashing through her and she had to avert her eyes.

'You mentioned that you lived in Paris too?' he said.

'Yes. A couple of years ago. I came here for cookery school and stayed about eight months.'

'You weren't tempted to stay longer?' he asked with an easy smile. 'Open a little patisserie on the Left Bank? Enjoy this view every day?'

'I was tempted—although where I lived, I did not have a view like this.'

Her father had not supported her ambition to cook, but he had offered up a penthouse for her to live in—an offer that Carrie had refused. After witnessing his chilling ruthlessness for herself, and having her eyes yanked open to see how little she actually mattered to him, she hadn't wanted to take *anything* from him.

'But I'm not sure I could really imagine being so far away from my family, unable to see them whenever I wanted. Plus…'

'Plus…?' he probed when she stalled.

'Plus, one of the reasons I came to Paris in the first place was to get away,' she continued with care, not wanting to say too much and yet wanting him to understand. 'To start over and be someone else. But I learned it's not that easy to do.'

She was staring straight ahead, but Carrie felt his gaze closing around her. Surveying. Deducing and then understanding.

'Someone hurt you?'

'Yes.'

But Carrie still didn't know who had hurt her more—Nate or her father—and which one she had been running from.

All she'd known at the time was that she hadn't wanted to be Carrie Randolph any more. The thought of spending one more day walking around with that target on her back had been unbearable. But she had been naïve, thinking she could leave her identity behind. That she could jet off to Paris, change her name, live in a tiny attic apartment and simply stop being a Randolph.

Her mother had tried to warn her, but she had been too desperate to hear her, and she'd had to learn the hard way that she couldn't change anything by trying to outrun it. All she'd ended up doing was inviting more hurt.

But she did not want to think about any of that with Damon. She didn't want her father or the past intruding on the happiness she felt with him. She just wanted to be simple Carrie Miller from Santa Barbara. And yet once again the complication and deceit had her insides twisting, as if poison was slithering through her bloodstream.

'All I will say is that he was obviously exceedingly stupid. And I suggest we don't waste a second talking about him,' he proposed, with a sinfully quick quirk of his lips.

Whether it was his words or the tantalising flash of his sexy smile, Carrie didn't know, but emotion pulsed in the air between them and she could have sworn she felt the ground beneath her feet actually shift. She could see that Damon felt it, too, but before she was even sure how to respond to the sudden flare of sensation Damon already was, extracting her glass from her suddenly limp hand and placing it on the table behind him.

'Maybe we shouldn't waste a second talking at all.'

He moved in even closer and slid his strong hands around her waist, lowering his mouth to hers slowly... slowly enough for her to stop him if she wanted. But Carrie didn't want to.

The languid kiss delivered a wicked kind of pleasure. It was thorough and purposeful, each slide of his lips telling her how much he wanted her, and knowing that it was just about *her*, the woman, and not the name or the opportunity, sent its effect spiralling even deeper into her core.

His hands moved up her back in a possessive slide, tunnelling into the long lengths of her hair as he slanted his mouth to both offer and take more. Her mouth opened beneath his, an invitation for the advent of his tongue which he accepted without hesitation. And his tongue playing against hers sent tendrils of electric sensation shooting in all directions, pressing her close to melting point.

She had not thought it a foregone conclusion that she would spend the night with him, but in that instant she knew there could be no other. They had set something alight that needed to burn itself out. Names, the past—all of it was suddenly irrelevant. All that mattered was that there was him and there was her. And they had found one another.

They had known each other less than twenty-four hours, and yet Carrie felt she *knew* him. She felt an ease with him that she had not been able to find with any member of the opposite sex since Nate. It felt as if she had been waiting for him, for this moment, this merging, for ever.

Her back bumped against something solid—the wall, she assumed dizzily—and then Damon's lips were running down her neck, his mouth wet and hot against her throat, and his hand was taking advantage of the low cut of her dress to slide inside and cradle her breast. After being untouched for so many years, she felt the skin-to-skin contact as a shock, and a startled gasp spilt from her lips.

Damon stilled. He didn't remove his hand—in fact his fingertips continued to stroke gently up and down the side of her breast—but he drew his head back just enough to allow his eyes to probe hers.

'Too fast? Do you want me to stop?'

'No.' The word fell instantly from her lips, but the shadow of a question lingered in his expression. 'I… It's just been a while since I've been with anyone.'

A beat passed as Damon scrutinised her expression. 'Are you sure this is what you want?' he asked, obviously ready to take a step back even as his eyes burned.

It only made her more certain.

'Yes.' The hand curled around his cheek guided his

mouth back down to hers. 'I want this,' she breathed between light kisses. 'I want *you*.'

I need you, she thought, with even more desperation.

This time when their lips caught Damon emitted a throaty growl and trapped her mouth beneath his, making the stroke of his lips slow, but deep. Carrie felt the effects of it all the way down in her stomach, and even lower in the sudden, insistent thrumming of her pelvis.

As he once again commanded the capitulation of her body, evoking feeling in every single cell she possessed, the fingers curled around her breast slowly began to explore her sensitivity. He brushed the pad of his thumb across her nipple and Carrie moaned into his mouth, bracing herself against the wall as his skilled fingers advanced to pinch and play.

Her hand curled around his shoulder tightened, and his tender exploration of her mouth quickly turned into a heated exchange that his tongue turned into a merciless plunder. Carrie loved every second of it. Being wanted so fiercely. Having someone be this greedy for her.

And then Damon's mouth was replacing his fingers over her breast. The straps of her dress had slipped from her shoulders, revealing her chest to the air, and Damon fastened his lips around her nipple, licking and flicking and sucking in a tantalising rhythm that had her head knocking against the wall and her teeth biting down on her lip, fighting the cries of hunger and madness building in her throat.

She could not fathom the forces he was unleashing within him. Could not understand how his worship of her breast sent her hips arching forward, rocking to a rhythm of their own. Could not figure out how he was making her body *his*. It did not seem plausible that the feelings pulsing through her could be real. Surely such delight, such brazen passion, could only belong in a dream or a fantasy. But she was both awake and alive, and Damon's incredible touch was driving her to places she hadn't known existed.

His mouth came back to hers and her body shaped itself to the hard planes of his. She was aware of the solid ridge of arousal just below his waist. She wanted to feel more of it. All of it. She was nowhere near experienced enough to be sexually confident, and whatever confidence she had once gained had been neutralised by Nate's deception, but in that moment it did not worry her. Everything with Damon was so instinctual—as if her body recognised him, recognised what to do.

Moving on that instinct, she brought her leg up, so their centres rubbed against each other. Damon's body acted on the same impulse, his hands shaping her bottom and pulling her against him, and the lethal rock of his hips against hers had her edging closer and closer to the beckoning oblivion.

They were scorching the air around them. Damon couldn't recall a time when he had been such a slave to his desires. He was controlled by one need and one only—the need for revenge. Very little else registered. Not hunger or thirst or desire. He ate and drank because food and water were placed in front of him. He took a woman to bed as an outlet—for relaxation and release. But he was *hungering* for Carrie. Greedy for her. Not only did he ache to know the secrets of her body, he craved the taste of her as if it had become his one and only life source.

A fire was beating through his blood that had been started by her and could only be quelled by her. He felt the flames of the gathering inferno lick higher as they moved together, his tongue sliding into the sweet cavern of her mouth, and he was unable to stop the thrust of his hips against hers as the honeyed taste of her on his lips made him crazy with longing, urging him to seek and take more of the delights she presented.

His hands slid down her back and curved around her perfectly shaped butt, pulling her in tight to his erection. And, feeling the answering way she moulded herself to him, Damon knew he could not wait another second to see more of her.

Pulling back, he smiled and tugged her along the terrace, reaching behind him to push open the doors that led into the master suite. As soon as she was inside the darkened room his fingers located the discreet fastenings of the dress and undid them. The dress slid down her body to pool at her feet.

Damon would have been lying if he'd claimed he had not envisaged undressing her when he had first pictured her in the dress, but the reality wildly surpassed the fantasy. Now Carrie was bare but for a pink lace thong and the strappy stilettoes and, looking at her, Damon couldn't catch his breath. He wasn't sure he even remembered how to breathe.

Her skin was flushed, glowing, and her eyes were dazzlingly bright. She watched him, watching her, her breathing shallow, and knowing that she wanted this with the same hunger and desperation that was driving him was a satisfaction Damon had not anticipated. Never had he expected to feel a connection so strong to another person. A connection that was so elemental.

She was like heaven on earth. One tiny piece of serenity and bliss amongst the blackness, the desolation and the pain. But if that tragedy, the anger and the pain, had been what he needed to experience in order to be in the time and place to meet her, then Damon felt he could accept that.

For her, everything might have been worth it.

Lowering his head, he pressed teasingly light kisses along her jaw, down her neck to her collarbone, feeding off the gasps of pleasure that broke from her lips. Her whole body quivered and Damon brought his mouth back to hers, swinging her up into his arms to carry her to the large bed.

Instantly he was mourning the loss of her body against his as he stepped back to rid himself of his own clothes. And as he did so he thought of all the ways he wanted to tease and touch her, pleasure her, this woman who had infiltrated his mind, his blood, his dreams, and whose body he could not wait to bury himself inside.

As she watched him undress, it felt to Carrie as if she was burning up from the inside out. First his shirt was dropped to the floor, revealing a solid expanse of chiselled chest and stomach, and then he was sliding his trousers over his strong legs, leaving only a pair of snug black boxer shorts on his body.

She could not draw her eyes away from his muscled physique and his skin which glowed with a godlike golden sheen. This feeling for him—it went way beyond lust. Deeper than desire. She did not know what to call it, but it had her reaching for him urgently as he came back to the bed, catching him between her open arms as he covered her body with his own. And then he was kissing her again, his hands moving over her with a reverent touch. A touch that was healing.

After the way Nate had used her, seducing her only to advance his own ends, Carrie hadn't been able to think of sex without her stomach churning with nausea. His lies had made it seem tawdry and base. But there was nothing sordid about what was unfolding between her and Damon. Their intimacy felt beautiful. And vital. Nerves fluttered beneath her skin, but they were nothing compared to the feeling of rightness that came from lying beneath him as he grazed his lips down the side of her neck, trailed a hot path between her breasts, down her ribs and over her stomach, seeking lower still.

But just as he was about to guide her legs apart he stopped, glancing up at her, and with a stutter of her heart Carrie realised he was asking her permission to carry on. Moisture sprang into her eyes and she nodded, suddenly aching to feel him touching her *there*, and then, nudging her legs apart, he buried his face in her and pressed an open-mouthed kiss to her delicate feminine folds.

Carrie was already balancing on a knife-edge, and the moment he pressed his tongue and connected it with her hidden core delight screamed through her body. She bucked and twisted beneath him, surrendering control of her own body to the feeling coursing through her, but Damon's firm hand on her stomach held her steady as he worshipped her, kissing and stroking and delving with his tongue, until the shocks shooting through her body became too powerful to resist and she shattered beneath their catastrophic force into a million sparkling pieces.

'Oh, my God… Damon,' she breathed, as the after-shocks zig-zagged up her body with alarming force and he began to kiss his way back up.

He covered her, his erection teasing her wetness. She was still quaking with the ripples of that first orgasm, but the moment she felt him slide against her she was hungering for another, her limbs tensing with anticipation, and she arched against him, unable to help herself, wanting to feel more of what he could do to her.

'Tell me what you want,' he whispered against her ear.

'I want more,' she panted, the words torn from her by a greediness that had his lips curling in a way that told her he had her exactly the way he wanted her. Wet and starving and begging. 'I want all of you.'

He responded with a devastating smile as he reached for a condom from the nightstand. He sheathed himself before positioning himself at her slick entrance, and then he was gently pushing into her, and her muscles were gripping his thick length in ecstatic welcome. A keening cry broke from her lips as with a final thrust he fitted himself fully inside her. He was so hard, his penetration so deep, and the feel of him so overawing, that Carrie struggled to catch her breath. She wanted to savour the moment, but the need for him to take her even further made her impatient.

'Damon…' she ground out, lifting her hips to intensify the feeling building in her.

He sank even deeper. By the strain in his face she

knew it cost him to hold himself still as she wriggled beneath him, but then she saw the moment her impatience became his. And then he was moving, retreating from her before driving back inside, his steady tempo intensifying as her hips met and matched his eager thrusts and they raced towards a peak.

She was on the very edge of coming but still holding back when Damon seized her mouth with a bruising kiss and sucked on her lower lip, and Carrie splintered apart in his arms before, with a shout of her name, he surrendered to his own shuddering climax.

Breathless and drained, he fell on top of her, breathing heavily, and Carrie ran a gentle hand up and down his spine whilst his racing heart evened out and the stars behind her eyes faded away. Raising his head with a languid smile, his dark hair messy from all the times she had dragged her fingers through it, he pressed a kiss to her lips, rolling onto his side and pulling her with him.

Just as he was enfolding her in his arms, a knock at the door had him pulling away. 'That will be the food I ordered,' he said, and laughed, sliding out of the bed and grabbing his trousers from the floor. 'Good thing we've worked up an appetite.'

He returned with two bags of food and several plates. They ate out on the terrace, devouring the dishes he had selected, him gloriously bare-chested whilst she wore only his shirt. His lips quirked every time he looked at her, as if he was appreciating the bare legs and the visibility of her breasts beneath the material.

When they were finished, he turned to her. 'Are you tired? Do you want to sleep?'

Under his beautiful gaze, her heart raced, and Carrie felt breathless just looking at him. She wanted to soak up every moment she had with him—wanted to know each and every part of him. If one night was all she could have, then she wanted every single second.

She leaned in, pressing a hand to his chest and bestowing upon him a lingering kiss. 'Let's not waste time sleeping.'

His answering smile told her she had read his mind.

Dawn arrived too soon.

The sharp early-morning light forced Carrie's eyes open and thrust her into painful reality.

Her one night was Damon was over.

An ache spread across her chest and for a small second Carrie considered an alternative scenario—one in which she didn't slink away, but stayed and told him everything. He would be annoyed, of course, but perhaps not as annoyed as she feared. After a moment of absorbing it he would draw her close for a drugging kiss and tell her he didn't care, that she meant more than anything.

But then she remembered his rawness when he had spoken of his father and knew she was withdrawing to one of her fairy-tale fantasies. Allowing herself to believe in it, even for a second, was dangerous. She would only end up hurting even more.

Because the truth was that staying was impossible.

A future between them was impossible.

Beside her, Damon was in a steady sleep, lying on his back with one arm flung behind his head and the sheet riding low over his chiselled stomach. Carrie could feel the heat rising from his body, and the longing to curl up against him, slide her leg across his and rest her head against his strong chest, as she had during the night, reared up within her.

She had to draw on every last drop of her willpower to slip out from beneath the covers and collect her discarded clothes. Once she was back in her dress, carrying her shoes in her hand, she tiptoed to the threshold of the bedroom, unable to resist a last look at him.

He was still sound asleep, his chest rising and falling in a peaceful rhythm. Her eyes throbbed and her throat burned with a new kind of agony. But it was her heart that ached most dreadfully.

She wished it didn't have to be this way…wished so many things were different. But she was a Randolph and he was a Meyer. That simply could not be.

'Goodbye, Damon,' she whispered, turning and leaving before the first tears could fall.

CHAPTER THREE

WEEKS LATER, CARRIE was still on Damon's mind.

When he woke on the day of the Caldwell pitch, his first thought was not of the crucial day ahead. It was of Carrie. Exactly as it had been every day since Paris.

Each morning he woke with his naked body tangled in the sheets, dappled with beads of sweat after yet another night spent languishing in a highly sexed dreamscape with Carrie Miller, delighting in the scenarios he hadn't been granted the opportunity to play out in reality.

Because she'd been gone by the time he woke after their night together. Which shouldn't have been a surprise. One night was all she'd been willing to give. One night was all that he had asked for. Usually that was enough. So it really shouldn't have bothered him.

Except waking to cool sheets and an empty bed *had* bothered him and, contrary to the reassurances he had issued to himself, that the strange feelings of angst over her silent departure were nothing more than a fleeting phenomenon, it was still bothering him.

He didn't understand why. As a general rule he didn't allow himself to form attachments deep enough that ultimately it meant he would miss a person when they were no longer there. And even if that had happened—and that was highly unlikely —he hadn't known Carrie long enough to actually miss her. And yet at times an uncomfortable feeling lodged within his gut, making him feel as though she had somehow infiltrated him emotionally as deeply as he had penetrated her physically.

He didn't like it.

Damon didn't want to be affected by another person. He didn't want his heart, or any other part of him, to be touched, softened. Weakened. Left open and vulnerable. He didn't want to have to feel the agonising pain of a loss that could never be replaced. He didn't want to live day after day with the edges of his heart burning and that inescapable ache threatening to burrow deeper with the slow passing of each second.

With the death of his father and his subsequent abandonment by his mother, Damon had already felt all that too acutely to ever want to relive the experience. And the protective walls he had built around himself were impenetrable.

Which made Carrie's continued lingering in his mind and his errant thoughts of contacting her once he returned to California unfathomable.

And intolerable.

She was nothing to him—nothing other than a beautiful distraction. It was past time he took control of himself.

Today was the day when he would present the final, all-important bid that would seal the Caldwell project and bring him within touching distance of his revenge. The day that he would look back on as the beginning of the end of Sterling Randolph. And that was the only thing he wanted to think about.

After all, he'd been working towards this day for ever. It had taken time to build his business to the point where he could challenge the Randolph Corporation. And it had taken twenty-hour days and endless networking to manoeuvre himself into a position of industry dominance. But he'd done it. He had achieved in ten years what other men had worked thirty years for, and over the past twelve months Damon had begun to shake the industry's confidence in Randolph.

But that wasn't anywhere near enough for him.

He wanted Randolph to feel his success slipping through his fingers as surely as his own father had felt his life slipping away.

And that was where the Caldwell project came in.

The Caldwell Banking Group in London were commissioning a new North American headquarters—a building that was to be a beacon of their global prowess and reputation. Everyone in the world, including Caldwell himself, believed Randolph to be the natural choice to spearhead the project. But for the better part of the past year Damon had been quietly cultivating the Caldwell executives, laying the groundwork to ensure that his bid was the successful one. And when he won it Randolph would be finished, cut down for all the world to witness.

It would not give Damon back any of the things he'd lost, but his father had been a good man, who had only wanted to use his intellect and talent to help people and make the world a better place, so to see the careless, arrogant man responsible for his death brought to his knees would deliver him an indescribable satisfaction.

When the important work of the day was done, he

would find some beauty with whom he could while away the evening hours—someone to shunt Carrie completely from his mind. But for the time being he settled for throwing back the sheets and standing under a cold shower, employing the ruthless discipline he'd spent a lifetime mastering to erase all traces of her.

Because there was no room for her—or anyone—in his head or in his life.

He had one focus, one ambition. And he would not allow anyone to stand in the way of him achieving that.

Because his revenge was what mattered.

It was *all* that mattered.

It was Carrie's day off from the bakery, but she was still working. Sitting back, she looked at the sketch of the five-tier wedding cake she'd been tasked with creating the day before. Pleased with the draft, she set it to the side before bringing up her list of special orders on the computer.

It had grown substantially in the past fortnight, and despite other people's concerns that Carrie was overstretching herself, her heavy workload was exactly what she wanted. And needed. She loved her thriving small business and she loved baking. The latter had been her salvation on a number of occasions, and throwing herself into her work was a key part of her plan to move forward, look only into the future and forget all about Damon Meyer.

Well, not *forget*, exactly, because that was impossible. There could be no forgetting the mind-blowing intimacy they had shared and all the ways he had touched and caressed her body that single night, healing the pieces of her that had still been emotionally black and blue. It was more about keeping her thoughts away from him, keeping herself so busy that she had no time to wonder about him, to wonder if he ever thought about her.

She was just reading through the notes that accompanied the order of a fiftieth birthday cake when a light knock on the window heralded the arrival of her mother.

'I brought you a smoothie, and a little something else,' Prue Miller announced with her usual bright smile as she walked through Carrie's door, setting down her gifts on the table and kissing her daughter's cheek. 'How are you feeling today? Is your stomach any better?'

'A little, yes,' Carrie answered, without taking her eyes off her notes.

'This is beautiful,' Prue said, admiring the cake sketch Carrie had just finished. 'A wedding cake?'

'Yes, I got the order yesterday.' Picking up the smoothie, she took a small sip and was relieved when her stomach didn't instantly heave. 'This is delicious. Thank you.' Reaching for the small bag next to it, she froze when she saw its contents.

A pregnancy test.

Swallowing her shock, but unable to quieten her quickening heart, she lifted her gaze to her mother. Prue was watching her with shrewd eyes, but her expression offered no hint as to what she was thinking.

'How did you know?'

Carrie just about managed to force the question past the tennis-ball-sized lump lodged in her throat.

Prue smiled. 'Because I'm your mother. And that stomach bug you've been suffering from has lingered a little too long for me to believe it really *is* a stomach bug.'

When Carrie made neither a move nor a sound in response, she sighed and retrieved the test from the bag herself, holding it in the air.

'Are you really going to keep me in suspense?'

Carrie trembled as the truth forced its way to her lips. 'I don't need to take the test. I've already done one.'

Her mother moved closer. 'And…?'

Carrie took a fortifying breath, fearful of the look she was about to see in her mother's eyes, and even more terrified of the reality it would become once she said the words aloud.

'It was positive. All four of them were. I'm pregnant.'

In the next second her mother's arms were around her, holding her tightly. 'Sweetheart, are you okay? Why didn't you tell me sooner?'

'I'm fine. I think. Actually, I don't know.'

She sighed, her thoughts and emotions far too jumbled for her to be anywhere close to identifying them.

'Have you given any thought to what you want to do?'

Carrie nodded, meeting her mother's eyes. 'I'm having the baby.'

Prue beamed. 'I'll help in any way I can. The bakery, doctors' appointments—whatever you need.'

'Thanks. But I'm not that far in my thinking yet.'

She was still trying to process the fact that she was pregnant and that it was not happening the way she'd always imagined it would—mainly because the father was a man she'd never anticipated seeing again.

Her mother must have read the struggle in her expression, for she moved beside her, hugging her again. 'It'll be okay, Carrie. You'll figure this out. You're not on your own. And, speaking of that…have you told the father?'

'Not yet.' There was no question in Carrie's mind that she would tell Damon, but she knew she would also have to divulge who she was, and she didn't expect either revelation to be met with delight. 'It's a little complicated.'

'Carrie, I understand the world we live in, and that some relationships happen quickly and are not always long term. I'm not going to judge you for having something casual. And you're certainly entitled to your privacy. So if you're not comfortable telling me, that is fine, but I really think you need to tell *him*.'

'It's not so much the nature of the relationship that makes telling him difficult. At least not only that,' she amended, thinking that one night together hardly amounted to a 'relationship', even if that one night had felt more fulfilling and substantial than any other day of her life. 'It's who he is.'

Alarm darkened Prue's face and Carrie could practically see all the horrifying options flying through her head.

The last thing she wanted to do was worry her mother further, so she took a deep breath. 'The father is Damon Meyer.'

'Damon Meyer? The son of Jacob Meyer?'

'Yes.'

Her mother blew out a stunned breath and Carrie knew she was thinking of the tragic way Jacob had lost his life.

The latest, highly anticipated Meyer-Randolph venture—a gentrification project in a run-down area of Chicago—had not been long underway. Jacob had made it a condition of his inclusion in the project that the existing homes and businesses were safeguarded and incorporated into the new development plans. However, not long after construction had begun, and he'd left to attend to another of his projects in Europe, Sterling Randolph had betrayed that promise in a bid to increase profits. The residents had been forced to leave their properties with little or no notice and with nowhere to go.

Anger at that turn of events had reverberated across the city, sparking enormous protests. When Jacob had learned of the double-cross, it had been too late to undo Sterling's actions, but he'd hastily returned to the city anyway, to try and set things right. When he had attended a meeting with the local community, one furious resident had shot and killed him.

'Well, that definitely does make it more complicated,' Prue said eventually. Seeing Carrie's miserable expression, she tightened the hand curled over hers in silent support. 'Does Damon know who you are?'

'No. And when he finds out I can't see how he will want anything to do with me or the baby.'

Damon left his team celebrating. They had worked tirelessly these past weeks, showing a determination and a focus that had almost rivalled his own. Their pitch to Caldwell had been flawless, so they deserved their night of jubilation.

He, however, would not be celebrating until he had a signed contract in his possession and Randolph's business obituary was being written.

But before he returned to his Mayfair home he stopped off at an exclusive bar for a nightcap.

A lone woman sat at the other end of the bar, and Damon remembered his earlier vow to find a companion to enjoy the night with. But the inviting smile of her deep red lips left him cold, and Damon turned away to savour his drink alone.

She wasn't Carrie. That was the problem.

Because, as much as he didn't want to admit it, there'd been something special about Carrie Miller of Santa Barbara.

Not for the first time a pang of disquiet chimed in him as he considered her. Something that prompted his brow to furrow…as if there was something about her he should have known but wasn't realising…the source of which he had been thus far unable to put his finger on.

But then, out of nowhere, it hit him.

Miller.

Wasn't Miller the maiden name of Sterling Randolph's second wife? The wife with whom he'd had a daughter?

Having committed every aspect of Randolph's life to memory, he scanned the recesses of his mind for her name.

Caroline.

Carrie?

A buzzing sounded in his ears.

No. It was not possible. It had to be a freak coincidence. Both Caroline and Miller were generic names. It was just an unfortunate quirk of fate.

Damon had almost succeeded in convincing himself of that when he recalled Carrie's adamant stance that nothing could or should happen between them and the way she'd tried to leave the chateau.

'It's complicated. You just need to trust me, Damon. It is better for both of us if this begins and ends tonight.'

They were the words she'd spoken that night. They had made no sense at the time, but in this new context there was no misunderstanding them. She had known exactly who he was, and the awful way in which their lives were connected!

The buzzing in his ears grew louder, accompanied by the heated racing and roaring of his blood and a bitter dread pooling in his stomach.

Picking up his phone, he called his executive assistant Isobel, who answered on the first ring. 'I need you to do a background check. The woman I met in Paris—Carrie Miller. Get me everything you can on her,' he instructed, finding it hard to speak with so much visceral feeling coursing through him.

Demonstrating an even greater efficiency than usual, Isobel delivered the report to him the next morning. Looking at the solemnity of her expression as she handed it over, he felt the tiny piece of hope he'd spent the night clinging to that it was all an error evaporate.

'Tell me,' he instructed, unable to bring himself to look and see it in inviolable black and white.

'She was born Caroline Randolph. The only daughter of Sterling Randolph and Prudence Miller. Started to go by Carrie Miller a few years ago. She lives in Santa Barbara...owns a bakery that is turning a pretty decent profit for a company that's less than five years old.'

'And her relationship with her father?'

Because that was what was really mattered.

'It's hard to tell. Her parents divorced when she was

nine, her mother relocated to California and retained primary custody. She doesn't court publicity the way her half-brothers do. If she does have a relationship with Randolph, it's a very private one.'

So it was unlikely that she'd been a spy—but not impossible! Perhaps Randolph had dispatched her to find out what Damon was up to…what edge he had with Caldwell or any other deal under negotiation.

'The two of you meeting in Paris could just be a crazy coincidence,' Isobel voiced, as though reading his thoughts.

'I'm not sure I believe in a coincidence that big,' he muttered, with quelling severity.

He couldn't afford to—not where the Randolphs were concerned.

'What do you want to do?' she asked, after a long silence.

Damon thought quickly, calculating all the different scenarios at play. There was only one course of action to ensure his plans continued unthreatened.

'Nothing. If she was sent to find information, she didn't get anything. And if it was, as you say, just a coincidence, then showing a reaction could tip my hand to Randolph. So I do nothing. Pretend it never happened. Never think of her again. Never see her again. Just make certain you get a guest list for any events I'm scheduled to be at—ensure she and I don't end up in the same place.'

'Of course.' Isobel nodded, getting to her feet and leaving him alone.

Damon rose from his chair, finally giving in to the nauseating agitation burning through his bloodstream.

She was Randolph's daughter. How could he have been so stupid as not to see it?

His chest see-sawed as he rewound through their encounter—all the ways she had mesmerised him, coaxed him into letting his guard down. But never again. From now on he didn't want to think about, lay eyes on, or speak to Carrie Miller—or Caroline Randolph…whatever her name was.

Even without her mother telling her so, Carrie knew she couldn't hold off telling Damon about her pregnancy once it had been confirmed by her doctor. Her calls and emails to his company headquarters, however, had gone unanswered, so when she heard that he was scheduled to attend a children's charity ball in Los Angeles she decided to drive up to LA, where his West Coast headquarters were located.

She left at the break of dawn, eager to get the encounter out of the way and to minimise the chance of being spotted. It was miraculous that they had gone without being sighted together in Paris, particularly since so many of Damon's social outings and female companions were noted in some tabloid or other or on a gossip site.

Since returning home Carrie had more than once suffered brief spasms of anxiety as she had belatedly considered exactly what their being seen together might have unleashed, and there was no guarantee she would be so fortunate again—especially not in Los Angeles, where there were more paparazzi in one square foot than anywhere else on the planet.

If she was caught with Damon and presumed to be

his new lover—subjected to the gossip and scrutiny his previous lovers had experienced—she knew it wouldn't take long for her real identity to be uncovered. And the revelation that Jacob Meyer's son and Sterling Randolph's daughter were lovers would be salacious enough to guarantee she would find herself at the centre of a new media storm.

The prospect of her life coming under such intrusive scrutiny for a second time, of being watched and followed and whispered about, was too harrowing to bear.

But it was still quiet when she arrived in LA and made the short walk from where she'd parked her car to Damon's offices. She'd viewed pictures of the building online, but the reality was even more impressive. The space was modern and fresh and bright. The striking glass-fronted building gave way to a contemporary interior with cool white and grey flooring and walls. Low-slung white seats and glass tables were clustered in the corners. An angular reception desk held central position in front of a large pond, and a back wall of windows led onto a lush green courtyard scattered with rattan tables and chairs and benches.

The whole building was a testament to Damon's design and architectural skill, and Carrie couldn't help thinking how it was the polar opposite to her father's more grand and oppressive creations.

But as she made her way to the reception desk she started to feel more jittery than she had expected, and almost wished she hadn't declined her mother's offer to accompany her in favour of facing Damon alone. Because the sudden tightness swelling in her chest was enough to make her want to turn around and speed back to the sanctuary of Santa Barbara.

But she reminded herself that Damon had a right to know he was going to be a father—a right to decide his own level of involvement. It was not her place to make that decision for him. And Carrie needed to know where she and her child stood, or she would spend the coming years wondering, always thinking of him and speculating on what might have been.

'Can I help you?' the polished receptionist asked as Carrie reached the desk, her voice almost echoing in the early-morning quiet.

'Yes,' Carrie said, before her fear of Damon's reaction overpowered her conviction that she needed and wanted to tell him. 'I need to speak to Damon Meyer. I don't have an appointment,' she added, anticipating the question. 'But if you could just let him know that Carrie Miller is here? Tell him I need to talk to him about… Paris.'

'Mr Meyer doesn't take unscheduled meetings.'

The girl delivered the stock line without a beat of hesitation and an almost pitying smile, and immediately Carrie realised she was probably not the first unsolicited female visitor who had attempted to breach the inner sanctum of Damon Meyer.

It was a timely reminder that she was just one amongst the many, and humiliation burned in her cheeks. But she kept her feet planted in the same spot, rooted there by the vow she had made to her unborn child to do everything she possibly could to reach its father, because it was what her child deserved.

'Please,' she heard herself say. 'I'm sure he has a very

busy day, but five minutes is all I need. So if there is anything you can do…'

The plea in her eyes must have been immense, because after a minuscule hesitation the girl picked up the telephone and spoke quietly into it before hanging up, the corners of her mouth tipped down.

'I'm sorry. His day is fully booked.'

Carrie felt like a balloon that had been popped. It had taken every ounce of courage she possessed to get to LA and prepare herself to face Damon. To think that it had all been for nothing and she would have to manage the ordeal all over again was exhausting.

'Okay. Thank you for trying.'

'But…' The girl looked around, then leaned closer. 'I shouldn't tell you this, but the elevator from the underground parking garage is undergoing maintenance, so everyone is having to come in the main entrance.' She gestured to the doors Carrie had walked through. 'Even Mr Meyer. He usually arrives within the next five minutes.'

'Thank you,' Carrie breathed, relief flooding through her that her exertions hadn't been for nothing.

She didn't have to wait more than thirty seconds.

She was still walking away from the reception desk when the doors parted and a man swept through them, enough power radiating from his tall, athletic frame to compel anyone in his path to take a hasty step back.

Damon.

He was exactly as he appeared in her thoughts, only better. A million times better. Tall and lean, but strong. His body was encased in a sophisticated dark navy suit, with a white shirt beneath. He wore no tie and his collar was unbuttoned. He carried his sensuality with ease, but it hit Carrie like a lash of lightning, making everything in her go weak.

He saw her straight away, and that burnished gaze of his landed on her. The fluidity of his movement faltered for the smallest second, and Carrie allowed herself a brief spark of hope that he would be happy to see her.

She was on the cusp of opening her mouth to say something, but then she saw the hardening of his expression—like flesh turning to stone. And her heart stuttered as the ice-cold recognition that at least one of her secrets was no longer so secret seeped through her.

He already knew who she was.

Anguish rolled over her in a single violent wave and she took a pleading step towards him. But Damon was already resuming his long stride, issuing words to the woman at his side and clearly planning to breeze straight past her as though she wasn't there…as though she meant nothing.

It was exactly as she had feared—her Randolph blood marked her out at his enemy, worthy of neither his time nor his civility.

It was the reaction she had readied herself to face—or at least she thought she had—but the dismay strangling her heart was a pain greater than she had known to prepare for.

'Damon, please. Wait. I came here to… I need to talk you. It's… It's important.'

He continued his stride, unmoved and unconvinced, reaching the elevator and stabbing the call button. It was on the tip of her tongue to shout out her pregnancy, just to make him listen, knowing that as soon as he stepped into that lift and the doors closed she'd have lost her opportunity, but she had not lost all her sense.

'Please.'

But he ignored her once again, taking a step into the elevator. And then the doors were sliding shut. Spurred by desperation, Carrie rushed forward and thrust her handbag between the doors, forcing them to part again. Damon's eyes moved to her with silent fury, but she stared fearlessly back at him.

'You will want to hear what I came here to tell you.'

Randolphs were liars. *Fact.* And Damon had witnessed first-hand just how convincing a liar Carrie Miller was.

Yet there was something about the weight in her words that prevented him from beckoning Security and having her bodily removed from his building.

What if the something 'important' was something she knew about her father? Something that he was planning? What if he had somehow learned of Damon's chances on the Caldwell project and was concocting a counter attack that would derail his whole revenge plan? Plotting something that would turn the tables on Damon? Something of that magnitude would surely account for Carrie's stricken and pale expression.

Making a snap decision, he turned to address Isobel, issuing instructions through clenched teeth. 'Reschedule my first meeting and make my apologies, please. Miss Miller and I will be in my office. Ensure no one disturbs us.'

Damon gestured for Carrie to step into the elevator. He stared straight ahead as the doors closed, determinedly not looking at her and resenting every moment of shared space and oxygen—especially when her scent infiltrated the air. Her betrayal still burned within his gut, and even if she was in possession of information that might be valuable, she had a nerve, showing up on his territory and demanding an audience.

Clearly she had inherited her father's gall!

But, sour though he felt, Damon knew he could not roll the dice on whether she was being truthful—not with so much at stake.

Forty seconds later they arrived at his top-floor office. Damon secured the door behind them before striding briskly to stand behind his desk.

'You have five minutes. So whatever information you came to here to impart, I suggest you speak quickly,' he instructed, with taciturn impatience.

Carrie stared back at him, her chin raised and her eyes clear. 'I'm pregnant.'

CHAPTER FOUR

'PREGNANT?' DAMON'S HEART, which had momentarily stopped, restarted at a pace that was worryingly similar to a train about to fly off the tracks. Of all the things he had been preparing himself to hear, that hadn't even made the list!

Through a rapidly descending veil of panic he scanned Carrie's face for any sign of the changes pregnancy wrought, but there was nothing—not that their necessarily would be at only a few months along. He knew little about pregnancy, but enough to know that.

'Are you sure?'

'I wouldn't be bothering you if I wasn't,' she replied, with a composure of tone and expression that was in direct contrast to the sound of his heartbeat pounding in his ears.

'But we were safe. I used protection.'

'It happened anyway.'

Her olive-green eyes continued to look unflinchingly back at him, and in spite of the quiet fury he had nursed since learning her identity, and in spite of all that he had felt when he locked eyes on her moments ago downstairs—a blaze of blistering anger and betrayal and hurt—something hot and heavy leapt into life in his stomach. The yearning to lean over and crush her plump mouth beneath his ripped through him, unexpected and intense.

'I'm ten weeks along. A recent blood test and a doctor's appointment confirmed it. I thought you had a right to know that I am pregnant and that I'm having the baby.'

And there it was again—the impact of those words striking him in the centre of his chest, punching pockets of air from his lungs, making his heart stop and start with a distress that threatened to be his undoing.

Gritting his teeth, Damon tried to breathe through it… tried also to steady his thoughts. But there was only a frighteningly familiar sense of the world spinning out of his control. He could feel the closeness of those inky black tentacles, poised to clamp around his wrists and ankles and drag him back into that abyss that had swallowed him as a boy, when he'd lost his father, and then his mother, and his whole world had been in a million pieces around his feet and there had seemed no way to put it back together again.

But he refused to return to that place.

'I know it's a shock…' Carrie said, watching him somewhat cautiously with her large eyes as he propelled himself to his feet.

His agitated stride carried him to the fridge for a bottle of chilled water and he snapped off the top with a frantic twist of his impatient fingers.

'Me showing up and telling you this… I did try to call, but whenever I tried to make contact I was stonewalled.'

She looked at him almost beseechingly, as if wanting forgiveness for… What? Her unexpected announcement?

Did she not realise she needed to repent for bigger sins than *shocking* him?

'You were stonewalled at my instruction,' Damon informed her indifferently, his feet moving once again on orders from his restless body, taking him back in the direction of his desk. 'Because I uncovered who your father was and I didn't want there to be any further contact between us. Naturally I didn't expect you'd be reaching out to inform me that our one night together had resulted in pregnancy.'

His chest heaved yet again at that word and all it implied. But rather than be overwhelmed by it he focused on the facts of it.

Ten weeks along, she had said. He didn't need to do the maths. He knew exactly how long it had been since they'd been together…since he had explored and tasted every inch of her incredible body. Seventy days. *Ten weeks.*

It wasn't inviolable proof, but nonetheless he found that he believed her. She had lied to him about who she was, providing him with ample reason to doubt every word that came out of her mouth, yet for a reason he could not fully comprehend he believed her.

'No. Of course not.' Carrie dropped her gaze to the floor, twisting her fingers together in front of her stomach. 'How did you find out?'

Because I couldn't let you go, he thought as his gaze moved over the delicate features of her face: eyes as large and captivating as an owl's, lips that were full and tempting, and satin-smooth black hair that was a striking contrast to her pale skin.

She was wearing a summery dress, a design with thin

straps and a flouncy skirt that brushed against her lightly tanned legs just above her knees, and that flash of toned flesh was mere inches from where he'd nuzzled her with his lips, kissing higher and higher until he had—

With a suppressed curse, Damon broke himself free from the intoxicating memory and pulled his eyes away. But it was too late. He had lingered in it too long to be unaffected, and beneath the heat of recollection blood surged through his veins and a thudding pulse ignited at the base of his groin.

He sighed, perturbed that for a second time she was appealing to him on a sexual level that was forbidden. 'Does it really matter?' he asked.

'I guess not.'

Her slender throat convulsed and the little colour she'd had in her cheeks seemed to fade. Approaching his desk uneasily, she perched on the edge of one of the duo of chairs facing him. It occurred to Damon that, given she was pregnant, he should have invited her to sit immediately. Irked by his uncharacteristic thoughtlessness, he rose from his seat, extracted another bottle of water from the fridge, decanted it into a glass and placed it in front of her.

She murmured her thanks. After a sip she raised her eyes to him. 'I'm sorry that I didn't tell you who I was.'

Surprise at such a forthright apology rendered him momentarily mute. In the two decades since the scandal, Sterling Randolph had never issued any words of regret or contrition for what had unfolded in the wake of his actions. It had been Damon's assumption that his daughter would have the same problem with atoning. But she offered the words readily and sincerely, and they carried more weight than he would have credited, loosening some of the tension straining his arms and easing the red-hot sting of anger swirling in the hollowed pit of his stomach.

'Answer me one question, Carrie—was our meeting in Paris a coincidence?'

He told himself he was asking because it was all that mattered. Because it concerned the plans he had in motion and he needed to know if they were in jeopardy... if Randolph had some notion of what he was up to. But deep down he wanted to know for himself. He wanted—needed—to know if it had been real, if the emotions and yearnings Carrie had provoked in him had been the product of a true and pure connection, or nothing more than a skilful emotional seduction by a manipulator as practised as her father.

'Yes,' she rushed to respond.

But the quick answer failed to satisfy the drumming ache within him and he didn't know why. It was the answer he had needed to hear after all.

'I had no idea you were at that museum gala. I had no idea who you were when we first locked eyes. I just felt a connection. I only knew when you introduced yourself—but everything I was feeling in that moment was so strong, so compelling, that it just got pushed aside.'

The impression of her words made his heart pump harder as she took a breath, her eyes resting gently on him, as though testing his response. He made sure to betray nothing of his conflicting feelings.

'It wasn't until later that night, maybe even the next morning, that it really hit me. I considered not going to the party at the chateau, but the thought of not seeing you again was.... I had a bad experience with a boyfriend. So these last few years I've avoided dating and relationships. But when I met you and felt such an instant connection I didn't want to walk away.' She sucked in a razor-sharp breath. 'I didn't set out to deceive you, Damon. I planned to tell you as soon as I arrived at the chateau. I wanted to tell you. I tried to tell you.'

'You tried?' His thick brows slammed into one another in condemnation of the fact that she had only *tried*. 'You didn't try very hard, did you?'

It should have been the very first thing she'd said to him. She should have made him listen—said it over and over again until he heard her.

'I did try,' she insisted, with a quiet and steady strength, and suddenly he had a flash of forgotten memory.

'There is something I should mention,' she had said, with a tiny flare of anxiety in her eyes.

Only he hadn't let her speak, not wanting to hear anything that would get in the way of what he wanted—her. His heart quickened with the disquieting recollection.

'And what about when you were so desperate to leave and I asked why? Did you try to tell me then? Because all I remember is you saying it was "complicated."'

'I wanted to tell you, Damon.'

For the first time Carrie's composure slipped. Her voice cracked with emotion, a stripe of colour bloomed across the tops of her cheeks, and the hands resting on her knees curled into fists. She pressed herself forward, her breasts swelling against the line of the dress, and the sight had fire licking a path through his stomach.

'I didn't want to keep it from you, but by that point it already felt too late. We'd connected…you'd opened up to me…and I… I was scared that once I told you Sterling Randolph was my father the only way you would look at me was the way you're looking at me right now.'

The anguish burning in her olive eyes made a knot form in his stomach—because, romantic dreamer that she was, she had imagined something that could never be. She'd craved something it was impossible for him to give and she would never truly be able to understand why. Because the truth of that day was something that very few people knew.

'You are the daughter of the man who got my father murdered,' he intoned huskily. 'You're *Caroline Randolph*. How am I meant to look at you?'

'I am not Caroline Randolph,' she asserted, in a tone that was far more venomous than anything he'd previously heard her use.

It made him wonder. Wonder why she lived her life under her mother's name. Wonder why she fought so hard against the name of her birth—a name that signalled privilege and wealth among other things. Wonder if that reason, like so many bad things did, originated with her father.

'The only person who calls me Caroline is my father. To everyone else I'm just Carrie. Carrie Miller. And with regard to my father, and being a Randolph—'

Damon held up his hand, cutting off her protest. Silencing his own curiosity. 'It doesn't matter. Whatever you call yourself, you're still Sterling Randolph's daughter.'

The daughter of the monster who had caused his father's death. Hungering for her didn't change that. Nothing could change that, however much he was wishing differently in this strange moment. And it was in that moment that Damon recognised that whilst it was the lie that had spurred his initial anger, it was not what had sustained it. It was what the lie had been about. She was a Randolph. That precluded anything from ever happening between them again, and his feelings on that were not quite so clear-cut.

'His actions put my father in a grave, Carrie. It's just that simple.'

She fought the emotion that was changing her expression. 'So that's it? What happened between us in Paris goes to the top of your list of regrets?'

Damon started to shake his head, but then stopped. He would never regret that night, but admitting it aloud would accomplish nothing. It *had* to be consigned to the past. Didn't it?

It felt as if his future hinged on this moment—this answer. He would either continue traversing the path he had started down long ago, storming towards his revenge, or lean into this sudden bend, leading goodness knew where. Back to all that she had made him want in Paris? But that, too, would inevitably end in loss and pain. *More* pain.

Clearly interpreting his contemplative silence as his answer, Carrie folded her arms across her chest. 'And the child we made together? Do you have any interest in knowing it?'

'It is not that simple,' he stated through his tightly clenched jaw, avoiding looking too closely at the dark emotion flaring in the green depths of her gaze. 'For the reasons we've just gone through, our circumstances are…complex.'

'I'll take that as a no.'

She was angry. The look on her face told him that. But she was also not surprised. She'd known his answer before he'd even issued it, just as she had known how he would look at her upon learning her given name, and her expected disappointment settled on him like a ton of bricks.

But what was the alternative option? They raised the child together, a Randolph and a Meyer? That was ludicrous.

'I will have an account set up in your name,' he said, surprised by the hoarseness of his own voice. 'Neither of you will want for anything.'

Carrie pushed herself to her feet. 'There's no need for you to do that. I'm perfectly capable of providing for us. I didn't come here to obligate you. I just wanted you to know.'

'There's every reason to do it,' he countered, standing too. 'We made this child together. I have a responsibility.'

Even as he uttered the words he recognised their laughable hypocrisy, and by the sudden flare of colour in her eyes, Carrie did also.

'Obviously I will require a DNA test at some point, to confirm paternity. But I'm aware there are sometimes safety issues involved with such tests, so that can wait until a point at which it doesn't pose a risk to you or…' His eyes dropped to her stomach and he was beset by the sudden desire to touch where his child grew, to splay his hand over her in some kind of paternal pride or possessiveness. 'Or the baby.'

'Fine. But whenever the test happens you should be prepared for a positive result. You're the only man I've been with in a long time.'

She'd said as much the night they'd made love, but to hear it again pierced him afresh. It had felt like a proprietorial caveman stamp on her, as if he had claimed her, taken her, made her his. That out of all the men on the planet she could have selected from she had wanted him.

When he tried to speak again, his throat was thick. 'Whatever you need in terms of doctors or accommodation, get in touch.' He offered her a piece of paper. 'This email address and phone number connects you directly to my executive assistant, Isobel. She will take care of anything you require.'

Carrie examined the scribble with a frighteningly blank expression. 'Well, I came here to tell you I was pregnant, and I've done that, so I'll let you get back to your day. Goodbye, Damon.'

She didn't wait for him to return the pleasantry. She turned and with her head held high strode from his office, leaving her scent in the air, an unsettled feeling scratching at the skin of his chest and a sudden rushing impulse to run after her.

Carrie jabbed at the button to call for the elevator, fighting the burning tears that were attacking the backs of her eyes. She did not want to cry. She wanted to be strong for herself, and for the child she carried, but every inch of her was wounded and aching with a disappointment she had little reason to feel so acutely. Not when the meeting had played out exactly as she had feared it would.

Damon had been angry that she'd lied. Shocked that she was pregnant. Reviled by her DNA and unwilling to be an active parent to a baby with Randolph blood.

He had every right to be furious with her, but the way he had turned his feelings off so completely had left her cold with shock. She'd believed they had shared more than that. But the man she had faced today had been cool and unyielding. Emotionally unreachable. It brought ugly, unbidden memories to the centre of her mind…memories of other emotionally unavailable men, hard and selfish men, on whom she had wasted too many tears.

Her father, for one.

How many times has she stood in front of him, desperately trying to reach him, to make a connection, only to be regarded by a blank stare? And that awful day when Nate's true intentions had become clear. She'd needed his support and his comfort but had been met only with his cold recrimination. She'd been crying, humiliated, her heart crushed, and he hadn't even hugged her.

Her fingers curled into a fist, closing around the card Damon had given her with the contact information written on—contact information for his PA, not even for him!

Her upset coalesced and hardened into an anger that throbbed in every inch of her body. She wasn't afraid of raising her child alone. Her mother had pretty much raised Carrie single-handedly, and she was a glowing example of what was possible. With the promised support of her mother and her grandparents, who were twin pillars in her life, she was in no doubt that she would successfully and happily raise her child in a secure and loving environment.

And yet Carrie was aware of the open wound left by not having a relationship with one's father. She would prefer it if the same fate wasn't inflicted on her child.

But Damon was making a decision that was all about him. He hadn't given a single second's consideration to the child they had made together and what was best for him or her. He was too consumed by the past to give any thought to the future, stuck in his uncompromisingly rigid position.

Just like her father, who had only ever seen the world though his own eyes, his own ambitions and greed. He had never donated a moment's consideration to anyone else—not his sons, nor his wife or his daughter.

With a ping, the elevator announced its arrival and the doors slid open, but Carrie's feet wouldn't move. She had always been cowed by her father's unyieldingness, never arguing with him. Because he was shockingly incapable of seeing another perspective from his entrenched position and because his favour was earned through silence. And more than anything she had longed for his favour. His love.

She had felt the same powerlessness in Damon's office, faced with his animosity, and had retreated to her default position of silence and acquiescence, hoping that if she didn't aggravate the situation further it would work out the way she hoped. But staying silent had only ever left her hurt and resentful. It hadn't enabled any relationship with her father.

Carrie didn't want to repeat that pattern with another person, and she didn't want to make the same mistakes—especially not when her child would be adversely affected. It was past time she learned to use her voice, to advocate for what she wanted and needed and what was best for her child.

Turning on her heel, she marched back into his office.

Damon spun with a startled look as the door crashed against the wall. 'Carrie, what—?'

'No! You had your turn to speak and I listened. So now you're going to listen to me.'

She drew in a fortifying breath, her courage wobbling as she felt the full force of his authoritative persona directed her way. He was clearly unused to being addressed so forcefully.

'I'm not under any illusions about my father. What he did to your father was awful, and you have every right to hate him. But that has nothing to do with this baby,' she said, her hands moving across her still-flat stomach. 'And it shouldn't have any influence on how you feel about this pregnancy.'

Pausing to draw a much-needed breath, she tried not to be diverted by the sheer magnificence of him, still and tall and straight-backed, polished eyes fixed on her. Their connection had been forged at first sight, and she felt its reigning power every time their gazes collided, making her shake and shiver all the way down to her toes.

'If you don't want to be involved, that's fine. I have no problem doing this on my own. But if the only reason you don't want to be involved is because one quarter of this child's DNA comes from Sterling Randolph, then you're acting like a fool and doing the child a huge disservice. Because you got one thing right—you *do* have a responsibility. To be there. To love it. To help it become the greatest and happiest person it can be, living a life that makes it happy. You grew up without your father, Damon. You know what that feels like. The emptiness, the sorrow… And you blame my father for taking yours away from you. Do you really want to let him be the reason you don't know your child too?'

The dark silence of his house greeted Damon when he arrived home from the charity ball. He tapped the control panel on the wall to bring up the lights before freeing himself from the tuxedo jacket, pulling apart the bowtie and ripping open the top buttons of his shirt.

Finally, he could draw a breath.

The children's ball was an important evening to him. It was the one event he attended without fail every year, often working his schedule around the date.

Damon had learned the importance of giving back from his father. When he'd lived, Jacob Meyer had been an actively involved patron of a particular charity that focused its efforts and resources on children in difficult situations. It had seemed only natural that Damon continued his efforts and, truth be told, Damon felt a great affinity for lost and struggling children. Having been robbed of his father, and then abandoned by his mother, he was aware of those struggles and the emotions that could be overpowering.

Anything he could do to ease those difficulties Damon was willing to do—including showing his face at the heavily attended ball to raise the charity's profile and boost the generosity of the donations given. As much as he sometimes loathed the inane small talk and huge egos, he was more than happy to help. But that night the function had seemed interminable, and from the moment he had arrived all he had been focused on was when he could leave.

Pouring himself a glass of smooth Cabernet, he walked out to the large terrace off the master bedroom of his house high up in the Bird Streets. As the name suggested, it was perched up in the Hollywood Hills, with the lights of Los Angeles glittering in the near distance. It was usually one of the few places he was able to find a rare moment of tranquillity and perspective, with his father's most famous construction standing proudly amongst all the other towers of downtown LA, its top light like a beacon just for Damon, but there was no peace to be found tonight.

Only noise.

Fatherhood had never been an ambition of his. Nor a consideration. He was too focused on bringing down Sterling Randolph to give any thought to the concerns of normal people, like marriage and children. No man could serve two masters, after all, and Damon had long known that his purpose in life was a pursuit that required *all* of him. And, whilst he had made himself enormously successful along the way, Damon would not consider his life a success until he had settled that score and avenged his father.

That was the purpose behind everything he did.

That was the cause to which he had dedicated his life.

And there was no place for a family amongst that.

Except now he had no choice about that. There was going to be a child. There already was a child, growing in the womb of the daughter of his enemy. A child with Randolph blood.

Damon took a long sip of his wine, his temples feeling tight.

He didn't have anything to offer—at least not emotionally. His heart had turned to stone after his father's death and had remained in his chest as a useless rock. And yet his decision to be uninvolved, other than financially, was not resting easily within him. He had not rested easily since the moment he'd made it.

A child deserved more than a big house and a healthy back account. It needed the security of unfailing, unconditional love and two present, interested parents. Every day of his life his father had demonstrated that to him. Jacob Meyer had always shown Damon how much he loved him, how important his happiness was to him.

Did he not owe his own flesh and blood the same devotion? Anything less than that would be unconscionable—especially when he knew the cost of parental rejection. How the child was always the one to pay the ultimate price in an inability to open up and trust and love. In the fear of doing so.

When he had needed her the most, his mother had turned away from him and left him behind. He hadn't been forced to contend with poverty or homelessness, so he had been luckier than many—and he never allowed himself to forget that—but it had still hurt and confused him. Would he really doom his own child to the same lifetime of confusion and questioning what they had done wrong, why they hadn't been enough for their parent to stay?

No, he could not pass on that pain. He would not author a legacy of heartache and mistrust.

Had he been thinking clearly earlier that day, he would have known there was no way he could be separate from his child. It was unthinkable. But he had not been thinking clearly. The decision he'd reached had been birthed by panic and fear. And not because Carrie was a Randolph but because when Carrie, in all her loveliness, had stood before him, everything she'd made him feel and think had been threatening.

Threatening to draw down his barriers and throw him off course.

Threatening the life he had built and shaking its very foundations.

And he had reacted defensively.

Blinded by panic, he had thought only of ending the discomfort, of making himself safe again, and he was ashamed of how selfish he had been in those moments, considering only himself and not the wellbeing of his child.

He certainly hadn't needed Carrie to march back into his office and tell him about the mistake he was making. On some level he had already known it. But her speech had crystallised it for him far sooner than he would have done it on his own.

To burden his son or daughter with the sins of its grandfather was wrong. And to miss out on the opportunity to know his child and be a steady and supportive presence, just as his own father had been, would be an enormous mistake.

But nothing else would change.

Carrie might not be his enemy, but she was still forbidden fruit. The only relationship he would have with her was one that was necessary for their child to be raised with both its parents.

And as for Sterling Randolph…

He still needed to pay for what he had done and Damon would ensure he did—and soon. The moment the ink of his signature was dry on the Caldwell contract was the moment when Sterling Randolph's world would collapse faster than a house of cards.

CHAPTER FIVE

CARRIE EXTRACTED THE tray of muffins from the oven and set it on the cooling rack, smiling at the sounds of delight from her young students. These informal baking lessons with a small group of adolescents from a local children's home had come about organically, largely because of Carrie's friendship with the woman who ran the home. She always felt as if she was doing something good in those lessons, paying something forward, and it was for that reason she had ignored the pit in her stomach the size of the Grand Canyon and forced herself up and out of bed that morning, refusing to be pressed into a wallowing misery.

Carrie had too many good things in her life to let Damon's rejection define her. And she would forge ahead with that life—a life that made her happy because it was what defined her. Her creativity. Her hard work. The community that supported her and which she gave back to. *Not* her name. And if Damon couldn't recognise that... well, *screw him*.

Carrie had wanted to believe that the connection they'd shared was strong enough to override the negativity of her name, but that had been just another wish from her hopeful, foolish heart.

Like many others who'd passed through her life Damon, the moment he had discovered her name, had thought it was all that mattered. But unlike all those others who had wanted to use her because of it, regarding her as some kind of chip with which they could bargain their way into a better life, Damon viewed it as a plague that needed to be avoided.

As much as she wished it was different, she would not bruise her knees praying for him to change his mind and show up on her doorstep. She refused to wait and hope, even though she was feeling the pinch of every silent hour and day that went by the way she had with her father when she'd been a young girl. She had waited and waited for him, hoping with every breath and every beat of her heart that he would show up and show her how much he cared—only to end up crying disappointed tears into her mother's shoulder.

There would be no more tears. She'd cried too many over men already. Her father. Nate. And now Damon. She was done with giving other people the power to hurt her.

And after yesterday she wasn't sure she wanted to see Damon ever again anyway. What she had seen of him made her think that she and her baby might be better off without him in their lives.

'Carrie?' Marina, the bakery's manager, popped her head around the door separating the café from the kitchen. 'Are you almost done in here? There's someone at the counter asking for you.'

Carrie frowned to herself as she helped the kids to box up the muffins she'd taught them to make. 'I don't have any appointments scheduled for this afternoon.'

She had deliberately been keeping her afternoons light, knowing that was when her pregnancy sickness and fatigue began to take their toll.

'I don't think it's about a cake order. I think this is a *personal* visit.'

Her busy hands stilled, her spine beginning to tingle at her friend's choice of tone. 'Who is it?'

'He didn't offer a name. But tall, dark-haired, a little Latin-flavoured and heart-stoppingly handsome about sums him up.'

Damon.

Her heart thumped so hard that her chest momentarily hurt. Some crazy part of her was joyous at the prospect of laying eyes on him, even as she recoiled at the thought of facing him again.

But surely it couldn't be him? He'd made his feelings painfully clear in his office, and when he hadn't been roused enough by her impassioned plea to chase her down before she reached the exit of his building she had understood the chance of him changing his mind wasn't just slim, it was non-existent. So it seemed highly unlikely that he had taken time out of his day to make the journey to Santa Barbara and was actually standing in her place of business.

Yet…who else could it be?

Heart hammering, Carrie took the few steps over to the doorway for visual confirmation, fully expecting it to be someone else. However, when she pressed open the door just enough to peep through she gasped as her eyes immediately locked on Damon. He was standing side on to her, so she could only see him in profile, but there was no mistaking him. No mistaking that proud and indomitable stance. Or the way her pulse fluttered and flipped in recognition of it.

In an immaculately tailored grey suit and a pale blue shirt that greatly enhanced the golden hue of his skin and the bitter darkness of his hair he looked frustratingly, mouth-wateringly good. Her heart caught as, even from afar, the impact of him pierced her sharp and deep, making her weak for him all over again, making her skin tingle with hunger to feel his touch. And she cursed herself for it. After yesterday, how was it still possible that her blood was singing at the sight of him?

Quickly Carrie released the door, taking a hasty step back from it as the tingles deepened to full-body tremors and her mind whirred. What was he doing here? Hadn't he already said everything he needed to say? Hadn't he inflicted enough damage upon her heart?

So what on earth…?

Unless…

Her frazzled mind could drum up only one reason for his unexpected appearance. But…surely not? Surely after everything he'd said yesterday Damon hadn't actually changed his mind about being a father to their child…?

Damon couldn't quite believe it. Not only had he voluntarily entered a business owned by a Randolph, but he also didn't loathe it on first sight. The space, simply named The Bakehouse, was actually rather inviting. The pale walls, wooden tables and chairs and modern, warm lighting all combined to create a welcoming and comfortable interior that relaxed its occupants without their awareness, making them want to sit and while away a few easy hours.

Casting his assessing gaze around as he was made to wait, he recognised Carrie's bright energy everywhere.

The gaggle of voices behind him had Damon turning sharply and eyeing the group of pre-teen youngsters emerging from what he suspected was the kitchen. Carrie was bringing up the rear, and as his eyes caught on her they stuck. She wore ripped jeans and a simple tee that highlighted her narrow waist, her slim legs and the generous curve of her breasts, which definitely had a new and welcome fullness, and the sight of her had him struggling against the instinct to reach out, pull her against his hard body and plunder her mouth until she was boneless and begging beneath him.

Seeing himself doing exactly that had him throbbing with agonising anticipation, even whilst simultaneously fighting a savage burst of annoyance. She was off-limits, and he couldn't comprehend why his brain was having so much trouble computing that message or why his body was failing to respond with obedience.

Burying his hand deep in the pockets of his trousers, where they would be prevented from reaching out and grabbing her on the orders of a wayward neuron, he watched with mounting impatience as she exchanged a few smiling words with the woman who was clearly the youngsters' chaperone before seeing them out through the door and waving them off with a promise for 'next time.'

Slowly, she turned and met his waiting gaze, folding her arms across her chest as she did so. 'You were looking for me?' she asked, her clear olive eyes and smooth expression offering no hint as to whether she was happy to see him or not.

He found that neutrality disconcerting. Not that he knew why. He was not there for her, but for their child, he reminded himself.

'Yes. I wanted to speak with you.' He glanced at their surroundings with a small frown, at the patrons too close for comfort. 'Is there somewhere private we could talk?'

Carrie led him to a small office. It was a bright and happy space, but she remained maddeningly neutral.

'Why are you here, Damon? Because it seems to me you said everything you needed to say yesterday.'

Her bluntness caught him off guard. 'I said a lot yesterday, I know. And I'm here because I think I was too hasty. As you said, the news was a shock, and I spoke under the pressure of too many emotions,' he admitted on a slight growl, as with rising agitation he could feel them stirring once more.

What was it about this woman that could make him feel so much in such a short span of time? He drew in a breath, but it was like attempting to steady a ship being buffeted by the violent waves of an approaching storm.

'The truth is there's no way I could live happily not knowing my child. It would be impossible.'

'So you're saying you've changed your mind?' Carrie surmised, with an enquiring arch of her eyebrow that managed to convey the depth of her disbelief.

Damon knew it was no less than he deserved.

'You *do* want to be involved?'

'Yes. I'm going to be involved,' he asserted, holding

her gaze and refusing to release it even as a treacherous heat stirred at the base of his stomach.

'Okay,' she said finally. 'Good.'

Damon didn't look too closely at the way her approval made him feel pounds lighter. 'Anyway, that's why I'm here. I thought we should talk again. Start the conversation over. Begin afresh.'

'Yes. We should do that…' With a nervous dip of her throat, she looked at her watch. 'Erm… I don't close up here for another few hours. But you can stay and have some coffee and cake—or I can meet you after?'

'Do you have plans for dinner?' Damon queried, the question catching him as unawares as it clearly did her. Because dinner had certainly not been part of his plan when he had decided to seek Carrie out in Santa Barbara.

But he did not want to conduct their conversation when she was working and they could be overheard or interrupted at any moment. It would be close to dinner time by the time she finished work, he argued inside his head, and, Carrie being pregnant, it was important she ate a decent meal. It had nothing to do with the way she was standing across from him, with her wide glowing eyes blinking up at him, making him long for a further opportunity to be near to her, to have the freedom to fix his gaze on her and watch her until his eyes were dry.

'No, I don't,' she responded, shaking her head tentatively.

'You do now.'

CHAPTER SIX

CARRIE WAS NERVOUS as she arrived at the hotel where she'd agreed to meet Damon for dinner. He'd messaged her a short while earlier, saying he'd booked one of the resort's luxurious private bungalows and arranged for dinner to be provided there, so she'd set off along the winding pathways through the colourful jungle gardens the resort was famous for. But with every step she took her pulse beat harder—too hard—in her veins.

She knew she should be happy that Damon had changed his mind, but all Carrie felt was troubled. Because how could she be sure he meant it? A day ago he'd declared the complexities of their situation insurmountable, so what had changed so quickly? And what was to stop him from changing his mind again tomorrow? Or in a year?

Carrie wanted to believe he was sincere, because she wanted her child to grow up with two loving parents, but she remembered all the other times in her life when men had spoken words with no real intent or emotion behind them. All the other times she'd trusted and been let down.

And it was not only her own heart she was responsible for now, but her child's—she had to proceed with caution if she was to prevent history from repeating itself.

Drawing in a steadying breath, she knocked at the

door of the bungalow. Damon answered it within seconds, flashing her a perfunctory smile and beckoning her in. His shirtsleeves were rolled up and several top buttons open, exposing his strong, hair-dusted forearms and a triangle of smooth gold chest, and that flash of skin had Carrie's throat drying even more as she remembered the hot smoothness of his body, the feel of him beneath her tongue.

For the briefest of moments everything else she was feeling rolled away, leaving only that delicious, stomach-tightening hum of attraction.

But it was only a moment.

Because she couldn't just forget the side of him she had seen yesterday. A side that was cold and rigid and selfish. All the things her father was.

'Can I get you something to drink?' he offered pleasantly, leading her along a corridor and into the body of the bungalow, then out through French doors to a red-tiled patio, where a table was already set for dinner with fine white china, crystal glasses and a vase of fresh-cut, short-stemmed pink and white roses.

'Water is fine, thank you.'

'The servers should be back shortly with the food. I hope it's not a problem, us eating here instead of a restaurant? But I thought this way we'd have more privacy.'

'No, it's fine. And you're right about the privacy factor. The restaurants are always booked to capacity.'

It was one less thing for her to worry about, at least—that they would be overheard and her secret exposed. At some point she knew there would be publicity—Damon's public status would ensure that—but it was something she was doing her best not to think about.

'You're familiar with the resort, then?' he asked, returning with their drinks.

The graze of their fingers as he handed her a glass of water detonated sparks all over her skin, making her hot and tingly everywhere. She took a healthy gulp, seeking to put out those small fires igniting in too many corners of her body.

'I make the cakes for a fair few of the weddings that get held here, so I'm here often enough.'

'You've clearly built a thriving business,' Damon complimented her. 'I thought your bakery was an impressive space.'

'Thank you.'

Carrie knew what he was doing with his easy smiles and courteous conversation. He was trying to charm her into forgetting all about the previous day. But it wasn't going to work. She wouldn't fall for charm again—not after Nate—not even if being the focus of Damon's clever mind and rich gaze was making her heart race. Making her remember all the reasons she'd wanted to go to bed with him in the first place.

Selecting a roll from the bread basket in the centre of the table, she began to spread a light layer of butter on it, needing to focus on something other than him and the heat sweeping across her skin as he continued to watch her.

'I can't help but be curious about that group of adolescents you had there when I arrived,' he said, startling her with the unexpected query.

'The kids? They're from a children's home down the coast. I host baking lessons for them every few weeks.' She took another cooling sip of water. 'Why do you ask?'

'Just curious.' Damon stared at her, long and hard, as if she was a knot he couldn't untangle. 'It's nice of you to do that.'

And because she was Sterling Randolph's daughter he thought she'd be incapable of doing something nice?

'It's not that big a deal. I just show them the basics. I started it just to give them a few hours of fun, but some have really taken to baking. I actually ended up hiring one of the older girls for a few hours on weekends.'

'I'm sure that to those kids, in the situation they're in, it is a big deal. To have someone give them that time and attention, to show an interest in them and be willing to invest in them…it will mean a lot.'

Carrie tilted her head, now curious herself. 'You say that like you have some experience of their situation?'

He lifted his shoulders in a nonchalant shrug. 'An organisation I support focuses its efforts on young people in tough circumstances. Most of them, for various reasons, are alone in the world. A lot of what we try to do with is show them that the future doesn't have to be hopeless, find them opportunities similar to what you're offering. Something to give them practical skills or experience… something to interest or excite them.'

'You said "we,"' Carrie blurted, thinking aloud. '"A lot of what *we* try to do." You're involved personally with those kids?'

Damon nodded slowly. 'I guess you'd call it big-brothering, or mentoring. Basically, I'm just someone to be there for them, to talk to them, give advice, offer support and ideas. You look surprised,' he commented, his eyes raking over the expression she'd failed to keep neutral.

'In my experience men of your status and success would much prefer to write a cheque with an extra zero on it than give anything of themselves.'

'I can't say that surprises me,' he bit back, streaks of hot colour flaring in his eyes like a warning shot, because he knew exactly who she was referring to and did not like the comparison. 'But I think you'll find I bear very little resemblance to the men you've experienced in your life.'

Carrie had to clamp down on her tongue to keep from firing back that he'd resembled her father pretty spectacularly yesterday. Because it would only antagonise him. And she wasn't there to fight, but to find some clarity. Either to confirm or dismiss her concern that he was woven from the same cloth as her father.

And learning that he didn't just support charities financially but actually participated in their work made him as different from her father as it was possible to be. More than that, he cared about those kids he mentored—Carrie had heard it in his voice. And didn't that say something about the type of man he was? The kind of father he would be?

It was certainly encouraging, but she needed more solid proof than that. She needed to know without a shadow of a doubt that she could rely on him and his word. That their child would be able to rely on him in a way she had never been able to depend on Sterling Randolph. And that was exactly what she was trying to discern as she matched his unflinching regard—almost as if, if she looked hard enough, she'd be able to see through to his heart.

A knock at the door signalling the arrival of their food pierced the terse silence, and without a word Damon rose to let the servers in. A few moments later they were gone again, and a feast of steaming dishes was spread across the table.

'How have you been feeling?' Damon asked as they began to eat. 'With the pregnancy? I should have asked that sooner. I apologise for not doing so.'

Touched by the apology, and the query after her well-being, she felt the stiff line of her spine soften.

'Not too bad. A little more tired than usual, and the morning sickness is disruptive. I'm not sure why it's called morning sickness when it lasts all day, but I'm getting through it.'

'You're okay to be working?'

'Of course. Besides, it's *my* business. I need to be there to run it.'

'Being on your feet all day is not a problem?'

'Not at this stage of pregnancy, no.'

'I only ask as you said you're more tired than normal.'

'The doctor said that's fairly typical, so I don't think being at work is the culprit. Obviously it may get more problematic as the pregnancy progresses.' She paused. 'I actually have my first ultrasound appointment tomorrow. If you're still around, you might like to come.'

'I'd like that,' he replied definitively. 'I'll be there.'

'Good.'

Carrie had half expected him to fob her off, the way her father always did, and she felt a small bubble of joy that he hadn't. That he was ready and willing to back up his declaration with action.

And suddenly she could not put off asking one of her pressing questions any longer. 'Damon, what changed your mind about…all of this?'

He spent a moment considering, lashes drawn down over his cocoa-rich gaze. Then, 'As I said earlier, it was a shock that I didn't react well to. I spoke in haste.'

From the way his brows drew together in a tight pinch, Carrie knew he really was unhappy with himself over his initial reaction.

'And you were right in what you said,' he went on. 'I lost the opportunity to have a relationship with my father because of yours. But there is no need for our child to suffer in the same way, for the past to claim another victim.'

The delicious morsel of food in her mouth turned to ash and Carrie had to force it down her throat. So it was about her father. Yet again.

The ease she had been starting to feel evaporated. Carefully, she set down her fork. 'I don't really know how ask this in a neat way, so I'll just ask it. In LA, you said you couldn't be involved because my being my father's daughter made it too complex. Well, this child is his grandchild. Are you able to separate those things? Are you going to be able to love this child?'

When Damon raised his eyes in response to her question and met her waiting gaze, the tension between them ballooned so thick that it would have needed a chainsaw to cut through it.

'It's my child. Of course I will love it.'

The look he dealt her could have sliced her in half.

'You doubt that?' he asked.

'I don't want to,' she answered earnestly. 'But you feel such animosity for my father… I don't want this child to be raised amongst bitterness and enmity. I only want it to know a happy life.'

'That's all I want too.'

Carrie looked away. There was so much nervousness jangling within her that she needed a second to compose herself. How could she frame her fears in the right way? How could she explain that she wanted to believe him but was terrified of how alive the past was in his present—a present that was complicated enough without being made murkier by ancient shadows?

'Are you really going to be able to deal with having a child with Randolph blood? Can you look beyond that? Because if you think you can't, or that at some point you may want to walk away, you should bow out now. I told you yesterday, I can do this alone. And having no father at all is better than having one who's uninterested, or hateful—or, worse, one who checks out.'

Damon's expression had hardened as she spoke.

'That's not going to happen. And I will not let you conjure these scenarios as a pretext to exclude me from my child's life,'

'I don't want to exclude you. I am the person who braved coming to see you so you would know about the baby. All I'm asking is if you're one hundred percent sure of your decision. Because if you're not…' she had to take a breath, draw on all her courage to speak the following words '… I have reservations about you being involved.'

For the longest moment he stared back at her without

moving, without even blinking. Then, 'Let's be clear. I *am* going to be involved. We can sort it out amicably, between us, or we can involve lawyers. But my involvement is not in question.'

Carrie felt her whole body react with a spasm of fear to the threat of litigation, and knew she must have paled, because a second later Damon speared his fingers through his hair and exhaled a heavy breath.

'I'm sorry. I didn't mean that to come out as a threat.'

'It certainly sounded like one.'

'The truth is, this is not a situation I ever expected to find myself in. Dealing with an unplanned pregnancy… Never mind being in it with—' He managed to stop his words, but a line of guilty colour streaked through his gaze before he could avert it, and it was that look that said everything he didn't want to say.

'Go on—say it,' Carrie urged, already knowing that he was thinking it each time he looked at her. That it was *all* he thought about. He'd changed his mind about the baby, but not about her. 'You didn't imagine being in this scenario with the daughter of the man you hate. The daughter of the man you hold responsible for killing your father.'

His gaze turned to granite. 'He *did* kill my father.'

'He didn't pull the trigger.'

This time it was anger that flashed in his eyes. Cold and lethal. 'So you're defending him now?'

'No.' She sighed, feeling the heavy weight of the past pressing against her chest and causing her anxiety to surge. 'I'm not. But don't you see you're proving my point? This should only be about the baby—about what is best for him or her. Not my father and what he is, what he's done. He has *zero* involvement in this.'

'He's your father, Carrie,' Damon scoffed.

'Yes, he is. Which, by the way, is something I have no control over. And, like I tried to tell you the other day, he and I barely have a relationship.'

Leaning back in his seat, Damon looked as if he was processing the information, but Carrie was not fooled into thinking that he was relaxed. She could see by the set of his body that he was still primed to pounce.

'So he won't be in the baby's life?'

'I won't prevent him from meeting his grandchild, if that's what you're asking. He's my father, and my door is always open to him. But as far as him being involved—that's unlikely.'

It was a painful truth, not made any less painful by the long years Carrie had had to come to terms with his indifference.

'Unless something is directly about him or his business, my father has very little interest in it. As this baby is about neither, I can't imagine him being any more a feature in its life than he was in mine. He doesn't even know I'm pregnant,' she shared, with a shrug to disguise the constant hurt she felt over the state of their relationship.

'He doesn't?'

'No.'

By the way Damon's eyebrows flew up with a surprise he could not contain, Carrie knew it meant that he was *finally* listening and hearing. And once he understood that her connection to her father was in a large part in name only, maybe his attitude to her would soften and they could start contemplating how to navigate the future, rather than arguing over the past.

'As I said, we don't have a close relationship.'

'Have you told anyone? About the baby?'

'My mother, of course. And my grandparents. They were surprised, but they're excited. They've all offered their help.'

'So you're planning on raising the baby here? In Santa Barbara?'

'Yes. This is my home. It's where my family is…my work is. It's where I'm happy.'

Damon nodded as though he had anticipated that. 'At present, I'm based primarily on the East Coast. But, as you no doubt know, I have offices in several cities—including Los Angeles. I also have a house there. Now, I have no problem making the West Coast my primary base, but I'm not sure my living full-time in LA is the most suitable arrangement,' he disclosed with a pragmatic tilt of his dark head. 'I think it would be far better for me to find a home here, near to you. Obviously I would need to commute to my LA office daily, and I'll need to travel for business. But so did my father, and he always made it work. As long as our child has a stable place to call home…'

Carrie held up her hand. Her head was spinning so fast she was liable to fall over, even though she was sitting. 'Wait—I'm sorry. You'll buy a house *here*? In Santa Barbara?'

'Yes. That way it will be easy for us to co-parent. The child can go between us without having any if its fundamentals change. Same nanny, same school, same friends…you get the idea. That way we'll be able to have a flexible arrangement that suits us both.'

Her mouth had gone bone-dry. He wanted to move to Santa Barbara? To co-parent? It was the last thing she had expected. She wasn't sure what arrangement she had been expecting, but it definitely wasn't this. Quickly, Carrie considered the implications of it—Damon being in her life, day in and day out—and her heart quickened, something she couldn't name thudding beneath her breast.

'So when you said you wanted to be involved, you meant…'

'That I want to be a full-time parent to my child, yes,' Damon clarified, eying her without concern. 'I have no desire to be a part-time father, Carrie. I want to be with my child on a daily basis. I want a relationship from the start. My father was a hugely important figure in my life. I always knew he loved me and was there for me, whatever else he had going on. If I'm anything less than that to my own child, I'll have failed.'

His passionate intensity left her speechless, and she could only stare into his handsome face, transfixed by the determination blazing there. Determination to be a good father, a good man. And in that instant Carrie trusted entirely in his promise to be present for their child. He was willing to change his life for it. To prioritise it.

It was a love she'd never known from her own father, and that made emotion stick at the back of her throat. Because for the first time she actually felt that it all might work out. That she and Damon would be able to make it work because they had common ground in wanting the best for their child.

'And since there is no possibility of you and I being together romantically, this seems like the best available alternative scenario.'

She went cold all over. Her heart clenched and her eyes burned. The sting of his words pierced so deep that for a moment she forgot to breathe.

'Right. Of course. It's the next best thing,' she agreed, hoping he hadn't noticed the beat of stunned silence before she spoke.

Then, picking up her fork, she moved it around her plate, keeping her hands busy and her eyes lowered.

'You're crying,' Damon stated, his eyes burning a hole in her.

'No. I'm not,' Carrie insisted, even as she kept her eyes downwards. It was bad enough that she was upset, but that he could *see* it…

'Yes. You are.'

Reaching out his hand, he extended two fingers under her chin and tilted her face up, baring to his gaze the sparkling moisture that sat on her lashes and blurred her vision.

Beneath her skin sensation pulsed where his fingers rested. It crackled through her, causing her pulse to leap, her blood to race, her skin to colour. But before the feelings could deepen, and she was forced to remember exactly how good it had felt to be touched and held by him, and before that hunger for him wrote itself across her face, she pulled herself free of his touch.

'Fine.' She braced herself to be honest. 'You said that you never planned on being in this situation. Well, neither did I,' she shared, her voice sounding as brittle as she felt. 'When I pictured having a child, I planned on being married, or in a happy, *committed* relationship at least, with someone who loved me and wanted to spend his life with me. So this is not the way I imagined it happening—separate homes, separate bedrooms, separate lives, with our child being shuffled back and forth between us. This is not what I wanted it to be.'

Damon was silent after she'd finished speaking, his fingers tapping out a slow beat on the table. Then, 'Carrie, even if there wasn't the obvious elephant in the room between us, I'm not sure it could be like that. I don't have long-term relationships. They're not what I want. And all you and I shared was one night.'

She held up a hand—a silent plea for him to stop. 'Its fine, Damon, I get it. I'm aware that what we had was just a one-night thing—just as I'm aware that Randolphs and Meyers are right up there with the Montagues and Capulets for families who shouldn't be together. I wasn't asking for the impossible. I just wanted to explain that this is hard for me too. Please don't misunderstand—I'm happy that you want to be involved, and we will find a way to make this work, but it is, nonetheless, hard.' She sucked in a sharp breath. 'One day I *will* find what I'm looking for. For now, I just need to adjust.'

She pushed back her chair, keeping hold of it as she pressed herself to her feet on legs that trembled.

'Thank you for dinner.'

His startled eyes followed her sudden upward movement. 'You're leaving? You've barely eaten anything.'

The last thing Carrie wanted to do was eat. Her stomach was twisted up in knots and the beats of her heart felt more like throbs.

Because she craved something that could never be. Belonging to a happy family unit had always been her dream, and when her parents' marriage had fallen apart she had directed all her hopes to the future…to the family she would build with the man of her dreams. She'd never lost that fantasy, not even after Nate. It had been a comfort to her, something she'd clung to as a promise of better days to come.

And even though she'd known there could never be anything more with Damon, her feelings for him had anchored deep from the moment they'd met, and because of that there had been a tiny kernel of hope that somehow…maybe…

But no! She had been foolish to allow that fantasy to build, and going forward she needed to maintain better control over her heart and her head. Going forward she needed to think of Damon only as exactly what he was—the father of her child. Nothing more.

'I'm all talked out and pretty tired—it's been a long day. But I'll see you tomorrow at the scan.' She spared him a brief glance as she hooked her bag over her shoulder. 'Goodnight.'

Damon rose to follow Carrie as she hastened to the door, his fists clenching as the impulse to reach out, catch her hand and stop her became stronger than the voice in his head screaming constant reminders that she was Sterling Randolph's daughter.

But what good would come from doing that? he thought irritably. Stop her and then…what, exactly?

She was a romantic. She craved the promise of a fairy-tale. He could not offer the words she so longed to hear, nor the future she'd pinned her hopes on. Even if she wasn't a Randolph his offerings would be limited. Relationships created an ever-present threat of loss and pain, neither of which he wanted. Therefore he could not act on the impulse heating his blood and making his heart thunder. It would be unfair to her.

He heard the door shut and stopped, cursing beneath his breath. Releasing a stressed huff of air, Damon wandered back out to the patio, looking up at the darkening sky and making every attempt to breathe through the longing that fogged up his head, to reorganise his thoughts into the correct order.

But ever since laying eyes on Carrie earlier that afternoon he'd thought of only one thing—losing himself in her once again. And every time he'd looked at her since, taking in the glossy waterfall of her ink-black hair, her luminous skin and glowing eyes and full lips—*those damnably kissable lips*—his mind had run wild with thoughts of surrendering himself to the delights of her body, to feeling how she arched beneath him as he found her sweet spot, to teasing her smooth skin with nips of his teeth and swipes of his tongue.

At one point it had become so unbearable he had been seconds away from shoving the table aside and pulling her out of her seat and into his arms. Only the last echoes of self-control had stopped him. Because he simply could not permit himself to do that. Taking her to bed once had been an act of betrayal. To do so again would be an even greater treachery.

Just because she was now carrying his heir, it didn't change what they could be.

It just complicated it.

Because now, for the sake of his child, he *needed* to have a relationship with her.

His own childhood had been gloriously happy. He had been safe in the love of both his parents and the stability of their solid, faithful marriage. He wanted his child to know something as close to that as possible, and his plan to co-parent should ensure that. Carrie had already shown that she would do what was best for their child, but he wondered suddenly and startlingly if she would continue to be amenable to that arrangement once his plan to ruin Randolph had succeeded.

By her own admission she and her father did not share a close relationship, but she seemed to have some tender feelings for the man, so how would she react to her father's downfall and Damon's role in it? His stomach lurched as, for the first time, he considered the possibility that she might reconsider his involvement in their child's life because of his actions.

The thought sat like a rock in his gut, even as he dismissed it as impossible. Carrie was not like his mother, who'd ignored his needs and flitted off with a new man to a new life that had no room for him. Carrie would put the needs and best interests of their child first, even if she was annoyed with him.

Wouldn't she?

Then, with another lurch, he recalled Carrie's words about one day finding a man to share her life with, and angry, scorching flames licked up the back of his throat.

The thought of her lying in the arms of another man…of that same faceless nameless impostor taking his place in her life, in his child's life…

But wasn't it inevitable? Carrie was young, beautiful, vital. She deserved a loving partner. What right did he have to resent the future she would one day find when he was offering nothing? When he had nothing within him to offer.

His throat tightened painfully.

When in a matter of weeks she would learn of the demise of her father's business and that Damon was the man responsible...

Damon glanced at the clock hanging above the door in the doctor's office. He'd slept fitfully, tossing from one side of the king-sized bed to the other. When he hadn't been tortured by carnal dreams of Carrie's perfect form rising up and covering his body, he'd been tormented by more dark thoughts of what would happen to his relationship with Carrie and the baby when his revenge on her father was complete.

As a result his mood was black, and waiting for their appointment to start in this airless room where his every breath was infused with the scent of Carrie was making it blacker. With his chest uncomfortably tight and his heart pumping as if he was running a marathon, he felt more on edge than ever, and was willing the appointment to start just so it could end and he could return to Los Angeles and be free of the constant temptation of Carrie Miller.

Finally, the door of the screening room swung open and a tall woman in her mid to late forties with fluffy blonde hair and a confident air walked in, aiming a smile first at Carrie and then at Damon. It went unreturned.

'Sorry to be a few moments late. I'm Elizabeth, your sonographer. You must be Carrie…' As she spoke she took a seat on the stool at the foot of the bed Carrie was reclined upon. 'And you must be the father?' She looked expectantly up at him.

'Damon Meyer,' he introduced himself tersely, speaking through the lurch of his stomach that had accompanied the word 'father.'

'Good to meet you. Do either of you have any questions before we start?' she enquired pleasantly.

They both shook their heads and with a glance between them she smiled, a knowingness shining in her expression. 'First baby?' When they nodded, she smiled again. 'Let's not keep you in suspense any longer, then. Just watch the screen.'

She pushed up the sheet draped over Carrie's mid-section, baring her still-flat stomach, and Damon gritted his teeth together on a hiss of breath as the exposed curve of her waist prompted bursts of tantalising memory. His lips had kissed that dip as he'd mapped her body with his mouth. His hands had shaped that very curve as she had sat astride him.

As the throb in his groin was reignited, he blanked the heady images from his mind and watched as gel was squeezed onto Carrie's stomach and then spread across her skin with a wand.

The screen filled with a surprisingly clear black and white image, and with her finger Elizabeth pointed to a small peanut shape in the lower left corner of the image. 'This is your baby.'

'It's so tiny…' Carrie breathed.

'Just for now!' Elizabeth laughed. 'Would you like to hear the heartbeat?'

Delight lit Carrie's face, and as she nodded eagerly Elizabeth twisted one of the dials on the machine beneath the screen.

And that was when it happened. The steady, rhythmic pound of a tiny beating heart filled the room and everything in Damon shifted upright in recognition.

That was the sound of *his* child. His child's beating heart.

'Oh, wow.' Carrie pressed a hand to her mouth, an abundance of love shining in her eyes. 'That's incredible. Don't you think that's amazing?' She beamed at him, angling her face to where he stood.

Unable to move, and with his amazed eyes fixed on the screen, Damon could only nod. Because as he looked at this first image of his child, and listened to its strong and steady heartbeat, it was not the roiling dread that he had expected to feel churning in his gut, nor that old familiar fear of love and loss, but something entirely different. Something brilliantly warm and wondrous. Something that lifted him up and made his chest feel like an inflated balloon, suffused with so much joy he feared it might explode.

And the longer he looked and listened, the more incredible he felt. Because there, in the middle of the darkness of the screen, was a tiny spot of bright white light, like a star in a storm, beckoning him on and guiding him home.

CHAPTER SEVEN

CARRIE HAD JUST heard her baby's heart beating and it had been the most extraordinary moment, wiping clear all the sadness that had settled in her bones after the previous evening's dinner with Damon and filling her with more love than she'd ever felt before.

She was still marvelling at the life that was growing inside her, so she didn't register the ringing of her phone until Damon prompted her.

'It's probably just my mom, wanting to know that everything with the baby is okay.' She lifted the device to her ear, wiping away the moisture beneath her eyes. 'Hi, Mom. Guess what I just heard?'

'Sweetheart, don't panic, okay?'

Don't panic. Were there any words more likely to cause panic?

The joy she had been revelling in was numbed by a rush of foreboding. 'Why? What's happened?'

Across the room, she saw Damon lift his eyes, alerted by her tone.

'It seems that a picture of you and Damon in Paris has emerged from somewhere. There are photographers outside my house right now, and outside your house and the bakery.'

Oh, God.

Panic closed its hands around her throat and set her heart racing like a runaway train.

'I don't think you should go back to your house, Carrie.'

'Where should I go, then?' she croaked. 'Grandma and Grandpa's?'

Prue hesitated. 'It will only be a matter of time before they make the connection and show up there too.'

The phone began to shake. It took Carrie a second to realise that it was her hand that was trembling, not the phone.

'I cannot believe this is happening,' she moaned, covering her eyes with her hand. 'I can't go through this again, Mom.'

'Sweetheart, just breathe.'

Carrie did as her mother told her, clinging to the calming familiarity of her voice.

'You can get through this. It will be all right.'

'What is it? What's wrong?'

Damon's sharp voice cut through the air and she uncovered her eyes, but all she could make out was his blurry outline towering over her.

'Carrie?'

Impatience made his voice a harsh rasp against her tender senses and she flinched.

'It's… I…'

But she couldn't form the words, couldn't find enough air to take a breath. All she could think about was the mayhem that was waiting for her outside the four walls she was currently surrounded by.

'Carrie, give Damon the phone. Let me speak to him,'

her mother instructed, and without another thought she held the phone out to Damon, who took it with a sceptical glance.

His eyes narrowed as he listened, his jaw hardening to such a degree she thought it could have cut through glass as easily as a knife through butter, but he held his composure—a feat that to Carrie seemed superhuman as she continued to shake so badly it wouldn't have surprised her if she'd actually started to crack apart.

'No, you're completely right,' he said finally. 'Being here right now is not a good idea, especially if we don't want them learning about the pregnancy. I'll take care of it. I know a place Carrie and I can go to lie low. No, I'll tell her. It will be a few hours, but we will let you know when we get there. Okay. Bye.'

Pocketing her phone, Damon didn't waste a second before springing into determined action. 'We need to get out of here. Now.' He picked up his possessions and quickly checked outside the window. 'Come on.'

Carrie heard the urgency in his voice and knew she needed to move. Only she couldn't. She was frozen.

'Carrie…'

The hand that curled around her cheek was strong and warm, its touch so tender that she felt herself leaning into it, sinking into the reassurance and security it offered. Damon was crouching to her level, his luxuriant dark eyes boring into hers, burning all the way down to her toes, burning through the fear and making it easier for her to breathe the longer she looked into that beautiful gaze.

'We need to leave. I will keep you safe, but we have to go *now*. I need you to trust me.'

Trust me.

He was asking for the impossible, but as his gaze held hers in a silent promise she felt herself nodding. He clasped her hand and gently pulled her to her feet, steering her out through the door. He didn't let go all the way out of the clinic and to his car, like a solid anchor keeping her steady.

He put her in the car, helped her pull the seatbelt across her weak and trembling body, and within minutes they were speeding down the freeway, out of Santa Barbara. By that time Carrie had regained some of her equilibrium, though she was still frightened and darting her eyes out through the back window to see if they were being followed.

'It's okay. There's no one following us.'

Damon didn't take his eyes off the road ahead as he offered his reassurance, and the speedometer was racing upwards at a frightening speed.

'Are you sure?'

He nodded, deftly darting into the neighbouring lane on the freeway, his strong, tanned hands steady on the wheel. 'I have some experience with this.'

'So do I,' Carrie muttered, twisting her hands together in her lap, an action she knew his alert eyes didn't miss even as she quickly pulled them apart and wedged them beneath her legs.

'Are you okay?'

Carrie glanced at him and then quickly looked away, scared that everything she was feeling, every ounce of her fragility, would be visible in her expression.

'What did my mother tell you?'

'That you suffer from panic attacks.'

Carrie stiffened. 'It's one of those things that sounds worse than it is,' she asserted, with a defensiveness she couldn't help. 'It's not a constant thing. I just have flare-ups in certain situations.'

'I'm not judging you, Carrie,' he said. 'I brought it up just to see if you were okay, so you could tell me if you're...struggling. So I can help.'

'I've been worse.'

'But you've also been better,' he stated, reading what she hadn't said. 'When did you start having the panic attacks?'

Crossing her arms, she directed her stare straight ahead, resenting that she had been thrust into a situation that demanded she share any of this with him. The last thing she wanted to do was open herself up to him. Secrets and scars were meant to be shared with those who loved you, and that definitely wasn't Damon. He'd made that clear the night before, and Carrie had spent the past twelve hours drilling it into herself how important it was that she guarded herself from him emotionally.

He was the father of her child, nothing more. They needed to be amicable, nothing more. Yet she could tell by the expectant silence that he would wait as long as necessary to get an answer.

'When I was eight,' she relented eventually.

'Eight?' he repeated, astonished colour darkening the line of his cheekbones. 'What could have possibly happened when you were that young to—?'

He broke off as his mind completed the calculation and came to the obvious conclusion. To the one thing their relationship always came back to.

'The scandal.'

Carrie watched his knuckles glow white as his hands tensed around the steering wheel.

'What happened?' he asked.

'Life went crazy. Everyone wanted a piece of my father...our family. Every time we set foot outside, the press swarmed. Basic trips to school and the shops became an ordeal. We were followed, photographed incessantly, screamed at on a daily basis. It was horrific.'

Even speaking about it brought it too close, and she momentarily closed her eyes to block out the memories.

'For me it became debilitating—our faces all over the papers, everybody watching us and talking about us. That's when the panic attacks started. I was too frightened to leave the house. I stopped going to school. It was the main reason my mom moved us back to California during the divorce.'

She suppressed a shiver, the memory leaving her chilled to the bone.

'I never want to go through that kind of insanity again.'

Inhaling deeply, and reminding herself that in this moment she was safe, she tried to focus on the landscape flying past the window. It was only then that Carrie realised she had no idea where Damon was taking her.

'Where are we going?' she demanded, with a turn of her head.

'Ojai. It's about an hour outside of LA.'

'Why there?'

'I have a home there,' he answered crisply. 'I lived there for some of my childhood.'

Carrie kept her expression neutral even as her pulse

jerked. He was taking her to *his house*? She wasn't so sure she liked the sound of that. She needed to be somewhere she could feel safe and calm—and he made her feel neither of those things.

And then an even more unpleasant thought occurred. 'Does your mother still live in Ojai?'

'No,' he responded after a brief hesitation. 'My mother never lived there.'

Carrie chewed on her lip in confusion. 'But you...you said you lived there for some of your childhood...'

'My father was from Ojai. When he was alive we visited often. But I went to live there full-time after he died, with my father's sister, my aunt Bree, and her family.'

'Why didn't you stay with your mother?' Carrie probed, peering at him more closely and noting the way his jaw was clenched, as though his memories were hard to contend with.

'She remarried very quickly and relocated to Europe,' he replied. She saw a nerve beginning to pulse in that solid jaw. 'She felt that, given everything that had happened with my father, it would be better for me to stay here, with his family. That it would be too much upheaval for me to leave.'

He was trying to paint a civilised picture of what had transpired, but Carrie was not fooled. She could see the ugly truth of it.

'She sent you away from her?' she gasped disbelievingly.

Judging others was not something Carrie liked to do—not after the way she had been scrutinised and judged just for being her father's daughter, over and over again, and goodness knew Damon and his mother's lives had been turned upside down with the sudden death of Jacob. But to willingly separate from her child at a time when he'd needed her most…

Carrie knew there was no universe in which her mother would fail to be there for her. Prue Miller had always put Carrie first, uprooting her whole life to safeguard her daughter. And, although she did not know her baby yet, Carrie could not foresee any hardship being so great that she would part from her precious child.

'It wasn't quite that stark or simple,' Damon expressed with a bite of irritation, his darkening gaze still fixed resolutely ahead. 'My father had lived to make her happy. He'd handled everything. She was cherished and insulated. But everything surrounding his death was so ugly that it was too much for her. She wanted to still be insulated, and she found someone who could give her that.'

'But you needed to be protected and insulated too,' insisted Carrie. 'You were just a boy.'

His admission the previous night that he had no desire for a long-term relationship had left her stunned, but it was little wonder after he'd learned at a young age that relationships offered no guarantee of for ever. How could he trust in any woman to stay by his side when his mother had so easily left him behind? How could she have treated him that way?

He glanced across at her and, expecting some kind of rebuke, Carrie was startled when those spectacular planes of his face that were always so hard in his regard of her softened, smoothing into something that edged towards tenderness.

'You're going to be a good mom, Carrie.'

Amazed, she could only stare back at him, trying to fathom what had prompted the high compliment and wishing he had not issued it. Because it had caused feelings she didn't want to feel for him to fizz in her stomach and at the apex of her thighs. Feelings which only intensified as his eyes turned molten with a sensual golden gleam.

Her bones shook. Heat swelled between them, surrounding them, and at once Carrie was aware of a tingling in her breasts, and the way her nipples were hardening into tight and begging buds.

Furious with how quickly she had fallen under his spell, she pulled her gaze away.

'I'm tired… I may just close my eyes for a little while,' she said, staring straight ahead but seeing nothing as waves of traitorous heat continued to crash through her.

'That's a good idea,' Damon agreed, clearing his throat. 'We'll be on the road for another hour or so.'

She turned her face away, bewildered that the glitter of his eyes had been enough of an invitation to send her body spinning out of control. It was exactly what she had instructed herself *not* to let happen!

Refusing to dwell on it any longer, Carrie slammed her eyes shut, determined to put him out of her head. But in the dreamscape of her mind Damon was waiting, and in his eyes was that intoxicating golden shimmer, and when he reached out to touch her she did absolutely nothing to resist him…

As he slowed the car to a stop at a red light, Damon took his eyes off the road to glance beside him at Carrie's sleeping form. Her chest moved gently up and down, her feathery lashes brushed the skin beneath her eyes and her deep pink lips were pressed firmly together.

She was so achingly beautiful that once it was on her he could not tear his gaze away. Nor did he want to look away. He was happy to simply stare at her, remembering how it had felt to be seated deep inside her, how she had come to life in his arms when he'd crushed those velvet-soft lips beneath his own. Each time he looked at her, feeling that all-over tug of urgent desire, he felt the will to resist doing so again eroded a little more.

He'd never known anything like it. He was used to liking a woman, pursuing her or responding to her pursuit of him, enjoying a brief, fun-filled affair and then walking away. Never had he been tempted to prolong any of those interactions. Never had he craved more. He'd never felt a *need* for a woman, as if she was critical to his survival. He'd never been physically incapable of drawing his eyes away.

With her it was different.

But everything was different with her.

She made him consider a different life…the pursuit of other priorities. Like family. Partnership. Love.

All the things that he had closed himself off from after his father had been killed and his mother had turned away.

All the things he'd decided he didn't want because they posed too great a risk.

But for reasons he didn't understand around her they felt…*possible.*

The sharp blast of a horn at his rear prodded him back

to his senses and, seeing the light had turned to green, he slammed his foot down on the accelerator and zoomed forward, now less than ten miles from the last place he had expected to find himself.

Damon retained his home in Ojai because the house was a connection to his father, a piece of his inheritance, but it was a bittersweet place for him. A place with a thousand happy memories of life *before* and a thousand bleak memories of life *after*.

But it was a location very few people knew to associate with him, making it a safe place for Carrie, and that was the most important thing—especially after seeing the fear that had overridden her every defence, infiltrating every inch of her until she was cold to the touch.

Damon had had no idea she had suffered so much in the aftermath of the scandal. He'd been so preoccupied with his own pain and what he'd lost it had never occurred to him—not even in the time since—that the scandal had created numerous victims, inflicted untold suffering.

At the first test it seemed he'd lost sight of all the lessons his father had worked to instil in him—consideration, empathy and understanding.

Just like his mother, he had been selfish in his grief.

For that, he was ashamed of himself. Ashamed that he'd been so blind and thoughtless. Ashamed that he'd not acted like his father, or the man his father would have expected him to be. Ashamed of the way he'd taken every opportunity to bludgeon Carrie with the hurt of his past when the whole time she had been carrying around her own burden of hurt.

But now he knew and he would be better.

Starting with Carrie. He would protect her the way she should have been protected as a child. As far as he was concerned it was one more crime to add to Randolph's docket that he had failed to ensure his daughter's physical and emotional wellbeing, and it made his blood bubble with fury. But *he* would not fail her. He would keep her safe, doing all in his power to ensure she was never made to suffer again—by the press, by her father, or by himself.

But even as he made that vow a voice in his head questioned how he would keep it.

His actions of revenge would guarantee that their families were swept up in a new media storm, and no amount of hired security could protect her from the trauma of that. Nor would he be able to protect Carrie from the pain of seeing her father's life in ruins. And what of the pain she would endure when she realised *he'd* been the architect of it all?

Randolph deserved everything that was heading his way. *But*, that voice in his head demanded, *if you also cause Carrie pain with your actions, are you any better than her father?*

CHAPTER EIGHT

OJAI HAD TO be one of the most beautiful places on earth, Carrie thought, as she admired yet another spectacular view from yet another window of Damon's home, this one stretching towards the mountains. Standing on the terrace of the guest room designated to her, she grazed her eyes over the majestic scenery, breathing in the scent of rosemary and lemon blossom as a soft breeze kissed her face.

She had just been stirring when they had arrived at the town limits, and although her sleep had been fraught with dreams of Damon and nameless figures chasing her, waking to the quaint and rustic glamour of Ojai had made her spirits lighter.

Then Damon had steered the car along a very quiet road, turning in at a set of high carved iron gates and following a brick driveway. And there, nestled amongst the abundant greenery of trees and hedges, had been the most beautiful villa. With bright white walls, terracotta roofs, and the trickle of a fountain hidden amongst the lush and colourful garden.

Carrie had loved the oasis on first sight, and inside had proved just as beautiful, remaining true to its Spanish colonial style with tiled ceilings, white walls and a flowing and open concept.

Damon had spared just enough time to give her a quick tour and show her to a bedroom before taking a call from his assistant and issuing instructions to postpone and re-arrange scheduled meetings. That had been over forty minutes ago, and she hadn't seen him since—which was hardly surprising, given that she was probably the last woman on earth he wanted to share his home with.

Whilst Carrie was grateful she hadn't been alone to manage her panic when she'd received that call from her mom back at the clinic, and was even more grateful that Damon's quick thinking had allowed them to escape unscathed, being far from home and an unwanted house guest was hardly ideal.

Carrie was still lost in those bleak thoughts when she was startled by a noise behind her. Twisting her head over her shoulder, she felt her heart jerk to see Damon in the open doorway.

'You settling in okay?' he asked with an easy smile.

She nodded, wishing he was asking because he cared and not because she was his responsibility by virtue of the baby she carried.

'My assistant has arranged for a selection of clothes and personal products and whatever else she thinks you may need to be delivered.'

'Thanks.'

But she was struggling to make her answering smile stick to her lips and Damon noticed it, surveying her with concern.

'What's the matter? Are you still feeling anxious?'

'No. I feel a lot better than I did. I just… I feel bad you had to get involved,' she admitted uncomfortably. 'I overheard the start of your call with your assistant…organising how to rearrange your meetings. I've completely upended your life with this.'

He advanced towards her, his body seeming more powerful, more commanding, in the casual attire of black jeans and a black tee.

'You haven't upended anything. Technology being what it is today means I can have meetings any time, anywhere.'

His kindness was unexpected, and his words sounded sincere, but they did little to expunge her feelings of guilt.

'Really, don't worry about it.'

'I just can't help but think that if I'd told you who I was straight away, none of this would be happening right now,' she blurted out.

Damon stilled, his eyes creasing at the corners. 'Is that what you wish you had done?'

'Yes.'

Because then her life wouldn't be under attack for a second time by a horde of paparazzi. Nor would she be a burden to a man who didn't want to spend time with her and whom she was loath to trust too much in case her trust was misplaced—*again*. On the other hand, if she had been honest with him they would probably not have shared that magical night together, and she wouldn't trade those memories for anything. And she also wouldn't be carrying his child.

The thought of that parallel world made her queasy.

'No,' she amended quickly, regretting her outburst and knowing that even if the chance was offered to go back in time and do it differently, she wouldn't. 'No, it's not. I just wish everything wasn't such a mess.'

'It's not a mess. The furore over this picture will die down. The press will find a new story to pick apart and they'll forget all about us. And until then you're safe here.'

'And after that?' she asked, hugging her arms around herself and wishing it was *his* arms tucked tight around her. But that only made her nerves feel more frazzled. 'At some point it will get out that I'm pregnant, and that the baby's yours, and when it does…' Carrie couldn't even complete the sentence without feeling overwhelmed.

'We'll figure it out,' he was quick to assure her, injecting his voice with a steeliness that garnered her faith. 'Whatever it takes, I will keep you and our baby safe. I won't let you go through what you did as a child. I give you my word.'

With a single step he closed the space between them, and she felt a tug low in her stomach at his nearness.

'We are in this together.'

She had to tip her head back to look at him, and the look in his eye set her heart pounding. 'Do you really mean that?' she asked, so badly wanting to believe in the promise contained within his words and his gaze, but so accustomed to words carrying no more weight than air.

'Yes, I do.'

And then he made the most remarkable move, stunning her into stillness. Reaching out, Damon brushed a stray tendril of hair behind her ear, the tips of his fingers lingering against her cheek. Sparks cartwheeled though her as a dusting of gold exploded in his gaze. Scared to move or breathe, in case she broke the connection, she waited for his next move, willing him to make one, to offer some signal that he felt everything she did…that she wasn't imagining these moments of pure physical, sensual connection.

But then her phone chirped from her bag, where she had dropped it on the floor, shattering the moment. Damon dropped his hand and with a sigh Carrie reached down to extract the offending item, her features growing taut as she checked the display.

After a brief hesitation, in which her finger hovered indecisively, she rejected the call.

'Who was that?' Damon enquired, eyes sharp.

'Jonathan. My brother.'

The phone rang again. Carrie took one look and jabbed it so it fell silent.

'And Wren. Obviously they've seen the headlines today. No doubt Xander will be next.'

Anxiety advancing once more, she collapsed onto the edge of the bed, dropping her head into her hands. She loved her half-brothers, but she wasn't sure she had the energy to give them the fight they were calling to have. She already knew they'd be furious with her. As ardent followers of their father, anything that displeased him, displeased them.

The phone rang again. Xander, as predicted.

'Exactly how big a problem are they going to have with this?'

Carrie raised her gaze to Damon. 'With the rumours about you and I? A pretty big one.'

'Which you knew would be the case,' he ascertained from her expression. 'And yet you still came to the party? To me?'

Carrie held her breath. She had risked her relationship with her brothers and her father that night in Paris, knowing that if they ever found out about any flirtation between her and Damon they would be uncompromising in their anger. But she'd been desperate to see him one more time.

Now Damon knew that too. And it caused her stomach to drop away. Because all she wanted was to protect herself, protect her heart, and yet he seemed to be accessing more and more of her.

A look so fleeting she had no time to decipher it shot across his eyes like a shooting star. He kept on looking at her, and she was powerless to do anything but gaze right back at him until her phone buzzed once again.

Not bothering to glance at the caller ID, she sighed. 'I should answer. They won't stop until I do.'

'Do you want me to talk to them?' Damon offered, making no move to leave.

'I think that would be the equivalent of pouring oil onto a fire. It's better if I deal with them.'

'Then I'll give you some privacy.'

With seeming reluctance he walked to the door, leaving Carrie with the impression that he didn't really want to leave her. But that was unlikely, wasn't it? Because he definitely didn't want to spend any more time with her than he had to.

But what about his promise to protect her, and that tender caress of her face…?

Her heart tripped at thinking about it again.

However, as her phone rang again, with more insistence, she put those thoughts aside, raised it to her ear and took a deep breath.

* * *

Damon retreated to the seclusion of his office and forced himself to remain there and not dwell on the conversation happening upstairs that was technically none of his business. He made himself sit at his desk and go through his emails, respond to the most urgent. To review plans. To sketch.

Even when he heard the gentle patter of her feet descending the stairs, and his body reacted with exhilaration, he made himself stay still, stay seated. To remain distant and detached even if it was only a physical distance, because he'd failed to remain emotionally disconnected.

When his nose detected scents of something mouthwatering being concocted by her talented hands, he battled the compulsion to go to her, to just be near her. Because he couldn't. Or, more accurately, he shouldn't. And he certainly shouldn't want to.

Yet he did, and none of the distractions he'd employed had succeeded in quelling that want, or in dimming his awareness of her being just a few metres away.

When, with a tentative knock, she appeared in his doorway, Damon devoured the sight of her, his hands curled into fists around the sides of his chair because he did not trust himself not to fly from his seat, pin her delicious body against the nearest wall and feast on her.

Despite the trauma of the day, and the strain hugging her eyes, she looked as beautiful as she had first thing that morning. So much had happened in the past ten hours. So much in his own mind had shifted and become uncertain.

'I'm not disturbing you, am I?' she asked, when he didn't immediately speak.

'No. How did the conversation with your brothers go?'

'About as unpleasantly as expected.' She shrugged her shoulders up to her chin. 'They were furious and they had lots of questions, which was not helped by my telling them that how I spend my time and with whom is not their business. They said I was being disloyal…that you have some vendetta against our father because of…everything.'

Damon stilled, his pulse stalling. 'I'm sorry it didn't go well.'

Carrie shook her head, brushing off his concern even though he could see she was troubled. 'I've made some food. I thought you might want to come and eat.'

He definitely wanted to devour her…all of her…very, *very* slowly. But since that was the last thing he should do…

'I'm not all that hungry, but thank you.'

Moving deeper into the study, she stood right on the other side of the desk, which suddenly seemed far too narrow. She was so close that with every breath he was catching the scent of her shampoo—something soft and calming. He had been hit by it earlier, in the bedroom, and once more the scent propelled his mind back to their night together and how, even as he'd half slept, he'd been conscious of that scent, using the arm anchored around her waist to pull her closer, so he could bury his face even more deeply against her fall of dark hair…

'Damon, my guess is you've not eaten since breakfast. If you're going to work for hours on end, then you need sustenance. So come on… I'm not taking no for an answer. Consider it a thank-you for all you've done today.'

'All right.' Catching himself smiling at her insistence, he got to his feet and walked in silence with her to the kitchen where the most delicious aromas swirled in the air, tempting his stomach. 'How many people were you actually cooking for?' he asked, seeing everything her busy hands had made.

The laugh that escaped her lips was self-conscious, but oh-so-sexy. 'I know… I went a little overboard. But whenever I feel anxious or stressed I cook,' she confided. 'It was my grandmother who started it. When the anxiety attacks were at their worst, she thought if I had something to focus my mind on it would help me take back control of my body. She was right. Measuring out ingredients, working through recipes, all that stirring and kneading… It helped me channel my energy and calm down. And it felt so good I wanted to spend all my time doing it.'

She had plated up their food as she talked, and it was only as she sat down that she looked at Damon's expression as he took his first mouthful.

'You don't like it?'

He swallowed. 'It's delicious. I don't think I've ever tasted anything so good, and I've eaten in some fairly high-end restaurants.' He sampled another forkful. 'Your talents are *not* limited to baking. With food this good you could be running a five-star kitchen.'

'Restaurant hours are a nightmare. And they wouldn't fit in very well with caring for a baby.'

'Is that why you didn't become a chef? The hours?' he queried, because he couldn't see what else had stopped her.

'Actually, when I first left cookery school I figured my path would take me to a restaurant. And I was actually offered a job as a pastry chef.'

'What happened?'

The light in her face dimmed. 'I very quickly learned that I'd only been offered the job because of who my father was.' Her eyes travelled up to his. 'The chef wanted to ensure her new restaurant was a success. She thought hiring me would earn the patronage of my father and all his wealthy acquaintances.'

'You wouldn't be the first person to get a job because of nepotism,' he pointed out.

'No, but it's not how I wanted to get that job—or any job. It's not how I wanted to live my life…always having to wonder if I was good enough or if I just had the right name. I wanted to earn it…to be the best. I wanted that job because there was no one else who could do it as well as I could. Not because I was someone's daughter.'

He heard her resentment and for the first time realised what a weight her father's name and reputation must have been to shoulder. 'And that's why you changed your name?'

She nodded. 'I just want to be able to be myself, to be free. I don't want to always have a target on my back. To always wonder if it's about me or my name.'

Damon frowned at her aggressive phrasing. *A target on her back?* 'The person who hurt you…the one you mentioned to me in Paris…that was to do with your name, too, wasn't it?'

'Yes.'

She fidgeted, making it clear she did not want to unlock that box of memories, and for that reason Damon knew that whatever happened had been bad—because she was inherently open. He saw that about her now. Saw how difficult she must have found it to know she had not been telling him the whole truth about herself.

'Let me get you more risotto,' she said.

Grabbing her wrist as she tried to rise, he prevented her from running away. 'You can either tell me yourself, or with a quick call I can have someone else find me the information,' he said, gentling the threat with a softer than usual tone.

Her agitation skipped up a few levels. 'Why do you even want to know? Why does it matter?'

'Because we're having a child together, and that necessitates us knowing certain things about each other.'

At least that was the convenient explanation. In fact, his desire to know was a lot deeper and simpler than that. He wanted to know. Wanted to know *her*. Her hurts, her bruises, her scars, her hopes and fears. He wanted to know everything.

Carrie sent him an arch look. 'Yet when I asked about your mother leaving you, *you* were not very forthcoming. Why should I share with you when you won't with me?'

Touché.

'I don't know how to talk about what happened with my mother,' he confessed, steeling himself for the searing pain that accompanied any thought or words about her. 'My father died and it broke her heart. I understand that. But the choices she made afterwards—to remarry so quickly, to send me here—I don't understand. I'd like to think that she did what she did because she thought it was in my best interests, but I'm not sure I believe that.'

'Do you ever see her?'

'She and my stepfather live in the South of France. She comes to the States maybe once a year. We have lunch.'

'Lunch?' she repeated, bewildered.

He nodded solemnly, struck again by the realisation that Carrie was as different from his own mother as it was possible to be.

She sighed. 'His name was Nate. The person who hurt me. He worked for my father and he was ambitious. He saw me as a way he could progress faster. I thought he was charming and kind. I'd always liked the idea of my own fairy-tale, so the thought that he'd fallen madly in love with me at first sight was intoxicating. But then he didn't get a promotion that he wanted, so he went to my father and attempted to blackmail him. He said he had photos of me that he would take to the press, along with details of our relationship, if he wasn't given an executive position.'

She paused, twisting her fingers together, her plate of food forgotten.

'He said he loved me, but all along he'd only cared about himself. I was just a means to an end.' Giving a tiny shake of her head, she pressed her eyes shut as though the simple act would erase it. 'I was so stupid not to see it.'

'No, Carrie.' Damon hurried to reassure her, hating it that she blamed herself for even a second. 'People like that are very good at what they do. *You* are not stupid.'

It was then that he saw the glisten of tears in her eyes.

'My father didn't see it that way. He was so angry that I'd exposed him and his business to humiliation. I'd always known his work mattered more to him than anything, that everyone else came second to the Randolph

Corporation, but knowing it and seeing it are two very different things. And that was the day I saw it. My heartbreak and humiliation didn't even hit his radar. He didn't even ask if I was okay.'

'That's why you don't have a relationship with him?' Damon asked quietly, suddenly realising their faces were only inches apart. Without his noticing, their bodies had inched closer together, their knees brushing beneath the table.

Carrie nodded sadly. 'I wanted to be close with him so badly. When I was younger and he didn't show up I told myself not to be hurt, that he was a busy man…he did important work. Then Nate happened. All I wanted was to know that he cared about me, but the only thing he cares about in life is business and success. It's all that matters to him. All he sees.'

Damon's gut twisted, because he knew the same ugly accusation could be levelled against him, and in the past it had been. It was a comparison that had his stomach writhing and bile climbing up his throat. Because if there was one man on earth he didn't want to be like, it was Sterling Randolph. A man who had respect for nothing and nobody except the almighty dollar. And it was the second time that day he'd realised he might be more like him than he cared for.

'The truth is my father doesn't have relationships. He has the Randolph Corporation. That's his only meaningful relationship. And waiting for him to open his eyes and see you is like waiting for rain in a drought.' She sighed, the sound carrying a lifetime of disappointment. 'And yet I still hope that one day he will open his eyes.'

'Why?'

Damon didn't bother to temper the harshness of his disbelief. He'd never been short on reasons to despise Randolph, but the way he had treated Carrie incited in him a fury that would have made the gods quake. So to hear her openly admit that she still harboured hopes of a reconciliation with the man was mind-blowing.

'It doesn't sound as though he's been any kind of a father to you.'

She lifted her shoulders in a small, non-defensive shrug. 'Because he is my father,' she supplied simply.

And, looking into her guileless gaze, he realised that it was that simple for her. In Carrie's view, no matter what sins he had committed, Randolph was her father, and that was a relationship she would always stand by with love and loyalty, even if it was unreturned. She was that open-hearted. That pure. Once she loved, she loved for ever. And that was a lot like *his* father. So like his father he felt a crippling twist of his gut.

'And because I understand why he is so infuriatingly single-minded…why he pours all of his energy and attention into the Randolph Corporation.'

'Why does he?' Damon asked after a beat. He was unsure if it was a sensible question to ask, but she'd piqued his interest.

'Because he grew up very poor. When his father died, my dad, as the oldest, got a job so the family wouldn't be homeless. He went to school in the daytime and worked at night at all of fourteen years old. Can you imagine that? Having the responsibility for your whole family on your shoulders when you're just a boy? Knowing that whether they eat that day depends on you?'

Carrie shuddered, and even Damon had to acknowledge the icy chill skating across his broad shoulders at the thought of such desolate circumstances.

'Eventually he dropped out of school entirely and worked full-time to take care of them. Even when he started his own company and began to make big money he never stopped taking care of them. So everything he's managed to achieve in his life is incredible. And I think he believes that if he takes his eyes off it, even for a second, it will all disappear. I think that fear is what drives a lot of his actions. It hurts me, but I think it's understandable.'

Damon reached for his water glass, taking a long swallow. His throat felt like sandpaper.

This was information he'd never had any desire to know. Damon had made it his business to learn everything about Randolph's business affairs, but the finer details of his life had held zero interest. It had been enough to know that the man had brought about his father's death, and seeing him like that, in black and white, had suited him just fine.

But the particulars Carrie had just revealed shaded him in colour. It was hard to align the man who had endlessly provided for his family with the villain who had traded his father's life for a greater profit, and it was hard not to feel some admiration for the man who had built his empire from dirt and air.

And that strange new feeling, wedged like a thorn in his side, was giving him uncomfortable pause for thought, raising quiet questions, for the first time ever, over what would happen to the man once Damon had succeeded in bringing about his downfall. With those facts of his life pinballing around his mind, Damon knew his vengeance held not only the power to bring his empire crumbling to the ground, but to cripple the man who sat at its helm.

It should have been a satisfying feeling. A few months ago it would have steeped him in elation.

But now…it didn't.

And that disturbed him more than words could express. Because thinking of Sterling Randolph as a human being… *No!* He could not afford to start thinking of Randolph as a person if he was to defeat him…not now…not when he was so close.

'You show a lot of understanding. More than I would argue that he deserves,' Damon intoned, clawing back his anger.

'I think everyone deserves understanding and compassion.'

'Everyone?' Her sentiment struck a flame to the emotions kindling within him and he eyed her with dangerously simmering outrage. 'Is this your less than subtle way of telling me to let go of my anger towards him? To find *understanding and compassion*?'

'What…?' Bewilderment clouded her expression. 'No. Of course not. I'm just… We're talking… I was speaking for myself… I—'

'Because that is never going to happen, Carrie,' he exploded, his breaths heavy, his words loaded with a fury that was pressing against his chest like a bar of steel. 'What he did is unforgivable. There's no way back from that.'

* * *

Carrie's throat was so tight with emotion she could barely swallow, let alone speak, but after a long moment, punctured only by Damon's furiously ragged breaths, the question tearing at her emerged.

'Is this how it's always going to be?'

Her voice was small and quiet, but the stare she directed at Damon commanded an answer.

'Everything I say, everything I do, you'll assume some ulterior Machiavellian motive?'

He looked away from her. His sharp cheekbones were ablaze with colour and a nerve pulsed in his jaw, but he made no effort to respond. And in that deafening and frigid silence Carrie knew she had her answer.

She pressed her lips together to lock in the cry of anguish that tore through her. Could she be any *more* stupid? She had thought something in him had softened towards her. She'd actually believed that over dinner and conversation they were forging a new connection. A tentative one, of course, but something new…something that was just about the two of them. But no, it could never be just about the two of them, could it? Damon would never *allow* it to be. His anger over the events two decades ago was anchored so deep in him that it spilled across all else like a flood of thick black oil.

Suddenly exhausted, drained by the effort of trying and hoping and being let down, Carrie scraped back her chair and pushed herself to her feet. She was no longer interested in hearing whatever answer he might concoct, or in waiting to hear it. Nor in giving him yet another chance.

The only consolation she could draw was that at least she now knew unequivocally where she stood. That pesky, hopeful part of her that was always waiting for the sunshine to break through the clouds had pushed her to hope that there could be more between them—even if only a friendship—that it might be possible for him to see her as Carrie the way she saw him as simply Damon. Not as the sum of his parts, or a victim of his past, or the face of his successes—just him. But no. Not possible after all.

Her eyes were well and truly open now, and the clarity was so bright it was blinding.

'Carrie…'

'Do not!' She pulled her whole body out of his reach as he followed her hasty retreat from the kitchen with a thudding stride. 'Do not touch me. Do not talk to me. Because no matter what you say it's never going to change. How you look at me…the way you see me. In your eyes I will never be anything more than his daughter.'

Even in that moment, even looking at him with exasperated eyes, Carrie thought how achingly beautiful he was. But all he ever saw was her father.

'The only thing I want you to do right now is to leave me alone. And stop pretending to care.'

Once again he made no response before she turned and launched herself up the stairs, firmly pressing the door to her room closed and resenting the lack of a lock on the door. Not that she thought he would make any attempt to come to her, but Carrie wanted to physically complete the action of locking herself safely away from him.

Realising that every inch of her was trembling, she set herself down on the edge of the bed and dragged a sheepskin throw around her shoulders. She fixed her gaze on the verdant valley beyond the window, and when she felt her hand was steady enough reached for the glass of water on the bedside table.

Hot, hateful tears scorched her eyes and rolled down her cheeks as the depth of her stupidity pierced her all over again. She had prised herself open and revealed to him her heart, her scars, her fears. And with that caustic reaction he had thrown her trust and vulnerability back at her. Would she never learn?

Carrie assumed he would apologise, the same way he had before. He would blame too many emotions, too much stress, maybe. But she didn't want another apology. She wanted him to be different, to be better.

And therein lay the problem.

She was waiting for him to be the man she'd met in Paris. Only that Damon didn't seem to exist. And she couldn't keep on waiting and hoping. Not again.

It was exactly what she'd done with her father—hoping and waiting for him to be a better man, a better father. A father who cared and who made time for her. She had waited and waited…and she was still waiting.

Carrie would not consent to subjecting herself to the same torment with Damon.

It might have felt like a fairy-tale when they'd met, but there was never going to be a fairy-tale ending for her and Damon.

CHAPTER NINE

IT WAS NO USE. Eyes wide, Carrie knew she wasn't going to achieve any more of the fitful pockets of sleep that she'd managed throughout the night, so she flipped back the covers, slid her feet from the bed and, trying to make no sound at all, crept across the floor and eased open the door.

Firing glances left and right, to make sure the corridor was clear, she tiptoed down the stairs, making for the kitchen in search of an activity to occupy her mind and her hands—the only activity that would satisfy in her state: baking.

But she came to an uncertain stop when she saw the kitchen was already occupied. The doors were pushed back entirely and Damon was leaning with one strong shoulder against the wall, his attention fixed on the horizon, where the sun was cresting the gentle slopes of the mountains.

Her heart thudding, Carrie started to retreat.

'Don't leave.'

She stopped, the words commanding her even though they were the very opposite of what she wanted to do.

'You don't need to leave.'

He turned as he spoke and the moment their eyes

locked Carrie felt all the pain of the previous night weave through her afresh, but the impact was dimmed by the sight of something dark harrowing his expression.

'You're awake early.'

'I haven't been to sleep,' he admitted, eyes pinning her with their haunted darkness.

Carrie nodded and averted her gaze, walking towards the cupboards. 'I was thinking of making some breakfast, if you're hungry. Maybe pancakes. Or bagels.'

Opening a cupboard, she reached in and retrieved whatever her hands touched, too aware of Damon closing the distance between them to be able to concentrate. She didn't want him near her because she didn't know what she would do. The urge to slap him was very real, but so was the desire to sink against him, cling to his hard body and cry out all her pain.

'I know you don't want an apology,' he began, sounding shaky and very unlike himself, 'but I want you to know that I *am* sorry for last night. For jumping to conclusions. And for hurting you.'

Tears pricked at her eyes. The words were kind, but as she had feared they were not enough. They weren't the words she wanted, nor the ones she needed.

'Let's just not dwell on it, okay?' she said, feeling exhausted at the thought of going round and round again and getting nowhere. 'It's not like it was anything new. Let's just focus on how we can work together for the good of our child.'

She was letting him off the hook, so she didn't understand why Damon's expression remained bleak, his shoulders pitched high with tension.

'But, like you said, it's there between us. Always.'

Crossing his arms over his chest, he dug his hands into his underarms and a ripple of foreboding shot through her.

'There are some things that I would like to tell you… to explain, if you're willing to listen.'

Carrie was only used to seeing him in supreme control, assured and solid, so that witnessing him on a lower vibration was unsettling. But it was clear that whatever was on his mind troubled him, and she wouldn't refuse him the opportunity to unburden himself. Nor would she deny herself the opportunity to maybe finally understand him better.

'I'll listen,' she said, meeting his eyes properly for the first time since entering the kitchen and feeling the expected shiver slither through her.

Damon gestured to the patio. 'Let's sit outside.'

Carrie instantly tensed at the thought of taking the same places they had the previous night, but Damon led her to a more casual seating space that overlooked the pool and towards the mountains.

As they both sat he leant forward, legs splayed, elbows balanced on his knees and his head bowed, as if physically burdened by whatever he was on the point of revealing. The forlorn sight hollowed out her stomach, and with a fretful leap Carrie's heart launched itself into her throat, its uneven beats escalating more the longer Damon went without speaking.

But whatever this was, she sensed that he needed to begin in his own time, when the right words came to him.

She only had to wait a few more minutes.

'The day everything happened in Chicago…the day

my father died,' he began, looking down at the ground. 'I was there.'

'You were there?' she repeated, floored by the confession.

How had she not known that? Since meeting Damon she'd scoured through everything she could find about the scandal, wanting to know it all, attempting to understand him.

'Nothing I've ever read about that day said anything about you…'

'My family kept it out of the press and convinced the authorities to do the same. They thought I'd been traumatised enough, witnessing it, without my name being in all the papers and having reporters clamouring for my story,' he explained dully. 'But I thought you had a right to know. And after last night, the way I reacted to the mention of your father, I wanted you to know. So you could understand why I…why I reacted the way I did. The way I always do.'

Her skin chilled as the truth sank in. He had been there. He'd watched his father die.

'Why didn't you tell me this sooner?'

'I've never talked to anyone about it.'

Being lumped in with everyone else hurt, even though Carrie knew that the momentous shift of emotion she had experienced upon meeting him had only ever been one-sided. For him it had been a bolt of attraction that, once fulfilled, had quickly expired. Not life-changing, as it had been for her.

'I never speak about that day. I rarely talk about my

father. That night at the chateau with you was the first time in a long time I've spoken to anyone about him.'

The memory of that magical night made Carrie ache all over and she hugged her arms around herself.

'All this time I've not really understood why you have so much anger towards him. But the fact that you were there, that you saw it—'

She broke off, pressing a hand to her mouth, incapable of saying anything more. She didn't know what she could say. Her head was buzzing, her thoughts too.

He'd been there.

At last it all made sense. Damon finally made sense. His hatred, his anger. That one moment, so destructive and yet so pivotal. All her questions answered in that hidden truth.

'It was awful. It was like a nightmare.'

He swallowed and looked off to the side, and when he drew a desperate breath it wasn't to draw the conversation to an end, as Carrie had fully expected, but to resume sharing.

'He would never have taken me with him if he'd thought there was any danger. He thought he'd smoothed over all the problems, that he could get everything back on track. It was meant to be a half-hour meeting and then he and I were going to spend the day together. He was going to take me to a ball game. But when we got there the crowds were already gathered. My father had security, and they tried to rush us in, but it was still chaos,' he recalled with a wince. 'The shouting, the protesting. The jeering. And then the firing. Just two shots. That was all. Everything went silent, like time stopped. And then it all came back into focus. I had been thrust to the floor. Everyone was screaming, bolting in different directions. I looked around for my father. He was lying on the floor, a few feet away from me. I thought he was okay… I started to crawl towards him, wondering why he wasn't getting up…and then I saw the blood.'

Damon's eyes swam, but his gaze was far off, back in that day. Carrie couldn't move, could only listen, even though she knew how it ended.

'All of his chest was red. I tried to stop it with my hands, but it was everywhere…pumping out of him. He said my name and reached out his hand for mine. He said "It's okay. I love you." I kept holding his hand. I didn't take my eyes off him. But he was gone by the time the paramedics got there. And I was still holding his hand.'

Tear-tracks scarred his cheeks and his breathing was uneven, and when he turned his head, his eyes locked Carrie under their dark spotlight.

'I felt his heart stop beating beneath my hands, Carrie. I felt it the moment his life ended.'

Tears flooded out of her eyes. How dark and frightening the world must have seemed to him in those immediate moments. How alone he must have felt, especially when his mother had abandoned him not long after.

She wanted to tell him she was sorry, but it felt so insufficient. She wanted to tell him she understood his pain, but she knew there could be no understanding the agony he'd been made to suffer. It made her feel useless, so achingly inadequate that there were no words that she could offer that would help or heal him.

All she could really offer was herself. Her empathy. Her emotion. The assurance that he was no longer alone.

But would he accept it?

Unable to bear the distance separating them any longer, Carrie moved to the seat beside him. She tucked her arm under his, laced her fingers with his and pressed her face into his shoulder.

'I'm so sorry, Damon,' she whispered against his skin.

His body was rock-hard with tension, the tendons in his strong arms standing out. He said nothing, and the only move he made was to rub the pads of his fingers against her knuckles. After a few moments of sitting like that, he unlaced their fingers. Carrie shifted upwards, bracing for him to pull away from her, but he kept hold of her hand and trailed his fingertips in dazzling, sizzling patterns along her palm.

Hot sparks ignited in her stomach, excitement shifting through her veins at the slight and simple caress. It shouldn't have been so provocative, but Carrie struggled to keep her breath steady—a feat that became even harder when Damon raised her palm to his face, curling it around his cheek. The skin-to-skin contact sent a jolt through her. His stubble-roughened jaw felt delicious beneath her hand and she exhaled sharply.

He turned his head, and his dark eyes bored into hers. She didn't blink, didn't dare to breathe, didn't want to do anything that would interrupt the moment. But the need to feel more of him beneath her fingers eventually won out, and gently she allowed her thumb to trace small circles on his skin. His eyes drifted closed, his lips curving into a facsimile of a smile. When his eyes opened again it was as if they were on fire, so bright and burnished, and all Carrie craved was to be kissed by that unique heat, branded by his flame.

As if he was reading her mind, he leaned in to capture her mouth, slowly drawing his lips across hers. Her craving awakened fully, she launched herself onto his lap, curling her arms around his strong shoulders and pressing herself to him as hard as she could, matching the urgent feasting of his deep, drugging kisses.

Her blood hummed with the intimate contact. Their physical reunion was everything she had been yearning for day and night for weeks. The slide of his lips and the stroke of his hands soothed every ache in her body and answered every wish of her heart. It was sweet and sharp, deep and needy. It was everything.

And Carrie wanted every second of it—along with so much more. She wanted the tight embrace of his arms, the weight of his powerful body above hers. She wanted him to drag down her top and bare her breasts to his mouth. She wanted him to rip off her underwear and ride her to sweet fulfilment.

But he didn't want that. In his eyes she was tainted.

'Damon, wait.'

Somehow managing to disengage her lips from his sweet mouth, Carrie braced her hands against his shoulders to stay out of reach. She made an attempt to slide off his lap, because trying to think with his enormous erection straining against her was impossible, but he held her too fast.

'We shouldn't do this,' she muttered, shaking her head and trying not to look at him. Because she knew that one look at his face would cause her to crumble. 'It isn't what you want—not really. You'll regret it…just like you regret that night in Paris.'

'I won't regret it,' he said, and there was tenderness in his eyes as he forced her to meet his gaze. 'And I definitely don't regret our night in Paris.'

'But…'

Silencing her with a finger across her mouth, he continued, 'The only thing I will regret is if I don't have you in my bed again.'

Carrie wanted to believe him more than she'd ever wanted to believe any words spoken to her, and even though she had convinced herself that all he felt about that night was remorse, the glint in his eyes and the feel of his hands on her waist told a different story.

As he slowly pulled her mouth down to his, Carrie didn't resist. Sinking into the hot, slow strokes of his tongue, she felt warmth suffuse her. Fear forgotten, she allowed her body to open to his, crushing her breasts against his chest, rubbing the apex of her thighs against his growing erection.

Through the thin fabric of her pyjamas his fingers burned where they touched, and she squirmed with her need to be free of the flimsy fabric. She reached for the hem of her top at the same moment he did, and together they pulled it over her head. Then Damon brought his mouth to her nipple, moving his tongue in a neat circle before suckling with such intensity that streaks of lightning shot straight to her molten centre. She could feel herself splintering as he offered the same worship to her other breast and knew his words had to be true. He had to want her. He could not caress her with such reverence if he did not feel something for her.

'Carrie, kiss me,' he commanded throatily, and she lowered her parted lips for him to drink from, loving the satisfied growl from the back of his throat when their mouths crashed together. 'It's not enough,' he growled against her mouth. 'I need to make love to you. I need to be inside you.'

'Upstairs?'

Her shook his head, his eyes burning with a fire she could feel thrumming beneath his skin.

'Here. Now.'

There would be no complaint from her.

Reaching down, she manoeuvred the fastening on his trousers so his erection sprang free and held his velvet length between her fingers, drawing her eyes up to watch how her touch commanded an instant reaction from him. His eyes were closed, face contorting with delight and resistance, and she grew even more bold, squeezing gently to see an even greater play of emotion, delighting in the power she possessed over him.

'Carrie…' He groaned. 'If you keep doing that you're going to kill me,' he said on a pained laugh.

She laughed, too, but released him as his hands firmly gripped her hips to rip away her shorts. She positioned herself above him, her pulse leaping with enthusiasm for what she knew was coming next, before slowly sliding herself down his length, his firm hands on her hips helping to guide her.

As she took him all the way inside her Damon's fingers bit into her skin to hold her still. His eyes locked on hers, the connection burrowing into her soul, and as he fitted within her so deeply, so perfectly, it was as though he was her missing piece.

When she could stand it no longer Carrie began to move her body, sliding up and down his remarkable length. Their mouths sought each other's, open and greedy, and as the friction built beneath Carrie's skin Damon began to caress her flesh where their bodies were connected, pressing the pad of his thumb to the bundle of nerves to intensify the sensations taking over her entire being.

His mouth sought her nipple again, coaxing it into a hard peak with the wetness of his tongue, and with those ministrations sending her hurtling towards a beautiful oblivion Carrie lifted and sank on his length with increased need. The joy of his thickness penetrating so deeply and sweetly inside her was all that mattered in the world. All she wanted was to savour their joining. To prolong it.

Damon braced an arm against the back of the sofa and thrust as she sank, and Carrie pressed her hands to his shoulders as his rhythm pushed her into territory that had her gasping and edging towards explosion. After a further thrust from Damon she tumbled over the edge in a shattering of emotion, to be quickly followed by Damon with only a single word emerging from his mouth.

'Carrie.'

CHAPTER TEN

DAMON STIRRED AND reached out an arm, only to discover that the bed was empty. His eyes flew open, his body tensing at the possibility that it had all only been another of his vivid dreams. But then he caught that light flowery scent on the sheets and knew it had been real. He and Carrie had spent the last twelve hours in bed together and, far from experiencing any guilt about that, all he felt was disappointment that he was alone amongst the tangled sheets.

Setting out in search of her, he headed straight for the kitchen, guided not just by his instincts but the scents drifting throughout the house. And sure enough there she was, her hands a blur as she diced and rolled and stirred.

Damon watched her quietly for a moment, shamelessly appreciating the sight of her in his shirt, her bare legs on display and the material made almost translucent by the slant of the late-day sun. Once again he tested his feelings, waiting to feel that sharp stab of guilt that he had broken his vow and bedded the enemy—but there was nothing of the kind.

In sharing the whole truth about the day his father had died he'd only wanted to enlighten her as to why his emotions got the better of him whenever her father was mentioned. But as he had confided in her Damon had realised he was giving her the ability to better understand him, and the freedom that had come with that, and the release he'd felt after finally sharing his harrowing experience, had been so profound that he'd wanted more of it. Had wanted to shine a light on the shadows that haunted him. To rip at the ties that bound him, the bonds of his own creation.

And kissing her had done exactly that. Kissing her had felt like freedom and peace. And it had felt so good to stop fighting his feelings and embrace them that he hadn't stopped kissing her. Hadn't stopped at all. And the surrender had been divine.

Coming up behind her, Damon slid his warm hands around her waist, liking the way she instantly melted against him. Brushing her hair aside, he grazed his lips against the tender skin of her neck, where she liked to be nuzzled, increasing the pressure as she murmured her pleasure. At the same time his fingers loosened a single button at the front of the shirt, so his hand could slide inside, teasing across her ribcage and up to her breasts. He cupped the generous swells, repeating the slide of his fingers across her nipples as her body arched in response to the sensation.

'That's the second time I've woken in a bed that you should have been in and weren't,' he whispered into her ear.

'You were sleeping and I didn't want to disturb you. I also thought you'd be glad of something to eat when you woke up,' she murmured.

'Hmm, I'm definitely hungry.' He continued the assault of his lips against her neck, shifting towards the lobe of her ear and the hollow beneath her jaw whilst his fingers played with her nipples until they were taut and she was squirming. 'You sure that's the only reason you didn't stay in bed?'

The minuscule hesitation in both her speech and her hands affirmed that his suspicion was correct. She was baking because she was anxious about something.

'I thought you might feel differently once you woke up,' she admitted, and he felt the sudden drum of tension beneath her skin. 'That you might regret…'

Damon held on to her tighter. 'I told you already… I don't regret anything.'

'If you did, I'd understand,' she continued, as though he hadn't spoken. 'You were upset, and in need of comfort, and…'

'Carrie.' He turned her, tilting her head back so their eyes connected. 'I don't regret a single thing that's happened between us.' It felt very important that she knew that. 'At one point I wanted to. Desperately. But I never did. And I don't regret today. I don't want to undo anything. I want to do it again and again and again.'

He punctuated each word with a kiss, revelling in every murmur she made before pulling her even tighter against him until there was not a single part of their bodies not touching.

'But nothing's changed,' Carrie breathed, fearful shadows dancing in her eyes. 'The past…'

'I'm not interested in the past right now.'

All that ugliness felt a long way away, and all he cared

about, for the first time in a long time, was what was right in front of him. The happiness that he could reach out and take. That he *wanted* to reach out and take. Everything else was irrelevant.

'I'm only interested in this. In us.'

And in a demonstration of exactly that he lowered his mouth, the searing hot slide of his lips demanding the capitulation of hers, and slowly Carrie's body relaxed, surrendering to the compelling pressure of his mouth, the hot and hungry sweeps of his tongue. And as she rose to her tiptoes to kiss him back with an equal fervour, feeding the hunger pounding through his blood, Damon caught her around the waist, lifted her off the floor in a single swoop and set her on the marble top of the island, trapping himself between her legs and holding her tight against him.

With impatient yet deft fingers he worked apart the rest of the buttons on the shirt and then pushed the sides open, so all of her was bared to him. He palmed her breasts as he continued his assault on her lips, before dragging his mouth down her neck into a fiery exploration of her chest. Curling his tongue around her nipple, Damon sucked until she cried out, and he would have kept up the pressure—except Carrie was reaching for him, placing her hands on either side of his face and pulling his mouth back up to hers, coaxing his tongue back inside her mouth.

As they kissed with a fiery rhythm, and Carrie's desire manifested itself in moans into his mouth, Damon's own fever began to throb more insistently, even though he would have thought it impossible for him to want her more than he already did, to want her all over again when he'd spent hours already tasting and touching her in bed.

But knowing how and where she liked to be caressed, and how it felt to slide inside her, was an electrifying familiarity. It was as thrilling to him to know the explosive orgasm that awaited him as it had been to touch her for the first time.

Too aroused, too crazed, to play any longer, he pulled her to the very edge of the counter and fastened his hands to her hips, feeling her wetness as he positioned himself at her entrance. To know that she was that eager, that ready for him, made him even harder, and as he drove powerfully into her Carrie arched, her hands clasping his shoulders, her nails biting into his skin and her green eyes exploding with dazzling emerald colour.

With each strong and claiming thrust she clung tighter to him, her moans ripped from deep within her throat, the sounds unleashing such a fire within him that Damon didn't know if he would ever get enough of her to put it out. But then he plunged into her a final time and they crashed into their climax together, and the storm that broke inside him was so intense that every inch of him pulsed with a fulfilment unlike anything else he'd ever known.

Carrie's heart pounded in a reckless, uneven rhythm, but it was matched by the frenzied beats pulsing in Damon's chest. Burying her face in the sweet-smelling nook of his neck, she inhaled the scent of his skin and splayed her fingers against the smooth, strong muscles of his back as she waited for the violent lashes of the orgasm he had given her to subside into pleasing, teasing ripples of silky sensation.

Damon had turned her inside out half a dozen times already, but none of those moments had been as passionately explosive at that one.

And she knew why.

'I'm not interested in the past. Only this. Us.'

They were the magic words she'd been longing to hear since… Oh, only since the first moment they'd met. And they had unlocked so much within her—everything she'd been trying to contain. Hope. Need. Desire.

Lying awake in his arms a short while earlier, Carrie had been thrumming with nervousness, convinced that, regardless of what he had said about not regretting anything, once he woke he would feel remorse for making love to her again. She had fled his bed solely to spare herself the hideousness of that moment. But then he'd come after her and issued those words, and with the promise of them glowing in his eyes, the truth of them burning in his hungry kiss, the uncertainty she felt had quietened, slipping almost entirely from her mind, leaving her free to give in to her need for him, her feelings for him.

She knew it was a risk, because she couldn't give her body without engaging her heart. But if there was a chance that they could be *something* to one another, a chance to explore all that moved and burned between them, a chance that she could better know the complicated, emotional, compassionate, sexy man that was Damon Meyer, that was a chance Carrie wanted to take. For herself and for their child.

She wouldn't waste time fearing it or questioning it. She would simply accept it. Embrace it.

In spite of the chaos happening in the outside world, Carrie and Damon enjoyed a blissful few days in the seclusion of his Ojai estate. Damon showed her all around the house and the gorgeous land surrounding it, walking her through orange and avocado groves and sunflower gardens. She felt such peace and contentment that in certain moments she even managed to forget about the media craze that had propelled them there in the first place, but generally it was never far from her mind, and when she emerged from the bathroom one morning, her body still humming from their steamy session in the shower, and saw Damon's frowning expression as he hung up the phone, her stomach clenched.

'What's happened?'

'Nothing bad.' Strolling towards her, he pressed a reassuring kiss to her forehead. 'It was my aunt Bree, reminding me about my cousin's birthday dinner tonight.' He sighed. 'I suppose since I'm here I should make the effort to go.'

'You don't normally make the effort?' Carrie asked, slightly surprised, as she'd seen the fondness with which he talked of his cousins. The most breathtaking smile had lit his face when he'd shared stories of growing up with them in Ojai, although it hadn't escaped her notice that most of those tales hailed from the time when his father had been alive, further proving just how much his world had changed, darkened, in the days after he'd died.

'I'm not in Ojai that often.'

'LA isn't that far away.'

'I'm not always in LA either,' he countered, turning away from her with a look that expressed aggravation at being questioned and striding to the closet, snatching the first tee shirt he touched.

'And that's what's stopped you from showing up? Geography?'

Carrie's eyes narrowed as he kept his back to her, his muscles tellingly taut, and her senses clanged with the warning that they had stumbled into difficult emotional terrain. And even though it was obvious that Damon wanted to retreat and hide from whatever feelings had been stirred up, Carrie wanted to know and understand them. To help him.

Closing the space between them, she ran her hand down his tense arm. 'Damon? Talk to me.'

It was a long moment before he spoke. 'I've got very good at keeping myself separate, okay?' he admitted roughly. 'After what happened, I didn't want to be close to anyone. I didn't want to take that risk.'

He was scared to love in case he lost again, Carrie realised with a painful twist of her heart.

'That's understandable. You went through something awful, losing your father and then having your mother walk away too. You're trying to keep yourself safe.' She paused, wondering how far her new privileges extended...if she could push a little deeper without scaring him into shutting her out too. 'The only problem is that doing that stops you experiencing good stuff too.'

Carrie knew that from personal experience. Fear had made her hide herself away and she'd missed out on so much… If she hadn't taken that chance with Damon in Paris she'd have missed out on something extraordinary. And if Damon couldn't conquer his fear, what did that mean for the future? Would he hold back from his child to avoid being hurt? And what about *them*?

He'd made no promises, and Carrie hadn't asked for any. They were simply acting on their mutual attraction and enjoying it. But if he remained a hostage to his fear of loving and losing she knew there was not even the hope of it turning into something more.

'I've kept my distance for so long, Carrie…' He sighed. 'I wouldn't know how to change even if I wanted to.'

She smiled, his words giving her hope that he *wanted* to change. 'I think you start by showing up at that party and let it go from there.'

He fired her a look of scepticism. 'Just show up? After years of not showing up?'

'Yes. And they'll be happy. The people who truly love you just want you with them, and everything that's gone before will become irrelevant once they have you back.' She slid against him, worked herself into his arms. 'They'll understand—even if you can never find the words to explain it to them.'

'Not everyone is like you, Carrie. Not everyone is compassionate and willing to forgive.'

'If your aunt didn't want you there she wouldn't have called. That was her telling you that she loves you and is there for you. Family is important, Damon. You have people who love you. Don't shut them out. And if not for yourself, do it for our child. Because he or she deserves to have family and love in its life.'

He looked away, but she knew he was thinking. Considering.

'Would you come with me?' he asked.

Carrie hesitated. Having trained himself to rely on only himself, Damon asking for her support was monumental, but as much as Carrie wanted to help him reconnect with his family, she was wary.

'Is that such a good idea? Me with your father's family?'

Nerves rattled beneath her skin at the thought. She didn't think anything could be as bad as Damon's reaction to her identity, but walking into a room where every single person had lost a cherished family member because of actions kick-started by her father would be unpleasant.

She would be *Sterling Randolph's daughter* once again.

'You'd have nothing to fear from anyone in that house tonight,' he promised.

The weight in her stomach lessened only slightly, but she smiled anyway. 'Of course I'll go with you.'

The truth was, she realised in that moment, she would go anywhere with him that he asked her to. Any time he asked. Even if it meant facing her own fears and experiencing discomfort.

Because supporting him was more important.

It was a depth of feeling that scared her, because whenever she had allowed herself to feel with such ardency in the past, her heart and her spirit had been crushed. And, with the way her feelings for Damon grew so rapidly each day, any damage to her heart by him could prove irreparable.

* * *

Damon had been right when he'd said she had nothing to fear from his family.

Everyone was warm and welcoming from the moment she walked through the door. If they were surprised that she, of all the women in the world, was accompanying Damon, they didn't show it.

She was ushered inside, the strawberry shortcake she had made especially for the dinner was gushed over and added to the waiting table of culinary treats, and her bakery business was queried with immense interest. Immediately put at ease, she transferred her attention to Damon, watching his interactions.

He was tentative at first, falling into what she imagined was his usual pattern of holding himself back and keeping everyone at a distance, but eventually he grew easier, laughing fondly with his cousin Noah and reliving long-ago boyhood exploits. And in watching his family, Carrie saw her words had been right. They were delighted to have him there and to have more of him than he'd previously been willing to share.

Happiness warmed her insides. Knowing how tough it must be to face that fear of loving and losing, she couldn't be more in awe of him for attempting to break the habits engraved in him over a lifetime.

After dinner, when the family had dispersed to different areas of the house, Carrie found herself admiring the display of family photographs on a sideboard in the large hall. In a gold frame was a picture of Damon and Noah, young and tanned, heads pressed together, smiling at the camera with such joy and the lightness that Carrie now knew Damon had lost when he'd lost his father. Then her gaze snagged on a different photo at the back of the display—a photo boasting a face that was easily recognisable: Jacob Meyer.

As she took in the lively eyes, bright smile and broad shoulders, the lump growing in her throat felt as if it was wrapped in barbed wire. Standing in front of him, with his father's arms loosely draped around him, was a young Damon.

'Damon's quite like him, don't you think?'

Carrie jolted. She hadn't heard his Aunt Bree approach, and to be caught red-handed, holding the picture of Jacob… 'I'm sorry. I didn't mean to…'

'It's fine.' Bree offered her a reassuring smile. 'You're only looking at the photographs. It's why I have them out.' She picked up the frame Carrie had set down in a panic, looked at it lovingly.

'You must miss him terribly.'

'I do. He was a good brother.'

'I'm sorry for what happened to him…for the part my father played.'

'Thank you.' Bree touched a hand to her arm. 'Although you have nothing to apologise for—you were a little girl. And your father—whatever part he played—didn't pull the trigger. It was a tragedy, and no one suffered for it more than him.' She stared intently at the snapshot of Damon. 'It's wonderful to see him finding some happiness at last—to see him letting himself be happy'

'I want him to be happy,' Carrie heard herself say, unsure why the subject of his happiness brought such sadness crashing down on her.

He had opened up to her and let her in, but there was still so much she didn't know, and the future seemed so unclear. Was Damon really ready to let go of the past and the animosity he carried because of it? Would he be able to regain the spirt of that laughing, carefree boy in the photograph? Would he ever fully open his heart?

And was Carrie risking her own heart by opening it to him?

CHAPTER ELEVEN

'THERE HASN'T BEEN anything new about us online today,' Carrie mentioned, taking a bite from her meal as they ate dinner on the veranda, the sun setting behind them.

Bathed in the dying rays of light, her black hair shone and her eyes danced with colour, and Damon ached for the moment when he would lead her inside, tease her from her clothes and tumble her onto the bed.

'I noticed. I told you they would move on.'

'I guess that means we'll be going home soon, then?'

Damon faltered at the question. He hadn't given any thought to returning home. He'd been too busy enjoying Carrie and the intimate routine they'd established in their hideaway to give any consideration to leaving. And as her question rolled around his mind the thought of returning to reality was an uneasy one.

'We could... Although I have another idea.' He thought quickly, the plan taking shape in his mind with such ease that he couldn't halt his smile. 'Come to Paris with me.'

'Paris?'

'Yes. I have a few meetings arranged, but I don't need to work the whole time, and there's Jean-Pierre's daughter's wedding at the chateau. It could be fun to go back there together,' he coaxed.

Carrie watched him, a smile tugging at the corners of her mouth. 'You really want me to go with you?'

'Yes, I do,' he replied, realising as he gave the assurance just how badly he did want her company.

A happy blush rose in her cheeks. 'I'll call Marina and my grandmother, and if they're happy to cover for me at the bakery for a little while longer, then, yes, I'll come to Paris with you.'

Three days later they were back in the City of Light, and Damon felt an unexpected pleasure in returning to the city where his connection with Carrie had been forged and their child had been conceived.

With the combination of jet lag and her pregnancy fatigue Carrie was exhausted when they arrived, so Damon insisted that she remain at the penthouse and rest whilst he attended his meetings. She laughed at his overprotectiveness, then agreed, and he parted from her reluctantly with a long kiss. But his concern for her meant that more than once during his meetings his mind strayed to her.

He returned to the penthouse to check on her mid-afternoon, when he had a short break in business, and was relieved to see the colour had returned to her cheeks and the dark crescents beneath her eyes were fading. By the following morning Carrie was back to her bright, energetic self, and after an early breakfast meeting Damon happily devoted the rest of the day to her.

Life was different with Carrie at his side. It was fuller, brighter. It had never occurred to him that he was missing out on something extraordinary by not sharing his time and his space with someone, but she filled gaps in his life and within himself that he hadn't known existed. With her, he saw a different way to be, a different way to live. He'd reconnected with his family because of her. He had faced those awful traumatic memories and felt their power over him lessen. She was light and air, breaking up the darkness that had surrounded him, and with her he focused on the good, dwelling less and less on the past and feeling less burdened because of it.

His feelings for Carrie had deepened and grown so substantially that increasingly Damon caught himself contemplating the future, looking ahead to when they would be joined by their little one with excitement running through his veins and a smile on his face.

But even as that sense of pleasure grew, a corresponding unease stacked in his stomach. The Caldwell deal winner would be announced any day, and Damon's certainty that vengeance was the right—the *only*—thing had slackened. He'd been unable to forget what he'd learned about Sterling Randolph. Those facts surfaced in his mind randomly, but always with the same prodding at his conscience, and then he'd look at Carrie and the stab would pierce even deeper.

He'd always looked towards the day of the Caldwell announcement as a day of triumph for him and a day of reckoning for Sterling, but Damon was starting to wonder if it would be his own day of reckoning instead…

As Carrie emerged from the bedroom Damon turned from his contemplation of the city below them and the look that filled his eyes threatened to unbalance her. No one had ever surveyed her with such unrestrained appreciation and appetite, and even though her first thought when she'd appraised herself in the mirror that morning had been that she looked beautiful, Carrie had attributed that to the hair and make-up experts who'd readied her for this exclusive wedding so she didn't tire herself. But the way Damon was looking at her made her feel as though it was far more than that. That in some way she was essential to him.

'You're ravishing.'

He smiled with a wolfish curl of his lips, leaving her in no doubt that he was envisaging all the ways he would like to ravish her. Carrie made a mental note not to let him touch her before they were out through the door, because given how turned on she felt under his heated attention, and how sensational he looked in his tuxedo, it was unlikely she would be able to resist. It was also entirely possible she would be the one to drag him to the floor and set about tasting every inch of his body.

'And you're mine.'

'All yours,' she breathed, melting beneath his words and feeling in that moment how very much she did belong to him, how she ached for him to be unequivocally, officially hers.

When he surveyed her with so much delicacy and awe, and uttered sentiments like that, it made her believe that was what he wanted too. But the truth was she just didn't know.

The future Damon saw for them, if any, was a mystery, and Carrie was too scared to ask. Her mind was alive with hopeful fantasies of the life they could share together—beautiful and blissful visions of family and love and laughter—but the memory of past disappointments was never far away. And although Damon had opened himself up to her, and given her reasons to believe in him, she found it a struggle to trust entirely. Especially when sometimes it felt as if he was still holding things back.

He'd unburdened himself about his father, but in certain moments he still seemed to carry leaden thoughts that cast his whole expression in anguish. When she asked him he'd tell her it was nothing, but Carrie was certain she could detect turmoil in him, and she was afraid it was about them…that even with the best of intentions the thought of a future with her—a Randolph—was too much to overcome.

Worries like that should, she knew, give her pause for thought, but it was hard not to want everything with Damon when their child's heart beat in her body, and when every time she thought of their child, or looked into Damon's burnished gaze, she was aware of how much of a capacity for love she had.

And those desires of her heart only grew larger in her mind later, as she watched the wedding at Chateau Margaux. As she watched the bride and groom clasp each other's hands, stare lovingly into each other's eyes and pledge their eternal and unfailing love to each other. With tears shining in her own eyes, Carrie knew she wanted exactly that. She'd always yearned for that kind of love, and ever since Damon had come into her life she'd longed for it with him.

It was all she could dwell on as they moved from the ceremony into the celebrations.

'You're quiet tonight,' Damon commented as he led her onto the dance floor, pulling her in close to the heat of his body. 'Are you feeling unwell?'

'I'm fine,' she assured him. 'I'm just enjoying the wedding. I never thought I'd be here again.'

'I've never wanted somebody as badly as I wanted you that night. I'd never wanted *anything* as much as I wanted you. And from that moment to this one that's never changed.'

His actions constantly told her that, but to hear it from his lips was an altogether different kind of delight, and Carrie felt herself blush.

'When we get back to California, I want you to look at properties with me,' he told her.

'Okay. I'd love to.'

'Good. Because I was thinking that you might have some interest in living there too.'

Stunned, she stopped moving and could only stare up at him. 'You're… Are you asking me to live with you?'

'Well, we are having a baby together,' he said with a deep smile. 'And I know what I said before…but it's different now.' He dropped his mouth so it brushed her ear and said, very intently, 'I don't want to miss a second of any of this, Carrie. And I don't want to be apart from you if I don't need to be.'

His admission gave her the freedom to speak some of her truth. 'I don't want to be without you either.'

'So that's a yes?'

It was everything she could want. Her heart felt close to bursting.

'Yes!' She beamed.

* * *

When Carrie woke the next morning she was curled up in Damon's arms. His fingers were absentmindedly stroking down her hair, and beneath her ear she could feel and hear the steady beats of his heart.

Memories of the previous night filtered through her mind: the way he'd held her as they watched the fireworks display at the chateau, how he'd carried her up to the penthouse from the car, the slow and sensual way he'd undressed her, kissing every single inch of her, and how her feelings of safety and happiness had deepened, settling across her like a blanket.

'I know you're awake. Your breathing's changed.'

She smiled, pressing a kiss to the warm skin of his chest. 'Good morning. Is it late?'

'It's a little after ten. What do you say to breakfast on the terrace and then a leisurely Sunday wandering around the Marais? You said you wanted to explore it a bit more.'

Resting her chin on his chest, she gazed up at him. 'That sounds perfect.'

She bestowed a kiss upon his lips, and then another. And as the taste of him was so good she couldn't stop herself from stealing another. But they could never stop with a single touch. Within seconds their limbs were tangled, their bodies curved into the shape of each other.

Carrie trailed kisses over his torso, scratching her teeth against his nipple and drawing from him that groan she loved so much. Her hands explored his taut, hot skin, seeking his hard length, and as she found it she stroked over him, feeling brave and bold and sure, and smiling as he bit out a ragged curse. Damon punished her laughter with a hard kiss, rolling her onto her back and moving her hands above her head, pinning them with his own. Teasing her body with his, he made her wait until she was squirming before sinking his length into her.

They made it to the Marais a short while later. One of the oldest districts in France, its narrow cobblestoned streets, hidden courtyards and tranquil gardens offered a glimpse of what Paris had been centuries ago, and Carrie was immediately enthralled by its beauty. They explored the maze-like streets and Damon was in his element, admiring the stunning architecture of the ancient aristocratic mansions. He showed Carrie the intricacies of the designs and she relished his enjoyment, his passion.

Hand in hand, they strolled through the Place des Vosges, the sunshine on their faces, before investigating the boutiques and galleries lining the square. With help from Damon, Carrie selected gifts for her grandmother and Marina, to thank them for taking over for her at the bakery whilst she'd been away, and Damon sought her opinion on works of art that he liked as he considered adding to what she learned was an extensive collection.

When their legs were begging for relief they stopped for an early dinner at a restaurant on the banks of the Seine and, closeted at a secluded corner table, they watched as the fading light sent its last sparkles across the slow-moving river and the city became illuminated as darkness descended.

It had been the most wonderful day, Carrie reflected later, when they were back at the penthouse. For the first time in weeks the future seemed clear. Like seeing far-off mountains on a cloudless day, she could see the life that lay ahead of her: making a home with Damon, welcoming their child in less than six months, becoming the type of family she had always wanted for her child. And for herself.

So what if he hadn't actually told her that he loved her? After everything he'd been through Carrie knew it wouldn't be easy for Damon to say those words. But all his actions showed how much he cared for her, and actions spoke louder than words, didn't they?

But if she truly believed that, why could she feel small frissons of apprehension skittering through her mind…?

Damon couldn't sleep, and the glowing numbers on the clock showed him just how long his tormented thoughts had kept him awake. Unable to stand it any longer, he extricated himself from Carrie's arms and slid from the warm bed, pulling on his clothes and heading for the building's luxury pool.

One hour and well over a hundred lengths later, Damon's muscles pleaded for a respite, but he continued to cut through the water, pushing himself harder, determined to excise the anguish from his mind.

The path before him had once been so straight and simple. Everything had been about organising Sterling Randolph's undoing. But now there was Carrie and their baby, and life with her was so good and easy. Every time she'd looked at him that day it had been with stars in her eyes and a smile brighter than the sunshine, and that had caused his heart to twist. Because he wanted to bask in the love she so readily offered, to take her hand and run into the future with her. But how could he when seizing that future with her would demand he abandon his revenge, let go of everything that had driven and anchored him for all his adult life?

Damon had imagined himself doing it—picking up the phone to make the call or send the email that would end it all—but, as much as a piece of him yearned to do exactly that, he knew he wouldn't. *Couldn't.* Because if he didn't finish this Randolph would get away with it. Again. He would never be made to pay for his sins. And Damon couldn't stomach that injustice. He deserved that victory—for himself and his father.

Carrie meant so much to him, but she wasn't more important than his revenge.

And it wasn't as though love came with any guarantees. Throwing away all that he'd worked for to be with Carrie didn't ensure them a future together. He could lose her, just like he'd lost his mother, and he certainly didn't have much faith in his capacity to love her the way she deserved to be loved. Look at how easy he'd found it to close himself off from his family and remain that way.

Carrie believed he could be redeemed, but he would only disappoint her in the long run, and if he lost both Carrie *and* his shot at revenge he'd have nothing. It would have all been for nothing.

Finishing a length, Damon came to rest at the side of the pool, his chest aching with exertion and the weight of his decision. He was at a crossroads. He could have Carrie and their baby and the promise of a bright future or he could have his revenge. There was no way he could have both. And if he made the wrong choice, he ran the risk of ending up with nothing at all.

* * *

The email arrived in Damon's inbox at ten the following morning.

He'd won the Caldwell contract. All he needed to do was sign it and Sterling Randolph would be ruined. Revenge would finally be his…

But suddenly Damon knew how wrong that was.

There was no victory in vengeance. There was only more pain and loss. And he wasn't prepared to lose Carrie just to settle a decades-old score. Because having her in his life was more important than anything else. *She* was all that he needed to be happy.

How he had ever doubted that he could love her was beyond him, because in that second he knew with blinding clarity that he could and he did. And to think of how close he'd come to destroying that—and to wreaking havoc on her father's life—was so horrifying he was almost choking on it!

But fortunately it wasn't too late for them. She had no idea of the monumental mistake he'd been so close to making, so he still had the chance to claim the future with her that he so desperately wanted.

And he wanted to start straight away by telling her how much he loved her and how grateful he was for her.

He was getting to his feet when his phone rang. Isobel's name was flashing on the screen.

Knowing with absolute certainty the way forward, Damon answered immediately, speaking before she did.

'Put a hold on that contract,' he directed her.

'A—a hold…?' Isobel stammered disbelievingly. 'But you only just—'

'I'll explain later. Just put the hold on it,' he repeated urgently, hanging up.

He located Carrie, sitting out on the terrace with the sun streaming over her, looking so beautiful his heart skipped a beat. She was staring at the phone in her hand. As he approached, his feelings ready to burst out of him, she lifted her head—and what he saw had his ecstatic heart slowing. Her face had lost all its colour and her eyes were clouded with a suspicion and anger that only sharpened as she looked at him.

With a sick feeling drilling down from his chest to his stomach Damon knew that he *was* too late. Somehow she knew everything.

He'd finally realised he loved her. Only now he was going to lose her. And there was no one to blame but himself.

Carrie stared up at Damon, the information that had just been communicated to her by her brother Xander spinning in her mind.

It wasn't possible, she thought frantically. It *couldn't* be possible.

But the dots were joining up to form a horrifying picture in her mind, and in her chest her heart was thundering with a dread that was quickly boring into every bone in her body.

'Carrie…' Damon started, his expression constricting.

'My brother just called me,' she said, managing to speak through the leaden weight on her chest. 'My father's in hospital. They think he's had a heart attack. Because you won the Caldwell contract and he didn't.'

She didn't take her eyes off him, wanting to see every flicker and flutter of emotion. Wanting to see the truth.

'Did you know that he was in the running for the project too?' she asked.

Damon hesitated only slightly before nodding once.

'And did you also know that there's been tension over his leadership at the Randolph Corporation? That he needed to win that contract to stay in control there?'

The silence between them stretched tight as she waited for him to answer. The weight on her chest tripled as she beseeched him to say something, *anything*, that would make more sense than the notions running through her mind. But hot, angry tears were already brewing in her eyes, because she could feel, like the tremors of an earthquake, that the truth was about to be revealed, and that it would bring the beautiful life she had been living crashing down.

Damon had been lying to her. Manipulating her. He was as bad as all the other men she'd ever known. And on some level she wasn't even surprised. She'd known all along that he was withholding something from her. Known she'd given over her trust too easily and freely... that she had pinned her hopes on a man destined to disappoint her. She should have listened to those repeated warnings from her head.

'That's why you wanted that contract,' she said, realising the extent of his deception. 'To get back at him. To ruin him.'

Carrie had expected it to strike her with the force of a wrecking ball, but it didn't. It was much slower, sinking into her like a thousand thorns, a pain that pushed in deeper and deeper until it was all she could feel.

'The board are going to vote him out. He's going to lose everything because of this, Damon. Because of *you*. How could you do this?'

She stared at him, but before he even came close to mustering up an answer, another thought barrelled into her.

'Am *I* part of this revenge?' she demanded, aghast at the thought that she'd somehow allowed herself to be used against her father. That she'd been a pawn in his twisted vendetta. 'Is that why you changed your mind about wanting to be involved with the baby? So you could take his family too?'

Damon opened his mouth, but she was already shaking her head, warding off anything he might say.

'On second thoughts, don't bother answering. It's not like I can trust anything you say or do, is it?'

Carrie paced away from him, sucking in lungful after lungful of air, but it wasn't enough. Every inch of her chest burned…every beat of her heart ached.

'At no point did you think about how doing this would affect me or our child…'

'I have thought about that—' he began.

But Carrie didn't want to hear his defence. It would only be more lies!

'No, you have not! Because if you had you would have stopped. You would have called off whatever you were doing before it got to this point. But all you've thought about is yourself. What *you* feel. What *you* need. If you loved me the way I love you—if you had any feelings for me at all—you wouldn't have done this.'

But he obviously didn't love her. Because, just like her father, he had placed his business and his thirst for revenge ahead of her and their child. Ahead of the life they could have shared. And that was shattering.

'You are a selfish man, Damon. You never deserved a single piece of my heart.'

And it was with that agonising realisation that the anger drained out of her and all she felt was the pain of her heartbreak, the disappointments of the past and the present colliding, and it was so excruciating it threatened to cleave her in two.

She knew she could no longer stay there. Without looking at Damon, she ran for the door.

'Carrie, don't leave...please.'

His anguished plea followed her, clawing at her already shredded heart.

'You don't understand everything. Let me explain... Where are you going to go?'

She threw open the door without looking back at him. 'Far away from you.'

CHAPTER TWELVE

DAMON STARED AT the gravestone bearing his beloved father's name. He was holding the Caldwell contract in his hands. But it was still unsigned and it would remain that way—because whatever triumph he'd thought he could achieve it would never have been more than a hollow victory.

He'd brought Sterling Randolph to his knees. He was attached to wires in a hospital bed, being forced to reckon with his mortality and the fallibility of his power, but it hadn't healed anything within him.

His father was gone, and nothing could change that. There was nothing in the universe capable of making that absence bearable. It was a loss that had to be borne, a grief that needed to be endured. That cavernous hole inside of him still existed and anger continued to roil in his gut.

He had realised it in time and yet also too late.

Because he'd not completely stained his soul, but he had lost Carrie. He had destroyed everything good between them, decimated all the faith she'd pushed past her fears to place in him.

Carrie, who had eased the burden of his emotions, who'd made every day bright and beautiful. Who'd shown him that the past was far less important than the present and the future. But when he'd had the chance to prove that to her he had failed.

He wished he'd realised the error of his ways earlier, halted his plans sooner!

He didn't blame her for storming off, refusing to hear him out. He had let her down in the worst way.

Something splintered inside him as he finally faced up to what a gigantic fool he'd been. He had clung to his anger when he should have been grabbing Carrie with both hands and holding on tight. Because having the person you loved in your life and by your side was the greatest gift imaginable. By refusing to let go of the past, he'd given away his future. *Their* future.

'Damon?'

He hadn't heard the car behind him pull up, and he didn't recognise its owner through the pouring rain until she hurried to his side and lifted her wide umbrella over him.

'Why are you standing here in this rain? You're soaked through,' cried his Aunt Bree, casting a horrified eye over his drenched clothes before examining his face. 'What's the matter?'

'He's gone,' he said, unable to move his eyes from the grave. 'I lost him and now I've lost her too.'

'Her? Who…? Carrie? Are you talking about Carrie? What happened?'

Through aching, gritty eyes—because he had not rested since Carrie had stormed out of the apartment in Paris—he looked at his aunt and saw that same willingness to listen and support that had always been there.

Only he had been too scared to accept it. Too scared to let her close in case he lost her too. But loss was a part of love, and Carrie was right. By closing himself off emotionally, he'd closed himself from so many other good things.

Taking a deep breath, he began to talk, telling her everything until there were no more words left.

'I was a stupid, foolish man, Aunt Bree.'

She sighed. 'You may not be able to change anything about your father being gone, but you can change things with Carrie. She's not lost to you, Damon, not if you don't want her to be.'

And suddenly he remembered Carrie's words. She'd said that people who loved someone—truly loved someone—would never stop waiting for them to come back. In that moment his aunt had proved how wise and right Carrie had been, and Damon found himself hoping they remained true of Carrie. Because without a doubt he knew that without her that hole in him would never go away.

She was the only one capable of making him whole and there was no one on the planet—*no one*—who could love her better or harder than he did.

But before he could go to her as a man deserving of her love and beg for her forgiveness, there was somebody else he had to face first.

Damon got to his feet as the door opened and Sterling Randolph was shown into the lounge. His heart thudded beneath his suit jacket. This was the showdown he had always anticipated, yet it would play out nothing like the way he'd once imagined.

Randolph reached the table and cast his eyes around—dark green, just like Carrie's—taking in the silence, the emptiness. When his gaze settled back on Damon, he arched a brushy eyebrow.

'You didn't want an audience for your moment of triumph?'

'There's no need for an audience,' Damon informed him levelly, retaking his seat. 'We're just having a conversation.'

'Really? How civilised. Ending it all with a conversation.' Sterling took a sip of the drink the waiter had deposited on the table. 'So, this is the part where you explain that you have me right where you want me?'

'No,' Damon said after a beat, looking him straight in the eye. 'This is the part where I tell you that I'm done.'

'Excuse me?'

'I'm done,' Damon repeated, feeling the last of that leaden weight lift off his shoulders as he breathed the words into reality. 'Done with hunting you, competing with you, undermining your business. Done.'

Carrie put down the phone, her body ringing with disbelief. Her father had actually taken the time and effort to call her to reassure her about his health and, whilst that was astonishing in itself, it was the information he'd shared about Damon that had left her reeling. He had withdrawn his bid for the Caldwell building!

He'd refused to say anything more, even when Carrie had pushed him for details, adding only that Damon was a good man and she should speak with him herself.

Which was easier said than done.

Because she hadn't spoken or communicated with Damon at all since storming out of his Paris penthouse.

Her hand moved to caress her bump, as it did every time her thoughts rewound to that awful day. To those awful, heartbreaking revelations and her own unforgiving reaction.

And didn't this just prove what she was already struggling with? That she had been too quick to judge Damon? That she had listened to her own hurt and anger and fear instead of listening to him, the man she had fallen in love with? He'd been in despair—she'd seen it with her own eyes—and yet still she'd walked away. At their first real test as a couple she had failed him. She'd accused Damon of destroying them, but Carrie could no longer hide from the truth that she had too.

She knew she had her reasons for reacting as she had—she was still suffering from the way things had been with her father and Nate and her fear of going through anything similar again—but Damon had already proved he wasn't like them. She should have trusted in that…in him.

And she needed to tell him that. Now. Before another day ended. She needed him to know how sorry she was for walking out on him when he'd so obviously needed her, and that she wanted to be there for him now. Because, whilst she had no idea what was going on, for him to have turned down the Caldwell contract she knew something was happening—something big!

She picked up the phone to call him before deciding against it. A phone call wasn't enough. She needed to see him, to touch him, to look into his beautiful burnished eyes as she said the words.

Snatching up her car keys, she hurried to her front door, trying to work out how long the drive to LA would take so late in the afternoon, but as she pulled the door open she froze—because there he was, his hand raised and poised to knock.

'Damon…' she breathed, stunned by the beautiful sight of him.

'You're on your way out?'

'Only to find you,' she said, her eyes drinking him in, feeling in her bones how much she had missed him. 'To apologise.'

He shook his head. 'You have nothing to be sorry about Carrie. I'm the one who needs to apologise. Can I come in?' he asked tentatively.

'Of course.' She moved back to let him enter and he followed her into the living space. 'How are you? Both of you?' His eyes had dropped to the bump beneath her loose tee.

'We're good. Healthy.' She smoothed her hands over her stomach. 'I'm starting to show now.'

'I see that. It's beautiful.'

As he raised his gaze to her face Carrie immediately fell headlong into the golden beam of his eyes…eyes that were no longer shadowed, but clear and serene. Her heart started to pound, trying to punch itself free from her chest and into his hands.

'You're beautiful,' he added.

With those words, her emotions started to unravel, and tears built behind her eyes.

Damon stepped closer, taking her hands in his and holding them against his chest. 'I'm so sorry, Carrie.

There are so many things that I want to say to you, but that's the most important. That you know how deeply I regret everything. I've made some big mistakes and I've hurt you badly and that was never what I wanted to do.'

Exhaling a shaky breath, he continued. 'You're everything to me, Carrie. When I think about the future, I think only about you and the life we could have together. A house here, overlooking the ocean, weekends in Ojai, our baby being born and growing up… I want that future with you. I want a beautiful life with you. I want to try every day to be a man deserving of your love, a man that you and our child can believe in and rely on, no matter what.'

Carrie couldn't stay quiet a second longer—not when the harsh words she'd levelled at him on that horrible day echoed between them.

'Damon, I should never have said that you weren't deserving of my heart,' she said, shame burning through her. She moved in closer, clutching at him. 'I was wrong to say that. I was wrong not to give you the chance to speak, to explain what you were going through, and I've regretted it ever since. But I got scared and I reacted. All I could see was that another man I loved had lied to me and put his ambition ahead of our relationship. All the fears I had about trusting you roared back to the surface. But you deserved better than that from me…because you've proved time and time again that I can trust you.'

He wiped at the tears on her cheeks. 'You had every right to be furious with me. I hurt you. I let you down. But I really hope that beautiful, understanding heart of yours has the capacity to forgive me one more time, because I am in love with you, Carrie. I have loved you since those very first moments in Paris. I was just too scared of risking my heart to truly let myself see it and feel it. But losing you in Paris woke me up, and I know now that the real risk lies in not loving you as hard as I can for as long as I can, and in not telling you how much I love you every single day.'

It was everything she'd wanted to hear, and all the sweeter for everything they'd been through.

'I love you, too, Damon. And I've missed you so much.'

With a sigh of relief he released her hands to curl his arms around her and, burying his face in her river of dark hair, he held her tightly against him. 'I'm sorry it took me so long to figure it out,' he whispered.

'No more apologies. The past is done. From now on we just look forward.'

His answering smile was breathtaking. 'I like the sound of that. And in that spirit…'

He caught her completely by surprise as he dropped to his knee, producing a small velvet box.

'I love you, Carrie. I love you more than I thought it was possible to love. And, having known the pain of waking up without you beside me, I never want to be without you again. All I want now and every day, for the rest of my life, is you and our child. To spend every day with you and to spend all those days making you as happy as its possible to be. So, Caroline Miller-Randolph, will you marry me?'

Carrie had so many loving things she wanted to say to him, so many feelings burning in her heart that she wanted him to know, but there was only one word she was actually able to say, and she knew it was the only word that mattered.

'Yes.'

Damon slid the ring onto her finger and sealed the move with a kiss, then another kiss to her stomach, and a final one to her lips.

'I love you,' he said again, and it was a promise.

Excitement exploded inside her like a constellation of fireworks. 'I don't think I'll ever get tired of hearing that.'

'Good. Because I plan on saying it a lot. And showing you a lot too,' he added, boosting her up in his arms.

Before she drifted into the paradise of his lips melting against hers, Carrie stole another look at the ring sparkling on her finger.

Maybe it hadn't always unfolded like the classic fairytale she'd wanted, but it had been their story—hers and Damon's—and she couldn't wait for the life of love and laughter and togetherness that would come next.

* * * * *

MILLS & BOON®

Coming next month

PREGNANT AND STOLEN BY THE TYCOON
Maya Blake

One night. It was only meant to be one night.

Genie only realized she'd said it out loud when Seve's whole body tightened, turning even more marble-like than before.

"Why are you doing this? You don't want even want a child. You said as much when we had dinner."

His eyes glinted, his incisive gaze tracking her as she paced in the small cabin. "What I felt a few weeks ago no longer matters."

"That's absurd. Of course it does."

He gritted his teeth. "Let me rephrase. The child you're carrying—*my* child—is now my number one priority. I'm not taking my eyes off you until he or she is born."

Continue reading
PREGNANT AND STOLEN BY THE TYCOON
Maya Blake

Available next month
www.millsandboon.co.uk

JOIN US ON SOCIAL MEDIA!

Stay up to date with our latest releases, author news and gossip, special offers and discounts, and all the behind-the-scenes action from Mills & Boon...

@millsandboon

@millsandboonuk

facebook.com/millsandboon

@millsandboonuk

It might just be true love...